The Dark Ship

THE
SEAGULL
LIBRARY OF
GERMAN
LITERATURE

The Dark Ship

SHERKO FATAH

Translated by Martin Chalmers

LONDON NEW YORK CALCUTTA

This publication was supported by a grant from the Goethe-Institut India

Seagull Books, 2021

Originally published as *Das Dunkle Schiff* by Sherko Fatah

First published in English translation by Seagull Books, 2015

ISBN 978 0 8574 2 839 4

British Library Cataloguing-in-Publication Data

A catalogue record for this book is available from the British Library

Typeset by Seagull Books, Calcutta, India

Printed and bound by WordsWorth India, New Delhi, India

For Samira

ACKNOWLEDGEMENTS

During the work on this book, I received support from the International Writing Program of the University of Iowa and the Friends of Villa Aurora in Berlin and Los Angeles. I would like to express my thanks for their interest and hospitality.

Sherko Fatah

PROLOGUE

It was a summer's day, hot, yet so windy that one didn't really feel it. Dark shadows of clouds hurried across plains and slopes, as if airships were gliding through the deep blue sky. Perhaps it was the most beautiful day of his life, not because of the mild light and the gentle wind, no, on this sluggishly fading day he for the first time felt the deep peace which beauty grants, and at the same time discovered its futility.

At this time of year, the old women went out to gather medicinal herbs. They knew when they had to go to a particular place for which plant. They did not have to climb far, only onto the hills. He saw them there, a little column, following, as so often before, the never quite overgrown paths. They were talking and laughing loudly, out here they were at last quite by themselves, free of rooms and rules for a couple of hours. Had they looked around, they too would have noticed the inviolability of the wild grasses, the clusters of flowers and the warm stones. But they swung their baskets and their long brightly coloured garments billowed in the wind, they were too caught up with one another. He almost envied them for it, for being set down there so obliviously in the day which was all around them like a giant, open window. He ran after them as they disappeared behind the hills, simply to go on seeing them, tiny yet not lost, and remained standing on the hill. He no longer felt the isolation out here or the harsh barrenness, he saw the landscape like an open hand. He breathed heavily. I'm still a child, he thought briefly, my lungs aren't big enough for this day. And even if they were, so he suspected, I could never go far enough into it.

The women had spread out in the distance and begun to pick the herbs. The sound rose like a weak echo, swallowed by the rocks rather than thrown back by them. It was a helicopter, and the late light shining on it made even its camouflage appear cheerful. He shielded his eyes with his hand and looked up. He saw the main rotor and the tail rotor and heard the swelling roar. But nothing, not even this machine was able to disturb the deep peace over the hills. The helicopter flew past, came back and flew in a wide circle above him. Two soldiers crouched in the open side hatch, one waved to him. Everything could happen on this day and so he waved back without fear. Slowly, with unreal slowness, the helicopter sank down to earth. Secretly he was aware of his childhood wish and now it was coming true—it was landing, a long way off, but it was landing. Perhaps they'll take me with them, was his next thought, perhaps I can fly with them.

He started running, waving and shouting, sharp-edged stones and thorny thistle bushes were in his way, yet nothing made him stumble and nothing pricked him. Far ahead, the helicopter was shrouded in whirled-up sand, dry stalks of grass sailed through the air. It's too far, I won't make it, he thought, as he saw the two soldiers jump out and, ducking low, run towards the women. They had put down their baskets and, hands on hips or at their temples, were looking towards the men. He saw the soldiers hurrying them to the helicopter, saw it hazily through the dust, and then he stopped. I won't make it, he thought once again regretfully, yet he was consoled that it had happened at all, something altogether out of the ordinary. He stood and watched them lift off, jerkily at first, then irresistibly, as if drawn up into the heavens, until they cleared the cloud of dust below them. The helicopter tilted very slightly to the side and again flew in its wide circle, gradually spiralling higher and higher to float away free in the sky. He continued watching it and waved again. And the machine really did approach once more, the roar became loud and louder so that he put his hands over his ears. Looking straight up he saw the women. There they were falling, one after another tumbled out of the hatch, arms spread out, they gleamed in the light and, as if to halt them, the wind tugged at their clothes.

PART ONE

1

Kerim remembered the never-changing ritual. His mother called him and his brothers. Together they brought out an old woollen blanket, threadbare from being washed so often, and spread it on the floor. Sometimes they also made do with sheets of newspaper. They put the pots and bowls in the middle and sat on the floor as if around a campfire. There were spoons but, as the family was usually alone, they ate with their hands. Everyone took as much as they wanted and reached into the pots without hesitating.

Sometimes, in weak moments, it seemed to Kerim as if the memory of this way of eating was all that had remained with him of his family. Because when he thought back to it, they all appeared before his eyes more clearly than they ever did otherwise—his mother who was always present, yet whom he hardly ever saw eat. He remembered her hands and her delicate forearms which were visible because she had pushed back her sleeves. He saw Imat in front of him, the older of his brothers, thin and pale, as he took tiny portions of rice and even picked out the ladies' fingers according to size before timidly pushing them into his mouth as if his lips were sore. Ali, on the other hand, was more like him, Kerim, and his father. Always hungry and close to his mother, he would grab the food. He liked eating and ate a lot for his age. Finally his father, tired, usually, after the long working days, also appeared before Kerim's inner eye. When he sat on the floor his heavy, protruding stomach made him look as if he had slumped into a heap. Kerim remembered the rings under his eyes, which bulged noticeably in the flickering TV light. Half looking at the screen hanging above their heads, half turned towards his family, always rather taciturn without appearing silent. That was how Kerim encountered him in his memories.

His father ran a small restaurant which was almost outside their town. It was no more than a hut, crammed with wooden benches and chairs. There was a big hole in the roof in one place, covered with a mat as a stopgap. Over time the mat had begun to come apart and, particularly in the early evening, let beams of gentle light, as Kerim thought, fall into the hut. But no one apart from him noticed.

Most of the customers were travellers stopping on their way through the mountainous north of the land. The restaurant was very close to one of the highways on which it was possible to cross the country from one end to the other. Kerim remembered the yellowish-brown room, the babble of voices and the drifting smoke above the customers' heads. Close to the mat, the smoke filled the slanting rays of light as if they were glass vessels. Kerim's mother was very unhappy that the hole in the roof was never properly repaired. But her husband didn't find the time. His life was determined by the preparation of the food. As long as

Kerim knew his father, food was the only thing that seriously concerned him.

Kerim already had to work before he left for school. He had to prepare the small kitchen which was in an extension of the hut. The day began at four in the morning, because that was the time the taxi drivers arrived. They were always driving around and paid special rates in the restaurant, in return they now and then undertook deliveries for Kerim's father. At that early hour there was only broth or skewered offal. That was usual; later in the day customers could choose between chicken or mutton and the broth that came with it. As accompaniment there was always rice which was cooked in great quantities in a huge black cauldron. His father left the steady stirring and finally the emptying and refilling entirely to Kerim. Later he was also allowed to take care of the gas cylinders which an uncommunicative man regularly brought up on a wooden cart. That was a little more expensive than fetching the cylinders from the shop, but the man connected them immediately and checked for leaks with a match. Kerim had known the man all his life without having spoken more than a couple of sentences to him.

As far back as he could remember food was at the centre of his life. He had an aversion to this recurrent ritual and to the great amount of work of which it was the cause. Sometimes he simply watched as his father, bent low and wheezing from the heat in the cramped kitchen, prepared at great speed the many plates which, half an hour later, Kerim's mother would collect again. And already as a child Kerim felt certain that he never wanted to do this work himself.

Behind the hut there was a windowless shed with a tin roof in which slaughtering was also done when necessary. Kerim seldom entered this dark room, because he found the stuffy heat and the smell unbearable. In the middle lay piles of sheep' heads, each with open glassy eyes and hanging tongue. A couple of boys from poorer families in the neighbourhood hired themselves out to Kerim's father and worked in the shed. They cleaned the heads and cut out the tongues. Once, just to make him familiar with what was done, his father explained it to him: the tongues had to be cut out through the soft part of the lower jaw, it would be too difficult to do it through the mouth. The boys squatted on the ground in their dirty trousers and shirts in the middle of the stench of blood and threw the long tongues into tin bowls beside them. They glanced up curiously at Kerim but didn't say a word. The sunlight only fell in a broad strip from the door over the dark floor and it was as if it bore the swarms of flies with it.

According to his father such work was not for Kerim, his oldest son. He taught him to cook, by the way, he had to be available to help in the kitchen. Nevertheless Kerim went to school regularly. His father even had an assistant who, when Kerim was away, accompanied him in an old pickup truck to buy supplies in the bazaar.

It seemed as if there was nothing his parents would not have done to ensure he got a good education. That is why his father didn't like it when Kerim went to the shed to watch the boys. Perhaps he feared that something of the oppressive, mute activity in that half light could infect his son and corrupt him. Kerim grew up with the feeling that he was intended if not for great things, then certainly for something better.

He began to be fat very early. It wasn't obvious at first, there were several plump children in the neighbourhood. But they didn't keep pace with Kerim. When he was seven he was the fattest child far and wide. His mother often told him not to take the leftovers. Finally she even sent him out of the house, so that he moved around more. She did it all secretly, however, at pains not to attract her husband's attention. Because Kerim's father had the girth of three men and nothing about it bothered him. He wasn't tall, in build he was rather slight, with delicate wrists and ankles. But the food had completely transformed him.

Kerim's mother had already known her husband when he weighed more than a hundred pounds less. Sometimes in the evening conversations she mentioned the memory of it in passing. She liked to dwell on the topic. Her face brightened, her almond-shaped eyes narrowed, she seemed pleased. When Kerim remembered it later, what he could not have known then was clear to him. This was the only small expression of disrespect his mother was allowed—and she enjoyed it just as much as she could. His father meanwhile sat hunched up on the bench cushions, smiling peacefully and breathing heavily as always.

'He was thin as a child when I saw him for the first time,' she said. 'Lean as our goat, you know, the little grey one . . .'

Kerim and his brothers listened attentively, even if they had heard it all before. Because for them it presented a chance to see their father differently from how they knew him. At least they could try. They looked furtively over to the wheezing man, trying to make sure that he didn't notice. Yet it was almost impossible to recognize in him the person she described.

'I had to force him to eat,' she said. 'I'm sure he was about to starve. Whatever I cooked for him, he only nibbled at it. Like a mouse. I had to look for the places he had taken a bite from.'

Kerim knew his father as a man of few words. Even when it was to do with the kitchen, he only gave instructions and explained no more than was absolutely necessary. But Kerim also remembered a feeling of security in his presence. When they walked down the alleys of the town at midday, he threw a huge shadow on the walls. His father held him firmly by the hand, and so Kerim could not escape the shadow and its extension even when he hung back for a moment and had to be pulled along.

Kerim would not have been able to say whether his father—and his family altogether—were well liked in the neighbourhood. Respected certainly, the restaurant business took care of that. Yet in the street people always greeted him with polite reserve.

Perhaps it was something to do with him coming from an Alevi family. Kerim learnt little about it, as his father seemed to have only few memories of it. The family had lived in Tunceli in Turkey—the word alone sounded as remote as a fairy tale.

'The village lay high up in the mountains,' related his father. 'Like a swallow's nest, so that from below one could not make out the path leading to it. That was very important, because as a result it was difficult for normal Muslims to make their way up. The Chaldaeans lived in the same fashion, all those who were different. But we feared the power of the state. Once a policeman came to our village and took a look around. The people showed him their houses and the assembly room where everyone, men and women, prayed and danced. When he was finished with his inspection, he said to the village elder, "You don't have a mosque." The elder replied, "We have our prayer house." "You need a mosque, let us build one," said the policeman. The village elder considered, because it was evidently an offer. Then he said, "What we need is a school for our children, we need books and teachers." At that the policeman shook his head, "First you must build a mosque and perhaps, at some point, you will get a school as well."'

His father rarely told such stories. He also conveyed only indirectly to his sons what he himself had learnt as a child—it was the feeling of not really belonging anywhere. In his childhood, Kerim envied his fellow pupils for their religious rituals. His parents expected something different from him, since they themselves hardly even prayed. That was nothing out of the ordinary; there were many families who prayed only on religious festivals. And yet for them belief seemed to be something taken for granted or was at least close to that. But what Kerim saw was a certain degree of dissimulation—in order not to bring the restaurant into disrepute, his father kept to the Muslim rules where it was necessary. Sometimes he even went to the mosque. His most important concession was to buy a live sheep for the Festival of Sacrifice. During the slaughtering, he carefully adhered to all the rules—he placed the animal with its head facing Mecca, said a prayer and let it bleed thoroughly dry, before distributing the larger part of the meat to the poor of the neighbourhood who every year gathered in the yard of the restaurant to wait for it. Some were the parents of those boys who worked in his shed.

Only much later did Kerim grasp what skill his father employed so that no one would notice what he really was in his heart—a man without Faith. The unobtrusive names for all his children, his behaviour towards his neighbours—it was fitting in. He lived for his family and his business, anything higher was alien to him. When Kerim, at about the age of six, began to pray in a corner beside the kitchen, just as he had seen the others do, he did so without knowing what one is supposed to say and how often one has to bow down. His father came to look for him and ended the whole thing as if it was a silly children's game, because he needed him in the kitchen.

Kerim remembered exactly that on that day, too, a sacrificial animal was standing ready in the yard. This time it was a dark brown cow. He watched the animal for an hour from the short flight of steps which led to the backyard. It was tethered to a wooden post, looked for scattered, dry tufts of grass and as it did so moved very slowly in a wide circle. Since the rope was winding itself around the post, the cow's radius became ever smaller. But the cow didn't notice, even when it jerked its head and the rope tautened. Its path led in a circle around the post. Finally it tied up a hind leg. But it wasn't capable of going backwards. And so it stood lopsidedly by the wooden post, one leg drawn up, and stared into space. It mooed briefly, but immediately fell silent again and lowered its heavy head as if it wanted to go on grazing. But it could no longer reach the ground.

Kerim didn't move. Leaning against the crooked railing, he looked silently down at the animal. He did not find the grotesque sight, which it provided for the next half hour, tied up like that, funny. He couldn't get the thought of the incident out of his mind. He had waited for the cow, half by chance, half because of the pain, to go in the opposite direction. Without pity he had waited a long time for it to happen. But the cow didn't do it. Only once did it seem close to the solution of its problem—flies had settled around the rims of its eyes and it shook its big head to get rid off them; at that the rope loosened a little, its flank won a little room for manoeuvre, and if the cow had only taken a single step backwards over the slackly hanging rope, it would have been able to move freely again, even turn around. Instead, it paused for a moment and used its little bit of freedom to press forward again. This time it bound itself for good.

2

Once they drove up into the mountains of Kurdistan to a remote vantage point. It was a damp day in winter. Fog hung between the mountain slopes and the further they followed the ascending zigzag road, the thicker it became. Kerim looked as hard as he could out of the side window but he couldn't see through the fog. Only very rarely did patches of rock face stand out from it, and it seemed to Kerim as if he was plunging into a pale river.

When he thought back to the trip, he was filled with a deep happiness. It must have been about the time he began to see the things around him in a new way. Kerim had a very clear memory of this inner experience, much clearer than of one or other of his relatives. In the beginning, he thought, all things were just set down around him. They were obstacles or they appeared beautiful to him, they hurt or they tasted good. But they always disappeared as they had emerged, apparently without leaving traces. All things were, in a certain way, light. And suddenly they changed. It was as if an invisible hand had given them soft shadows. That alone was enough to make the world, the landscape around him accessible. And there was always a hill beyond the hill, a path which at some unexpected point crossed the one Kerim was following, seeming to tempt him to a yet-unknown place.

As Kerim watched the fog slide along the mountainsides, he was waiting for this pale veil to lift and show him, here and there in the rock, the outlines of stone animals and monsters, or contorted faces.

At the time, it was one of the few occasions on which he travelled alone with his father. As the family virtually never left home—because the work in the restaurant always came first—this excursion into the mountains was something special.

They had set out early, the muezzin had just made the call to morning prayer. His father sat tired and taciturn at the wheel, repeatedly yawning. The road kept going further and further up, and they drove very slowly because of the poor visibility. That made Kerim even more excited, so that he rocked back and forth in his seat until his father had to tell him to stop. The fog flowed along by the car windows.

After hours, they finally emerged from it and reached a flattened mountaintop. There was a car park and a wooden house that looked abandoned. When he got out, Kerim noticed how cold it had become. The dampness immediately got into his clothes and made him shiver.

His father went ahead, and the way he walked and his posture seemed to Kerim so solemn that it was as if in the next few moments a secret would be revealed to him. But behind the door which his father held open for him, there was only a restaurant, smaller than their own. Hesitantly, Kerim crossed the threshold and looked around the room. Long shadows stretched across it. The stone floor, the tables and wooden benches standing this way and that, everything was submerged in the grey morning light falling through the dirty windows. Just as at home, it smelt of fat and smoke, a sweetish, sharp smell which to Kerim would always be associated with the early morning, the time before the first guests came.

But up here on the mountain, it was already forenoon and no one was coming to eat. His father strode purposefully through the room and knocked on a tiny wooden door which seemed to conceal a shack. That must be the kitchen, thought Kerim. The door was pushed open, it was as light as if made of cardboard. A short man stepped out, even he had to bend in order not to bump his smooth skull on the doorframe. Kerim fell back involuntarily because he expected to see an ugly or just even a frightening face when the man raised his head. Yet then two friendly eyes were beaming at him and, smiling, the man was scratching his unshaven cheeks.

'Kerim, this is Anatol,' said his father. 'He's an old friend of mine. Say good morning to him.'

Kerim obeyed and even after that did not take his eyes off the man. The latter noticed and winked at him as he talked to his father. Yet all the man's friendliness could not pacify the boy. Kerim stared, waited for him to drop his mask.

'Why are you watching me?' Anatol asked at one point and there was an uncomfortable pause.

Kerim didn't know what to say but immediately felt ashamed. The feeling was like the shudder of a fever. Helplessly he looked at his father, who finally broke the silence.

'He's a little fearful,' said his father, still looking at his son. 'I don't know why. Recently, he's hardly even gone out into the street. Just sits in his corner and stares at the customers.'

Kerim suddenly felt offended and shook his head vigorously. 'I'm not afraid,' he burst out and looked at the floor as he did so.

Anatol stretched out his long thin arm and placed his hand on Kerim's head. The boy started but didn't shake the hand off. He didn't know what disturbed him about the man and that unnerved him even more. So he simply said nothing and kept still. The hand lay on his head for a long time, before it finally tousled his hair and was raised.

'But perhaps you're hungry,' said Anatol.

Again there was a pause. Kerim nodded just to satisfy him.

'Well, I can do something about that. I've got something good for the two of you.' Anatol got up and added, 'Something unusual for special guests. I've already prepared everything.' Then he quickly withdrew and disappeared behind the little wooden door.

Anatol cooked and he took his time. The smell of fat and onions began to pervade the room. Kerim was still uneasy and quiet. He felt the empty room in which they were sitting to be strange, but at the same time it made him curious.

'What is the man doing?' he asked.

'He's cooking for us,' said his father, 'and that is a great honour, because he is a very good cook.'

When Kerim thought back, he believed that he had necessarily expected that this excursion with his father would also be devoted to food. But it wasn't so. At the time he had expected nothing.

'Why is he doing that?'

'I asked him to,' his father replied. 'So that you learn something.' He had half raised his finger. 'Only you. Your brothers are still too young.'

'Can I walk around?'

His father nodded and Kerim began to explore the room. But he found nothing that interested him. The things around him lay there like empty husks. He remembered having made a half turn because of it and to have sighed deeply once. He stepped up to one of the windows. The sky was still grey, his father's old Toyota stood lost on the empty lot in front of the building. A brown cat was sitting motionless underneath with wide-open eyes. In the distance the fog that filled the valley could still be made out. In summer, with the view, it must be beautiful. Now, however, everything about the scene was cold and forlorn.

'Why are there no other people here?' he asked without turning around.

'So that no one disturbs us,' replied his father. 'Anatol is on holiday. That's why he put a sign on the door.'

Kerim looked at the dark rock which rose up beside the house. The stone gleamed damply and in some places water even seemed to be running down it. A car came up the road. Four people were sitting in it. The car approached the restaurant, stopped, and the driver stuck his head out of the side window. He looked at the entrance, briefly raised a hand and then turned around again.

'People come from far away to eat in his restaurant,' said his father, as the sound of the engine faded away. 'Anatol is famous.'

After half an hour, the cook appeared again.

'The meat isn't ready yet,' he said apologetically. He looked about the room with a disgruntled expression. 'It's cold, isn't it?'

'Not especially,' said Kerim's father. 'Are you feeling the cold?'

Kerim bravely shook his head.

At last. Anatol brought the food. He must have worked quickly to prepare this meal. The aroma of rice, cooked meat, green and white beans filled the room and warmed it perceptibly. Kerim's father didn't offer to help and nor did he send his son into the kitchen, not even to bring in the plates. Anatol did everything himself. Probably that's exactly how it had been agreed.

Gesturing ceremoniously with his arm, the cook pointed to the spread table, as if he was at that moment causing the food to appear there by magic. Kerim's father thanked him several times.

'Eat slowly,' he instructed his son.

Kerim really was hungry meanwhile and had to restrain himself so as not to eat as usual, hastily and almost without chewing. He concentrated and so truly did enjoy the food. Yet he was quite tense because he was waiting for something. The food, as good as it tasted, was nothing out of the ordinary. There was only one thing that struck him—the cooked lamb was unusually tasty.

Nevertheless, he shook his head when, after he had gripped his hand, his father asked him about it.

'Eat of the meat,' said his father calmly and watched Kerim's movements, looked at him as he chewed. 'Eat some more of it.' He nodded gently but firmly.

Under the observant glances of the two men Kerim thoroughly chewed the next titbit but didn't dare say anything.

'This lamb,' said Anatol, 'was not yet born.'

Kerim went on chewing mechanically, not really understanding.

'It was still in the womb.'

'That's why,' added his father, 'it's so tender. Eat some more.'

Kerim was still chewing, yet under the eyes of the others he could no longer taste anything. The meat seemed to dissolve in his mouth and disappear immediately after.

His father gave him a sign to pause. What he said then Kerim hardly remembered. At first, it had to do with the meal. Finally, however, it expanded into a kind of sermon. It was about youth and purity. The reason this lamb tasted so good was that it had absorbed so little time, he said. It was still very close to its origin, its creation. Then he turned to look straight at his son. After a pause he went on, 'Everything that lives always remains linked to its origin, that is, God the Almighty. The more remote it gets from this origin, the weaker and uglier it becomes. It loses its youth, the strength of its origin, and must finally die and crumble into dust.'

Kerim still wondered about the meaning of this mystical address and felt a disappointment that he had never found anything that he could learn from it.

Then he sat at the table without moving and stared at the plate with the remains of the meat. What he had already eaten now lay heavy in his stomach with all the significance it had taken on. For the first time, he felt an aversion to food altogether that would never leave him. And, so at least he thought in retrospect, he was from that moment on a prisoner of time.

If he paused and paid attention, he could feel himself becoming more distant from his origin and weaker and he felt what Anatol said, more or less by the way and to end the oppressive silence, to be a quiet warning: 'God doesn't let you get too far before he fetches you back.'

Kerim never discovered why, but one day his father took him to Najaf, the most important place of pilgrimage for the Shiites. Even if he observed no rules of Faith, his father did nevertheless have a special relationship to the past, at least as far as it concerned him and his family. That was evident both in the stories he occasionally told and also in the second trip he undertook with his eldest son. At any rate, Kerim later explained it to himself in that the Alevis were after all a schism of the Shiite creed and his father wanted to draw his attention to that. But what Kerim then saw had absolutely nothing to do with anything he knew—it was a completely unfamiliar world of Faith.

After a long drive, the shimmering city rose up from the yellow clay desert. There were groves of tall date palms around its edge; among them stretched extensive cemeteries, countless gravestones of various forms protruded from the ground like multicoloured shards of glass. The nearer they came, the more the cemeteries resembled the fragments of a huge, smashed vase. The alleys of the town lay unprotected in the scorching sun. His father halted outside an old house whose wooden beams stuck out under the roof and were snow-white from dust and light. They still had a bit to walk to the golden entrance of the mosque. Kerim remembered the wide courtyard of big rectangular flagstones which were so hot that he felt the heat in his face as he walked. He saw women, their faces veiled in black, and his gaze was immediately caught by the huge golden cupola and the minarets. The place was crowded with white-bearded men wearing prayer caps. They emerged from the main door without shoes, Kerim remembered their white-and-blue socks.

'Do everything I do,' said his father. And, as always, he showed skill in fitting in. He raised his shoulders, lowered his head a little and so transformed himself without any fuss into one of the many Believers.

The half light began right behind the entrance. An old man took their shoes. They continued on the gleaming, cool floor. Cupolas and massive pillars, hung with glass teardrops in which the light of the candles was reflected a thousand times over. Voices and sounds came from the room with the tomb of Ali. As they entered this central space his father kissed the doorpost, Kerim copied him. Inside there was a crush, the pilgrims proceeded anticlockwise around the tomb—a dark wooden box protected by a heavy silver railing. They were pushed and shoved forward, always towards the shrine. They were still several yards away from it as his father was already stretching out his hand in order to touch it at the first possible moment, and Kerim also raised his arm. The pressure of the crowd increased, women clutched the metal latticework, were squeezed against them yet spoke unceasingly. An old man, his prayer cap slipping, was pushed backwards along the railing. As if he didn't care that he was facing the wrong way, his hand stroked the metal. There were tears in his eyes. Kerim looked at the calloused hand and had some sense of how much sorrow, how much fervour Imam Ali had aroused over the generations through his martyr's death.

Most pilgrims tried to kiss the grating but, because of the shoving, their puckered lips slid along the grille. Suddenly the man in front of them slipped to the side, Kerim was pushed forward, and as if of its own accord, his mouth fell on the metal, warm from all those who had touched it. Kerim glanced around and saw people's fingers thrusting into the mesh of the grating, saw their noses squashed against it when they touched it with their face. And there stood what all were pushing towards—the dark shrine with its smell of old wood. Kerim tried to see more of it, looked through ever-new spaces in the lattice, as if at some point there would be a larger one. They were constantly pushed forward and were already on the other side when they detached themselves from the stream of people. Kerim looked at the old men who sat cross-legged on the floor, shaking their heads, on their knees the holy book that he knew from his few Koran lessons. There, however, he had got to know, if anything at all, only the Arabic letters, and more than that the sound of the holy words. But never had he encountered such fervour, never such people with a Faith so full of urgency.

He followed his father back through the glass vault, their shoes were returned to them and they stepped out into the hot midday light. Whenever he thought back to it, this mosque seemed to him like the container of an unprecedented event, long past and repeating itself, at once sad and uplifting.

3

He had lived with war since early childhood. The first had begun before he was born. After a surprise offensive against Iran, the Iraqi troops were quickly pushed back to the border. The leadership in Baghdad ordered the use of poison gas on long sections of the front, so that their positions would not simply be overrun by the enemy soldiers and, rushing ahead of them, the children's battalions, contemptuous of death. But those were news items. In the restaurant, the customers talked about other things, for example, the numerous Egyptian guest workers in the south, some of whom had got too friendly with the wife of a soldier and been sent home in a coffin.

Shortly before the end of this war, something occurred which Kerim remembered with particular clarity. It was a spring day and they were on the road going in the direction of the Iranian border. They wanted to visit the family of his mother in a village a little more than ninety miles east of the town. The old people were meanwhile living alone and hadn't left the place for decades. What they knew about their children, they learnt when the latter visited. Kerim was looking forward to seeing his grandparents, he enjoyed the journey. He pressed his forehead against the window and let the jolting of the car go through his body. The small, roughly-put-together stands of traders lined the road.

The further they drove, the rockier the landscape became. They passed small settlements, no more than a few, scattered low huts, surrounded by half-ruined walls. All the people who lived out here appeared to try to be close to the road. Even their animals, cows and donkeys, stood or knelt close to the road, at its edge where the surface crumbled into sand. The open country around them, the grey rocks waveringly blurring in the forenoon heat and the yellow-brown hills in front of them—everything was deserted, appeared abandoned and untouched. Even the wooden electricity poles seemed fragile, as if they could at any time be dismantled and removed without much effort.

They had put the greater part of the journey behind them when an agitatedly gesticulating man forced his father to stop.

'You can't go any further,' panted the man and leant far enough through the car window to see Kerim and his brothers on the backseat. 'An air attack, I don't know exactly where.'

Kerim remembered the desperate expression of the man as he turned around and pointed across the wide sand-coloured plain which stretched away from the road.

His father steered the car to the roadside, turned off the engine and got out. Although his mother wanted to stop him, Kerim followed. Before she could hold him back, he had opened the door, jumped out and was standing beside his father. Like him, he put his hand in front of his forehead to try to make out what was happening on the plain.

He saw two shapes which, at first, he took to be clouds of dust. Their core was dark against the landscape. The clouds stood in the valley like trees of smoke, the light wind that morning was enough to shred the edges of their crowns.

'When did it start?' asked Kerim's father.

'Twenty minutes ago, maybe less,' said the man, his voice trembling. 'There were three or four explosions, not very loud, a long way off . . . . Perhaps they'll come again.'

'Perhaps,' muttered Kerim's father. 'Were they helicopters or aeroplanes?'

The columns of smoke gradually melted away in the wind. Although no victims were to be seen, the silence was alarming. Not even birds were circling over the plain.

Kerim turned away and went back to the car. He hadn't expected anything more and so was not disappointed. His hand on the door handle, he didn't even look back. The steep mountain slope beneath which they were standing bulged out a good way over the road. It was dotted with little gravestones of every shape, most no more than simple lumps of rock. Yet from their even distribution and the little flags and banners, it was clear that there was a Muslim cemetery up there. The slope must have begun to slide. Kerim looked up at this now-inaccessible graveyard which seemed to want to burst against the background of the dull blue sky. Flocks of black birds had settled on the rounded mountaintop above the graves. Kerim was sure that they had flown there when the plain sank into that deathly silence from which it had not yet re-emerged. And for a moment, Kerim saw the birds fly up and he believed he could clearly hear the rumble of the slope finally giving way, saw thousands of pale grey bones crashing down on himself, his family, onto the Toyota and the young man they didn't know.

'They've attacked Halabja,' said his father, after he had got back into the car and shut the door. For some reason, he held on tightly to the door handle as if he was afraid it could open again. 'But it's not like usual,' he said quietly.

'What do you mean?' his wife asked him, her face full of fear.

'I don't know myself.' The young man's car had turned around and drove past them down the road they had come. A brief toot of the horn sounded as farewell. 'But I think it's better to go back.'

***

School meant nothing but trouble for Kerim, he was always tired and impatient. He only discovered a pleasure in learning later on, with his English teacher, and that had something to do with English being far away. His father had so often told him about his brother Tarik that although he had never met him, this uncle was as familiar to Kerim as someone he knew personally. Uncle Tarik lived in the distant German capital, he had emigrated there to seek his fortune when still a young man and had later brought his young wife to join him. The mere thought of someone leaving his home and starting a completely different life somewhere else had electrified Kerim since childhood. Of course it was much easier to find an English teacher in the town than a German teacher. But his parents assured him that the languages were similar.

He learnt quickly. If he had been asked to say why, then he would have referred to the fascination he had for giving everything a completely new name. It seemed to him that he was looking at familiar objects with a different pair of eyes or at least from a new place on earth. Looking at the pictures in his textbook, he felt like one of those British colonial soldiers advancing on Baghdad, a tremendous effort that ended tragically for them. He took an interest in the fate of these soldiers because he was reading about them in their language. He also learnt, of course, that, even if largely from India, they were representatives of the former colonial power. But that interested him much less than their aimless and yet dogged struggle not only against a superior enemy but also against the sun which ate the skin from their bodies.

'Their commanders could not accept that the sun would kill them,' said Kerim's English teacher with deliberation.

He was slim with the faint shadow of a moustache and a pale skin. At some point, he had spent a lengthy period of time in England, had studied there, until his family ran out of money to support him. He took poorly paid casual jobs and encountered a world before which he finally capitulated. He never told what exactly he had experienced. If asked, he shook his head, looked away from the faces of his pupils like an offended boy and stared at the bare, blotchy walls of the small room which served them as classroom. No one dared pester him any further.

'These men,' continued the teacher, 'were very brave without being particularly cruel. And yet God did not reward them for it.'

'Why were they unable to understand the heat?'

It took time for Kerim to formulate the question, because it had to be put in the foreign language.

The English teacher leant back slowly on his wooden chair and smiled almost gleefully. Kerim had always had the feeling that he was a favourite of the teacher. That's also why at home he stubbornly insisted on getting the English lessons. No one could contradict him when he said the language might be useful to him one day and he secretly understood his parents' consent as an indication that they planned to some day send him abroad.

'The white commanders did not know the sun,' asserted the teacher. 'Where they come from, the sun does not shine as hot as it does here—it's as if it was farther away.'

'And is it smaller?'

The English teacher was no longer smiling. His head rocked from side to side.

'I don't know. Have you ever looked at the sun to find out how big it is?'

'No.'

'Well then. Don't ask silly questions.'

That was the other side of this essentially patient man. If the discussion got off the point, he became stern.

After a couple of seconds he added, 'I say that to you because you are such a good pupil. You must not waste your energy.'

The image, however, stayed in Kerim's mind—although he had never seen it, he was convinced that the sun in Europe was smaller than it was here. It must be different because under it a world completely different from his own had come into being. The pictures in his book showed it—the land was green and full of tall houses, and the people there were as white as if they were all ill.

On one of the early evenings after the English class, the pupils stood around outside the building a little longer than usual. The oldest of them, Ahmad, was already driving his father's car and was very proud of that. The other boys surrounded him while he, arms folded, leaning against the car radiator, enjoyed their glances. A scrap-metal dealer slowly pushed his heavy metal cart past them. His lips were pressed tightly together and he looked at them sceptically. Kerim gazed at the big, slowly turning wheels of the cart, the spokes decorated with brightly coloured plastic rings which were supposed to attract the attention of passers-by. Suddenly, the idea that this man was really pushing his cart seemed very funny to him.

Audible, if not very loud, music was coming from the car's tape deck. It was very old Western pop music on a cassette which Ahmad had found somewhere.

Together they tried to understand the English text of a particular song. Ahmad would sit behind the wheel and spool the cassette back again and again. They could half make out the words but they didn't understand it.

After a while, their English teacher stepped out of the building. He was no doubt on his way to his evening teahouse visit and was smoking a cigarette. The pupils waved to him and he joined them in front of the car, frowning as he realized what the boys were doing.

'Do you understand it?' he asked the group, and all of them immediately nodded.

'But what does he mean?' asked Kerim.

The man said nothing, lowered his head and said to Ahmad, 'Play it once again, from the beginning.'

After a brief musical introduction, the voice came in. The teacher had them translate it simultaneously.

'Oh-oh, here she comes . . .' they hummed in chorus. The first line was easy. At the second, they were in difficulties and began to stammer.

'Stop the tape,' said the English teacher and Ahmad obeyed. 'Play it again.'

They tried yet again.

'Watch out boy, she'll . . . .' They didn't get any further.

'You don't know that yet,' said the teacher laughing. 'She'll chew you up,' he added and looked expectantly around the group. 'Go on,' he said.

'Oh-oh here she comes,' they all repeated, 'Oh-oh here she comes, watch out, boy, watch out, boy—she's a man-eater.'

When the song was over, it was their turn to look expectantly at their English teacher. No real answer seemed to occur to him, he crushed his cigarette underfoot.

'Why does he sing that?' asked Kerim, disgruntled because he didn't understand something in the new language that came so easily to him after all, even though he knew the words.

'What?'

'That she eats people.'

'What else could it mean?'

Kerim didn't need to think for long and was first again.

'That she eats men.'

Only Ahmad behind the steering wheel burst out in a wheezing laugh, all the others waited for an answer.

The scrap-metal dealer came back, he pushed his cart forward even more slowly. When he had drawn level with them, he stopped, stood up straight and looked over observantly. Then he made signs and pointed with his big, knotted hands at the baskets and bundles he was transporting. Wherever there was a group of people standing, whether under the tin awnings or by the shop windows with their film of dust, he tried to do business.

'He doesn't mean it literally,' said the English teacher finally. 'She's—she's simply hungry.' He left it at that.

Dismissing the dealer with a curt gesture, the teacher walked away.

Ahmad pressed the play button once again. With a driving rhythm, the song boomed from the car. They all nodded or rocked back and forth to it, as the scrap-metal dealer got behind his cart again, hesitantly bent forward as if in pain and set the cart in unbelievably slow motion.

All the boys in the neighbourhood admired the lanky and always good-humoured Ahmad. Not only because he could already drive a car but also because he was head and shoulders above them all in a in a quiet and cheerful way that no one could really find unpleasant. But there was also something else that drew Kerim to Ahmad and to the house of his family—Shirin, his younger sister.

Everything about their first meeting was chance. He had come to pick up Ahmad. Shirin had opened the gate to him and had immediately gone back to her work. She was taking laundry from a long line stretched zigzag across the courtyard, carefully folding it and stacking it in a green plastic basket. At first, Kerim hardly took any notice of her. He looked at the shirts flapping in the wind, spreading their soft arms as if in greeting, stared at the low house with its dark kitchen windows, and the two plump cats under them which had fled the midday sun into the shade beneath a wooden bench. The longer he waited, however, the more frequently his eyes came to rest on the young girl. He did not know why, there was nothing about her that could have captivated him and yet he scrutinized her. Of course, he tried to make sure that she didn't notice and looked away at the very moment she looked over her shoulder at him. She did so fairly often, he thought. She said nothing and did not even appear friendly. Yet to Kerim she had become, from one moment to the next, the most attractive being he had ever seen. He registered the contours of her body when she stretched up to the washing line and bent down to the basket. He was ashamed of his glances, at the same time he blamed her for them, because the power which she attracted in fact emanated from her. He was bewildered. What he felt was new to him and he wanted to get rid of the feeling. Insofar as he had known himself up to this point, it didn't belong to him, it was something foreign that wanted to seize him that afternoon, and all that he knew about it was that it came from outside. Although Shirin behaved as if she didn't notice anything, Kerim was certain that she was laughing at him. He began to catch her sidelong glances and saw how she screwed up her beautiful dark eyes as if she were smiling, yet without really doing so. He saw her raising her bare arms and asked himself what in all the world was so special about them. She was only a girl, like so many he had already seen in his life. Yet something had transformed her. It wasn't anything she had done, yet in front of his eyes she had turned into another being.

Ahmad at last came out of the house. He ignored his sister, hurried past her to the gate and beckoned to Kerim who immediately followed him. Already almost on the street, he looked around once more and his presentiment was fulfilled—Shirin was watching him as if he had forgotten something important. Kerim felt his ears becoming hot as he called over the wall, 'See you soon.'

The new feeling didn't leave him. He could only forget it now and then, something he managed best while learning. Yet it was inside him like an unfamiliar restlessness which awoke when he had no work and none of his friends to distract him. He had no proper appetite any more and everything that he did and experienced passed him by, leaving no trace. As he didn't know what to do, he asked Ahmad several times after his sister, with a great deal of skill, however, and without showing any emotion. Finally, he couldn't stop himself and went alone to the house of Ahmad's family. He did it without any goal in mind, just to be near her.

Standing in front of the courtyard gate again, he began to feel embarrassed. He went to the other side of the street and waited there. It was hot and there was no shade anywhere on the street lined with low buildings. So he sat down close to one of the walls, drew up his knees and stared across.

After a while, a boy appeared spraying water on the ground with a hose. A conspicuously well-dressed man came past, laid his prayer beads on the boy's head, for the lack of any other possibility, and let him rinse his hands. After that, he picked up the beads again, pushed the hose aside and walked on. Kerim watched the man and wished he were him.

4

At school Kerim discovered that a new war was imminent. It was not, however, his teachers who told him but his fellow pupils. No one else talked about political matters, at least not in public and not in front of children. Kerim's parents, too, were cautious. Members of the secret police were everywhere and were assisted by an army of informers.

Somewhat later, it was officially announced that the government in Baghdad had decided to preserve and defend the historic and natural rights of the country. That meant invasion of the smaller southern neighbour which long ago had indeed once been a province of the country. According to their teachers, the notoriously decadent ruling dynasty of this dwarf state propped up by the West had hardly deserved any sympathy.

At first, the events in the south seemed very remote. It was the highway that brought the new war to the front door of Kerim and his family. At the beginning, all tank and troop transports were moving south. Then they came back, a few at first, finally whole columns. Sometimes the drivers of the transporters stopped at the restaurant. They had always been driving for a very long time and were happy to have got away from the desert in the south. The transports were evidently intended to secure the country's borders. Most of the drivers were anxious. The attack had led to international outrage. No one openly criticized the leadership but in the men's conversations, there were often abrupt pauses which no one interrupted, just as if what they said had blacked-out passages.

Kerim remembered the pictures of a white-haired man on TV. He stood behind a wooden lectern and at certain words his head jerked forward. At that time Kerim already understood some English, but it was hardly any use since, after a few seconds, an Arab commentator spoke over him. But he knew this was the American president, emphatically nodding through cigarette smoke and food smells and smiling with hardly visible lips.

It was not only the situation in the country that changed. Kerim saw stray dogs everywhere. Earlier their number had remained tolerable, they were shot if they appeared in packs and many of them always perished on the roads. Now nothing seemed to curb their numbers. They trotted along the alleys of the suburb, crouched in the shadow of the houses and rummaged through the piles of refuse near the market stands.

One day, on his way to school, Kerim found himself among them. A big, grey dog with a crippled front paw hobbled in front of him and didn't want to let him past. At first, Kerim thought he was mistaken, walked faster and came very close to the animal. The dog dodged to the side, ran around a metal canister lying there, as if to take a run-up, and attacked Kerim. Its teeth were dark and protruded from its mouth like little hooks. Yet what frightened Kerim much more were the eyes. Framed by bald patches, they lay pale between deep folds like remains of dirty ice. The first time the jaws snapped shut, they just missed Kerim's hand. Taken by surprise, Kerim backed clumsily away to a garden wall. In doing so, he bent forward a little and, already at the next moment, felt the heavy paws on his chest. Standing on its hind legs, the dog was taller than Kerim and stared down at his face. It was only for a second that he hesitated before shaking the animal off, but it would have been long enough for it to bite at him. He must have instinctively jerked away, because he didn't know how he had got his neck out of reach of these jaws. He quite clearly heard the sound of the teeth snapping together, it ripped apart the atmosphere of unreality that still surrounded him. With all his strength, he pushed the heavy body of the dog away and ran back down the alley. For a moment, he wanted to cry out but there was not a soul to be seen. Not a single silhouette was visible at the end of the lane, the morning light lay heavy on the sandy ground and nothing seemed to leave traces on this surface. Kerim was still moving as if in a dream, at once lightly and with a racing heart. And he couldn't believe his eyes when he looked back in the direction he had come from. Four more dogs emerged from the light, indistinct shapes, at first, becoming more solid and making straight for him.

The grey dog had not followed him. It was still standing by the wall and waiting, while the others drew closer. Kerim thought quickly. He had never been in such danger before. And yet he first of all had to get it into his head that the huge dog over there had just attacked him. He resolved to use his bundle of books as a weapon.

The four dogs were only a few yards away from him. A reddish one was so thin that it resembled a greyhound, it was as if its ribs ran over the fur. Another was stronger with long legs on which it approached head down. As the dogs distributed themselves around him, Kerim dared to utter a brief cry. The dogs started and the loud high tone from his throat scared Kerim himself. Without warning the grey dog attacked him. This time he jumped up. But Kerim reacted quickly and struck its head with the bundle of books. Howling, the dog fell into the dust, immediately got back on its feet and withdrew a couple of yards.

This success encouraged Kerim. He leapt towards the reddish dog and kicked it. Either he surprised the animal or it was simply too weak to evade him. Kerim struck it with full force on the side of the stomach. The dog didn't howl, instead it arched its back in pain and the next moment opened its jaws unnaturally wide. Kerim had actually by now wanted to be running back down the alley but the sight transfixed him. The dog's body twitched convulsively and Kerim immediately realized that it was about to vomit something up. The effect of his kick surprised him—he almost forgot the other dogs and had to force himself to keep an eye on them. The grey one had not yet recovered from the blow, it was wandering aimlessly around. The two on the other side were ready to take flight in an instant. Kerim had got the upper hand and immediately felt safer. A light wind rose and whistled gently in his ears. He was still alone in the lane with the dogs, yet life seemed to be reawakening, as if he had bobbed up to the surface from the depths of a lake.

He stared at the dark clot which the red dog had brought up onto the sand. The dog briefly sniffed at it again, before making off, hesitantly, as if it perhaps wanted to swallow it down again. Flies had settled on the clot at once. It took a little time before Kerim recognized the fingers among meat fibres and residues of blood. Later he wished he had not looked so closely but what he saw imprinted itself in every detail in a fraction of a second. It was a hand or at least part of one, and what he recognized it by was a golden gleaming ring on one of the three fingers which lay slightly bent in the sand in front of him, as if they still belonged to a living human being.

With an effort, he tore himself away from the sight and ran back without paying any more attention to the dogs. The wind in his ears swallowed every sound, and even if they had followed him he was no longer bothered about it. But the dogs remained behind.

At home they only wanted to believe half of everything he told them about this encounter.

'Why do we eat animals, in fact?' Kerim abruptly asked his father, after the latter had just been trying to reassure him, because of the business of the swallowed hand.

'What's that got to do with it?' he responded, since no answer occurred to him.

Kerim remained silent. The question was the only thing which really preoccupied him after the incident with the dogs. No one anyway believed that he had been in serious danger. At least that was the impression he got, because his mother simply nodded all the time when he talked about the big grey dog, his father said nothing. His brothers, on the other hand, found just that part particularly exciting and asked after every detail until Kerim grew tired of entertaining them with it.

And he also became fed up with the assurances of his father, who tried to convince him that the hand had simply been a piece of meat and the dog could also have found it somewhere. His face, however, revealed aversion and also uncertainty about the affair.

Kerim was familiar with this kind of hushing-up all around him. It usually happened unintentionally, was more a reflex than anything else. If someone had seen anything odd and was reckless enough to talk about it, then he got answers such as: It was certainly only this or that. It also happened—Kerim had observed it in the restaurant—that simply no one replied, which was very unusual and would necessarily alarm the speaker.

'What else should we eat apart from animals?' his father smiled.

'Plants perhaps.'

'But we eat plants, too. Is that not enough for you?'

'Yes, but I feel sorry for the animals.'

His father sighed. 'And you say that after they had almost eaten you. You should not feel sorry for them. It's God's will that we eat them. If it were otherwise, we wouldn't do it.'

With that, the conversation was over. But whenever Kerim recalled it, it was clear to him that something quite different had concerned him. He just did not know how and, above all, to whom he should say it. On the way to school or in front of the house, he would often stop and not just to catch his breath. He looked down at himself and at his broad shadow. Then he looked at other boys of his age and occasionally even grown men. I'm fat, he said to himself, and others are thin. The conclusion satisfied him and only later did he realize—he had begun to be at odds with himself.

The feeling was like being dizzy and it was related to everything he knew. He had doubts not only about himself but also about his family, and, above all, about his father. That was why he asked him several times about the hand the dog had vomited up and carefully observed his reaction. Kerim knew what he had seen and so he only paid attention to the attempts to talk him out of it. It began with disbelief, then followed forced laughter and finally it ended with speculations about who the poor victim could have been. But it was never serious. The story came from another world, a kind of foreign land, and Kerim suspected that as far as his family was concerned this foreign land only existed inside his head.

The school was at the northern end of the town, it was a long way on foot for Kerim. Even after the incident with the dogs, he bravely went down the alley. Sometimes he almost wished that the pack would turn up again, so that he could show it to everyone. But it had disappeared like an apparition.

After the alley, his route took him straight to the edge of town, where the gently rising treeless hills of the surrounding countryside began. Although one could see a long way, Kerim was obsessed by the idea that the dogs were hiding there and waiting for him. At night, he lay awake, heard the regular breathing of his sleeping brothers and, surrounded by their fearlessness, felt himself abandoned.

He saw the dogs emerge out of the clay colour of the ground, at first transparent as phantoms on the pale, shimmering, around hilltops, then evermore clearly. In his vision there were twenty of them. Led by the big grey dog they made straight for him, disappeared in the hollows only to reappear even larger than before, more defined each time, until he could hear their breath. Cars occasionally glided soundlessly past but, apart from him, no one noticed the dogs.

Kerim summoned up his courage and told his mother about it. She was just rinsing dishes in the yard. When he had finished, she briefly held her hands in the stream of water and turned off the tap as if to make sure there was the necessary quiet for her reply. She looked at him but hesitated for a moment. Kerim hoped fervently that she would find a solution. He had not found it easy to open his heart to her, yet he saw no other way out and he felt a little ashamed. It was only bad in the morning, he added right away. In the afternoon, on the way back, he wasn't afraid.

She found a solution. For the next two weeks, his father reluctantly accompanied him to school. They made their way at a very slow pace, two ponderous figures, their arms sticking out away from their bodies. The coolness of the morning made them shiver. And suddenly, the streets were busy again. People Kerim had never noticed before greeted his father and engaged him in short conversations. So it took a long time before they finally reached the school. His father never failed to pause briefly at the main road and look over to the hills. When nothing happened, he silently walked on. That was his way of dealing with Kerim's night-time terror. Astonishingly, it helped.

The school was an inconspicuous building, separated by a high fence from the street on which, further up, the booksellers spread out their goods on the pavement. In order to reach it, one had to cross an almost-circular open space. In the middle, a tall mast with the national flag was surrounded by a symmetrical arrangement of flower boxes. Kerim liked this square. When he passed it in the morning, it was always peaceful and still, although there was also a small teahouse in which, even at this time, the old men were sitting and smoking their water pipes. He knew a couple of them from the restaurant.

When he came to the square, he always bore to the right. Since there was little traffic at this end of the town, he could walk on the road.

That's what he did one morning, accompanied by his father. After the latter had conducted a few fleeting conversations at the tables of the teahouse, he suddenly turned around and walked quickly back to his son who was standing a little distance away. He even took him by the hand before urging him on. They went around the flagpole.

'Don't look over,' were the first words his father said to him that morning.

Behind them, the voices faded away, in front of them lay the empty space. Isolated clouds drifted across the deep blue sky. Their shadows wandered over walls, houses and asphalt. Although Kerim was determined to keep his eyes on the road leading to the school, he nevertheless turned his head. His gaze was drawn by the other side of the square, where the House of the Communist Party was. With its grey-brown colour and the row of uniformly high windows, it resembled a factory building. A red flag fluttered on the roof, much smaller than the national flag on the square, yet visible from some distance. Normally, a tired guard sat dozing on a plastic chair in front of the entrance gate. This time, however, a dark green army transporter blocked the gate. It was parked right on the street corner. On the load space was a large container-like box without windows. Instead, narrow slits could be made out just under the roof.

'You mustn't look over there,' his father warned him again.

Yet Kerim couldn't help but look. That morning, they belonged together. The seemingly abandoned party headquarters, the two big crows on the wall in front, whose heads moved jerkily, as if they, too, were listening for the sounds from the transporter. These sounded like hammering from a shaft deep down in the earth and they came at regular intervals.

'What is that?' asked Kerim

'I don't know. Don't stop.'

Shortly before they reached the street, the school was already visible in the distance, Kerim heard the crows' wing beats. He looked back and saw them flying off. They had been alarmed by a dull rumble from the transporter, followed by further sounds which were louder than before.

'There are people inside,' said Kerim, more to himself than anything else.

'Yes,' replied his father hastily. When they had walked a few steps further, he added, 'The street over there—you know where it leads, don't you?'

'To the big prison.'

'Exactly. Those are prisoners to be taken there.'

Kerim said nothing.

His father stopped suddenly and drew him close. 'Promise me that you won't go near it. Whether the truck is still there afterwards or not. Promise me.'

Surprised, Kerim nodded.

'I'm counting on you,' said his father. 'Or do I have to pick you up from school?'

'No,' said Kerim quickly, because he wanted at all costs to avoid appearing childish. 'I won't go near it.'

'Good,' said his father, gripped Kerim's hand more tightly and pulled him along.

5

The transporter with the prisoners stood on the square for another day. On his way home from school, Kerim walked slowly and cautiously past it and listened as hard as he could for the now hardly audible noises. The square was completely deserted. Kerim looked around surreptitiously and saw draped windows and doors which seemed as if they had been shut and barred for the last time. Even the teahouse at the corner appeared to be closed. At any rate, the wind blew veils of fine sand over the empty tables on which the cats slept curled up but with alert and mobile ears.

Kerim was still firmly determined to obey his father's instruction. He made for the far end of the square, past the flag in the middle, and did not take his eyes off the transporter behind it. It seemed to him as if he would have to circle it with agonizing slowness. He stared at the ventilation slits, dirt caked around them, and still he tried to make out noises coming from inside.

He didn't know what finally caused him to slow down and walk over. When he thought about it later, it was probably above all an excess of a feeling of security that made him brave. It was not as if he wanted to disobey his father. Rather, his father himself through his presence on the square had opened up a secure space—where he had been with him, nothing really bad could happen to Kerim.

The red flag hung limply over the building, twitching only occasionally in the light wind. He crossed the square taking care to look in all directions. The desertedness spurred on his curiosity. When he was standing in front of the transporter he briefly paused and didn't quite know what he should do next. Ready at every moment to recoil, he placed his hand on the metal side wall of the container. It was hot, as he had expected. After a few seconds, he became aware of the stench coming from the truck and filling the air around him. He hadn't expected that. He resisted the impulse to run away now after all and crept around the back of the transporter.

The big door at the back was bolted with a metal bar. There were no ventilation slits in the other side-wall, bare and smooth, it faced the building of the Communist Party. Kerim did not understand it yet—the transporter had been parked there as a threat, as a gesture of power.

He went around the vehicle again to the side with the slits. He waited for a moment, then tapped on the metal wall. Nothing happened. He tapped again. This time more firmly. As he was about to give up, he heard a banging sound from inside. Someone was moving and bumping against the wall as he did so. Kerim knocked again. He could hardly breathe with excitement. What had he started here, he asked himself, and clearly felt how the forbidden attracted him, opened up to him like a dark room, far larger than he had expected.

Now he clearly heard a tapping signal. He placed his hand flat against the tin wall and felt the taps. He knocked in reply.

'Who are you?'

Kerim recoiled in shock. The voice was quiet but clear. It came from above. He looked up to the ventilation slits and realized that the man was speaking to him through them.

Kerim said his name but the man didn't understand him, so he had to repeat it.

After a short pause the man said, 'Don't talk so loud. For yes, knock once, for no, twice. Have you got that?'

Kerim tapped the wall gently once.

'Go to my family,' said the man, repeated it and waited for Kerim's sign.

He described exactly where they lived. Kerim made an effort to retain everything. But he was distracted, without, at first, really noticing it. There were quiet footsteps approaching the transporter. Kerim couldn't see anyone but he was seized by an anxiety which made it difficult for him to go on listening.

'Tell Alia that I love her. Do you hear me?'

Kerim gave no sign. He looked towards the rear end of the transporter and knew that at any moment, someone would appear and discover him.

'Do you hear me?' asked the man inside. 'Tell her that I love her and will come back.'

Kerim had already begun to move. He wanted to quickly disappear and would no doubt have managed it but he couldn't bring himself to leave the prisoner behind just like that. His voice sounded dull and suffocated, his despair was evident in it. It lay in the haste of the words he gasped out, each one squeezed out through the metal wall. So Kerim darted back after all and banged against the wall once, louder than before, to warn the man.

As he turned around to finally leave the transporter behind it was too late. With a few long strides a man in uniform was beside him. He wanted to grab Kerim by the shoulder but the latter stepped back in time. Yet he didn't dare flee.

'What are you doing here?' The man was neither a policeman nor a soldier. He wore sand-coloured trousers and a dark green shirt. They were parts of a uniform that Kerim had never seen before. The heavy boots and the belt made a military impression.

'Nothing at all,' said Kerim quietly. He looked at the ground, then immediately looked the man in the eye and tried to assume an innocent expression. 'I was only curious,' he said.

'You've no business being here. Has no one told you that?'

Kerim shook his head and lowered his eyes in the hope of looking more like a child than he really was.

'What's your name?' asked the man.

Kerim told him and in his head was already preparing his next answers. Nothing stirred in the transporter, perhaps those inside were listening.

'Where do you come from? What is your family called?'

That was the feared, the always-dangerous question, and it was immediately clear to Kerim that he must on no account answer it. This man who was evidently uncomfortable in the heat of the square was not only a stranger in the usual sense—he stood on the other side, came from another, dangerous world. He must find out nothing about me, thought Kerim. He considered whether he could run away but instantly dismissed the idea. I'm too fat, he said to himself, he'll catch up with me. He saw himself locked up in a cell in the big prison, thought of his father and what he would say. For a moment he was overcome by despair. He wanted to start crying but he couldn't any more, not the way he had done it before, perhaps only a year ago. Something inside him had hardened—his eyes remained dry, the light was dazzling him but it didn't make them blur. He saw the narrow face, the moustache with its many grey hairs and the angrily narrowed eyes.

'Answer me!' The man wiped the sweat from his forehead and shook it from his hand. Drops audibly struck the tin wall of the transporter. 'What is your father's name? Tell me, or . . .'

Kerim was still staring at him but without seeing anything. He searched feverishly for a solution, perspiration stung his eyes.

Suddenly, he relaxed, raised his head and gave the name of Anatol with whom he had eaten the unborn lamb. The man wanted to know more and Kerim claimed that Anatol was his father. Later he again and again asked himself why he had done it and never found an answer. At the time, however, every word he said about Anatol was a relief to him, he spun this made-up story around himself like a protective cocoon.

'So you're not from the town?'

Kerim nodded and again put on an innocent face.

'Well, you seem to have enough to eat there . . . .' The man looked down at him.

Kerim nodded again. To his relief, the man was now tired of the business. His boot scraped the dust of the street and he spat in front of him. Abruptly, he struck the transporter with his fist, as Kerim had done, only much harder. He turned back to the boy.

'I won't ask you what you were talking about to those in there. Tell it to your father, because perhaps someone will ask him about it. I don't know. Clear off now and never do anything like that again.'

Kerim was already making off before the man had finished. Then at last he turned away and whatever happened now would not have made him hesitate. As if freed from a shackle, Kerim felt himself to be light and almost nimble. But this state did not last long. Hardly had he left the square behind than he began to have doubts about what he had done.

He had to force himself, yet he did go to Alia as the man in the prison transporter had asked him to do. Without saying a thing to his parents, he set out after school.

On the way, he was overcome by fear at this visit. What should he tell the wife apart from the little that the prisoner had managed to say? He did not even know whether she would believe him. The street led him ever deeper into the poor settlements at the edge of the town. Unplastered walls with grey or blue metal doors, isolated young trees planted here and there in small holes in the pavement. In the heat, which fell upon the town with the gusts of wind from the hills, they seemed to be dying more than living. Children squatted close to the gates. Kerim didn't know any of them, and they took hardly any notice of him. Sometimes holes in the walls revealed narrow courtyards with smooth stone floors swept a thousand times, as if made ready to receive supplies, but there were only washing lines and tin stoves. The homes, too, were mostly empty and their doors stood open as if they were unoccupied.

Then he came to narrower, winding alleys leading uphill, with sewage channels running along the middle. The walls were close on either side and warm and he realized with astonishment that he had never been here before. He studied the forest of antennae above the flat roofs, the improvised wooden electricity masts at every corner and the occasional very old houses whose upper stories were supported by knotted wooden posts. It made him feel a little proud that he was carrying out his mission on his own account.

Just as the prisoner had described it, the alley led to a small square. At once fascinated and satisfied, Kerim looked at the old building in which there was a furniture shop. In front of it, plastic chairs were stacked up, and on the roof, visible from a distance, were dozens of unvarnished bedsteads and shelves. Kerim had been looking for this conspicuous house as a guide. He had forgotten another one but now he saw it and remembered it again. On an old stretch of wall right next to the furniture shop was an inscription in big, almost faded green letters. '7up' it said—the prisoner had repeated it more than once. Kerim wondered whether he had forgotten it because this old advert was so out of place here.

It was only a few more steps to Alia's house. When he was standing in front of it, he called over the wall until the door opened. The young woman looked at him with a smile, she stood there calmly, one hand on the gate. Kerim ran his hand over his stomach, wiped the sweat from his forehead and made sure once again that she was the person. When she nodded, his agitation caused him to fall silent for a moment. He would gladly have brought her other, better news. He asked whether her husband was at home. She quickly said no, they had heard nothing from him for weeks, did he know anything? He collected himself, looked in her face and tried to speak slowly, but everything the prisoner had told him, everything that he, Kerim, had repeated to himself gushed out.

He saw the colour draining from her face. She rested her arm on the gate, yet recoiled from Kerim as if he was threatening her. The gate opened wider, two small children, much younger than Kerim, and an elderly man hurried out of the house. All three stood wordlessly beside the woman and stared at Kerim who, for his part, took a step backwards into the street, since he didn't know what to expect from these people. But he wanted to tell his story to the end, because it was important, after all, that Alia understood in what circumstances the man had spoken the words intended for her. And so he continued as the woman's knees gave way and she sank down by the gate. The elderly man leapt to help her, at the same time glancing angrily at Kerim. The latter still had to pass on the final words. Astonished at the power his message gave him, real power over people, he spoke more loudly than before.

When he had fallen silent the woman was weeping and the two children were also beginning to whimper. The man, however, came at Kerim. His face red with rage, he raised his arm to strike but then stopped himself.

'Go away!' he shouted. He reached out for the gate but couldn't shut it because of Alia.

Because he thought he could protect himself by doing so, Kerim forced himself to cry. He managed little more than a grimace. What really preoccupied him was the effect of words, something he had encountered for the first time that afternoon.

On the way back, he wiped the remains of the false tears from his face like flies. He didn't really have an explanation for what had happened. He had done nothing wrong and yet he was left with a bad conscience.

***

The bad news reached them about three weeks after the meeting with Alia. They were about to eat their meal late in the evening. With his brothers, Kerim had already laid the blanket on the floor and placed pots and plates on it. Now all of them were squatting around the edge of the blanket. Kerim was on the brink of putting a handful of rice in his mouth. As always in those days, he felt ravenous but also knew that others didn't eat as he did. Only in his own family was he sure of not disturbing anyone with his greed. His father stopped chewing, raised his head and said Anatol had been arrested, early in the morning, and no one knew anything. After that, he continued his unhurried chewing.

The news struck Kerim like a blow. He was hardly able to swallow anything. He picked up his glass of water, looking anxiously around at the others as he did so. But it's over, that was what went through his head. He had passed on the prisoner's message, with that his experience with the transporter had been consigned to the past as far as he was concerned. And now everything was there again, it had followed him, as the dogs had once followed him, and he felt himself to be guiltier than ever.

His mother came over to him, pushed back her sleeves, reached out to his chin and raised his face in order to look at it. Kerim did nothing to resist, he wanted to but he couldn't smile with her.

'What's wrong?' she asked him. 'Doesn't it taste good?'

'It does,' he muttered.

How he would have liked to start crying, throw himself at her breast and confess everything he had done. But something told him that it was too late, perhaps only by two weeks, but for good. He looked at his mother's so-familiar face, at her very dark eyebrows and the pointed nose and he knew she could do nothing more for him. At the same time, he saw Anatol clearly before him—the small, strange man, who now had to suffer because of him and would probably never find out why.

He heard his father and his brothers eating noisily and thought, No one can help me any more. The best thing I can do now is to say nothing about it.

Yet Kerim felt a need for a confidant to whom he could confess his wrongdoing and all the appalling things that would quite certainly result from it. But no one came to mind. He thought of his friends, but they were all much too close to his family, it would have made no difference telling them or his parents. His English teacher was always willing to listen to him, yet Kerim didn't quite trust him. Then he thought of Shirin whom he secretly still adored. As if his trouble could bring her closer, he prowled around the house of Ahmad's family and waited for her on her way to the girls' school. He had made up his mind to talk seriously to her and to find a way of describing his problems to her. Yet it all proved to be pure fantasy. When she was standing in front of him in her school uniform of dark skirt and glowing white blouse, nothing at that moment was more remote than talking about what had happened to Anatol. She looked at him, expectant yet carefree, and made him forget what was weighing on him. Always at such moments, and also when she came to the restaurant with her family, she transformed him into the man he had not yet become. This effect, too, Kerim ascribed to her alone, came to believe finally that he could only change if he were close to her and then only if her constantly joking brother was not around. The gangling Ahmad, his parents' joy, never appeared more foolish to Kerim than when he sat at table there in the restaurant. Compared with Shirin, whose profound thoughtfulness—he was firmly convinced of this—was only hidden by her cheerfulness, as by a veil, Ahmad was someone completely taken up with what was around him. He fulfilled almost every demand, and if for once he did not manage to do so, then he gained the sympathies at least of those who saw him lose. Everything seemed to give him pleasure—food, driving, learning, life. He simply got by without striving for anything higher, there was nothing that would have caused him to reflect longer than need be, still less brood about it. In Kerim's eyes Ahmad was an image of present-day life—he embodied everything from which he felt increasingly excluded. Yet that was not all he felt as he waited on the family. When he looked at Ahmad, smiled and waved at him, he felt as if he himself had somehow come out wrong.

6

Kerim experienced the course of the war like a distant thunderstorm and what impressed him most strongly about it was his parents' helplessness. His father acted as if nothing had happened, although every one of his guests talked about nothing else.

His mother on the other hand changed. When the tank transporters drove past on the highway right in front of the restaurant and the ground shook, she didn't want to go out of the house any more. She helped her husband with the work. But when the taxi drivers came with the deliveries, she didn't even greet them any more—she withdrew, as if they were complete strangers. Many of the men had known Kerim's father for years and he had difficulties explaining his wife's behaviour.

'It's the war,' Kerim once heard him say. 'She's afraid of the tanks, and everything that's still to come.'

The man to whom he was talking owned a chicken farm at the other end of town. He threw one of the full cages he was just unloading to the ground. Then he stretched and rested his arm on the side panelling of his pickup. The other dirty hand he raised to his forehead. Anxiously, he looked down the wide road which disappeared to the south between undulating ground and thickets.

Through the panic-stricken cackling of his hens he said loudly, 'And she's right. This time it will be worse.'

Kerim picked up the cages and stacked them against the wall of the house. His father turned to the chicken farmer who looked depressed.

'Why do you say that?' he asked.

'What?'

'That it will be especially bad. Compared to what?'

The other scratched his forehead and sighed. 'Worse than everything we've known.'

Kerim's father became impatient. Chicken feathers flew through the air around him, he rubbed his stomach nervously. The farmer looked straight at him.

'Don't any of you watch the news?'

'Sure.'

'Then you must know that this time the whole world is attacking us. My brother in Basra says they've assembled so many tanks and troops at the border that one can no longer see the desert floor. They're going to overrun us.'

'Why us? They're going to overrun our beloved and indispensable leader.'

The chicken farmer shook his head. 'And who's going to follow on their heels? The Iranians—they're already painting the signs which say, "Three cheers for Ayatollah Khomeini."' He went around to the open load area, opened a cage and skilfully pulled out a hen. The white bird twitching in his arm, he continued, 'For us here things can only get worse. It would be best if you lay in supplies.' He winked, wrung the chicken's neck and gave it to Kerim's father. 'That's for you this evening.'

When he drove off, they kept on watching him until he could no longer be seen in the haze hanging over the road. Kerim felt his father's worry about what he had heard, but his father continued to act as if he were unconcerned and merely said, 'He's always been telling stories, for as long as I've known him.'

But the man proved to be right. A couple of weeks later, the whole country was sliding into civil war. The president in Baghdad appeared to be overthrown in a few days. There were no more histrionic speeches on TV, no announcements of triumphs, not even news any more. Performances of Arabic song ran unceasingly—soloists, choirs, now and then very large choirs with small soloists who stood in the foreground. Parts of the normal hour-long medal-award ceremonies in one of the presidential palaces were still scattered in-between. Then there were no broadcasts any more, white noise covered the TV screen.

'Now the light has gone out in the presidential palace,' commented Kerim's father as the whole family stared at the flickering TV.

Instead evermore ragged people appeared on the road. Families, individual old people, finally a wave of refugees pushed up from the south. Kerim only had to step outside the door to learn the latest news from one of the dust-covered figures. He shouted out his questions from the yard gate until someone gave him an answer. The foreign troops had not conquered the capital, they had turned back at the last moment.

'We could already see the dust raised by their tanks,' said an older man bitterly. He was wearing a threadbare jacket, his little turban was askew. His eyes lay deep in their sockets, it was unclear whether their expression was due to horrors experienced or to exhaustion.

From him, Kerim learnt that the old government was in power again and was deploying all still-available troops against the Shiites. The latter had risked an uprising in the hope of being supported by the international forces. The help failed to materialize; now the tables were turned.

'It would be better,' said the man and thoughtfully pushed his fingers under the turban, 'if the Kurds were to react quickly. When he's finished down there he'll come up here. And soon you will be refugees, too.'

This prediction also came true—after the refugees, carried by the same shock wave, came the soldiers.

After weeks of flight, they entered their house again. All still felt the night-time cold of the mountains in their bones. They had spent many days in emergency shelters on Iranian territory just on the other side of the border. It rained often, and the ice-cold water penetrated their clothes. It was the first time that Kerim was glad to be fat. He had seen his mother sitting under several layers of clothes and blankets on a stone outside the big refugee tent and heard her teeth chattering.

The yard gate was wide open as in all the other houses in the neighbourhood. Cautiously, his father went in first, inspected the yard and then crept across the terrace into the kitchen. Kerim stood in the street with his mother and brothers. All were full of uneasy anticipation. On the way back, they had seen destroyed houses, abandoned trucks of the government troops and the dead by the roadside, their faces barely covered by cloths. The Kurds really had risen up and they had succeeded in keeping the government troops in check.

The house had been neither looted nor wrecked, it did not even seem to have been entered. Pots, crockery, glasses and pans were lined up in the kitchen just as neatly as Kerim's father had left them.

But one problem became evermore intense in the days that followed—the meat deliveries no longer came, because many of the peasants in the area had abandoned their farms and stalls during the fighting. Finally, the restaurant had to be closed.

'I have rice and vegetables but without meat I can't cook,' his father said to Kerim one evening. He had two big kitchen knives in his hands and was gesticulating with them. Helplessness was written on his face.

Kerim looked over to his mother. Her face was swollen, for days it had seemed as if she was crying, yet there was never a tear to be seen.

'I have a plan,' his father continued and didn't take his eyes off Kerim. 'But I need help to carry it out.'

Kerim nodded.

'I need someone who is not afraid and who doesn't behave like a child, do you hear me?'

Kerim again nodded silently, yet he felt uncomfortable.

'Take me with you,' shouted his brother Imat and stood in front of his father.

'No,' said the latter, 'only a man can help me.' It sounded so serious that the younger boy was immediately intimidated.

Kerim took the two knives and held them behind his back when he gave his mother a goodbye kiss. Her face expressed complete disapproval, she turned quickly away and pulled the cloth over her head to cover her face. Yet her husband was standing impatiently and determinedly at the door and avoided her surreptitious glances by staring at the car key in his hand.

'Push the knives under your seat,' he said to Kerim when they were at last sitting in the car.

In order to be less conspicuous, they took the Toyota instead of the pickup. They drove south. Darkness was already falling, but in the present situation that was an advantage. His father drove very slowly. They glided past the poorly lit houses. The electricity had just failed, people were making do with oil lamps and candles.

'We can't go straight along the highway,' explained his father and Kerim felt proud that he was being treated like an adult. 'What we are doing is not allowed. We're only doing it because we have to,' he added and gave Kerim a sideways glance. The latter merely nodded seriously.

The lights of a checkpoint could be seen further along the street. They turned onto a narrow side alley in time. Kerim's father accelerated and then braked abruptly at the exit. He switched off the headlights and waited for a minute. They glided further out through the darkness. Among the last remaining houses, Kerim saw another checkpoint, a rectangular brown tent in the middle of a heap of sandbags. He could even make out a kind of hatch, whose soft cover hung down, a piece of cloth with a zip around it. The old Toyota bumped violently along a stony track, then went cross-country and up the gentle rise to the highway. They drove into the darkness that pressed against the windscreen. Only after driving blind for several minutes did Kerim's father switch the lights on again.

About twenty miles further on, they stopped by the side of the road and got out. Kerim's father went to the middle of the road and looked across the now lower hilly landscape. The boy did the same. Before his eyes, the first contours were emerging out of the night, when his father startled him.

'I know where we are,' exclaimed the former hurriedly. 'Get in, it's not much farther.' In front of the car, he paused. 'Do you have to go?'

Kerim proudly shook his head.

The next time they halted, a track that branched off, no more than an unusually wide goat path, had led them to the middle of a flat valley bottom. This time his father switched off engine and lights and for a moment they sat silently side by side in the unfamiliar silence.

'Give me one of the knives,' said Kerim's father then, 'and don't make a sound.'

Kerim understood that they were on a hunting expedition. The rocky floor of the hollow, strewn with small stones, made his every step audible, no matter how hard he tried. Kerim was guided by his father's dark silhouette and paid attention to his signals.

They climbed up to the crest of the next hill, gradually their eyes became accustomed to the darkness.

Kerim thought himself transported to that same moon which shone above him as a crescent in the night sky. The ground around them was grey, yet in some places, deep black patches spread out. Here stood burnt-out wrecks of cars, the paint of which had been turned into a spotted reptile skin. Sand and stones were covered by a layer of ashes in which they left pale footprints. Nothing suggested the presence of other people, the wind alone dominated the silence; restlessly, it blew across the valley, constantly changing direction.

Once at the top, they had a view of the karstic steppe with mounds on it like tumuli. Kerim's father raised his arm and pointed, uncertain at first, at something that looked like a house in the distance. A low wall could be made out in front of it and the weak reflection of the tin roof in the moonlight. Kerim immediately thought of one of the remote farms of very poor people, but he did not know what business the two of them should have there. This time he asked his father, because he thought he had a right to know before they got there.

His father squatted down in front of him. 'Do you remember our picnic in the mountains, when the helicopter came and took away the old women? What did I tell you then?'

Kerim thought.

'If I never talk about it, then in time it will be no more than a dream.'

'And is that what happened?'

Kerim answered in the affirmative.

'It was different with the dogs, wasn't it? You're still thinking about them, because you talked about them so often.'

Although it wasn't true, Kerim also agreed with that.

His father nodded. 'One doesn't forget it, but it's no longer important. It's just the same with what we're doing here. Don't talk about it, to anyone. You know,' he whispered, 'we don't have any meat.' Kerim stared at the knife in his hand. 'There aren't any people over there. All the farms here are abandoned. I only want to see whether we find anything.' Uncertainly, he tried to meet his son's eyes.

The latter knew that his father was lying. Why did they have the knives with them if they were only going to take a look at something? His suspicion was straightaway confirmed by the way his father stalked the farm, while he, Kerim, cautiously followed him.

They crept around the wall and peered through the windows. Then they entered the house. Unlike their own home, this one had been looted. Someone had also attempted to set it alight. Plastic chairs with melted legs stood crookedly in the living space, as if they were sinking into a swamp. There were long trails of soot across panes and metal window frames, lamps and ceiling, as if a huge, black flower was closing around the intruders in the room.

Kerim was afraid of finding bodies. On entering one of the smaller rooms, he stepped hastily back at the sight of a charred bundle. But it was only bedclothes, still exuding the smell of burning.

Relieved, he went back into the yard. He breathed in deeply and briefly enjoyed the coolness of the night. Far in the distance, low over the humps of the hills, the last weak glow of the day could be made out. Kerim strained to hear a noise but there was nothing apart from the gusting night wind which blew over him.

Through this silence echoed his name and he started. His father must have gone quite a distance from the house. Kerim ran in the approximate direction, the wind made it hard for him. So, at first, he searched like a lost dog before finally following a half-tumbled wall. It must be the remains of a much older farm, because after twenty yards, it had no shape any more and a little further after that, it disappeared into the ground.

He saw his father again as a broad shadow. This time, however, his arm with the knife could be clearly recognized, sticking out oddly from his body. Kerim called but his father didn't hear him. As he came closer, Kerim realized that his father was looking down at a large black lump on the ground. He stood still for a moment and gripped the knife in his hand more firmly. He was trembling with excitement and fear.

Hardly had Kerim reached his father when the latter grabbed him and pulled him down. They crouched, each on one side, over a white donkey; its limbs were still twitching and blood was pouring from its opened throat. The blood spread over the ground like a flimsy piece of cloth, rapidly growing larger, and it was darker than everything dark in that night, with an iridescent gleam on its surface.

'Look carefully,' said his father and Kerim's gaze wandered over the bony flank and the hard coat of the donkey, bushy at the back of the neck. 'The eye, look at the eye!'

Kerim looked into the big, moistly shining eye which was still rolling, even if weakly.

'It's still alive,' said Kerim and felt pity and a quiet terror inside.

Then the flat of his father's hand struck him in the face—once, twice.

'Look, I said. What do you see?'

Kerim didn't think he could see anything, he felt only the heat of the blows in his face. The flow of blood lessened. The eye no longer rolled, yet there was still life in it, something was still looking up at them, who were squatting above it. The next moment it had disappeared, nothing had changed in the eye, except that it was now empty as the houses over there, sunk into itself like a thing.

'Did you see it?' asked his father.

'What?' Kerim was uncertain.

'Did you see the life?'

'Yes, now it's gone.'

'But it was there.'

'Yes.'

His father rose to his feet.

'That's all,' he said and looked around.

Kerim didn't understand. 'What?' he repeated.

'All that was and that ever will be. Remember that—it comes and it goes. That's all. Now help me.'

They cut the best pieces out of the body and unhurriedly carried the meat to the car. There they wrapped it in plastic foil and put some in the boot and some on the back seat. Hardly an hour later, they were back home.

7

The meat of the stray donkey did indeed help them to get through the difficult period. His father offered it for months. In all that time, there was only one complaint. An elderly man called Kerim's father over and said that the meat was so tough, he couldn't chew it with his old teeth. The way he spoke, it sounded more like an observation than a reproach.

Kerim had just entered the room and glanced anxiously over the sparsely occupied plastic tables to his father. The latter raised his arms, as he always did when he was agitated. He affirmed each word he spoke with a nod. In this way, he appeared more impressive than what he had to say.

'What do you want? The meat of a calf, pale and tender—or do you want lamb, yes, do you want lamb?'

Kerim was afraid that he was now going to tell the truth, get it off his chest in front of the people there, because no one suffered more from the deception than his father himself.

But his father had only paused for dramatic effect before concluding his scene, still with his arms raised.

'Then bring me lambs and calves. If you can't do that, you have to eat what I have. The cow was just old, do you understand me? These are bad times.'

With that he lowered his arms, turned around, threw the towel over his shoulder and disappeared into the kitchen.

The old man had not dared contradict. Instead, he now gave the son of the cook an appeasing smile which turned into a broad grin when Kerim likewise smiled. He could clearly see the long, pale grey fibres of meat sticking between the man's dark tooth stumps. The sight gave him a bad conscience and so he was friendlier than necessary.

They drove through the abandoned countryside again quite often, always setting out as darkness fell. They saw the sand rise in gusts. In the headlights, the drifting veils of dust appeared like ghostly herds of game. They learnt to observe the huts, to judge whether people were present. Sometimes there were fresh trails on the sandy tracks leading from the highway to the farms. Adolescents stumbled around behind blind windows or crouched in the yards like unarmed occupiers. Then his father always accelerated.

'In this damned country,' he said once, 'nothing works except the traffic. Everything else is unsafe. You can't—are you listening to me?—trust anyone any more. There's no order any more—every stranger can be your murderer.'

* * *

It was around this time that Kerim overheard the conversation of two strange men who came to the restaurant one afternoon and who, merely by appearing, silenced all the other guests. The pair did not give the impression of being hungry. One might almost have thought they were brothers, so alike were they in their dark, dust-covered jackets and white shirts with a rim of sweat on the collar. Kerim had never seen such guests before. Unobtrusively, he went close to a window and peeked out to catch sight of their car. Cars were always significant. Ordinary people, if they had a car at all, drove up in ancient-looking Nissans and Toyotas. Even the tyres with their almost-smooth treads showed that these cars had driven enormous distances. Luxury cars or even just bodyworks that had been looked after were virtually never seen.

Kerim knew at once that the big new Range Rover belonged to these two men who were now noisily pushing their chairs into place and talking loudly to each other, unconcerned about the listeners in the room. A family left the room as unobtrusively as possible, without having finished their meal. The three small children, too, had fallen silent.

The two men didn't interrupt their conversation even when Kerim's father came up to their table and placed the water glasses in front of them. Leaning back, relaxed, their legs stretched out in front of them, they laughed and declaimed. They were evidently glad to be leaving the Kurdish region and returning to the safer south. Only after Kerim's father, looking down on them without saying a word, had waited for some time did one of the two briefly raise his head.

'Bring us whatever occurs to you,' he said slowly and quietly, yet so emphatically that it sounded like a warning.

Kerim's father merely nodded and he went quickly to the kitchen.

Kerim was still standing by the window and, like all the others, was unable to do anything except listen to the men. At first, they just went on joking, but then after one gave a sideways glance they suddenly changed the subject. Kerim looked at them more closely and now he noticed that although they were more or less the same height and also behaved in a similar way while talking, one was quite clearly older and took the lead. Although unshaven and sweaty, he gave the impression of taking care of his appearance. Like someone who works in an office, thought Kerim, high above the dusty streets. When the man wasn't talking, his jaw muscles moved constantly and threateningly under the skin. His gaze always rested only briefly on his interlocutor, then roamed across the room but remained focused. This man was waiting for something, more for a violent response than for a reply. Yet no one moved as he spoke.

He told the story of a man in Europe who managed to place information and leaflets hostile to the regime in the embassy postbags. He had a contact man in Baghdad who received the bags and sorted the mail. He secured the illegal material in order to put it into circulation later on. For a long time, everything went well.

'It was really only a minor matter,' said the man, and a smile played around his mouth. 'But the secret service could not put up with it, because this damned spy in Baghdad was sitting close to the government officials. Word got around. The highest circles became aware of it. And so we came under pressure.'

The man paused. The 'we' seemed finally to have paralysed everyone, including Kerim, who likewise sensed the suddenly rising fear. It was very similar to that around the prisoners' transport. He scrutinized every person in the room, looked up at the roof with the hole in it and again towards the kitchen. The sounds from there cut through the silence. Kerim heard the fat hissing in the huge pan, plates were being readied. He looked cautiously at the man who was speaking, saw the bulge of the shoulder holster under his arm.

'So we had to think of something,' the man continued. 'The one in Germany was less important. These exiles talk and write a lot, it's mostly a waste of time bothering about them. No one really listens to them. But we could use him to get at the other one.'

He leant forward, reached for the water glass and, slurping loudly, emptied it in one gulp.

'What did you do?' asked the other. He, too, was smiling and rested his chin on his hand like an attentive pupil. The other hand, however, lay on his thigh, his fingers drummed gently on the trouser cloth and it wasn't far from there to his gun.

'We sent a woman to the one in Germany whom we suspected. I only know her from photographs, but she was beautiful, well built . . .' He outlined a figure in the air with his hands and both men laughed knowingly. Then the speaker looked around and repeated the gesture to the guests staring at the tables in front of them. 'She looked good—you know what I mean, eh?' He turned back to the other. 'She asked around a bit among the diplomats and then got to know our man right away, one evening in a bar. He simply couldn't resist her. And she was so skilful that he fell in love with her. Imagine, after their first night, she didn't need to do anything at all any more—he was running after her. I envy him, you know, we had put a present in his bed.'

Restlessness was evident among those present, but the man simply raised his voice and addressed the room, 'What do you want? Every one of you would have been weak, believe me. But what do you peasants know about life?'

After a couple of seconds which he allowed to pass, as if he were waiting to be contradicted, the man went on, 'In less than three weeks, we had the name of the other in Baghdad.'

'And?'

The older man raised his shoulders. 'The usual procedure, but for months. The best thing about it—all that time, until we were finished with the spy, the other in Germany was happy with our present. Two sides of one gift.'

Kerim's father stepped up to their table. He was holding the two plates with fried donkey and rice. It occurred to Kerim that he had taken an unusually long time for the two portions. The men made no effort to push their glasses aside. Instead, the younger asked, 'What happened to the Baghdad spy in the end?'

Again the other raised his shoulders, before announcing, 'We played football with his head.'

Slowly, as if he was only now noticing him for the first time, he looked up at Kerim's father. The man narrowed his eyes and nodded at the plates. 'Don't you want to put that down?' His voice sounded quieter and strained.

Kerim again saw the jaw muscles working, their movement radiated up to the temples. At that moment, he realized the danger his father was in. All eyes were on him as he slowly lowered the plates onto the tabletop. Under the man's watchful gaze, he pushed the glasses to the side with the rims of the plates. Immediately after that, he let the plates fall an inch or so onto the table, enough to make a small bang.

The men, just like the people in the room, stared at his father. He remained standing at the table. Kerim remembered exactly the expression on his face—helpless and proud at the same time.

Finally, the older of the two men noisily pushed his chair back and stood up.

'Thanks,' he said, 'but unfortunately we don't have any more time.'

With that, they left the restaurant. Several guests rose immediately and came to the window. They saw the men strolling unhurriedly to their four-wheel drive.

What they didn't see was Kerim's father, who was still standing by the table and staring at the plates. He was wiping his hands on the sides of his trousers without stopping and seemed to be thinking feverishly as he did so. Kerim finally turned to him and asked what was wrong. His father didn't react. He stood there like that for a while longer, then took the plates and carried them back into the kitchen. Kerim looked back at the two men. They were taking their time, had still not got in, but had opened the tailgate and were looking for something. While the younger man bent over and rummaged around, the older man leant casually against the vehicle, frequently changing his position because of the hot metal. He looked steadily over to the restaurant, straight at the window, as if he wanted to commit the faces there to memory. Kerim looked at him very carefully. On the one hand he feared and loathed the man, but on the other he was filled with quiet admiration. His movements were so utterly different from those of the people he knew. He walked around as confidently as a hero in a Western, his gun always in reach, and seemed to fear nothing and no one. On the contrary, he challenged others to a fight whenever he could. It was this very attitude that impressed Kerim. How he wished it for himself—to be afraid of no one, to have to obey no one's orders, to be free. No one here is like this man, thought Kerim, as he stood there at the window, and yet he also guessed that this freedom was linked to something terrible.

His father's heavy footsteps startled him and all the others at the window. He had evidently just washed his hands, was still drying them and, as he went, threw the towel onto one of the tables. He headed straight for the door, his lips pressed together, his face stony. Everyone sensed the danger.

A quiet family man, who had managed to keep his children quiet during the appearance of the secret policemen, was first to react and stood in his way. He tried to block the door. His wife began to wail, as she looked around for help. Now Kerim's mother also emerged from the kitchen, alarmed by the renewed noise. She shouted at her husband, asked what he was intending to do, repeated the question a number of times. Several men tried to hold him back. After a moment's hesitation Kerim, too, forced himself to jump over and reach out for his father's shirt. Now his brothers were also standing in the room and whining. The men managed to push his father up against the wall by the door. Kerim leapt back to the window, worried that the two outside could hear the noise. He was sure they would come back. But they hadn't noticed anything yet. They had meanwhile finished whatever they were doing, the younger one shut the tailgate and they exchanged a few words.

For a short time, it seemed as if his father had calmed down, but then Kerim saw him free himself. Silently, he swept and pushed the hands from his body and started moving again. The heavy man wasn't to be stopped, he reached for the door and opened it. At that same moment, as if at a command, everyone let go of him. They released him into the bright midday light of the open space in front of the restaurant, as if it was forbidden terrain, firmly in the hands of the two secret policemen, towards whom Kerim's father now walked unwaveringly.

The older policeman detached himself from the vehicle and took a relaxed step towards Kerim's father. He even made as if to open his arms and said something. From the window, Kerim had the impression he was greeting his father. The latter stopped in front of the man and began to gesticulate and shout. What he was saying could not be made out, yet one could see that after the scene in restaurant, he was getting something off his chest. The younger of the two men took little interest in the argument. He glanced at the two on the other side of the vehicle and then got in. At that, the other immediately turned around. Kerim's father raised his voice, now individual words were audible. He angrily demanded that the two pay for the food they had left lying. His interlocutor opened the door of the four-wheel drive. Only now did he briefly lose his temper. He pushed the fat man away and with outstretched arm pointed at the restaurant. Kerim saw his dark gleaming eyes and couldn't bear it any longer.

He pushed past the other people and went out. His father caught sight of him and motioned to him with his hand to stay where he was. The door of the four-wheel drive was slammed, the engine started, slowly the Range Rover began to move. Then everything happened very fast. His father ran to the exit of the lot and stood in the way of the vehicle. Kerim saw only the dark-tinted panes, heard the roar of the engine and, immediately afterwards, the dull, soft thud of the impact as the Range Rover struck his father. Rumbling, it rolled over the body, which was tossed around and came to rest in a cloud of dust. A cry made up of many voices came from the restaurant, now everyone came running out. The women covered their faces with their hands, the men ran over to the lifeless body. Kerim stood as if paralysed, the only thing he could do was watch as the four-wheel drive disappeared southwards down the highway.

PART TWO

1

His father's death changed everything in Kerim's life. At the moment of the shock, during the period of mourning and even when they opened the restaurant again, he still felt like the boy he had been before. But that passed quickly, once all responsibility and all work had passed to him as eldest son. Later, Kerim didn't like to think about that time. He avoided remembering the arguments with the string of lazy helpers, the last of whom he sacked after a fierce shouting match, although he knew that his father had been under an obligation to the lad's father. The incident then did indeed give rise to unpleasant talk in the neighbourhood. Without consideration for the recent death, without showing any understanding for the new situation of the family, a couple of people, always the same ones, stirred things up against them. In their eyes, Kerim's family were probably destined to suffer.

Nevertheless, the food-supply situation gradually improved after the country was divided into zones and kept under surveillance from the air by foreign warplanes. Little by little, peace and quiet returned. The old regime was still in power but its influence no longer extended to the north.

Only occasionally did Kerim employ new assistants. He was dissatisfied with all of them. What was he supposed to do with people who held up the work instead of making it go faster and whom, on top of that, he had to pay? He directed his energy to making the work as businesslike as possible. He also retained the custom of slaughtering an animal for the Festival of Sacrifice. He did it reluctantly but he instinctively trusted his father's long experience as far as conforming to tradition was concerned.

It was not the cooking or the trips to the bazaar that he found burdensome in those years. He suffered rather from his mother's grief. No matter how hard he tried to replace his father, it was no use. They were marked for ever by misfortune, and he wasn't the only one who thought so. Kerim doubted that he was still a candidate for Shirin's family, if he ever had been. Ahmad, at any rate, talked about her admirers with suspicious candour, and after the death of Kerim's father his family no longer turned up in the restaurant as they had done before. On their now-rare encounters on the street, Shirin sometimes looked at him as if she was trying to remember someone whom she had once known.

The thought made him feel unsure, yet he knew he could not resign himself. To Kerim, it would have meant that everything in his life had already been decided.

Whatever his mother did, whether she was rinsing the great quantities of crockery or sitting with the women neighbours, she hardly ever addressed him directly. It was as if she was angry at fate. Sometimes he observed her behaving just as before with his brothers. Only Kerim seemed to have become another person to her since that event, someone whom she now only gave brief instructions and at whom she never smiled. Later, he often told himself he had probably misunderstood her and done her an injustice. Perhaps she simply could not come to terms with his new role as head of the family.

He felt lost, however, and at the same time, light, ready to leave everything in the past behind. It was a dangerous feeling.

During many of his already short nights, he lay awake until four, despite the hard work in the kitchen. In order to avoid making the very old springs of his bed creak, he lay there without moving and looked at the ceiling or the dim twilight that penetrated the curtains. Then everything became unreal—the kitchen, the endless monotony of the conversations, the bad news from the south. In the semi-darkness of the room, he let his gaze wander and saw his old English books. He had tried to go on reading them for a long time. He thought about how, since his father's death, he had not gone to school. In the new situation, that didn't seem to bother anyone. He asked himself if they had all really forgotten him.

Although he only had a little time before he had to get up, he just lay there and tried to feel his body. Once he had managed it effortlessly, once his heavy body had been like a solid shell around him. But now he was only aware of the beating of his heart. He felt it not only in his chest but also in his neck and in his ears, felt the incessant beating and the effort his heart made against the numbness in his limbs.

Suddenly, he started, because he was certain, it had stood still. It had missed at least two beats. But what alarmed him even more—there was no certainty that it would go on beating. It could stand still at any moment. In order to distract himself, he stood up and crept barefoot around the room. He got cold feet on the stone floor, yet he didn't mind. He went to the window and looked out into the yard, to the street, to the wrapped-up figures hurrying to morning prayer in the dawn light. On the horizon, the night sky opened like the lid of a huge chest. Yet nowhere was there a path for him.

After such nights, the work was even harder for him. By the afternoon, he was already feverish with exhaustion.

I have grown up without noticing it, he sometimes thought later, the work has made the time fly. He imagined that he was evermore like his father, waddling from kitchen to dining room. When he remembered it, he was astonished—for everyone except himself, things were as they always had been.

Kerim repaired his father's old Toyota and drove it. The car gave him a little of the freedom he so urgently needed. He enjoyed driving and when his mother asked him, he readily agreed to take over the annual visit to his grandparents who lived near Halabja. He was all the more glad to do so since, this time, he would drive alone.

The news was meanwhile full of reports about an imminent American attack on the country. Here in the north people feared it less than in the south. Because of the sanctions the problems of the regime in Baghdad had become remote to people. Nevertheless, there was a general feeling of tension which made a family excursion appear too dangerous.

Such a visit was no small matter. Kerim was disgruntled as he watched the boot of the car gradually fill up with all the things his mother wanted him to take to her parents. She pretended that evermore new things were occurring to her, yet in truth she had long ago bought them in town and had them ready for the coming journey. The boot was overflowing with bags full of clothes old and new, packets of soap, toothpaste, shampoo and boxes with foodstuffs, sweets, pistachios packed in little bags, dates, and she also added a sack of flour. Kerim said nothing, a discussion with her would have been pointless. He knew that each of these gifts was not intended as sustenance for the old people but was an expression of her love for them, which, it occurred to him, must have grown greater from year to year.

He didn't have much time. For the sake of courtesy, he would have to spend one night at his grandparents' house. He wanted to be back at work in the late afternoon of the next day. Until then, the three of them would just have to manage. He was looking forward to the hours he would spend alone and so he calmly let everything happen, even if his mother was holding him back. When she was finally finished, it took some effort for him to shut the boot. He had placed a bottle of water on the passenger seat. Leaning against the car, he asked himself if he had forgotten anything, then he turned around, embraced his mother, went over to Imat, who was by now almost as tall as himself, and pinched little Ali's cheek.

He drove off, saw the three of them stand in the dust of the courtyard and raise their hands, waved back through the open side window. As always, at the gate, he thought about his father.

***

He left the town behind, driving east, passed the checkpoints of the Peshmergas guarding the road and listened carefully to the guards, quizzed them. One hinted at disturbances in the valley but was cut short by his commander. The latter said, if it was important one could drive but at one's own risk—nowhere was completely safe at the moment. Kerim sensed that things were more dangerous than the guards were admitting but he didn't want to turn back. On the contrary, the uncertainty excited him, he longed for a little adventure.

So he finally stepped on the accelerator on the highway to Halabja, enjoyed the wind rushing through the open window, the eternal frying smell of the kitchen forgotten for a while.

Glad not to have to expect the heat now in spring, he passed the peasants' donkey carts at the side of the road, had to overtake a couple of trucks, then the hilly landscape opened out to one side of the road. As the sun wasn't shining on it, the earth appeared dark, as if it were damp. On one of the sandy sidetracks, a herd of white geese moved unworriedly towards the road. Kerim drove more slowly, the tanker behind him began to sound its horn. The road was in good condition and it was the best route to Halabja. It led past a low, rocky massif on one side, shabby settlements of huts on the other. Some of the houses appeared to have been knocked together from scraps of one kind or another. Although the land with its thistles and bushes looked poor it was fertile nevertheless. The district around Halabja was famous for its walnuts and pomegranates.

The traffic that day seemed normal to Kerim for the early hour of the day. Perhaps there were fewer cars than he had expected but nothing suggested a threat.

He made good progress up to the halfway point of the journey, he was already looking forward to seeing his grandparents again. Then a traffic jam built up behind a broken-down tanker blocking the road at an angle. The business of bypassing it took time. The sun had meanwhile dispelled the morning haze, the folds of the hills lay in deep shadow, and Kerim saw each of the wooden electricity masts, each of the antennae sticking up on the tin roofs of the huts and each of the trees shaking off the sand in the forenoon wind. Everything was scattered as if by chance across the stony plain to his right and yet everything was in its right place. The route had become so familiar to him over the years that he only paid attention to what was unusual. A man, kneeling on a hillock, his raised hands beside his head, praying under a lonely, majestic poplar. A cow seeking the shrinking shadow which a pointless, isolated concrete wall provided. The animal stood close up against this remnant of a building as if it was leaning against it.

On the last part of the drive, he also saw the cemetery on the slope again. The dead still wanted to slip down and bury the road beneath them. Kerim would not have been able to say whether the cemetery had increased in size over the years. It seemed to him to be exactly as it had been then, on the calamitous day of the gas attack.

Before him lay Halabja, a collection of huts and houses pressed deep into the yellowish-red expanse, divided by the broad highway, narrow alleyways running through it. Black birds circled high above the plain which was enclosed by a semicircle of mountains rising up in the distance. Step by step, the low earth ridges turned into tree-covered slopes, marked by furrows and bare rock. The earth around this plain towered up like a natural fortress wall. That was the Iranian border. It ran between the rock peaks up there and no one could have said where exactly.

He reached the river which was crossed by a low concrete bridge and left the road by a track which ended seven, or eight, feet lower by the edge of the stream. Here he stopped the car and got out. It hadn't taken him long and in order to enjoy his brief freedom even more he wanted to put in a rest. The river was broad and shallow, more like a sluggishly flowing puddle. A herd of floppy-eared brown sheep were standing in the water but Kerim saw no sign of the shepherd. He stretched, took the few steps to the bank and squatted down. He looked through the concrete tube of the bridge to the other side, turned his head and looked up to the rocks, to the bushes which stretched up into the clear blue of the sky at the top. He was amused by the slapping sound of the sheep's ears when the animals shook their heads, only the flies bothered him. He heard shots in the distance, single ones at first, then whole salvos. They briefly startled Kerim but were nothing out of the ordinary. He dipped his hands in the water, then stood up and shook them dry. He looked around once again and abruptly it occurred to him that since he had come down here, no more cars had passed over the bridge. As if he had been the last traveller to Halabja. He began to feel uneasy, the desertedness of this place so close to the road now felt threatening.

I'm getting hungry, he said to calm himself and patted his round stomach. He went over to the car, already had the car keys in his hand when he saw the man on the bridge. Quite suddenly he was standing there, alone, gaunt and dark, not because he was standing against the light but because he had a magnificent black beard which reached down to his chest. Slowly, the man raised the barrel of his Kalashnikov, pointed the gun at Kerim and released the safety catch. Kerim instantly froze at the sound of the click, and for two long seconds he thought he was going to die.

The man didn't fire, however, but with a small movement of the gun barrel indicated that he should step back. Kerim was breathing heavily. He took a couple of steps closer to the riverbank and slowly raised his arms. The car keys jingled in his hand. The man on the bridge lowered his gun a little but it was still pointing at Kerim. The gunman said nothing, his mouth was hardly visible in the beard, and Kerim didn't dare to be the first to say anything.

He did not know to what circumstance he owed his life, why the man didn't simply shoot him but guided him to the car with the gun, where Kerim remained standing and waited till the gunman came down the slope to him. The man wasn't interested in the contents of the boot; all he wanted was the car itself, and Kerim was to be his chauffeur. He had him drive along the road. They crossed the town, which appeared deserted. In a side alley, which led uphill past sheds and homes, the man told him to stop. He gave two long whistles and a little later, three more armed men emerged. Apart from their height, they looked to Kerim almost identical. In their dirty, earth-coloured clothes and with their long beards, they merged into a uniform group. Issuing brief commands, the man beside Kerim instructed him where to drive. The three on the backseat talked loudly to one another, the smell of sweat and dust filled the car. They were Kurds, and Kerim listened silently to them as he followed the highway, passing the monument on the right, which the Kurds had erected in memory of the victims of the gas attack. Hardly had they left the town behind than his passenger told him to take a side road leading up into the mountains. When the road began to zigzag, he ordered him to drive faster. The dust-coloured mountains here were bare apart from occasional collections of bushes, oval bundles which looked as if someone had laid them on the naked rock. The road quickly deteriorated, shook them about so badly that the men stopped talking. As far as he had been able to make out from what they had been saying, they had been on their feet since early morning. There had been a rearguard action after they had tried to destroy smaller Peshmerga positions to the west. Now they were withdrawing from Halabja, back into the mountains. Kerim was now dumbfounded that the guards at the checkpoint had simply let him drive on. He said it out loud to himself and the men behind him began to laugh. One leant forward and rested the barrel of his Kalashnikov on Kerim's shoulder.

'Your people don't want to alarm you, hey? Don't want to make you any more frightened than you already are in the godless town.'

Kerim understood the allusion to the imminent invasion by the Americans, which the official Kurdish politicians welcomed. He said nothing and waited until the man removed the gun barrel again.

The serpentines became steeper. Behind his passenger, a view opened up over the whole valley. Kerim thought feverishly and regretted his decision to drive that day. He thought of his grandparents, not so very far from here at all, of his mother, his brothers, of everyone he knew, and was certain he would never see them again. Probably, he thought to himself, they will kill me as soon as we've arrived, they only needed me as driver, in order to get away more quickly.

They came to a plateau which lay like a vast step before the mountains, a dusty surface, dotted with lumps of rock and dark metal wrecks which looked like the remains of crashed cars. To the left, surprisingly unprotected, like observation posts above the valley, there appeared the huts. Kerim was overcome by a sadness which made him sigh. With every foot closer, the feeling grew stronger. He tried to remember everything he had still intended to do, what had been important to him and was astonished how little occurred to him. I must have been asleep, he thought, a long, long sleep. I have completely forgotten to look to the future, and now that I'm waking up, I have to die.

They left the track which led past the desolate settlement, climbed another couple of hundred yards and disappeared behind the next rocky ridge. The men ordered him to halt close by the huts and get out. One asked whether he had anything in the boot, Kerim nodded and unlocked it. While they rummaged in his things, he looked around. The huts were arranged in a semicircle like a small fortress. The corrugated-metal roofs were covered with earth, the rough clay walls hardly distinguishable from the ground. A donkey on a long rope trotted around behind the houses. Kerim didn't see many people. A couple of dark figures squatted on a threadbare blanket in front of the entrance to the largest building. An old Toyota pickup was parked close to the track. His kidnappers were finished, they banged the boot lid shut and motioned him to follow them.

Only when they had reached the open space in front of the houses did one of them stick a gun barrel in his back, as if to show everyone that Kerim was a prisoner and not perhaps a guest. They directed him past a pyramid of stacked sub-machine guns and to a hut a little distance away from the others. They passed through a front room empty apart from an ancient wooden chair, opened a trapdoor in the wall. Here they locked him in a windowless cell, just big enough for him to sit on the floor and stretch out his legs. The man who then secured the barred door said nothing and didn't look at Kerim but gripped his wrist and removed the wristwatch. The trapdoor was shut and the sounds grew faint.

Kerim sat there for a long time without moving, felt the wall against his back and tried to control his fear by breathing regularly. If it hadn't been for his fear, this pause would have done him good. A beam of light, fine as a blade in the darkness, came through a crack and formed a dazzlingly bright patch on the wall of his cell. After his eyes had got used to it, the darkness around him turned to twilight. He could even see the marks on the flaking metal bars, the gleam of the shackle on the padlock. He sat like that for a long time, listened to the quiet shouts that could be heard outside from time to time—mostly they were brief commands. He rubbed his face, was glad to be sheltered from the sun but felt thirsty and hungry. He slid lower and leant his head against the wall. But the posture was too relaxed, his agitation much too great to lie there like that. So he sat up straight again and leant his hands on the ground. He heard the sound of a car engine—it was his own car that someone was driving away.

He had already known for some time that there was a group in this area which called itself Followers of God. They were holy warriors who caused the Kurdish militias great problems. Again and again, there were skirmishes and ambushes, there were even rumours circulating about thwarted suicide-bomb attacks. These people, so it was said, had entrenched themselves in the mountains around Halabja; in tiny villages and checkpoints, they had themselves set up, close to the border. They were also in the Americans' sights since the latter's invasion preparations had got under way. It was said of them that they had good contacts abroad and there was speculation about their equipment and what they were capable of doing. The area around Halabja had long been dominated by strict Believers. And there had always been radicals among them who threatened to split off from the rest. In recent years, however, the latter had grown unusually strong. That was all that Kerim could scrape together about them. Yet he knew it was they who had seized him and that, sooner or later, they would ask themselves what they should do with him.

He brushed the palm of his hand across the sand until his fingers slipped into a sticky fluid. He stared at his hand and didn't dare smell it, just let it fall and leant his head back again.

2

When he heard them coming, he stood upright in his cell, then immediately shrunk back into the farthest corner. Darkness must have fallen by now, the patch of light on the wall had moved a good distance before it had finally faded. Kerim's mouth was dry, his eyes were stinging. In his fear, there mingled the quiet hope of something to drink. The trapdoor was opened, the swaying light of an oil lamp fell through the bars into the cell, mild and flickering. That was the moment at which Kerim saw the Teacher for the first time. He was of average height and slim build, wore a baggy pair of combat trousers and a pale kaftan. He had put a woollen blanket around his shoulders because of the cool of the evening. He came briefly into the cell and raised the lamp so as to be able to look at Kerim. This man, like all the others, had a long beard with long silvery strands. Kerim saw him squint and frown. Then his face relaxed and took on an amused expression. There was something like astonishment in his gentle brown eyes. He scratched his hollow cheek and asked Kerim his name. With that he stepped out of the cell. The man who had come with him shifted impatiently from one foot to the other. He was a head shorter than the Teacher, was wearing a bleached military jacket with many pockets and in his left hand carried a Kalashnikov which he swung around as if it were part of his body. Faded, rust-red spots and little splashes spattered his woollen shirt as if it belonged to a dead man. His face was framed by a thick, dark beard which, becoming thinner, also covered his cheeks. On his long hair was a cap with a broad border. Kerim was afraid of this man from the moment he looked into his face. The big, hooked nose, the deep-set eyes under the bushy eyebrows, his mouth with its narrow lips, an expression of contempt about them—Kerim knew immediately that he was dangerous.

The man asked the Teacher what they should do with Kerim and seemed nervous as he did so. There was a brief silence while the Teacher stroked his beard. He leant his head to the side and raised the lamp. He scrutinized Kerim for a couple of seconds and Kerim observed his patient thoughtfulness. It calmed him that this seemingly gentle man had so much authority.

'Is there anything special you can do?' asked the Teacher in a soft voice.

Kerim thought frantically. He was still standing hunched up in the corner but to answer he took a step forward. Hastily, he said the first thing that came into his head.

'I can carry the weapons.'

The hook-nosed man breathed out loudly. 'You're so fat, we'll have to carry you instead.'

Kerim knew that the reply had been a mistake. He strained to think, cooking came to mind, driving the car. Yet everything seemed too unimportant, at least, not important enough for the group. He looked at the floor for a moment and all his courage faded as he realized that nothing would occur to him. Slowly, he raised his head and said with desperate boldness.

'I can do everything, because I can learn everything.'

The Teacher looked at him in silence, the lamp in his hand swayed and the light it cast flitted up and down the walls. The hook-nosed man grew restless again and grumbled once more that Kerim was too clumsy. But the Teacher paid no attention and motioned to Kerim to follow him. The latter hurried to leave the cell, waited briefly at the bars until the hook-nosed fighter had passed him and followed the men through the dark hut. When he stepped out into the night he drew in the cool air and a quiet hope began to rise in him. Walking quickly, he tried not to fall behind the others, yet he had to slow down because the hook-nosed man limped. He placed the soles of his boots flat on the ground but at every step hardly bent his knees. This curious gait made him sway, stiff as a puppet. On no account did Kerim want to overtake this man for whom he was so clumsy, he wanted to do nothing that could provoke him.

***

His car had indeed disappeared without trace and so, from now on, Kerim lived with the Holy Warriors without raising any objections or asking dangerous questions. His fear gave way to relief when the Teacher gave him a cloth to cover his hair. Never before had Kerim worn a turban; to general amusement, he needed help to wrap it around his head.

In the evenings, he sat with them on a spread-out plastic sheet. While they ate their frugal meal, rice and chickpeas from tin bowls, they all remained silent. After that, however, until night prayers, the men and boys told stories. A small wood fire close by warmed them. The well-worn metal of the rifles, always stacked within reach, gleamed in the flickering light. A fast-flowing river could be heard in the distance.

They all ate very little, and at the beginning Kerim suffered from that. Instead, they drank great quantities of black tea which was as strong as a drug. The nights here were clear, the stars closer than Kerim had ever seen them. This stream of light flowed slowly yet steadily from the dark silhouette of the gently curving mountain chains in the west as far as the deep black, threateningly jagged rock blades in the east. Sometimes Kerim leant back and stared up for so long that he lost his orientation and thought he was looking down into a monstrous abyss, bottomless and cold, filled with fires extinguished for aeons.

Many of the men had families whom they had left behind in a nearby town called Khurmal. The town, like the whole valley, was controlled by fellow Believers who had come to terms with the unbelieving, as one thought here, Kurds of the district capital and did not consistently apply sharia. At agreed times, they allowed the Holy Warriors to come down from the mountains into the town to visit their families and buy supplies. Over time, a tacit understanding advantageous to both sides had developed. The Holy Warriors only attacked the Kurdish militias and spared the people in the valley.

In the first few days, Kerim already found out almost everything about the life and the plans of these men. They talked candidly, as if he had been with them from the beginning. For the near future, they were planning suicide attacks on Kurdish local politicians who were in league with the American devil. It was evident to all that the Kurds supported the imminent invasion and would ensure that the devils also destroyed them, the godly here in the mountains.

The men were full of contempt for Kerim's hometown. To them, all its inhabitants were infected by Western unbelief.

Since the arrival of satellite TV programmes, they said, the young people had gone crazy. Because they wanted to look like some Americans they had seen on TV, the boys smeared grease in their hair and schoolgirls walked around dressed like whores.

Then there were the Internet cafes that had opened everywhere. Kerim remembered the many pictures of naked women and men Ahmad had once shown him there. They were shocking images, Kerim had only quickly looked at the close-ups of body openings, then he had been overcome by shame and the fear that someone might notice what they were both looking at. But these pictures stayed with one, they literally stuck in one's thoughts.

When they talked in the evening, the Teacher regularly intervened to make clear to them that the blow was imminent and it was only a question of time, perhaps a few days, before they would have to move into the mountains. Everyone knew what that meant. It was the beginning of March and bitterly cold in the mountains. But only up there, not here in their camps, only in the immediate vicinity of the border were they safe, because there were the caves in which they could hide when the devils sent their airplanes. The Teacher used the opportunity to describe it to them as if he had often experienced it. He pointed to the dark sky and imitated a soft engine sound, described the vapour trails of the giant eight-engine B-52 bombers. After that, he indicated with his finger the flight movements of the smaller jets which would try to target the caves directly.

'It will be terrible,' he said. 'But you already know that, you can prepare yourselves.' Then he fell silent and left the conversation to them again.

The only one, apart from Kerim, who didn't wear a beard was the childlike Hamid. He maintained that he was eighteen but Kerim guessed him to be fifteen. Hamid was the first in the group to whom he felt a closeness. He made it easy for Kerim because of his candid, light-hearted manner.

Hamid, just like the Anwari Brothers, two men about the same age as Kerim, almost like twins, always together, made it clear to Kerim how the war propagated itself. They were all war orphans, like so many in this country. The Holy Warriors had financially supported their mothers. As soon as the boys were old enough, the Holy Warriors took over responsibility for their schooling and upbringing and for their upkeep. The burden on their families was thereby reduced. Kerim, too, felt a little bit like an orphan.

Hamid was responsible for the lesser tasks, he fetched wood for the fire and he prepared the tea. He was full of pride at being recognized as a member of the group. Sometimes this pride got the better of him, for example, when he got on the men's nerves with his readiness to help and they chased him away. But it never took Hamid long to recover. He was good-natured and did not hold anything against these men who had accepted him as a comrade-in-arms. Yet he was also garrulous, as Kerim soon found out. After he had discovered that Kerim was prepared to listen, the boy began to pass on his observations, always in a whisper, and gradually everything that he knew about the others in the group. Kerim meanwhile knew that the hook-nosed man, whom he continued to fear, was called Mukhtar. Hamid told him that the latter had already fought in Afghanistan. That gave him unlimited authority in all military questions. Only the Teacher, the spiritual authority of the group, could raise objections, but he rarely did so.

***

About a week after Kerim's arrival in the camp, the fighters were woken in the middle of the night. They lined up in front of the hut and were informed of an operation they had to carry out before they went into the mountains. Only Mukhtar and two of the older men took their guns with them. In addition, a heavy hammer, a field spade and a plastic bag were brought along.

From the Teacher, they heard that that night they would be able to show how free they already were of everything the people in the valley believed, how far they would go to follow their true Faith which disdained this earthly life in the face of that of Paradise. Shivering in the night-time cool, they stood there and listened to his words. The Teacher admonished them yet again, urging them to forget everything they had learnt from their parents, in school or even in the mosque. None of it was true, it all only served to idolize suffering here on earth, to accommodate to it, to fearfully bear it, in order to reach, at the End of Days perhaps, Paradise after all, like an animal in a herd, pressed in among all the other animals, hoping not to be noticed and to get through.

Led by Mukhtar, they set off westwards. They formed a column and from time to time took turns at carrying the tools. The night was cold and still. The wind brushed over the rocks; in some places, it produced a quiet sound, almost a humming, as if an invisible child was observing them on their march. No one said a word, no one wanted to know anything more about what they had to do, no need, they would be told and they would simply do it. Tiredness made their steps heavy, allowed each of the men to become immersed in his own thoughts. All made sure to stay close together because it was pitch dark around them. Even the rock beneath their feet seemed no more than a footbridge, stretching in a long arch high through the night.

Kerim had no idea how long they had been going when the column halted and Mukhtar softly gave instructions to remain silent. Two men crept ahead, came back and confirmed there was no one there. Satisfied, Mukhtar gave the order to go on. After about thirty yards, they were standing at the top of a slope. Below, they could just make out the plateau, to which they now descended. There they found themselves on a kind of lookout platform from which, by day, one could look across the whole valley. Only the audible depth of the wind made them suspect that the darkness into which they looked from the platform was nothing but emptiness. In the centre of the place rose a small mausoleum, nothing more than a covered space with walls of roughly layered stones and a frequently repaired roof. Kerim also discovered the end of a narrow road which led up here from the valley. He knew that people came here from far away out of reverence for this tomb.

The room was empty and cold, the floor consisted only of a stone slab. The men knelt on it, felt it and the characters engraved in it. Inside, Mukhtar now risked switching on a torch. The inscription told them something about an old Sufi sheikh who lay buried here, but Mukhtar didn't give them time to read. Instead, he ordered the man who had last carried the sledgehammer to begin the work. He gave the stone slab a couple of powerful blows and it gave way a little. When Mukhtar shone the torch on it, no more than large cracks could be made out, the inscription was still completely legible. The man struck it several times, then passed the hammer on to another and so they took turns until finally they had smashed the slab into small pieces. Again and again, Mukhtar ordered them to pause and listen, asked Hamid, who had remained outside, whether everything was all right and then told them to continue. They collected the stone debris, carried it out and threw it in a pile in front of the mausoleum. A heavy smell of earth rose. Now they took turns at digging. Mukhtar shone the torch into the gradually deepening pit and suddenly Kerim became aware of the dreadfulness of what they were doing. This coal-black hole in earth, buried for centuries, under the stone filled him with horror. When it was his turn, he already had to climb in. He tried to breathe as little as possible as he dug up the earth and flung it up to the edge. Kerim knew that the superstition of the mostly older people who came here prevented them from ever changing anything at such a place out of fear of disaster. Now he was standing here and digging for the bones of such a man, dead so long ago.

And it was he who then found the skeleton. The light of the torch passed over long, brown bones and remains of wood. Mukhtar immediately told them to look for the skull. The Anwari brothers jumped down to Kerim in the pit and with bare hands, they burrowed in the sticky earth until one of them came upon an oval object under the bones. Kerim enlarged the hole with his hands. When the beam of light fell on his fingers, the first thing he saw was a row of six large teeth and, immediately after that, the earth-filled eye sockets. The skull stared at him with half a grin, the lower jaw was missing.

They gathered the bones together and passed them up. There they were put in the plastic bag. Finally, Mukhtar briefly looked around the space, then said they should leave everything as it was. They made their way back with the bag of bones and the tools.

At the camp, Mukhtar handed over their haul to the Teacher who, for a moment, held it up in the light of his oil lamp and, with an expression of revulsion, immediately threw it in the direction of his hut. Kerim never found out what happened to the bones of the sheikh.

'Let them worship the hole,' the Teacher had added. 'At any rate, they'll never see their idol again.'

They could also consult the Teacher if they had problems of some kind. They could visit him for a brief talk in his hut, where he listened and gave them advice. Kerim took advantage of the possibility more than once. Their meetings grew into little discussions. The Teacher tried in several ways to make clear to him what was new about their movement.

'You know this story perhaps,' he said once—it was already late in the evening—'about the mullah and the two cows. It's an old story. One day, a peasant came to a mullah and spoke to him: "Mullah, what does the Koran really say when the cow of one man kills the cow of another with a thrust of its horn?" The mullah did not think for long. "The matter is quite clear," he said, "the owner of the living cow must pay for the dead one. Because after all, he is the owner." At that, the peasant said the mullah's cow had just killed his own cow in the meadow. The mullah was astonished, but quickly recovered himself again, raised his finger and said, "Now that is a special case. To decide it, I must first of all look in my black book." That is how people talk and they do so because secretly they know that this kind of cleric has long ago made his peace with the earthly life. When at the Festival of Sacrifice, an animal is slaughtered, who then gets the best piece of meat even before the poor? If they are invited to a festival, whichever one it is, don't they sit in the best place and receive the largest portions of food? You know that is so. We are different, and also want to change that. That is what I try to explain to you all the time—we have nothing to do with that frivolous kind of religion. For sure, we have to cooperate with the clerics in the villages, we need their support and that of their people. But believe me, the difference between us and them is immense.'

The Teacher also inquired about Kerim's past and interpreted it.

'Consider, your father was killed by the henchmen of the regime which the Americans supported for a long time. Remember that. Out of respect for him, you should think about the consequences of that fact. If that is the peace of the rulers, the one they have and give us, then we don't want it. Then we want war.'

***

For weapons training, they left the hut settlement and walked about half a mile up the gently rising rocky ridge. In the swiftly fading coolness of morning, they worked their way through dry bushes and loose scree until they came to a broad, flat depression, at the far end of which stood a row of targets riddled with holes. Only when they were completely shredded was Hamid sent to replace them. Then he ran, swift as a hare, ignoring every obstacle, across the hollow and was back before one looked twice. Here Kerim got to know the group's preferred weapons, above all, the famous AK-47. Although Kerim was new, Mukhtar took no notice of him. He lay like the others in the dust on the hot ground and tried, as well as he could, to take aim while the sweat ran into his eyes. After each round, Mukhtar hobbled from one man to the next and from a distance, one hand over his eyes, inspected the result. It remained a puzzle to Kerim that he was able to distinguish the new bullet holes from the old ones in the targets; his judgement, however, was decisive. But he never assessed or punished Kerim. This wilfully preferential treatment was intended to belittle Kerim in the eyes of the others.

Nevertheless, he soon learnt to shoot and he even enjoyed loosing off automatic-fire salvos. He was never sure, however, that he was becoming familiar with the weapon. He could take it apart but always had difficulties reassembling it. Hence he soon had the feeling of being no use as a soldier. Mukhtar let him be without a word and did not even look at him, yet his expression told Kerim that he had expected nothing else. Luckily, Rashid, the only one here to wear spectacles, helped him unobtrusively and quite as a matter of course. He was from Kirkuk and had even attended the Technical College before breaking off his studies and joining the Holy Warriors. Kerim didn't find out why, as he had quickly learnt never to ask anyone here about his reasons. Rashid was the group's bomb expert and had little to do at the moment, since here they were at an outpost and the 'laboratory', as he called it, was further up in the mountains. He assembled the Kalashnikov without looking, screwing up his eyes the whole time despite his glasses, and took the opportunity to admonish Kerim to learn how to do it as quickly as possible as it could be important for all of them.

At first, Kerim was also a failure at close-combat training. He had to learn to avoid his opponent's lunges with the huge combat knife, had to try to grip the other's wrist. In time, he got better and better at it. But at the beginning it so happened that Rashid drew the knife back too quickly and through Kerim's already closed hand. The cut was deep and Kerim bled so badly, he thought the wound would never heal. In the evening, the Teacher saw his bandaged hand. The blood was still soaking through the dressing. He ordered that for a while, Kerim should fetch the water during the close-combat lesson. When Mukhtar grumbled, the Teacher explained they would have to change their strategy because there was new information. The Americans' air reconnaissance had intensified. Since they could attack at any moment, the pickup, which they had been using to fetch water from the river, was too conspicuous. But they would hardly start shooting at someone walking around in the mountains.

The Teacher was indeed well informed about the latest developments because he had a mobile satellite TV. Sometimes all the men, sitting in a circle as around a fire, were allowed to watch the news but when that could happen was decided by the Teacher.

Whenever Kerim drove the donkey up the stony path with a switch, he thought about his family. How had they been getting on? he asked himself, were they at all able to keep the business going? While the donkey in front of him bore the two big, empty water canisters up the next rise, Kerim saw his brother Imat sweating in the kitchen, saw little Ali carrying out the plates and his mother lamenting her fate to the families of the neighbourhood. She was right, it was a great misfortune for the family, thought Kerim, and suddenly he realized that they must believe him dead. Perhaps they still hoped he would return, yet secretly, they were already mourning another death. The thought did not let go of him. It made him melancholy, yet there was also something strong, invigorating about it.

Once the donkey had left the pass behind and was descending the slope on the other side, the panorama of the landscape opened out in front of Kerim. He stopped for a moment to take in the view. The zigzag path cut across the rocky ridge like a scar. He could already see the rushing, blue-green river on the valley floor, snaking through the sand-coloured rock in wide curves. The foam on the water glittered white. Above the rushing water hung the absolute stillness of the afternoon like a vast, light blue, infinitely delicately blown vessel. The donkey trotted on single-mindedly. Kerim looked at the river and the veined rock landscape beyond it. Here ended his country, he knew that—somewhere beyond the river lay the frontier. Suddenly, the fierce pain in his hand vanished, he even clenched it. I'm dead, he thought, I've died on a day like any other and I've only realized it now because there was so much work. I'm dead and I'm free. The hand began to throb and Kerim spread out his arms as if to push the pain away from him. A shudder which seemed to flow down from the glittering lustre of the heavens coursed through him at that moment from the back of his head to his groin. I'm free, he thought once again, gasping for air, and then threw himself in the dust, wanted to make himself small before the power of the one God. He was so small that he trembled and drew up his shoulders, pressed his forehead against the pebble-strewn ground. This was what the Teacher meant when he preached to them, 'You must die, in order to achieve life, each of you must have dug his own grave here, in order to become something that no one can kill.'

Below at the stony riverbank he cooled his hand in the water. Then he took the canisters from the donkey's back. He had to wade into the river up to his stomach to immerse the large containers so that they filled up. He had to be quick, too, because the donkey kept going further along the path. Kerim heaved the canisters onto dry land and hurried after the animal. Finally, he had with some effort loaded them onto the animal, yet now, under the weight, the donkey refused to move. Kerim had to beat it with the switch until it eventually got going. He would have liked to stay longer by the river. The isolation awakened his imagination which had gone to sleep in the regularity of the day-to-day schedule of the camp. At the same time, it dispelled the quiet fear that constantly gnawed at him. Since he knew the return trip with the water would take longer, he set off.

Later, in the evening, the Teacher called all the men together after prayer. They sat in a circle in front of his hut. Evidently worried, he walked up and down in front of them and stroked his trimmed beard. He informed them that strangers had been seen in the valley, Americans. Not ordinary ones, but heavily armed paramilitaries who had considerable technical equipment with them. These people, explained the Teacher, were CIA agents. Some dressed like local people and so tried to remain undiscovered, others had pigtails and coloured pictures incised on hands and arms. They distributed sweets to children and pretended to be harmless. But, in truth, they were making measurements and made use of a technology they called GPS in order to locate the camps. Everyone knew what that meant. The Teacher made it explicit nevertheless.

'They will feed their computer bombs with this data.'

The men looked out into the dark valley where the distant scattered lights of the houses were gradually going out. Once again, the Teacher reminded them of the foundations of their struggle as they had repeatedly learnt them.

'Think of the rule—we are setting a small group against armies, we are setting the light against the heavy, the simple against the complicated. If they use these bombs, we will use the knife. They kill us from the air, we kill them in the street. If they employ GPS, we use messengers with handwritten notes. The small against the big. And—we are all standing at Heaven's Gate while they cling to the earth in which they will be buried as if there were nothing above it.'

The Teacher ordered that they must leave this outpost in the direction of the border immediately after the next morning prayers. Not across the river, however, but—he pointed eastwards—into the mountains. He glanced quickly at Mukhtar who merely grunted and nodded.

After the meeting, the Teacher called Kerim to him once again. He allowed him to enter the hut first and sit down on the sandy carpet in the middle of the room. He lit a lamp. There was a scratched wooden table in the room, a satellite phone on it. A map also hung on one of the clay walls but it was so frayed that one could hardly use it any more. In the Teacher's bed niche, Kerim saw a blanket and a straw-filled sack and a stack of four books in front of the gun.

The Teacher asked to see Kerim's hand but Kerim could no longer open it, because the dressing had turned rock-hard from sand and blood stuck together.

'I am not a good soldier,' said Kerim softly as the Teacher began to cut open the bandage.

'What are you then?' asked the Teacher as he concentrated on the task.

Kerim told him that he did indeed feel the power of Faith inside him and was altogether ready to make sacrifices. But he also told him about his fear of the heavy PKMS machine gun, of firearms in general. Finally, he reported his experience by the river to the Teacher.

The Teacher paused. He looked intently at Kerim, his pointed nose gleamed in the lamplight and there was a sad expression on his narrow face.

As so often, the Teacher interpreted what had been experienced. 'Up there, you were quite alone and free and yet you became aware of the all-powerful order—it flung you down as if in prayer. The core of freedom is the law.' He stared thoughtfully in front of him. 'Yes,' he continued in a hoarse voice, 'war and Faith are two different things. But wait a little,' he said and put a fresh dressing on Kerim's hand, 'you don't know everything. It will get much more difficult. But you stayed with us.'

Kerim was completely surprised. Bewildered, he said he had thought he was going to be killed.

The Teacher shrugged. 'We were only interested in the car.' And without another word, with only a silent nod, dismissed him.

That night, Kerim lay awake for a long time. The great quantities of black tea stopped him from falling asleep. He heard the snoring of the men and, behind everything, the quiet, fine murmuring of the border river. Hamid, who was lying beside him, was likewise awake. He turned to Kerim and began to whisper.

'Why aren't you sleeping? Are you afraid?' he asked.

Kerim took his time over the answer. 'I don't know—perhaps.'

'It will be cold,' said Hamid.

'Yes,' said Kerim, 'go to sleep now.' Yet he thought that he feared the cold least of all and he envied Hamid for having such a practical problem.

Far away, there was the sound of an aircraft. Kerim closed his eyes and saw this long-drawn-out thunder as a razor-sharp straight line, drawn inexorably through the white noise of the night.

3

At first light, all the men stood ready, wrapped in woollen blankets, and waited for the Teacher. They left the car and the donkey behind; the animal would find its way down to the water, said Mukhtar. The tools and the heavy machine guns were distributed among the strongest, the others carried the lighter weapons. Kerim slung a Kalashnikov over each shoulder. The Teacher came out of his hut holding his books in his arm. He laid them on the ground, knelt down and began to dig a hole with his bare hands. Two men immediately jumped over and helped him. The Teacher pushed the books into the hole, filled it in again and stamped the earth flat.

Although he limped, Mukhtar went first and set the pace and he didn't walk slowly. He was followed by the Teacher. Behind him, in single file, the men. Hamid and Kerim were the last. Kerim didn't mind bringing up the rear. Here he had the task of keeping an eye on the surroundings. They climbed up in the dawn light. Despite the noise made by all the feet in front of him, Kerim could make out the murmuring of the river. They followed its course through a moonscape peeling out of the grey night which looked as if it was strewn with children's skulls.

Later, when the sun was already shining into their faces, the landscape changed. Fertile slopes replaced the rocky wasteland. Stunted deciduous trees rose between overgrown rocks, tall bushes obscured the view of a mountain scene that seemed heavenly to Kerim. Here the smell of water was in the air, and they were just able to breathe it in now, in the morning, before it retreated into the ground.

They rested at a bend in the goat path they had been following for hours. Before them lay a green valley, a torrent rushing through it. All the men removed their woollen blankets and tied them up.

The Teacher sat on a stone close to Mukhtar whom the march must have tired out most. Kerim only glanced at him, saw the dark glow in his eyes and the compressed lips—it was as if something had put him in a constant rage. The men chewed their dry bread, sat with their heads hanging, stared at the ground between their crossed legs. They rinsed down the bread with water, and when they were finished let themselves fall back into the grass. At a sign from the Teacher, they all rose and went down to the stream. There they performed their ablutions. For the length of the prayer, all exhaustion went from Kerim. The deep, soft voice of the Teacher opened up an inner space for them, a flight of word chambers and niches in which they could not get lost but, safe as in their own house, could walk from entrance to exit.

Around midday, they reached a projecting rock massif, at the side of which they halted in order to get their bearings. From this point, there was once again a view of the broad valley. Closest to them was the small town of Khurmal. They looked down on the earth-coloured mosque and the tin roofs, on the dusty fields and green-yellow meadows. A broader main road that cut through the settlement led in one direction to the open valley, in the other as far as the steep rocks where it branched out into many small paths that led up into the mountains.

The silence of midday lay over the valley; in the distance, a couple of cars glided along the tracks. Then the men again heard the sound of aircraft. Three silvery gleaming jets, followed by dull rumbling which immediately after that filled the blue dome above the valley. The Teacher looked up calmly. Just as the rumbling was fading away, three of these aircrafts appeared once again. The Teacher brushed his beard from his lips, the wind caught its long strands, and, for a moment, Kerim loved him like a distant father. Everything depended on him—as long as he was there, their way remained visible.

With a start, the Teacher came to life. Swiftly, he detailed Hamid, Rashid and Kerim to go down to the town unarmed. They put down their sub-machine guns.

'We have to know what's been happening in the last few hours,' he said. 'Ask the people about it. Go to Ismael in the mosque and then follow us to the caves above the river. And don't be afraid, the Unbelievers will not dare attack the town. What they hate most are ugly TV pictures.' With that, he glanced at Rashid who merely nodded as a sign that he knew where they should go.

Shortly before the group split up, restlessness arose, because some men were determined to pass on news for their families. Names were called out, the three tried to memorize everything but soon there was too much. Finally, Mukhtar stepped in and ended it all with an abrupt gesture, following which he stretched out his arm and pointed towards the valley and, without another word, they set off.

During the descent to the town, all pressure on them melted away. They were able to talk freely, Hamid no longer whispered. Since no exact time for their return had been agreed, it was as if they had briefly been released for this excursion. The path led them though ever-denser undergrowth and over ever-darker rocks. From time to time, Rashid made circling motions with his arms in order to relax his shoulders and Kerim, too, was glad at last to be rid of the guns.

Then Rashid talked about the smell of chemicals, something he missed. He described one in particular in every detail.

'It makes you drunk, you hover above the work, and even though you know you have to concentrate, because you could be blown up at any moment, you're grinning like an idiot, do lots of unnecessary things. It's a dangerous intoxication,' he said laughing.

It was on the tip of Kerim's tongue to ask him how it was that he had come to carry out this kind of work and what he thought about it. Instead, for no reason, he told him about his uncle in Germany. Rashid quickly changed tack, affirmed that he too had friends there.

Hamid interrupted to ask what kinds of bombs he had already made. Rashid's enthusiasm for the technical side of the work immediately took hold of him. He listed all the types, named the components and also added right away that they got all of it from the other side of the border. Then he explained that there were only two essential aspects—the mixture and the fuse. It was easy to learn the right mixture but dangerous to produce it. The fuse was a different matter— it had to be varied depending on whether, as often happened, found projectiles, like anti-tank shells, were connected up and so transformed into a bomb, or whether one made the whole bomb oneself, as with explosive devices for cars. These had the great advantage that simple fuses could be used, because the driver could trigger the explosion whenever he wanted, one only had to explain it to him. Rashid's face brightened as he described how attentively the martyrs followed his instructions shortly before the attacks, what great peace the certainty of death gave each of them. He spoke of huge arms dumps the regime had established everywhere in the country. Many of them had already been abandoned.

'And we'll find more as soon as the Unbelievers invade.'

After an hour they reached the town. Kerim was running his hand over his beard, which was still short and had gaps, when he saw the men, all in dark clothes, standing in the shadow of the houses and looking at them. They were indistinguishable from the Holy Warriors and yet they did not belong to them. They were devout but they did not take up arms. They sympathized with the warriors, also supported them, but they did not kill. The dark outlines of completely veiled women appeared in windows and scurried past in the alleys. It was time for prayers, the faithful were gathering in the mosque. Kerim saw the huts' projecting roofs, made of knotted tree trunks, covered with branches and dry foliage. On the ground in front of the door, pumpkin-seed shells covering the sand. Women squatting on a blanket around two stone slabs, grinding corn.

In front of the small mosque, everyone immediately saw that they were strangers; the men cleared a passage for them. Rashid asked for the Ismael who could give them news and eventually a small, fat man came up and greeted them warmly. Only now did they realize that there was great agitation here. Ismael put his hands together, he glanced around nervously. He reported hastily—the Americans had bombed the capital in wave after wave. He spread his hands in order to convey the size of the explosions. The news broadcasts were reporting it without interruption. The invasion would come next. There were airplanes in the sky all the time, and the godless—he pointed in the direction of Kerim's hometown—could hardly wait for it.

He opened his arms, let them go first and led them to the small restaurant as his guests. There they sat on old but very soft cushions, drank water and tea. Every ten minutes, Ismael sent the mosque attendants for nuts and repeated the details. Rashid explained to him that they were gathering up in the caves and that, if things got really bad, they would go over the border. He asked whether anyone knew about Iranian troops on the other side but Ismael shook his head. They passed on to the imam all the messages the warriors had given them for their families and left it at that because, by now, time was beginning to run short.

Unsettled by the news, all three felt a need to deliver it as soon as possible and they cautiously brought up the question of departure. The imam waved his prayer beads in front of their faces, invited them to eat with him, offered them places to sleep, first at his home, then in the town.

Rashid thanked him, waited a little and began to talk about their plans again in order to emphasize their lack of time. The sequence was repeated, they drank another tea, then they slowly rose, one after the other, without any haste. Even if time was pressing, it was important to avoid appearing in a hurry. They were successful in this, and Ismael, who finally let them go, had the satisfaction, as host who had offered everything, of remaining behind only because the circumstances demanded it.

Not until they had left the town did Kerim realize that now they would mainly be going uphill, so it would take longer than he had anticipated. Thanks to their replenished water reserves and because the sun was already low in the sky, they did not find the first part of the way very difficult. At the point where the group had divided, the sweat-inducing and, in parts, dangerous ascent began. Rashid went first, Kerim last, always concerned not to let the gap between him and the others get too large. Hamid looked around to him at regular intervals, which, on the one hand, touched Kerim but, on the other, also put him under pressure. Although he had already lost some weight since finding himself with the Holy Warriors, he was still heavier than the rest. He had begun to feel embarrassed about it, above all, during the close-combat exercises when his corpulence got in his own way, and during the march when the grumbling of his stomach became clearly audible. Angrily, he battled with his handicap and as he did so, he quite often thought of Mukhtar and his limp.

Gradually, the path became steeper and stones slipped down behind Rashid and Hamid, which Kerim repeatedly had to avoid. Shortly after, he already had to use his hands to climb, a darkening abyss gaping to one side. His wound began to hurt again. The sun had disappeared behind the mountains and the colour began to drain from the rocks echoing to their feet and their panting. They climbed up through a dark grey landscape filled with huge but shapeless silhouettes. Stubbornly, they went step by step, each time instinctively testing their hold. If they slipped, they dug their fingers into the path, froze for a moment to breathe out their terror and then went on.

Kerim had lost all sense of the duration of the ascent, and was glad not to be making this effort with the whole group while being observed by Mukhtar and the Teacher, when Rashid paused and, with a hiss, drew their attention to something that was still invisible. Kerim only waited until Rashid got moving again. Later he learnt that there were mines scattered here on the slopes, which Rashid wanted to warn them about.

The climb soon came to an end. Now they had to descend a rocky ridge. This was less of an effort but difficult in the dark. Kerim stumbled forward and now felt his exhaustion. Somewhere in front there was the river, the water gurgled and thundered through the narrow rock gaps. The closer they came to it the more Kerim began to shiver.

A crooked wooden bridge, which swung alarmingly, led across the river. When Kerim stood on it, saw the foamy strips of the water rushing past, he doubted whether it would bear his weight. But it did. On the other side, they had to start going up again. This time they climbed. When Rashid reached a jutting ridge, he stopped, because he was looking straight into the muzzle of the sub-machine gun of the sentry whom the group had posted there in front of the caves. His woollen blanket pulled right over his head, the man crouched there and simply raised his gun as a sign that they could come up. Kerim reached the protruding rock and sat down exhausted but satisfied. The sentry, one of the silent brothers from a village near Halabja, nodded to him without changing his expression. A pair of wood pigeons rose from the black mass of bushes below, their pale stomachs shot past and sank back into the darkness.

***

The news from the valley caused considerable disquiet in the group. Precautions were quickly taken—immediately after morning prayers, they brought weapons, sandbags and food supplies into the cave. There were several entrances of which the group used only a smaller one—in it, the rock opened into a deep, not very wide space with a low ceiling. A long crack gaped in the middle of it. The cave was cold and damp but could be readily heated with a fire. To sleep, the men laid their blankets in a row, one next to the other.

If one followed the ridge outside around the rocks, then behind the next ledge, one came to a path that led, after about half a mile, to a mountain hamlet by the river. It was one of the many isolated settlements here and on the Iranian side of the border. They were all controlled by those true to the Faith, nothing diverted people from prayer. Traditional law was in force everywhere, and up here, every family head, even clan leaders, supported the Holy Warriors, gladly or not. The greater part of the next day was taken up with sending messengers to the people in the hamlet to convince them to leave the place, at least for the time being. Now the Teacher and now one of the older Holy Warriors tried to convince the village elders of the impending danger. Finally they gave up, because the villagers didn't want to take one step away from their homes. To drive them by force over the nearby border seemed pointless to both the Teacher and Mukhtar.

Television had been strictly forbidden in the village for years. There was no distraction whatsoever, there was a calm, such as Kerim did not know from the godless city. Threatened with cruel punishments because of their protectors, the people were strangely withdrawn, as if they wanted to recede into their huts, into the landscape. Hardly ever did Kerim see one of the completely veiled women.

Yet there was an electricity generator which they could use for the satellite TV. It took until evening, then they had the device set up in the open on a folding table and could receive the broadcasts. There were international news programmes—if they were in English, the Teacher and Kerim took turns to translate. The invasion of the Crusaders had begun and the bombing had continued in many parts of the country. More cruise missiles were being constantly launched from ships, aircraft were in action uninterruptedly.

In the evening, the villagers slaughtered a sheep in their honour and Kerim offered to prepare it. He did it well and, for a short while, everyone seemed to be fond of him. Then, however, Mukhtar detailed men to go in turn to Khurmal on each of the following days, should it become necessary, and come back with the latest news. Kerim would be last to go and was happy about it. Mukhtar and those men who still didn't quite trust him and kept their distance were basically doing him a favour.

At night, however, they huddled together. The rock under them gradually cooled down and the entrance to the cave gaped darkly before them. Kerim saw himself looking out through the mouth of an astonished giant. On the first night, he took Hamid's hand in his own before falling asleep and he was overcome by profound melancholy, although it did him good to touch a human being.

The next morning, snow had fallen. The sparse whiteness covered the low tree crowns, the bushes along the riverbank, the grass and even the knotty rock outcrops. Long after the morning prayer, the messenger to the town was already on his way—Kerim saw the Teacher close to the hamlet. Kerim was just bringing firewood up to the cave. With the huge bundle tied together on his back one couldn't help but see him. The Teacher waved him over and Kerim threw down the bundle. Together they walked a little way across the mountain meadow. The Teacher was looking down at the ground, as if he were admiring the greenery covered up by the snow and yet breaking through in many places. Talking to Kerim with unusual candour, the Teacher did not look at him. Once he stopped abruptly, turned around and pointed to one of the huts of the hamlet. The sun fell on the roughly layered walls, each irregular stone, each crack, each snow-covered twig of the brushwood roof seemed to take on a glow. Kerim saw the hut, the cold, rushing river and the end of the rocky valley, and the night-time sadness, which until now had made his heart heavy, lifted away from him in a second. All his exhaustion and fear gave way to a warm awareness of the present.

Finally, the Teacher dismissed him with a wave of the hand. Kerim went back to his bundle, shouldered it and carried it to the cave. From the entrance, he saw Mukhtar sitting by the river holding his feet in the water. Kerim's heavy footsteps startled him. He called Kerim over, who took the bundle into the cave and then hurried down. There he immediately squatted down beside the commander but Mukhtar said curtly that he only needed help to stand up. He pulled his legs out of the water and dried them carefully. Kerim stared at Mukhtar's chafed, completely crippled toes which were like excrescences on his feet and pointed upwards. With some effort, Mukhtar wrapped the foot cloths as tightly as possible around the remains of his toes, pulled on his shoes and had Kerim help him to his feet. Since he had noticed Kerim looking, he said to him,

'I may hobble but I can cross mountains and seas.'

As he spoke, he gripped Kerim's arm so firmly that it hurt and only let go after the other had agreed. Then he pushed him away. Kerim stumbled across the stones by the riverbank. Keeping a respectful distance, he trotted along in front of Mukhtar towards the wooden bridge.

Later he was no longer sure whether he had really heard it but the detonation was preceded by a sucking noise. It was impossible to localize where the missile had struck but its impact made the ground under Kerim's feet shake. Cries could be heard on every side, Mukhtar ran past him with big unsteady strides, then stopped, grabbed Kerim by the shoulder and pushed him up towards the bridge. Dozens of birds were in the air around them, sailing around like lumps of rock, before finally leaving the valley. Kerim was just able to see that the hamlet, and with it, the hut, had disappeared.

The group had gathered in the cave when the real attack began. The men pressed themselves against the walls of the cavern, Mukhtar remained close to the entrance and looked out. Like scared animals, they listened to the very different-sounding explosions. To begin with, they were distant, came closer and then moved away again. The rolls of thunder ploughed through the rocky valleys. In the cave, it was as if thrusting out of the stone from all sides. In a gap, they heard the sound of a jet. Mukhtar crouched down and looked up into the sky.

'Hornet,' he muttered.

Now there were many small explosions, coming closer. Mukhtar glanced over at the men and Kerim knew—the only thing that concerned the commander's hunted, restless spirit at this moment was fear of perishing in this hole. Mukhtar's fingers drummed nervously on the breech of his Kalashnikov. After a short pause, the sound of explosions grew louder again, and this time they were so close that the mountain really was shaken, sand trickled from the crack in the roof. Kerim saw the many wide-open eyes around him, saw Mukhtar, his lips moving—he was saying a soundless prayer. His hands gripped his sub-machine gun, now in one place, now in another, yet he didn't move from the spot. The tension became unbearable and it was only a question of time before the first man leapt out of the cave into the open. Then the Teacher stood up, kicked the now-scattered firewood aside and stood in front of the entrance. His Kalashnikov was slung over his shoulder.

'What did you expect?' he began. 'I told you they would come with all their hellish power.'

The explosions crept closer to the cave. Mukhtar positioned himself between the exit and the Teacher's back.

'But our concern is not the war of the others out there,' the Teacher pointed behind him. 'Our concern is not the war whose beginning and end, whose motive and outcome they alone determine. What counts is your own war. The war you are beginning and which no one else apart from you can end. Understand this, they have left us nothing except war. All of you, don't you hear your brothers, your sisters crying, do you not see them in the dirt of the streets, in the middle of ruins—while the others in their clean cities claim to know nothing about it, while they remain silent and only humiliate us even further by their behaviour? You know the feeling, you know the pain when you see them remain silent—while their lips appear to remain tightly shut, they are in reality spitting on you, on us all. Do you know that?'

The men nodded. The explosions were now giant fists striking the mountain. Smoke drifted in, veiled the figure of Mukhtar who had not moved.

'For how long do you want to bear it? How long shall we crawl in the dirt which the Zionists pour out over us? They hate us. They're racists. They despise us because we have no modern planes and tanks. And they will let us feel that again and again. How often do they have to bomb us, how often will they buy our corrupt governments, how many more of our brothers will they kill before each Believer understands that he himself dies in each of them? How long are you going to allow yourselves to be consoled by the empty promises of the West? You will never, never be happy without God!'

He seized Rashid by the shoulder, who looked up into the narrow face in which the dark eyes glowed as in a cold fever. The Teacher gripped his shoulder more tightly.

'And God grieves—He grieves over each one of His faithful. How can you remain idle, how can you continue looking on for even one second more? The sword speaks, the war of wars has begun, and if it should last centuries—the Unbelievers will lose it. We may not have planes, but we have the Faith which is stronger than any machine and any shell. Yes, calmly raise your head, all of you raise your heads.'

Kerim saw the Teacher coming to him out of the smoke, felt his soft hand under his chin. Gently the Teacher pulled his head up. He breathed in the acrid smell of gun lubricant.

'Their end has already begun. They don't know it yet—or they don't want to know it, they still gorge and wallow as if there was nothing that threatened them. If they were not so cowardly, then they would see the black horizon. They could see coming what will inevitably annihilate them.'

He was still holding Kerim's chin, the latter's breathing was shallow and he didn't dare move. The Teacher's voice changed. In a tone of lament he continued, 'Do not say to me that you were not filled with grief at the death of your brothers in Afghanistan, in Palestine. Don't say to me that you did not feel for your violated sisters in the Occupied Territories. Don't say to me that Palestine is not part of your souls.'

The men began to shake their heads, one after another, they rhythmically and silently struck their thighs.

'Don't say to me that your own small life is worth more than that of our martyrs. Mukhtar has seen boys like you tied to the tracks of tanks and slowly crushed to death while the Unbelievers, the Russian dogs, laughed.' Quickly, the Teacher went over to the Mukhtar and drew him before them through the smoke. 'Say, did you see them?'

Mukhtar, coated in pale grey dust and with terrifying dark eyes, answered, 'I saw them die and they did not make a sound.'

The Teacher shouted through the thunderous roar, 'Don't say to me that you're worth more than they are! Not one of us must live! Only the Unbelievers can't let go of it, because that is all they have. But we have Paradise—we, all of you are certain to reach it. So what more do you want? Or are you faint-hearted, deaf to the Words of God?'

The men shook their heads.

'Can He not reach you? Do you turn away when His Word is brought to you? Do you have no heart for the suffering of which He speaks? Do you not want to hear what He has to say? Is that how you are?'

All shook their heads.

'It is your war. Each one of you has his war, each one of you knows what he has to do. The battle begins as a struggle of the soul and ends with the victory of the Faith. This world is the work of the Almighty, it is His Work—not one millimetre, not even a ray of light separates it from Him and it can only belong to His Believers, His warriors. Today, the Unbelievers still laugh when the mothers of the devout weep, today they still pretend they want to liberate our women, your mothers, your daughters. And in truth they turn them into whores, that is what they want! Because their own women are whores. Today, they still soil the Faith, because like that, it appears to them to be weak and ridiculous. But already tomorrow, they will run, they will flee to the shore of the wide and silent ocean that will swallow them up.'

The Teacher turned to the entrance and pointed outside, where the world had disappeared in smoke; there was a weak trace of light amid the think clouds.

'We are on God's path, even if it is a streak of blood. Not a word more is necessary.'

4

He returned home at the end of the summer. His clothes were tattered and the soles of his shoes had so many holes that his feet touched the ground. He had finally taken off his head covering and shaved himself as best he could in a mountain spring. Since, however, he had used his combat knife, his face around the chin was covered in small cuts, tufts of bristle still sprouting among them. The people in the alleys took fright when they saw him and gave him a wide berth because he was so dirty and matted. The Peshmergas stopped him several times on the road, but he always convinced them with the story about his family who were waiting for him, the lost son. He had left behind all his weapons, was carrying only Rashid's dirt-caked cloth bag, which he pressed to his hips with one hand. In it, he had the money, more than 6,000 'greenbacks', US dollars. They were tied in bundles, which seemed to secrete something greasy that stuck to the fingers. The money made him at once calm and nervous. He knew what he had done to get it and he also knew that everything he did from now on was dependent on this money.

Kerim had lost so much weight, no one recognized him. He left the dusty road, went through the gate of the restaurant, passed the spot at which his father had died and finally stood at the door. He paused for a moment. In the past months, he had often imagined what it would be like to come back. And the overwhelming feeling of familiarity had always given wing to his thoughts. Yet now there was nothing of that inside him. He saw the shabby house, the bleak parking lot, the old pickup, the antennas and clotheslines in the neighbouring yards and through the windows the few customers who had stopped off at this time in the early afternoon. The news was on the TV and it occurred to Kerim that he knew nothing of events in the world, in the country. And he became aware of the indifferent silence which enclosed and sealed all the things around him and which from now on would separate him from them.

When he stood in front of his mother and his brothers, there was only astonishment in their faces. They looked at him as if he had risen from the dead.

'Have you been sleeping in the street?' asked Imat and there was a quiet reproach in his voice. He had to go back to work right away.

But his mother was already weeping. Hesitantly, she placed her hands on his shoulders, wanting to embrace him. Instead, she pushed him into the kitchen like a big, strange present.

Kerim related nothing of his experiences, he did no more than hint that he had been kidnapped on the day he went to visit his grandparents. His mother asked no more questions but insisted that he ate something immediately and set to preparing it. Kerim wanted to draw little Ali to him, yet his youngest brother looked at him with horror. When Kerim stretched out his hand to him, he took flight.

Later, at the first available opportunity, Kerim took advantage of an unobserved moment to hide the money. He took the bag into the kitchen and deposited the bundles of money in a cupboard in which his father had collected very old, rusty tools. He had carefully wrapped the bundles in plastic bags beforehand. He placed a heavy metal box on top. He knew that no one had gone to the cupboard for years, ever since they had found mouse droppings in it. After that, his father had been responsible for this niche. When Kerim was done, he glanced around the room and knew very well that he had not returned, as the others believed, and that this money was the sign of that.

***

In the time that followed, he didn't reflect much on the flood of events in the country. He was constantly exhausted. Since he again passed most of the time in the kitchen, he only saw the news in the evening when, sweaty and tired, he sat down to eat at one of the tables. The latest headlines from world politics, sports and stock exchange ran along the lower edge of the CNN images. They always covered up the ground of the yellowish landscapes, the lower part of dust-covered date palms, bushes or the gates of far-away houses. Kerim imagined his former fellow fighters hiding just behind these ribbons of text, which seemed permanently to limit the occupiers' sight. A channel like CNN was like the window of a space ship orbiting the earth at a great distance and zooming in on Kerim's country from time to time. What he saw there was for him, too, an alien world of washed-out colours, curiously scaled-down and commented on by reporters who sometimes wore bulletproof vests and even helmets. Spacemen, in fact, thought Kerim. Yet at the same time, he felt a fear which soon hardly allowed him to sleep any more. The Holy Warriors were achieving their goal of creating a network with many other groups. This uprising was growing ever larger, was spreading everywhere in the country and would quite possibly reach here. He was lost if that happened, they would find him.

The time came when even the long-distance drivers began to be afraid of the highways. They no longer drove to Baghdad because all the news from the south was threatening. The kidnapping and murder of a Turkish truck driver, the video of his beheading were an unmistakeable signal to every one of them.

As usual, some of them stopped off at the restaurant around midday, ordered their big portions of rice and chicken and animatedly discussed events from the news broadcasts or ones they had heard about on the road.

In this way, Kerim learnt about Fallujah, a stronghold of the rebels which had first been besieged and then captured by American troops. The town on the

Euphrates, in fact, unimportant in itself, lay about seventy miles west of the capital. Fallujah and the district around it had always been dangerous territory, a centre of smuggling and bandit gangs. This was where the 'insurgency', as reported by CNN, was concentrated. It began slowly. First of all, the American soldiers on their patrols discovered more and more slogans—'Kill the Foreigners!', 'Free the Fatherland!'—which had been written with sheep's blood on the naked walls, covered only by a layer of desert dust, of the city centre. For some time, there had already been reports of the presence of Emir Zarqawi and there were also indications that jihadists from abroad were gathering there.

The drivers said, all of that had, at first, been uncomfortable news for the Americans, which is why they had played it down for a long time. Then, however, the violence had exploded. A highway with the number ten ran through the town from one end to the other before continuing on a bridge across the Euphrates. For reasons about which all could only speculate, a group of contract workers and secret service operatives had taken a wrong turning, managed to get back on the main road from the labyrinth of streets and were finally killed close to the bridge and dragged out of the vehicles. The pictures of their burnt and mutilated bodies, hanging from the steel girders of the bridge, went around the world.

Enveloped in the smoke from their cigarettes, three truck drivers leant back in their chairs, waiting patiently for their food. In his mind's eye, Kerim saw everything the three men were talking about. While without thinking, he carried out the familiar movements in the sweltering heat of the kitchen and ordered his brothers around, only one thought was going through his head—they were all leading their normal lives here, almost as if nothing had happened all that time, while a couple of hundred miles further south, a war was taking place, even if it was a small, limited war for a dirty industrial town. And here they were all simply waiting for it to blow over, as if it had nothing to do with them. Only the little feeling of disquiet that the violence could reach as far as here, the occasional tremble of suppressed agitation made these events appear closer and more threatening than the many other news items from other, unfamiliar parts of the world. In Fallujah, the rebels had made use of their time to set up a small kingdom. This had been presented to them on a plate by the occupiers who simply did not want to admit that there was a full-blown uprising. They broke off an initial offensive because the world TV audience was outraged by yet more pictures of war and destruction.

Kerim listened to the men talking; surrounded by the hissing of the fat, he pricked up his ears. Finally, he himself brought out the three plates to the table. The men sent him back for bread and water. After that, he remained standing beside them.

'You've grown thin,' said one of the drivers. Unlike the others, he had not yet begun to eat. He scrutinized Kerim sympathetically and scratched the thick stubble on his cheek. 'You and your family have had a great deal of sorrow since what happened to your father . . . We all feel sad about it.'

The other two nodded in agreement and went on chewing.

Kerim said nothing. Many had already commented on his loss of weight and always concluded that it was due to the grief working deep down in his body. He himself felt differently about it. He enjoyed his new agility every day, it was as if he had at last removed a coat that was far too heavy. It was true that it had begun inside him when his father had died before his eyes. Yet it was less grief that had taken possession of him than a sense of the transience of life. In a single moment, he'd lost his past, everything that until then had seemed to have grown as part of him had loosened and fallen away. What had begun then had continued, and it'd made him lighter with every passing day—it had changed him and it felt good. He looked at the men's plates and remembered the greed with which he had once pounced on food. He didn't miss the feeling.

The driver had meanwhile started his meal. Eating noisily, he continued.

'You all know, at the beginning of the year, I still used to drive to Fallujah quite often,' he said. 'I also know some people there. At any rate, what the Americans have brought to an end for the time being was already beginning then. Fallujah—I don't envy anyone having to try to control that town. Once when I was driving through it—that was still before they had hung the Americans from the bridge—everything appeared calm and peaceful. The people were as they always were. I stopped for a break. It was midday and I was eating in a restaurant just as I am now. Through the window, I could see a crowd gathering in the street outside. Young people mainly and more and more of them the longer I looked. I had the feeling something was going to happen, not necessarily anything bad. The people weren't making a noise, there were no shots to be heard either, and no one was armed. I was curious nevertheless, so I ate up quickly, paid and went outside. The restaurant was in a poorer quarter at the edge of the town. It could have been that a robbery had taken place. When I asked one of the boys, he told me, however, that the Americans were building something in an open space at the end of the street. He was, like all the rest, very excited, waved his arms about. So I thought, it must be a military post or some other kind of heavily defended installation, perhaps even a prison. Gradually, the whole crowd began to move, slowly, as if everyone was afraid of the building site, and I went along with them. The noise of the bulldozers could already be heard from quite a distance away. One could see the cloud of dust. Then we were standing in front of the place and saw the men who were working there. I still remember exactly what I was thinking—how crazy to be slaving away in this heat. There were perhaps twenty soldiers there. They must have been working for some time and had first excavated a deep pit into which they had thrown all the refuse which they had collected in the open space. Now they were levelling the site and none of those around me knew why they were doing it. Everyone was staring and wondering. There were also a couple of guards for security, but not many. The Americans wanted people to see the work being done, to follow what was happening. The soldiers had to take a lot of breaks. They had lots of plastic bottles with water—there was a whole palette full at the edge of the site. Whenever they were thirsty, they went over and drank a whole bottle. Then they continued working. I think we watched them for almost a whole hour and no one understood what they were doing. It was simply interesting to observe the Americans. Normally, they only drive past, I've seldom seen so many together in the open.'

He interrupted his story, drank a glass of water and turned his attention to the salad. Kerim wondered how he had managed to empty his plate while entertaining the other two men. He must be used to talking while he ate. The driver allowed a few seconds to pass, knowing full well that everyone around him was waiting for the end of the story. He smacked his lips with pleasure, cleared his throat, drank some more water. But he only continued when one of the others broke the silence and asked,

'Well, what were they building? Go on, tell us.'

The driver raised his greasy shining hand and admonished his listener to be patient.

'Two days later, I was in the town again and the Americans were still working at the site. I drove straight there because I wanted to know what they had done. Again it was blazing hot. The bulldozers had disappeared but a dozen men were still working there. Again many of the young people of Fallujah were standing at the edge of the space and looking on. You won't believe it.' He looked around his listeners and once more let seconds pass.

Now the others stopped eating and stared at him expectantly.

'It was a football pitch, a brand new football pitch with everything that goes with it. The pitch was marked out and the goals even had nets.'

The anticipation faded from the drivers, they went on eating silently for a while. Then one of them said,

'Well, that was presumably a present for the boys of the town.'

The man who had told the story leant back and lit a cigarette. He nodded and said,

'Most of them only knew something like it from TV. The Americans had seen the boys playing football on this field of refuse, using the piles of rubbish as goals. And so, without further ado, they made a proper football pitch for them.'

He took a deep draw and looked at the two others, who had still not finished their food and glanced quickly at Kerim.

'And do you know what happened?'

Now the men put their spoons on their plates and likewise reached for their cigarettes. They did so simultaneously, as if they had foreseen that the story was not yet over and had saved up this gesture for the real conclusion.

'After the soldiers had withdrawn,' said the driver, 'the place was empty for two days. No one went there. As if it was secured by an invisible lock to which no one had the key. Then one night, two hundred people from the town suddenly turned up. They went to the rubbish pit, and with their bare hands took everything out and spread it over the football pitch. They destroyed the goals and the markings and then left.'

5

It was a late afternoon, and Kerim, as usual not concentrating, had burnt himself at the stove. His thumbs hurting, he carried the plates to the table at which an elderly gentleman was sitting with his bodyguards. In his suit, the man looked like a civil servant, to go by the guards, however, he was more likely to be a local politician stopping off here on his way to Kirkuk or Arbil.

As he was approaching the table, Kerim noticed a figure close to the entrance to whom he paid no attention at first. He exchanged a few words with the customers and looked over again since the man made no move to come any further and sit down at one of the tables. When he recognized him, Kerim shrank back. The careworn figure with a pale layer of street dust on the shoulders of the tattered jacket was no one but Anatol.

Kerim quickly looked away yet instantly understood that he had to greet Anatol. But he remained where he was, incapable of going closer to him. A secret fear, but even more the shame related to it, paralysed him. Finally, Anatol nodded and took a step in his direction. Now Kerim looked at him and didn't quite manage to hide his feelings.

'Why do you look so scared?' said Anatol with a calm expression when they were standing in front of each other. 'Have you seen a ghost?'

Kerim was tempted to answer yes, but he raised his shoulders a little for a moment and said nothing as they embraced.

Anatol smelt of forlornness and fear. It was as if he had brought the prison with him. His cheeks were sunken, his eyes seemed lifeless, although he was trying to smile in a friendly way.

'How are you, my boy, how are you?'

At last Kerim was able to take the initiative. He drew Anatol away from the customers and led him to a smaller table close to the kitchen. As soon as he was seated, Kerim asked what he would like to eat. But Anatol didn't want anything.

'Just tea,' he said, 'I don't want to stay long. Sit down with me,' he requested firmly.

Kerim looked uncertainly around, yet he already sensed that there was no escape from the situation. So finally he nodded and sat down.

'I know you bear all the responsibility now, after what happened.' Anatol's big, dull eyes were on Kerim. 'You've changed. You've become thin now and tall,' he said thoughtfully.

Kerim called his brother over and told him to bring two glasses of tea and a portion of rice and chicken.

Once Anatol had also greeted Imat, Kerim turned to him.

'Where have you come from now?' he got out, although there was nothing he wanted to know less.

Anatol stared at the tabletop in front of him and something like a smile played around his lips.

'I was in prison for a while,' he said then and suddenly looked Kerim in the eye, as if he wanted to see what effect the sentence had.

Kerim merely nodded and nervously stirred his tea. And it became clear to him what mattered now.

'Why?' he asked. 'What happened?'

Anatol raised his drooping shoulders and looked as if he was too weak even to do that.

'I don't know,' he replied. 'They came early in the morning and took me away. You know how it was always done. No one tells you why.'

Again he stared at Kerim for a long time, and that he began to feel that the Anatol was about to spring something on him, confront him with a truth which, however, he could not possibly know.

'Believe me,' Anatol continued, 'I have often, very often thought about how it could happen. But I still don't know.'

Kerim made an effort to look sympathetic and understanding, and observed himself at the same time. He would gladly have confessed everything to Anatol, revealed his monstrous but no more than childish weakness on that day, explained to him that he was simply afraid of the policeman. Yet something inside him refused honesty. A voice, quiet and nevertheless strong, had awakened, whispering incessantly that he must not betray himself and simply accept that this ragged man had nothing to do with him and everything that lay before him.

Anatol changed the subject.

'I feel very sorry about the business with your father. You know we were good friends. I only heard about it when I was free again.' He raised his narrow hands. 'But you see how it is with me—I have little left. That's why it took so long until I could come here.'

Kerim thought about what he might want. He tried to find some clue to it. Does he suspect the truth? It went through his mind again, but he at once firmly rejected the idea, convinced it was impossible. And yet he asked himself why he found Anatol's behaviour so reproachful. Why was his stare so weak and needy, why was he wearing these threadbare clothes? Did he want to make a show of his suffering or make everyone who had had more luck than he feel guilty?

Imat brought the food and placed it in front of Anatol, who immediately pushed it a couple of inches to the side. Kerim looked up at the ceiling, where the big hole, repaired in a makeshift way, could still be made out. All of a sudden, the thought occurred to him—his father could have left it like that, the way it was, all those years, as a pointer to a way out, perhaps even for his son.

He thought back to the visit to Anatol many years before, of the esteem in which his father had held this small man. But none of it made him feel nostalgic, quite the opposite—he sensed very clearly how these memories and this figure from the past were becoming evermore remote. In truth, so he believed, it had all died long ago. He only put on an act, a pretence of familiarity. Now he was ready to flee, he thought about it at every moment, and that alone unburdened him.

Kerim's mother came to the table. Anatol looked sadly up at her and, with an effort, rose to his feet. It was a sad reunion. Kerim knew that his mother saw in Anatol someone who was linked to her husband. He listened attentively to the two of them. In the end, he even forced himself to cheer Anatol up a little.

'My father did tell me how highly he thought of you,' he said. 'And that you are his friend.'

At that, the emaciated man collapsed into the chair. For a moment, he seemed dumbfounded, beside himself. Kerim feared an outburst of rage. But then Anatol lowered his head and tears ran down his cheeks, leaving pale channels on his dust-covered skin. Kerim's mother comforted him while Kerim got up abruptly and took his leave, saying he had to work. Anatol just nodded mutely. Later Kerim saw him wolfing down the food. He was still weeping, taking big mouthfuls and swallowing them down with a visible effort.

* * *

The very next day, Kerim began the preparations for his flight. He counted the money once again. Then he set off on foot for the old town.

It was a hot day, Kerim walked past tall, new houses and the shells of buildings under construction and thought that he would never see them completed. He passed through the archway where the old bazaar began. The street was crowded, cars drove at walking pace. The further he went, the more people there were. Passageways, winding alleys and streets led off to left and right. From a small bridge, he had a view of the bazaar with its water tanks, half-ruined roofs, the web of cables, the children playing with cardboard boxes, the casual labourers under the tin awnings, smoking, waiting for work as they did every day.

In the shops, he saw the glowing yellow, red and green fruit juices in long-stemmed glasses standing on the cooled dispensers. He hurried over the big flagstones in the covered part of the bazaar, stepped over the deep waste-water drain in the middle and saw the many different cloths, the pieces of clothing and household appliances on offer. Briefly, he wondered whether he really should go away from here, where life went on despite the troubles in the south. There might be another change for the better and so a future for him in this country.

But then he was already standing in front of the shop of Nasir the tailor, an old friend of his father. He was a discreet man with extensive connections, his father had once said admiringly of Nasir. If anyone did, then he knew a way to get Kerim out of the country.

He stepped inside and his gaze wandered over the counter, weighed down with cloth, and a row of empty plastic chairs in one corner. He became nervous. Now he would have to tell Nasir about the money, would have to reveal his plans to flee.

When the tailor emerged from the back of the shop, Kerim was hardly able to speak. It was the first time in his life that he was making such a far-reaching decision. He returned Nasir's greeting, glanced out into the street through the window with its grille and said nothing.

'I know you,' said the tailor. 'Tell me who you are.'

Kerim told him and immediately fell silent again but, in his desperation, looked straight at the man. The latter responded and offered his condolences. Yet something in his plump face changed, he no doubt suspected that the young man in front of him had something important on his mind. He lowered his eyes, picked up a piece of tailor's chalk and began to work. He simply waited, because questions weren't going to get anywhere here.

The sound of the shop door opening broke through the silence lying heavy in the room. A veiled woman entered; without greeting, she made ready to wait. Nasir immediately turned his attention to her, so Kerim could collect his thoughts.

As soon as the woman had left the shop, he burst out with his problem.

'I want to go over the border,' he said. 'I have an uncle in Germany. I have money.'

Nasir brushed over the cloth with the palm of his hand and looked thoughtful.

'Why do you come to me?'

'My father advised me to do so. When he was still alive.'

'You will need a lot of money,' said the tailor calmly. 'And it's dangerous.'

Kerim didn't have the feeling the man wanted to warn him. What he said sounded too casual. More that he wanted to prepare the field for the necessary negotiations.

Nasir took hold of the rolls of cloth on the counter, pushed them aside, raised the top and came out into the front shop. He pushed past Kerim, went to the door and locked it. Then he indicated to Kerim to follow him. In the back, a kind of box room with drawn curtains, he took a plastic chair from a stack and put it down for Kerim. He disappeared through another door and a couple of minutes later, brought two glasses of tea on a tray. He sat down opposite Kerim, dropped two sugar cubes in his own glass and stirred thoughtfully without saying a word.

After he had emptied the glass, he leant back in his chair, crossed his legs and scratched his cheek.

'Because I knew your father, I have to tell you once again. It will be dangerous. I hope you know what you are doing.'

Kerim only nodded dumbly. Nasir rubbed his chest and looked at the ceiling.

'You know,' he continued, 'shortly after the Americans invaded, the government had already been overthrown. There was a Bedouin further south, who was in luck. One day he discovered an abandoned car park in the middle of the landscape. A whole fleet of cars was standing around there, all of them new, Mercedes, BMW, you know the kind. The Bedouin didn't waste a lot of time thinking, fetched a very, very long rope and slung it around each car as he would around a camel. From now on, it was his herd. Then he began to sell them, cheaply at first, but in time, evermore expensively. Each time, he removed the rope from the car he had just sold. The smaller his stock became, the more his prices shot up. The man grew wealthy as a result. Well, and now he's in his much bigger tent and sitting there chewing like a camel. Do you know what cars those were?'

Kerim shook his head.

'They were Saddam's future presents for deserving comrades. What I'm trying to say is: you can get rich here too and have a good life, if you act adroitly and perhaps hurry up a bit. Why do you want to go away?'

Kerim listened to the steps of passers-by, audible through the curtained windows. He found the dusty smell of the bales of cloth on the shelves unpleasant. He didn't know what to say in reply and didn't want to think about it either.

'Good,' said Nasir finally. 'You must know what you're doing, and I won't ask any more questions. When can you bring the money?'

Kerim drank the last mouthful of tea and became animated.

'I have it with me,' he said.

Nasir made every effort to talk his new customer out of his haste but Kerim couldn't be stopped. In the weeks that followed, they met regularly in the shop and the tailor reported on the progress of Kerim's business. He explained that the matter was not as simple as Kerim imagined. He did not have enough money to pay for a complete and safe journey to Germany. In that case, he would only have to wait till a sign came from the organization. Then they would have put him on a plane and flown him to some country or other, Argentina, for example, where he would perhaps again have had to wait for weeks or months in a hotel. The reason was that the organization bribed officials at airports worldwide. The waiting time depended on the different shifts these people worked. Only when the position was such that a trouble-free transfer from one location to the next to Germany was possible, could he begin his journey. The whole thing was organized like a normal tourist trip, except for the illegality. And, so Nasir explained to him, there was an even more luxurious way—with really a lot of money, one could have got hold of a German passport for him. The document wasn't forged but bought from someone who had come back from Europe, from Germany in this case. Kerim could have changed his identity and slipped into the role of this returnee. If such an operation succeeded, then he would have become a German without further ado and would never have had to fear problems with the authorities.

Kerim was sitting opposite the tailor and noticed how he enjoyed laying out all these facts before him. At the time, Kerim did not yet have any idea of what Nasir described as a problem with the authorities. He listened in silence and didn't even ask questions about the astronomic prices.

His case was anyway different. While Nasir could guarantee that he would get to Berlin with the sum he had available, the journey would nevertheless have to be made in stages, some dangerous, some not. At each of their meetings, Nasir impressed on him how important it was to make contact with Athens, no matter where he was. That was where the headquarters of the organization was, the hub of the whole thing. They would make sure that someone was sent to Kerim who could take him on. The tailor therefore suggested to Kerim that he take on the hard slog of going on foot through Turkey into Greece.

'It's not so far from home,' he said encouragingly, 'you know the landscape. Imagine what it would be like going illegally across the border into Austria and to creep through the forest in a really foreign place at night and perhaps in the snow.'

At the mere thought of that, Kerim was ready to agree to the other variant. Yet again the tailor urged patience. He raised his hand and shook his head.

'Wait until you've heard everything. It will be dangerous, because you have to cross the sea. There's no other way of doing it, I've made all the calculations. Not such a great distance, but still . . . do you think you're up to it?'

Since he was unable to imagine it, Kerim simply said yes.

'There's something else very important we have to do,' the tailor immediately went on, 'that is, invent a story.'

Kerim already knew that he had to apply for asylum when he arrived in Berlin. 'You need a good reason, otherwise they'll send you back home right away. They want to know exactly why you had to leave your country and they won't believe you and will keep on asking you about it. Your story has to be good.'

Nasir explained that the readiness of the authorities to recognize a request for asylum depended on the mood at any particular time. 'A year ago, several women were accepted who said they were lesbian and were threatened with death by their families for it. It was true of some, not of others—at any rate, for a while it was successful. Now it's changed again. Who could threaten you?' Nasir paused significantly and looked thoughtfully at the curtained window.

Kerim waited but, finally, in broad outline, he spoke about his kidnapping and his time with the Holy Warriors. The tailor raised his head and looked at him.

'We've discussed it and everyone thinks that it really would now be best if Islamists threatened you.

At any rate, you're an Alevi, your father was—that's very unusual here.' He again looked thoughtful before continuing,

'According to what you say, you really are in danger. But we can't tell your story like that, because then they would send you back right away. What if you say that you're being persecuted for religious reasons and your father was killed by the Islamists? You don't need to look so shocked. It's only a story, a fairy tale, and your father would certainly have agreed to it.'

Doubtfully, Kerim consented. From now on, this story was a constant topic at their meetings. Nasir did not tire of telling it to him in every detail and reminding him that it would possibly secure him his new life.

Smiling, he said,

'The Germans aren't stupid, you know. They, too, have people here whom they can ask, believe me. But we'll make sure that the story is confirmed. It's a good story, it fits the times.'

Sometimes the tailor talked about the strange transformation in the people who came to see him in order to leave the country. In his opinion, they got into a kind of frenzy, a frenzy of transformation, which made them give up everything they had achieved thus far in order to set out for an uncertain future. He spoke of a lawyer, much liked here in the town, who lived in a big house, drove several cars and nevertheless could not be talked out of fleeing to Sweden where now, after a long time, he had at last found a job as a dish washer in a railway-station restaurant.

'I talked to him on the phone last week,' said Nasir. 'And you know what he says? He is very happy to be finally working. It becomes an obsession and they lose all self-respect.'

Kerim was aware how much trouble Nasir was taking with him. He even felt Nasir's dissatisfaction with the remaining dangerous part of the journey and repeatedly had to reassure him because of it. To Kerim, this favourable treatment seemed like a legacy of his father and a good omen for his journey.

6

After five long weeks, the moment had come. Nasir sent a messenger, a boy of perhaps twelve, who remained standing at the entrance to the car park and waited shyly until Kerim finally saw him. He went out to the lad and was told he would leave tonight. Kerim sent him away and hurried back into the restaurant. He did not say anything to anyone about the imminent journey. Everything important he wrote in a letter that he left behind in his room.

At about one in the morning, he sat up, swung his legs out of bed and tried to get up in one swift movement so that the springs didn't creak. There wasn't much he could take with him—his only piece of baggage was once again Rashid's bag which he had brought with him from the Holy Warriors. For a moment, he stood still in the room and listened. It was quiet in the house. He looked out of the window onto the street one more time, as he had done so often, and made an effort to take in what he saw—the pavements with their long kerbstones gradually sinking into the ground, the cracks running across the road in many places, visible through the dust blown across them, the dark water tanks towering up and a thick, dark cable stretching along house walls, held up by screwed-on and frequently shifted iron hooks. I will never see it again, he thought, the words lagging behind his feelings. A small degree of melancholy was mixed with a greater amount of anticipation, making him uneasy.

Very carefully, he opened the door of his bedroom. He couldn't be completely silent and he knew that his mother would hear every one of his steps. She never slept so soundly as not to register the tiniest disturbance in the night, she had even heard the mice in the pantry. Kerim left the door ajar behind him and went down the stone steps. He remained standing for a moment at the entrance to the kitchen and considered whether there was anything else he needed or wanted to take with him, something small perhaps. But nothing occurred to him. He stuck his head through the kitchen door and saw the huge rice cauldron for the last time. It curved darkly in the room, and Kerim thought of how often, stirring dutifully, he had stood beside the cauldron. He breathed in the heavy sweetly sticky odour of the kitchen, then hurried into the dining room. The empty wooden chairs crouched in the darkness like beggars who had nodded off. This room was banished into silence.

Once he had shut the restaurant door behind him and was standing outside, an image involuntarily came to Kerim's mind. He saw his mother's head on her pillow, her big, dark eyes wide open and, like her, he heard the clicking of the lock again and again. At that moment, feeling the night wind on his skin, he was in silent agreement with her that he had already left her. She would remain lying in bed and wait until she could no longer hear him. He, however, walked across the car park and into the street, filled with the idea that he would have become someone else when he—and he was firmly convinced of this—saw her again one day. He also thought of Shirin. First I shall change myself, he thought, and then, as another, call everyone, even her, and, who knows, perhaps she'll follow later.

That same night, Nasir the tailor drove him to Zakho. He proved to be very adroit in dealing with the sentries at the checkpoints. For each, he had a different version of the story about Kerim's father who was seriously ill in Zakho and waiting for his son. Otherwise, too, he was in his element when telling stories. He again briefly touched on the true fate of Kerim's father, as if it was a comfort, telling of a special assassination attempt. Immediately after the uprising, when the Red House in Suleimaniyah had already fallen and all the representatives of the regime were either dead or had been driven out, there was still one particular thug around. He was notorious for his cunning and cruelty and the Kurds absolutely wanted to punish him. He was in Kirkuk. Many Arabs lived there and it was a kind of last enclave of the regime in the middle of Kurdistan. Since he knew all the tricks, he had an army of well-trained bodyguards around him. A direct attack would have been too dangerous and so the Kurds resorted to a ruse. A Peshmerga pretended to be a madman. He put on a dirty woollen sack and the oldest boots he could find. He let his hair and beard grow long like a dervish, practised grotesque movements and even drooling. He prepared very thoroughly for the operation before he eventually came to Kirkuk and began to wander the streets there. At midday, in the marketplace, he suddenly cried out in the middle of the crowds, he stole fruit from the traders and pestered the people for long enough until they all knew him. Night after night, he slept in the street, by day, he began roaming around again. People got used to him and put up with him as they put up with a sandstorm or rain. The man also hung around the alley which the thug took with his bodyguards to go to his office. Often he threw himself in the dirt in front of the men or stood in front of them with outspread arms. They stepped over him or pushed him aside. He always claimed to have some important message from God to tell the evildoer and he always carried out his strange movements as he did so. One morning, the moment finally came —the still powerful and dangerous man seemed in a well-disposed mood. He wanted to hear from God, he said.

The bodyguards opened their cordon, looked attentively around and the Peshmerga at last came close enough to the man. He began to whisper, but he already had the dagger in his hand and the next moment he thrust it into the thug's heart. 'God has had his fill of you,' he said.

And the best thing of all, concluded Nasir, the many bodyguards had been so surprised that the man was able to escape into the next alleyway, not a shot was fired.

The story took Kerim's mind off the pain of departure and his fear of everything unknown that lay in store for him. When he heard the story of this belated assassin, he could not help but think of himself as he had been not too long before and he quickly distracted himself from that by looking out of the car window.

Towards morning, they reached the centre of the little town, situated between bare, gentle hills on one side and beneath a long stretch of rock faces on the other, close by, the little river and the ancient bridge, enchanted according to legend, which looked as fragile as the bone of a bird.

In front of the hotel, Nasir embraced his protégé and repeated all the instructions, checked the money and the slip of paper on which all the telephone numbers and addresses which could be useful were noted. Nasir pointed to a particularly important mobile number, in case he should get lost somewhere, and put everything back in a small, closable plastic pouch that Kerim from now on carried next to his body. Nasir further gave him the advice not to use the traffickers' boat but, at the harbour, to look for another, larger ship. With a little patience and skill, it was possible to get on board unnoticed. He described again the harbour in every detail and impressed on him that it was no great distance and all that mattered was reaching Greece. Then he said goodbye and drove off.

Kerim did not remain alone for long. Four other Kurds were waiting at the inn for their transfer. They had already been living here for weeks on the little money they still had left over and had pooled. They killed time over tea and cigarettes. They immediately accepted Kerim as one of the group. Even at the breakfast table—he had hardly slept and was not in the mood for conversation—they surrounded him and sounded him out. Kerim had to concentrate in order to sum up his story in the way that seemed best. Again and again he took an olive from the bowl in the middle of the table and delayed his replies by chewing for a long time. As he had no appetite, he drank three glasses of tea and himself began to ask questions. Here, in the group, it was evident to Kerim that he must have changed. Something threatening must emanate from him because these young men didn't behave with him in the way he was used to. They cautiously inquired about his life, as if they were afraid of making an unpleasant discovery. They accepted everything as he said it. If he was silent, they were too. Kerim did not ask himself what could have caused this change in the effect he had on people—what concerned him was whether it would be useful to him in future.

Later he took his leave, not discourteously, although abruptly. He stood up, took the flat bread out of the basket and tore it in half as if it was a sign of his separating from them. He took his half with him to his room in the hope that he would not have to come down again very soon.

He was in luck—the trafficker who would take them across the border into Turkey turned up the next morning. Kerim crouched, crowded together with the others in the minibus as they drove into the mountains to the east. The trafficker, a burly man, who looked about sixteen stone, soon began to sweat in his too-tight, well-worn suit. During the drive he smoked one cigarette after another and seemed very nervous. He had not told them his name but talked incessantly. First of all, he described the risks of the sea passage to them. Many had already drowned, he said, but that wasn't the fault of the traffickers—none of the refugees could swim. But recently, in particular, very many had got through and had all made it to Europe. He went on about the cities in Germany, Sweden, in Denmark and the Netherlands and tried to get them in a good mood by describing street cafes that were always full of people who had plenty of money and didn't have to work much because the state gave them an income. The young men beside Kerim made enthusiastic remarks. But he couldn't stop thinking about the water. It had never occurred to him that in an emergency he might have to swim, and now it was too late.

To begin with, the journey was still on a normal road. Kerim was reassured at the sight of the cloud shadows on the gently curving hillsides, the sunflower fields and the yellow, harvested fields. They drove past the endless line of tankers backed up from the border crossing. The drivers sat in groups on blankets at the side of the road or right under the trucks and trailers eating breakfast. The hatches of the tankers were open. Below the road, in a kind of concrete tunnel, he saw an old man with a stick squatting in the shade. There were simple stands everywhere, four poles with a roof of plastic sheeting. Dogs roamed by the road. Donkeys stood alone in the open fields. There were settlements of clay houses built high up against the rock walls.

* * *

Kerim only had a patchy memory of what happened next. On a godforsaken path in the hills, the man passed them on to another, not, however, before they had paid him for his part of the operation. They immediately set off again, went on through the border country with their new guide. He was a young Turk from Adana who had more or less just reached adulthood, they didn't get any more out of him. He remained taciturn throughout the virtually endless march, perhaps also because they, the refugees, were talking to one another and the guide could only understand with great difficulty, if at all, what they were saying.

Once deep inside the Turkish part of Kurdistan, he did speak after all. On the previous, first day of their march they had rested in the shadow of rock ledges and trees before setting out towards evening. The big man in the car had already explained that it was too dangerous for them to cross the territory during daylight, since the Turkish soldiers patrolled the border territory hunting for terrorists. Now night was falling, the sky over the mountains glowed magnificently in orange and yellow. They walked in single file along an extended hill ridge. Kerim looked down into the shadow-filled ravine beside him and to the dark hills looming up on the other side. A tall, isolated deciduous tree rose up there, grave stones around it, many tilting to the side. Suddenly, a jolt went through the group, because the guide at the front had come to a halt. The moment of fright was followed by the man giving an all-clear sign with his hand. Along the hill-crest on the other side of the ravine, a column of men and women with shouldered guns was coming towards them. Only by their dark outlines could Kerim see that they were wearing uniforms, he recognized the women by their posture and gait.

'PKK,' whispered the guide, who was standing close to Kerim. Then he turned right around to him and said in English, 'Some of them over there come here especially from Germany. You're going to Germany? Isn't that odd? Why don't you stay here and fight with them?' There was a humorous undertone to his voice.

Kerim looked at the group moving past in silence. He imagined them seeking shelter in caves, perhaps in the very same ones in which he had lived with the Holy Warriors and which, before them, had already given shelter to the Kurds in their fight against the regime in Baghdad. The cold evening wind blew through the valley and the evening glow faded. Kerim became aware of the smell of autumn, he glanced briefly at his silent companions whose eyes were on him, as if they were waiting for his command.

'Get me to a harbour,' he said to the guide, 'then I'll be happy.'

PART THREE

1

It was the noises that scared him most. In the dark and cramped hold, they enclosed him like the heavy, toxic-sharp air. Kerim tried to get used to it, tried to reassure himself. But the prospect of having to bear this dull roar for days almost made him despair. It came to him out of the metal of the floor and the walls and into the brief sleep that repeatedly enveloped him. He had vivid dreams in these bare half hours and the dreams were accompanied by the rumble. In the noise, he fled through the streets of Mersin, wanted to hide from the glances of the youths hanging around but didn't manage it. He hurried through a fog of electric light. Only when he woke up, panting from the exertion of dreamt movements, did he know that he had not stumbled, that he had not fallen deep into the noise of the street. It was the rumble that had crawled into him and been transformed there. He crouched amid the chests attached to the walls with broad straps. When he was awake, he recalled how he had taken possession of his kingdom down here. It had been a moment of rest as if after a long walk. He had found a noise-filled but dry, little place. There was even a light which, however, he didn't dare switch on. A small torch was the only souvenir he had bought in the town. With it he had explored the hold. He crept around among the huge wooden cases and metal containers until he had enough of their dead surfaces.

When he had switched the light off again and hidden away in his niche, he thought about what he would do to pass the time. He could walk around in this space, perhaps even open the door to the main deck now and then. It was only a few yards to a companionway from which he was able to see the sky. He resolved to do something as dangerous as that only at night, if at all. At any rate, so he thought, the noise also protected him if he opened the outside door.

He stretched out his legs and leant against the wall. Its unceasing, delicate vibrations went through him, he felt them down to his toes. He started and was not certain whether he had nodded off again. The door was opened and the light switched on. Soundlessly, Kerim pushed himself deep into the niche between chest and wall. Just as he had practised it, he had disappeared from sight in a second. He heard two men talking in an unfamiliar language. They spoke quickly and so softly that Kerim was beginning to fear they had noticed his presence. He heard heavy steps. One of the men was evidently giving the other instructions. After that, a squealing sound filled the room, as if they were pushing something heavy across the iron floor. Kerim tried as hard as he could to remember whether he had left something lying around outside, and again and again he thought about his food store. But he reassured himself as best he could with the thought that the two men had a better chance of finding him than the linen bag behind one of the metal containers. The seamen chatted for a few moments longer, then they left the hold and darkness fell upon Kerim.

He was just about to crawl out from behind the chest as the floor seemed to give way under him and the wall against which his back was pressed tilted away. The chest admittedly did not begin to move but it rose up beside him and that alone made it difficult for him to breathe. Groaning, he forced his way out of the hiding place and was sitting as he had before just as the ship tipped to the other side.

It was no more than a gentle rocking, yet in an instant it put Kerim in a state of fearful excitement. The ship was casting off at last. For a little while, he was relieved. He leant his head against the wall and smiled in the darkness. Now I just need to stick it out here, he thought, now I need to do nothing more but wait. Every hour he passed here brought him closer to his goal. He thought of the cramped, dark lorry in which, hidden behind sacks full of hazelnuts and almost suffocating, they had spent many terrible hours on the way to Mersin, and immediately he was reconciled to his situation here.

The noise around him was only a little louder but had become less regular. A few minutes later, he was overcome by fear and he became so restless that he had to stand up. He stood there swaying. There was no going back any more—he was leaving the harbour behind, the town, indeed the continent. He was now all alone on this ship with these men he didn't know, and that thought made him shudder.

The ship tilted gently to one side, before swinging back immediately. Kerim observed himself. After some time—he could no longer judge how much—he waited for the signs of seasickness. He had definitely taken account of that in his plans when he had come on board that night. The moment he set foot on deck, he knew that in this place he had no choice but to fall ill. As he stumbled over the pipes and covers and almost fell, because he had to avoid the dull safety lighting, he already hated the idea of hiding away in this huge, deserted metal shell. Standing in one of the passageways, he heard a television. The sound of unceasing panting and blows echoed along the iron tunnel. The set was probably in a kind of lounge far away at the other end. Kerim thought for a moment, then he was sure that someone was watching a karate film. He hoped he would be immune to seasickness. If so, he would regard it as a sign from heaven.

He wiped his sweat-covered face, felt his eyes stinging and took a deep breath of the thick air of the cargo hold. It was as if he had to swallow it down. He forced himself to listen carefully to the sounds. He did so periodically, because the seconds the sailors needed to open the door were his only chance. Yet to do that, he had to penetrate the steady noise, had to pay attention to what lay beneath it. There was a state of concentration which forced open the rumble. If he was certain that he discerned nothing but the faint trembling of the metal, he distracted himself again, because he did not want to waste his special gift, as he believed it to be, of attentiveness.

He felt hunger but forced himself to remain sitting in his niche. He could have looked at his watch but would have had to switch on the torch to do so. But like his food he also rationed his portions of light, he wanted to use only what was absolutely necessary.

Kerim shook his head in order not to fall asleep. Yet like his dreams, since he had hidden away on the ship, his thoughts, too, were stubborn and oppressive. He couldn't shake them off. His fear alone made him start, it was strong enough.

He stared in front of him. Sometimes it seemed as if he could see in the dark. At certain points, it thickened around him, at others again, it became somewhat paler, thinner. It was an illusion but Kerim retained the idea of a fog, because in a way it was comforting: he could find a way out of the veiled landscape—there were hidden paths he could walk on. This time, however, the rumble didn't seem to want to open to his ears, it remained a solid wall. So he placed his hands on the metal floor and absorbed the rocking of the ship. It was a steady, almost good-natured rolling. Only very rarely was there a disturbance of the pattern, then the arc of the movement was curtailed on one side, as if far below the rump of the ship was being pushed away by something soft it encountered.

Gradually the sound changed again. It released nothing except the deeper levels of the rumbling and a kind of mechanical creaking, soft and very remote. There was nothing threatening about the constancy of the noise. Whatever endures doesn't attack you, thought Kerim. It might possibly turn out to be dangerous, even fatal, but it didn't require any swift reaction. After he had made sure of the situation, he began to feel his way forward. It wasn't far to his food bag but Kerim wanted to remain as close as possible to the floor. If someone came, he would still have enough time to take cover behind the chests. All he had to know was where a gap was to be found. That was why he stretched out his arms and used the palms of his hands like feelers with which he brushed over the cracked, dirty surfaces of the chests.

He crawled forward and reached the tank behind which his food supply lay. He had seen it only briefly when he sneaked into the hold. Through the open door, the electric lighting of the lower bridge had illuminated the space. This container was not freight but part of the ship and behind it there was enough room for his bundle. Kerim didn't want any baggage that proved to be a hindrance.

Now when he took out his bread and took a small mouthful from his water bottle before eating, for a moment he had a feeling of satisfaction. But even as he was chewing the second morsel, it gave way to renewed fear. He knew his supplies would not last long. Furthermore, he had to find a place to relieve himself. He had hoped the hold would be larger. At the harbour, when he had been on the lookout from behind the barrier before finally choosing the ship, it had not occurred to him that he would end up in a space like this. He had expected to have to hide in an extensive maze-like hall, between cars or even stacks of containers. Instead, he found himself in a store room which was big but also so crammed full that it reminded him of a cellar.

But he had had no choice; sooner or later, he would have been discovered in the dock area. The long shadows of the patrolling security guards slid over the dusty ground and through the fence behind which he had hidden. The pit in which he spent the second night was like a long groove in the ground. He remembered how quickly night had towered above him, not dark and still but restless with the rustling and whirring of insects. They rose with hard, dry wings and crowded in clouds around the glaring harbour streetlights. When he looked up from his pit and, dazzled, screwed up his eyes, he looked into these circles of light and thought of soundless explosions with swarms of countless small ruins in them. And suddenly, he saw, far beyond the beams of light, the outlines of the dark ship, blurred as if under a layer of ice. The deep red rump loomed up behind the harbour mole; Kerim could follow the outline from the tip of the bow down to the bollards. The ship with the name *Sea Star* had appeared as if from nowhere.

He drank a last mouthful of water before stowing the bag away again. Then he tried to estimate how long the food might last. If he was very careful, perhaps two days. He planned to hold out as long as that and then show himself. Of the crew he had so far heard only two men and seen a deck guard from a distance. What would they do when he finally came out of his hiding place? Merely the thought of that moment agitated him so greatly that he involuntarily froze. Perhaps it would have been better after all not to undertake the journey alone. On the other hand, this way the risk of being discovered was much less.

Kerim leant back once more and breathed heavily. He closed his eyes and quickly opened them because he realized that, sitting next to the tank, he was in the exact line of vision of possible visitors to the hold. In order to remain undiscovered, he had to hide among the stacks of boxes on the other side of the space. He had realized that as soon as he had crept into the hold, now he warned himself to be cautious. It was the profound darkness he had not counted on. A room without windows is as secure as a cell, he thought.

He took out the torch. Somewhere there must be a corner where he could relieve himself. He wished he would find a hole in the floor or at least a small drain.

The thin beam of light scanned the scratched metal of two huge containers right next to him and penetrated dark crevices, the few unobscured parts of the walls gleamed like dust-covered windows. On the floor around him, only deep grooves and dry dirt could be made out.

He tried to memorize his surroundings and switched off the torch. Then he crawled between the two metal containers and ran his hands across floor and wall. He felt the regularly distributed small humps in the floor and the strange warmth emanating from the wall. When he was certain that he wouldn't find anything here, he crawled backwards and investigated the next gap. To his great relief he already struck lucky. What he felt under his damp, sweaty fingers was something like a frame with a wire netting across it.

He sat down and switched on the torch. Broad slats, thick with dirt ran horizontally across and overlapped so that nothing of the space behind could be seen. It must be a ventilation shaft. Kerim switched the torch off. He grasped hold of the grille and shook it. Yet the wire was so strong that it didn't give a millimetre, and even if he had been able to loosen the netting, there were still the slats.

About half an hour later, however, he was crouching in front of the frame again. His search had been in vain. There simply was no opening in the floor, at least none that he could have reached. Finally, he had urinated behind the chests, far enough from his hiding place, carefully, in fits and starts, as if he was in danger of flooding the hold. He felt the grille again before making as if to strike it with his fist. Once again he crawled towards where his food was hidden, stopped there and pointed his torch into every corner. Despondency made him heavy. Yet suddenly, he was tense again. He stood up and once more investigated one of the walls behind the stacks of boxes. The torch's small cone of light slid trembling over the metal, and what he had, at first, simply overlooked now came together bit by bit—the arched outline of a door. I should have gone on board a ship before, he said to himself, then I would have known what to look for. Kerim sat down and switched off the torch. It was time to concentrate again. This time he found it harder than before, because his attention was drawn to the door.

2

The door could not be opened from his side. He did find a lever but couldn't make it work. Disappointed, he withdrew. He would have gladly kicked the door which was perhaps only jammed. But since he had to avoid making the slightest sound, there was nothing else to do except force himself to be calm.

During the hours that followed he stared into the blackness and registered himself gradually becoming empty. Empty of feelings and memories, even empty of thoughts. He asked himself whether this was not the best state of mind in which to hold out in a dark room. Yet he was also afraid of the emptiness, because for him it was certainly a preliminary stage to disappearing. He crouched in the cloud of dull noise and stink of machinery and when he moved his head, his gaze only wandered across darkness. Finally, he longed for sleep and closed his eyes. Yet, despite the emptiness, he remained awake for a long time, counted his breaths and felt the trembling of the floor. At least, he said to himself, it isn't cold. Cold—he was sure of that—would have finished him off here. He imagined the cold, as he knew it from the mountains. Snow on the slopes and on the hill paths, ice-cold rivulets in front of the clay huts. Over that, he nodded off in the end.

He started, woken by a sudden new sound which clearly came from somewhere threateningly close. There is someone here in here—that was Kerim's first thought. As a reflex, he made himself small in his niche, drew his legs up and ducked his head down. The noise was, at first, like a scratching, then it became a loud cracking. Finally, it stopped. Kerim strained to hear steps, breathing, anything that would betray the presence of a human being. He held his breath but heard nothing, no sound detached itself from the drone of the machinery.

He waited a couple of minutes. Then he cautiously crawled forward alongside the boxes. He had to know where these sounds came from, the thought of crouching in the darkness and simply waiting was unbearable. Perhaps it was an animal, locked in with him. At the end of the stack of boxes, he stopped. Again minutes passed. Nothing moved, everything was as before. Kerim wondered if he had only been dreaming. He thought it possible, given his condition.

Finally, he switched on the torch and shielded the beam of light with his hand. He could discern no change in the hold. He switched the torch off and crawled further, the very same way he had taken before, on his search. When he was able to touch one of the big containers, he pressed the button of the torch again. He moved the patch of light over the floor in front of him and slowly raised his hand. The next moment, he started and immediately recoiled. The torch almost fell from his hand and the beam of light strayed erratically through the hold. The door he had discovered was open—for a fraction of a second, Kerim had been able to look into the dark space behind it.

Breathing heavily and stiff with fear, he did not know what to do. His hand clasped the torch, as if it could be torn from him. He did not want to switch it off, on no account did he want to be blind.

For a moment, he still hoped the crew had opened the door and disappeared again. But immediately after that, the beam of light met a man's chest. The man breathed out with a hiss in surprise and shielded his eyes. Kerim knew at once he was not a member of the ship's crew. He lowered the torch a little, so that the other could take his hands away from his face. Kerim now clearly saw the frayed shirt and the dirty jeans. Apart from that, he noticed the man was barefoot.

'Who are you?' Kerim whispered in English, when the other had lowered his hands. He did not get a reply. The man stared dumbly at him. There was fear and mistrust in his eyes, and he seemed only with difficulty to repress an impulse to flee, his long legs trembled. He was altogether very thin, Kerim established, and that made him feel a little more secure.

'Do you not have any shoes?' he asked.

This time the other said he didn't.

By God, thought Kerim, I would have risked a lot but I would never have climbed barefoot onto this ship. The mere thought of this kind of defencelessness made Kerim shake his head.

'I am a refugee like you,' he whispered, 'so say something.'

The other moved nervously. Finally, he knelt down.

'The room back here is safer,' said the man quietly. 'What is your name?'

Kerim told him.

'I'm Tony.'

Kerim nodded quickly. Now at last he could switch off the torch.

'Why is it safer over there?' he asked in the direction of the man.

'They don't come in there so often.'

'How do you know that?'

Tony didn't reply but the sound from his reaction suggested a gesture as response. 'Do you have anything to eat?'

'No,' said Kerim just to be on the safe side. It was at any rate possible that this man could still cause him problems. Perhaps they would have to separate again.

At the same time, he asked himself whether Tony really had come on board not only without shoes but also without a supply of food. What recklessness, he thought. It was not very auspicious for their time together on the ship. Kerim switched on the torch again when he became aware of Tony's movements. Involuntarily, he wanted to call out to him, 'Quietly, quietly,' but from now on, he had to get used to the sounds of the other.

Dazzled by the beam of light, Tony gestured forcefully with his hands.

'Save the batteries,' he hissed.

So Kerim crawled after him, uncertain whether this meeting would be of advantage to him. At the door Tony whispered, 'Here they would certainly have discovered you very quickly.'

The other hold was considerably larger. Kerim asked what kind of door it was and used the opportunity to briefly pass the beam of light around the space.

'The door can be opened at any time,' said Tony. 'But what do you want in there? That hold is much too full.'

Not necessarily a bad thing, thought Kerim.

In the light of the torch, he again saw long rows of stacked boxes, also thick hosepipes on the walls and heavy pieces of equipment. Smaller boxes were piled up on palettes. With relief Kerim ascertained that the sound of the engines was weaker here. He asked the other about the equipment.

'Probably for cleaning. What's the point of a question like that?'

Kerim put the torch back in his pocket and responded silently, It's better to know what's around one. If he's right, then I ask myself how often they go about cleaning.

Tony reached one of the walls. He sighed and signalled to Kerim by doing so that he was sitting down.

'This is a good corner,' he said. 'Come over here. There's something I have to tell you.'

Kerim noticed that the other was talking at normal volume, and he asked him about it.

'That's what it's about,' said Tony and began to chew something.

'I thought you didn't have anything to eat?'

A soft sound was repeated several times and Kerim believed he could see the other in front of him as he gently tapped the floor nearby with the palm of his hand.

'OK, I'm ready,' said Kerim impatiently.

'How old are you?'

Kerim hesitated. 'Twenty-five,' he lied. The years that he added to his age didn't count in his eyes.

'You're still young.'

Kerim didn't know what to say to that.

'Explain to me why you're here.'

Kerim felt a reluctance in the face of the other's forward manner. 'Because I want to get away, that's all.'

'Almost everyone wants to at your age.'

'Are you a schoolteacher or something?'

Tony gave a gasp that could also have been a suppressed laugh. 'Yes, how could you tell?'

'By the way you talk. Why aren't you wearing glasses?'

'Do all teachers wear glasses?'

'Almost all.'

Again there was the wheezing from Tony's corner. 'You're right. But I don't wear them in the dark.'

Kerim was glad that he, too, had asked something. 'What kind of teacher are you?' he added.

'English, history.'

Kerim tried to find a comfortable position. When he leant on his hands, he felt the greasy film that covered the floor. He wiped his hands on his trousers and sniffed at his fingers.

'It's some kind of oil,' said Tony. 'Everywhere here, even on the walls. Switch on the torch.'

Just to be stubborn, Kerim waited three seconds before he responded. Tony let him light up two huge rolled-up green hoses.

'We could use the hoses to lie on. But they're heavy.' Kerim crawled over to the rolls and tugged at one. The material was rubbed off in many places. He pulled down enough to cover a sufficient area of the floor, immediately lay down on it and switched off the torch.

Tony was evidently about to begin talking again when steps could be heard. The sound came from the wall right beside them. Tony immediately fell silent. Kerim had sat bolt upright and waited for the other to make a move. He didn't stir, however, and Kerim didn't dare speak. The steps grew louder, someone was making straight for this wall. Kerim had not looked at it and now asked himself whether there was a door there. He held his breath as the sound of the footsteps ceased and there was a new scraping noise.

Perhaps there were pieces of apparatus on the other side, which the man was only taking from the wall. Kerim hoped it was so but he could no longer control himself.

'What do we do?' he whispered.

'Be quiet,' hissed Tony and still didn't move.

In the middle of the blackness, there suddenly appeared a glaringly bright, curved crack. It was as if the wall was being cut through by the light, then the oval door was open and, dazzled, Kerim shut his eyes. He put his hand in front of his face and squinted through his fingers. As through a veil, he saw the shadowy figure of a man, behind him an iron stairway onto which the sun fell from above as down a shaft. He could make out the rust-coloured dirty steps and the flaking yellowish-white paint. A tremendous feeling of happiness flooded through him while his eyes hurt from the light. Cool, salty air penetrated their room, Kerim wished for nothing more than to climb up the stairs and reach the railing.

The man remained standing in the doorway and didn't say a word. Instead he looked to the side once more, listened for sounds from the stair shaft. Then he stuck his head into the hold. He was holding a bundle in his arm, something like a plastic bag wrapped around something. Tony was squatting not far away from him, the man must already have seen him. Kerim was ready at any moment to disappear behind one of the now-visible tanks.

The man was still staring into the room.

'Another one?' he asked suddenly. His voice sounded choked and irritable.

'Yes,' replied Tony hastily. 'I didn't know. He was in the other hold.'

Kerim was astonished at Tony's change of tone, it sounded as if he wanted his words to be light, floating, without any emphasis. The man stepped into the hold and closed the door behind him. In the darkness, Kerim again felt heavy and let his head drop.

'Are there any more?' asked the man.

'I don't know.' Tony hadn't budged from the spot.

'That's dangerous, dammit.' The man breathed with audible heaviness. 'That's not the way it was planned. Do you know what's going to happen when they find the two of you?'

'No,' said Kerim quickly and cut Tony short. 'What will happen then?'

The tapping of the steps told Kerim that the man was moving towards him.

'You little bastard, where do you come from?'

'From the harbour.'

'Where do you come from?' The man sounded angry.

'Answer him!' Tony's voice was sharp.

Kerim hesitated. 'I've forgotten,' he said then.

'How did you get onto this ship?' asked the man but didn't expect an answer. Instead went on, 'OK, one or two . . . but I hope for your sakes, that there aren't any more on board. And don't make a sound.'

Kerim heard him put the bundle on the floor.

'I'll try to come again tomorrow,' said the man and made his way towards the door. 'And then you'll tell me where you come from.'

3

Kerim breathed heavily. He didn't know whether it was because of these new surroundings or perhaps just because of Tony, yet he felt weak and threatened. When he heard the other wheezing, twice in quick succession and then again after a few seconds, he asked himself whether Tony, too, was perhaps feeling something similar, was possibly even more desperate than himself.

'How long have you already been on the ship?'

Instead of a reply, there was only a grunt from Tony's corner, a sound like a suppressed sneeze.

Kerim involuntarily saw the other in front of him, laughing at him in a superior way. He decided not to ask him anything more, only to answer when there was something urgent.

'A long time,' Tony then did mutter finally, 'too long. I sailed from Port Said. Do you know where that is?'

'Of course,' asserted Kerim. 'But if you don't want to, you don't have to tell me.'

Tony paid no attention. 'Well, then you can imagine how long I've already been here. So far everything has gone OK.'

Kerim said nothing. He thought about the fact that he still didn't know what Tony looked like. He knew only his figure more or less and his voice. Strangely, he imagined him as that gaunt man who at home had come along their street twice a week. He sold sunflower seeds which he carried in front of him on a big, round metal tray. He always emerged from the veil that sand and light formed in the distance over the far end of the street. His shadowy outline gradually became a figure as he slowly approached Kerim, who waited for him as often as he could. The man never spoke, but his dark, hollow-cheeked face twisted into a grimace and he uttered a growling sound when he saw Kerim. It was presumably an exhortation to buy but Kerim usually only shook his head and looked at the flat seeds that resembled the layers of a dark plumage. I always only looked at him, thought Kerim, as someone who walks past me and leaves something behind.

'It was difficult to organize the thing. I had to pay a lot of people at the harbour—and this Filipino here.'

'Where did you work as a teacher?'

'Everywhere. I was in a lot of countries, a lot of cities. And I had a girlfriend in each one.'

Kerim ignored the remark. 'You must have money.'

'A little, sometimes. Deals. But it's more important to know something and to be able to teach it to others.'

'What's so important about where I come from?' asked Kerim.

Tony had begun to undo the bundle, a gentle rustling could be heard.

'You should answer him when he asks you something. What counts is that we need him.'

The rolling of the ship had increased. In order better to control the slight feeling of nausea rising in him, Kerim lay back on the hoses.

'He's brought us water.'

'How do you know him?'

'It's a long story. But I hope you understand that we are now both dependent on him. He knows that you're here.'

Kerim closed his eyes and thought. 'What happens if they see us?'

'I wouldn't even bother thinking about it.'

'Why not? It's a big ship. There must be other hiding places.'

Kerim heard Tony crawling around, the bundle rustled as he did so.

'Give me some water,' Kerim said, 'I don't feel well.'

Tony paused. 'No,' he replied.

Kerim was so surprised that he sat up straight. 'Why not?'

Tony crawled towards him, the tapping of the palms of his hands on the metal floor could be clearly heard. Kerim felt him very close and recoiled as best he could. Tony's hands felt for the hosepipes and up to him. He grabbed Kerim's throat and pushed him to the floor. His grip was so tight that Kerim began to struggle. Yet the stranglehold only became all the tighter, he couldn't move an inch. Tony shifted his weight to the arm that pinned Kerim down.

'It seems to me,' he gasped, 'you haven't understood what's happening. You're not alone here. And I swear to you, before they get me, I'll kill you. Have you got that?'

Kerim tried to nod but his head only twitched.

'Have you got that?' asked Tony once again and squeezed more tightly.

Kerim was hardly able to breathe and as his larynx was pressed together, a wave of panic swept over him. He struggled again and braced his body upwards. Tony loosened his grip somewhat. 'I didn't organize all this for an idiot like you to destroy it now, do you hear me? You'll give this man—he's called Justinus—an answer to every question he asks. And yes, you'll be friendly to him—you got that?'

This time Kerim could give something like a nod.

'Don't make a noise and listen to what I tell you.' With a final brief pressure, he let go off Kerim.

Gasping for air, Kerim jumped up and put his hand to his throat. He felt Tony's hand so tangibly, it was as if he still had to prise it loose. Tony had already withdrawn to another corner. He spoke slowly and surprisingly loudly.

'I know what you thought, you little fool. You hide away for a bit and then the crew will take care of you and set you ashore. But that's not how it works. You've no idea what you've let yourself in for.'

Kerim had begun to retch. Wheezing, he tried to breathe in deeply again. When he finally managed it, he had to vomit. Stinging stomach acids shot into his mouth and nose. What he brought up was hardly more than a handful of water. Much worse, however, was the crushing feeling of being completely abandoned that overcame him. He sensed, more than knew, how true Tony's words were.

After a couple of intakes of breath, his heartbeat slowed again. The fading panic was followed by something like exhaustion, strong enough to make him lie down. What he needed most of all now was light. He placed his hands over his eyes so that the darkness he was forced to see was his own and no longer that of the hold. Only after he had lain there like that for a couple of minutes did anger begin to rise, accompanied, however, by the fear that Tony could immediately attack him again.

He roused himself and crawled forward on all fours. He didn't care whether he bumped into anything, all that mattered was to get away. To his surprise, the other let him be. After a few yards, his hands felt a metal pipe which, contained in a kind of channel, ran across the floor. He followed it until it disappeared under a wall. Reaching upwards, he found he had indeed discovered another door. Without hesitation, he worked the handle, although cautiously.

The door didn't lead outside. Even when he had opened it just a crack, the new room seemed brighter than their own space. Kerim recognized the contours of a water tap and a washbasin, several layers of oil-cloth things hung in one corner. He crawled into the room, the door closed behind him. Trying as hard as he could not to make a sound, he stared at the tiny window close to the washbasin. Spellbound, he stood a few feet away and looked up to it. Behind the veils of dirt on the thick glass there really was the last light of dusk.

Finally, he dared creep closer, first crouching and then slowly rising to his feet. His hands on the edge of the basin, he brought his head higher and higher, ready to take cover at any moment.

Although already indistinct in the twilight, what he saw was at once liberating and terrifying. A part of the ship's deck, pale, with the railing, ended in front of the wide, dark surface of the sea. In the distance, the horizon, as if blurred by rain. For the first time, he was able to imagine the ship racing along on this dark ocean. Even if he could not actually see the movement, he knew now he was on his way, and simply the thought that this journey, like every other journey, must sometime come to an end gave him confidence.

He remained at the window even when he heard the door behind him and with a glance saw that Tony had followed him into the room.

'Dammit,' hissed the other, 'be careful.'

'It's already dark,' mumbled Kerim. 'No one can see me here.'

The next second he retreated a couple of steps and ducked down. A man had walked past the window hardly a yard away from him. Kerim had been able to make out the back of his light-coloured jacket and was certain that he was going out on deck. Nevertheless he strained breathlessly to hear a sound.

'What is it?' whispered Tony.

'There was someone there.'

'Did he see you?' Tony's voice almost failed him as he spoke—and that in turn unsettled Kerim.

He had to risk another look and still saw the man's back, now some distance away.

'No,' he said.

Tony crawled over to the washbasin and, like Kerim, slowly stood up. They watched the slightly swaying figure close to the stack of containers. The man was moving at an almost leisurely pace, his movements appeared controlled. He kept his arms a little bent and away from his body.

'That's the bosun,' muttered Tony. 'They call him Aldo. They say he's as moody as the wind. Don't get in his way.'

* * *

Once again they sat in the dark. Tony inquired if Kerim was going to sleep. When he answered no, Tony seemed relieved and began to pass the time telling little stories which he remembered.

He described a wall he had once seen in a schoolyard. It was a chalk-white wall, the upper corners already dark and eaten away by damp. The pupils had planted flowers in front of this wall. One could think it was tombstone. Yet it was only an inscription in clumsy, childlike letters that was being honoured here: *Learning is the only wealth. A good education is our right.* It was a Christian school. Right next to the wall, a small Madonna with tiny raised hands and a dark face stood on a pedestal. Only when one came close did one see the thousands of ants which welled up from the flowerbed, crawled up the Madonna and, for some reason, gathered on her face.

'Do you have a girlfriend?' Tony asked abruptly. And Kerim was sure he wanted to provoke him with the question.

And yet he listened intently, heard of places he could hardly imagine. He briefly had the thought that he was like Hamid. Like him, he knew almost nothing of the world, and when he thought of Central Africa, where Tony came from, it was always only the picture of a giraffe that came to mind. The other told him about a nightclub which was in the basement of a hotel, about the crush of people at the entrance to this Lonely Hearts Club which was really an improvised disco. Kerim was unable to picture it in his mind. Tony realized that and illustrated the scene for him as best he could, described the few people sitting on wooden benches and the many standing around in groups, the second room which was in semi-darkness and where only the dance floor was illuminated by a couple of weak spots.

Distorted reggae rumbled from suspended speakers. Tony's girlfriend for the evening wanted to dance immediately and pushed him through the people into the middle of the crowd. He tried to do as they were doing, briefly wiggled around uncertainly, but then he didn't need to do anything any more, as she took him firmly in hand. She wrapped herself around him and her hands ran over his back. He felt them so forcefully on his back, on his thighs and in his crotch that he shrank back with a yelp. She pursued him and drew him close, immediately shoving her fingers inside his waistband again. He really tried his best to manage something like a dance, wanted to gyrate his hips, but her hands were in the way. He twisted like a captured animal, until finally he grabbed her. Panting close to his ear she threw herself against his chest. He felt her forward, thick tongue first at his nostril, then at the corner of his mouth. In close embrace, they twitched, rather than danced, to the music. So far he had hardly exchanged a word with her but her broad laughing face was already familiar to him—the low forehead with the two gentle bumps, her pencil-thin, almost-absent eyebrows. Tony pressed mouth and nose against her head and breathed in the smell of her hard, tightly combed-back hair. Gradually, he felt it to be unbearably hot, sweat flowed from every pore and he stopped resisting her hands. The woman whispered short sentences in his ear, she said everything that came to her mind, and Kerim was ashamed to hear it out of Tony's mouth, she said it in a voice that at once offered and demanded and which gradually robbed Tony of his reason, as he put it. Only when nothing else at all occurred to her did she throatily gasp, 'I love you.'

Kerim had become restless during the story, had turned to the side and, surprised at the strength still inside him, had listened to his accelerated heartbeat. But Tony also related other things. He described the broad flat roofs of the town, the metal scaffolding of huge hoardings on top of them, people sleeping stretched out amid flapping bags and cloth remnants, their faces covered by the palms of their hands as if they were weeping, old houses in the Indian style—a term which didn't mean anything to Kerim—and between them, ruins left over from some war or other. He described the heat and a strange object made up of six large marabou wings which pushed into one another and separated again as the three birds hacked at the remains of a fish, and how the fish head with its two staring eyes, which seemed to have been stuck on, twitched and flew through the air between the open beaks.

Tony told him about the huge unofficial refuse dumps everywhere, about the brownish-red earth, about the ash flying around and how the Lonely Hearts Club was no longer enough for what he wanted. At some point, in some city, he was standing in front of the exit of a Daihatsu car salesroom and saw street children surrounding a minibus. The driver had wound down the window, and one of the boys, perhaps fourteen years old, harangued him. He was wearing a ragged corduroy jacket, a dirty T-shirt and two pairs of jeans one on top of the other, the pair that was too short over the larger pair. The driver said something and the boy lifted his T-shirt and displayed his naked torso, pointed with his finger at his chest and, as he did so, constantly repeated the sentence, 'God bless you.' He was joined by a small boy. When the latter realized that the begging was futile, he squashed his nose against the window on the other side of the minibus and licked it from top to bottom.

It was a little, unimportant story, Tony said about it, but he couldn't get it out of his head. What, he asked himself, had the bigger boy been pointing at? He had thought about it for a long time and was finally certain that the boy didn't want to show how undernourished he was, because that was true of many. He wanted to tell the driver of the minibus something else, he wanted to remind him that under their clothes they were the same.

'According to what I learnt as a child at the Christian school, that boy was Jesus Christ. What would he be where you come from?'

'A beggar,' said Kerim and in his mind asked himself what was the point of deifying a human being in poverty if it was of no help to him.

'I thought for a long time,' Tony continued, 'and I often hated all these poor people. It would be better to be an animal, I thought. Animals can provide for themselves. But we, half-animals, who have nothing and need everything, we seek the closeness of other human beings because we have no choice except to live off their pity. But this pity can become exhausted. It's particularly bad in the cities.'

'Is that all they do—beg?' asked Kerim.

'Some sniff glue,' said Tony and explained it to Kerim.

'It helps them fall asleep. And then at night, they sit around in the dark streets like the dead of Pompeii, frozen in the act of what they were just doing.'

After Tony had also explained Pompeii to him, they slept for a couple of hours.

Their provider appeared again the next morning. Kerim passed the time until then crouching in a corner. He kept his distance from Tony and didn't exchange a word with him. Once he secretly crawled through the rooms back to his provisions bag and forced down what was left. He felt a grim pleasure in not having to share the dry bread with the other and also in drinking the last plastic bottle with flat water alone. The know-it-all could drop dead. He washed down each bite with water that by now tasted poisonous, but swallowing was nevertheless an effort. The thundering noise and the damp air, smelling of chemicals, almost numbed him. For some hours now, the ship had been pitching so violently that every second he thought he would have to vomit. He stared into the darkness and all his courage evaporated.

He stuffed the empty bag and the plastic bottles behind the tank. Then he crawled back. He could by now manage that without any problems, if he bumped into something, he knew instantly in which direction he had to go next.

'Shh,' hissed Tony as Kerim came up.

At that moment, the door opened again. Kerim remained lying on the floor, screwed up his eyes and made ready to take a deep breath. The air blew into the hold like a strong gust of wind and with it a fine spray of rain. Their provider leant against the door-frame, Kerim tried to make out as much as he could. He saw the metal stairs again, this time, however, there was no light shining on them, the rust patches were dark with damp. Kerim opened his mouth wide to suck in the fresh air just as the man switched on the torch.

'What's the matter? Are you sick?' he asked.

Kerim closed his mouth and shook his head. The man shifted the beam to Tony and then switched it off.

'The two of you have to be careful. Aldo's playing up like mad. He's got a stick, hitting the walls with it, sniffing around like a dog, thinks he can smell stowaways. He'll come here and look for you.' The ship rolled to the side, the man staggered back for a moment.

'What happens if he finds us?' asked Kerim.

'They'll throw you overboard.'

'Which way is east?'

'What?'

'Show me which way east is,' said Kerim.

The man raised his arm and pointed. Then he threw a plastic bag into the room again and looked up the steps behind him as he did so.

'You must try to get below.'

Tony was already at the bag. He looked up and held his hand in front of his face.

'How are we supposed to do that?' he asked in a high, agitated voice.

The man looked around once again, stepped into the room and shut the door behind him. Kerim lowered his head, put his cheek to the metal floor and felt the vibrations going through him. He thought of ants. The return of darkness made him despair, he could have wept at the thought of the rainy day outside.

The man's voice now sounded determined, even hostile. 'You must disappear from here. Aldo will search everywhere. His suspicions have been aroused and he hardly even lets me out of sight. I'll leave the door open. Don't try until its night—but be careful!' They could hear him breathing in and out. 'Keep to the left and follow the passage as far as the next stairway. Go down it and hide in the large hold.' The man seemed to become nervous at the mere thought of this action. 'Perhaps it's better if you separate and go one at a time. Just don't go on deck, is that clear?' He cautiously opened the door. Kerim raised his head. 'If you run into someone, I can't help you any more.'

'Thanks,' said Kerim and meant it.

The other misunderstood him. 'No one invited you,' he retorted.

Tony quickly intervened. 'He doesn't mean it like that.'

'You can make it if you're careful. The next time, I'll come down to the hold. I don't know when exactly. Be careful with the water.'

After their provider had gone, Kerim crawled along the wall and already felt agitated. He closed his eyes and had images in front of him he had never seen before. The passageway beyond the door that was now open, the visible part of the ship in the daylight as he imagined it. Metal surfaces and stairs, tiny and rocking under the great milky dome of the sky. Was he dreaming it? What he had seen of this ship before he set foot on it was at any rate not enough to show him this iron labyrinth as he saw it before him now. When his inner eye roamed over the deck and out across the never-ending, restless surface of water, fear rose up so powerfully in him that he could hardly keep still. Suddenly it became clear to him where he was.

'I can't swim,' he whispered to himself.

A little later, he switched on the pocket lamp. He wanted to find a spot facing east. Tony looked wearily, almost apathetically over to him.

'What are you doing?' he asked quietly.

Kerim knew by now, that the question was more or less a reflex and didn't really have to be answered.

He found a spot and took up his position accordingly. Then he switched off the torch and began to pray. The familiarity of this observance gave him back his calm. It no longer mattered where he was, the darkness and the constant pitching lost their terror. He stood up and knelt down, he spoke out loud and included all his fear in the prayer.

When he was finished, he felt strong enough for what might lie before him. Anything could lurk behind that door, perhaps even death. Nevertheless he impatiently shone the torch on his watch again and again.

'We have to go now,' he said loudly, when he thought the time had come.

'No, we'll wait a bit,' replied Tony firmly.

'What for?'

A wheezing sound came from the other corner. 'It's only evening. We'll go in the night when everyone's asleep.'

Even the thought of spending more hours in this space was unbearable to Kerim.

'I want to go now,' he responded. 'It's the right moment.'

'How do you know that?'

'I just know,' said Kerim quickly and surprised himself. Everything in him was prepared for this dangerous walk, he couldn't wait any longer. 'I'm going,' he said determinedly.

'You will not. Dammit, you'll get us both killed.'

He breathed in deeply. He had guessed it would come to this. But this time he wanted to defend himself.

'You can't stop me.'

'We'll see about that.'

Kerim already heard the other crawling towards him and got ready to meet him. Tony seemed to notice and paused.

'What do you want to prove?' he asked, his voice sounded almost whiny.

Kerim made a last effort to come to an understanding.

'What can happen? I won't say anything about you if they catch me.'

'But then they'll really start looking.'

'This man is already looking now. He can be here at any moment.'

Tony gave no answer, only his uneasy breathing could be heard. Yet Kerim knew he had convinced him without having wanted to. He didn't leave him any time to think about it.

'We'll do it like this—I'll go first, exactly the way your friend described. You wait. If they catch me, I'll try to make a noise. If you don't hear anything, follow me. Just give me enough time.'

'No, I don't want to stay here any longer either.'

Kerim was already at the door. Hastily his fingers reached out for the lever. When he had found it, he drew his hands back and turned around once more. He whispered, 'They're more likely to discover us if we go together.'

With that, the matter was settled. He felt it but had no time to enjoy the elation of his first victory over Tony. When he had opened the hatch just a crack, he ducked down to the floor like a frightened dog, and not even the fresh air could distract him—he concentrated all his attention on what he could hear. Once again he forced himself to penetrate the rumble of the machinery and he believed so firmly in his ability to do so, and in the small inestimable advantage that it would grant him, that he crawled forward without hesitation.

What he saw in the semi-darkness was an empty, narrow passageway. The floor was so damp that Kerim involuntarily drew back his hands. The coldness of these puddles of water briefly deterred him. But he immediately got over it again, crawled to the stairs and squinted up. The metal steps had holes, and right at the top, above the last one, a heavy grey sky drifted past very close, surprisingly bright in the moonlight.

He carefully worked his way forward. The passageway was pitching but his real problem was the darkness together with the roaring of the wind in his ears. Kerim realized that, out here, it was impossible to spot one of the crew in time. The thought threatened to paralyse him. He shut his eyes for a moment. All he could was to trust in his luck and get below as quickly as possible.

He moved forward, pausing after every little calculated stretch. This precaution was pointless but he was unable to do without it. His hands splashed through the water, the evenly distributed little bumps in the floor hurt his knees. His only regret was that from this passageway he couldn't cast a glance at the outside world.

With relief, he made out where the stairs began. Yet as he crouched in front of them, he was unable to start climbing down, to disappear once more into a stuffy, dark space. Before that, he had to be free, even if only briefly. He rose and leant with his back against the wall. Above him, a lamp flickered on, just long enough for him to make out the wire casing. He was alarmed for a moment, he felt his heart beating in his throat, but the light was merely defective. After a few seconds it cast its wan light on the passage again. Kerim wiped the sweat from his forehead and, at the same time, began to shiver in the wind which swept unceasingly along the passage.

On the spur of the moment, he went back to where he had began. He was just about to climb the stairs he had looked at so longingly when the provider had come, as the door behind him opened. Kerim started, his hands clutched the railings of the flight of steps. But it was only Tony, wanting to follow him. Kerim saw the dismay in the other's face. He immediately raised a hand to reassure him. The hatch closed again.

Cautiously, Kerim climbed the stairs. The closer his head came to the opening, the more powerfully it attracted him. But finally, he risked it—he emerged into the open air and looked out across the indefinable grey-black mass of the sea. He climbed further and crawled on hands and knees as far as a new railing which safeguarded the narrow gangway on which he found himself. He held on tightly, felt the crumbling rust on the palms of his hands. When the ship dipped on one side, he thought he was going to tumble head over heels onto part of another broader passageway beneath him. He didn't dare stand up, yet what he smelt, the wide-open expanse, filled with the salt of the sea, that was enough for him. Admittedly, he still feared the dark water, of which he saw no more than a piece of surging and dully gleaming surface, more than everything else—but for this one moment, he was free. Cowering down, he looked for the stars, opened his eyes wide and forced himself to see them, as if he could lose track of their positions.

Emptiness and loneliness allowed him to gather his thoughts again and he hated the idea of having to return to the prison of some enclosed space. He was himself again and immediately memories rose up which he'd otherwise try to shake off. This time, however, he allowed himself to fall into them, they carried him away from the ship.

It seemed like a dream to him when he thought of the night on which he and Hamid were woken up. None of the men in the hut stirred when Mukhtar prodded them with the stick and told them to go outside. Shivering, they stood in front of him. Another man, whom Kerim had never seen in the camp, stared with a stony expression. He was probably an informant from the nearby villages. Mukhtar, leaning on his stick, briefly described the situation to them. An enemy, as he put it, was hiding in a cave not far away. He evidently wanted to flee across the border, after inhabitants of the village from which the informant came had occupied a local school for girls and finally closed it. At first they had let the teacher go but now they were determined that the One Law should prevail, and that he should be punished because he had offended the commandments of the pure Faith.

A smile played around Mukhtar's mouth as he gave them this information, as if he wasn't taking the story quite seriously. Kerim thought about why he and Hamid were being chosen for this spontaneous operation and came to the conclusion that it must be some kind of test.

They were instructed to take a torch and their combat knives and to track down the teacher. Mukhtar didn't waste any words on what they were to do with him, only came close up to the pair and repeated, 'This man is an enemy.' After that, the informant joined them, anxiously concerned to keep his distance from the leader. He described the approximate position of the cave in which the teacher must be hiding. Kerim paid close attention to the hoarsely stammered words of the man whose face remained lowered, as if didn't want to be recognized.

They set off in the night in almost pitch darkness. As long as they followed the track, they made good progress. After about an hour, however, they had to change to a steep side path. Hamid recognized the place immediately. He moved almost as surely in the dark as in daylight, was not dependent on the pocket lamp which was switched on from time to time. They climbed up the dark slope. To Kerim, it was as if they were climbing into the night. They didn't say a word to each other, both concentrated entirely on the path beneath their hands, knees and feet, their shivering had long given way to a feverish heat. They were so lost in a landscape, Kerim felt loneliness heavy in his stomach. Their monotonous scratching, scraping and stamping had for some time been the only noise in the night, until Hamid suddenly grabbed him from behind. Kerim reached for the torch, but the boy didn't need it this time either, merely climbed past him, went ahead for a couple of yards, came back and gestured to him with his hands that they were close to their goal. Kerim was surprised. He had expected that it would take much longer and a dullness had taken hold of him, which now evaporated in an instant. He had thought they would have to creep up, take someone by surprise. But none of that was necessary. Behind the next shadowy rise, he recognized the light of a fire emerging from the black mountainside.

Hamid drew his knife and hurried ahead. Moments later, they were standing at the entrance to the cave. There was no escape from it, since it was not much more than a hollow in the stone, perhaps three square yards in size. The fire had heated up the space, they could hardly breathe as they entered. Nevertheless, the man sleeping on his side was wrapped in a blanket, his head lay on his hands. Kerim had already gone around the fire and, knife in hand, had squatted down. The man was still sleeping, he must have been very exhausted by his flight. When Hamid kicked his legs, the man opened his eyes, looked at Kerim in surprise for a moment and then immediately smiled. Kerim was taken aback, rose and took a step backwards. The man sat up, wiped his sweat-covered face with his hand. When he saw Hamid, his face took on a hunted expression. Only now did he grasp what danger he was in.

Kerim stared dumbfounded at the face. There was nothing he had expected less than to meet someone again, here, in this desolate place, and from a time in his life that seemed so remote to him. The man pulled the blanket closer around him as if he was cold, his fingers dug into the woollen material. He quickly glanced at Hamid, then turned to Kerim, speaking insistently, 'But we know each other, don't you remember me? I was your English teacher. You had classes with me. Don't you remember?'

Kerim couldn't answer.

'You're older now,' the man went on, 'but I recognize you anyway.' He briefly examined Kerim and there was astonishment in his eyes. 'What are you doing here?'

Kerim still didn't say anything.

'What is it?' Hamid intervened. There was nothing childlike in his voice any more, nothing but determination.

Kerim had no idea what to do. He saw the flickering of the fire reflected in the boy's knife blade, looked once again at the black, greasily shiny hair of the teacher and caught his desperately appeasing smile. Kerim was quick-witted enough to raise his arm to forestall any hasty action on Hamid's part.

'Let's go outside,' he said in almost pleading voice to the boy. 'Come, I've got to talk to you.'

They stood in front of the cave and felt the cold of the night on flushed skin.

Hamid played around with the knife and said, 'You know the man from before.'

He wasn't curious, he merely stated it as a fact, and Kerim knew that it was clear to Hamid what that meant. So he quickly said, 'I can't kill him. I can't make a prisoner of him. I can't do anything.'

Hamid became nervous, he repeatedly brought the flat side of the knife blade down on the palm of his hand.

'We must. He's an enemy,' said the boy. 'You stay here, I'll do it, alone.'

'I can't,' said Kerim.

The smoke from the fire, which was gradually burning down, was now around them in the air and the warm orange glow enclosed them and the man in the cave like a room without walls. Kerim felt cold sweat on his forehead, he looked out helplessly into the encroaching night.

Hamid made a last attempt, half-turned to him and said, 'We'll take him with us. He's an enemy.'

Kerim reached out for Hamid's arm and gripped it.

'He's not an enemy,' he said, 'believe me, he's not an enemy. Let's just go. No one will find out. I beg you.'

Hamid squinted and looked back into the cave. He let the knife sink down and, lost in thought, raised a hand to his chin. Suddenly, there was despondency on his face. His shoulders drooped, the tension left his body. Hamid had not made any decision but Kerim took advantage of the opportunity to draw him out of the cave, slowly, step by step.

They disappeared into the darkness, as if they had been nothing but phantoms, the man in the cave had still not moved.

When Mukhtar asked them after morning prayers about how their mission had gone, Hamid said nothing but Kerim knew very well that he would not keep his secret to himself. Kerim replied, 'We played football with his head.'

4

Kerim lay in the darkness of the lower hold and heard the knocking. To master his agitation, he began to imagine Aldo, how he struck the walls of the ship and unhurriedly worked his way along. His image of the man became so vivid, he thought he could see him at every blow and at every step. He imagined what the man must be feeling. No doubt he knew that people were afraid of him and didn't want it any other way. He received instructions and carried out his duties just like everyone else. But no one sent him around the ship, perhaps even the captain lowered his gaze when they met. The latter he could only imagine as a man in a white cap and with a mysterious badge on the front of his shirt. Hence Aldo didn't disturb anyone when he picked up the wooden club reserved for these occasions and began the search on the starboard side. Experience showed that stowaways were most likely to be found in the holds. The fact that he also searched every corner of the decks and between the containers was part of his game more than anything else. Finally, however, he did come down the narrow stairway and got ready for a surprise.

He had a big torch with him, long enough so that it could also be employed as a truncheon. But he didn't switch it on. The powerful white beam certainly gave its user a feeling of security as he poked around in the corners with it, but Aldo was no policeman, for sure he was more a hunter. The strong, thickset man paused on the half-landing of the stairs and rubbed his chin with the back of his hand. He shone the torch along the passageway, to see if there were any clues. But there was nothing. Now the real part of his work began. At regular intervals, he struck the walls and railings with the stick, not too hard, not too soft. He liked the dull yet clear sound of his signal. It was not penetrating but unsettling. Perhaps Aldo liked to imagine how stowaways perceived the knocking, emerging from the general noise, at first hardly audible, slowly evermore distinct. Then they knew that he was coming, then they crawled behind the chests and would gladly have disappeared into the cracks. Presumably, he thought, No one hides on my ship, no one can hope to survive here like a rat in the dark.

He moved with the caution of a burglar. From time to time, he stood still, took shallow breaths and listened. These were moments in which he felt like part of the ship, indeed that he was the ship itself. This state didn't last long, he was completely alert soon again, took pleasure in raising his club and struck the wall once more. He didn't care less what the others thought and said while the same Jackie Chan film was on in the TV room for the twentieth time.

Suddenly, Kerim started. He had no longer been at the centre of things, had crawled into another man's head, had looked through his eyes and lost himself.

That seemed to him like a certain portent of his death and he quickly pulled himself together, wiped the greasy skin of his face and wanted to be himself again.

***

The lower hold was larger than the one they had left. But it was also closer to the engines, so that here the chemical smells and the shaking of the floor and walls were incomparably greater. At first, Kerim believed he wouldn't be able to bear it for even an hour. He crept far into the space before he paused, took out the pocket lamp and briefly looked around. In the beam of light, he saw the half-empty hold. There were stacks of wooden chests either towering up singly one on top of the other or placed in groups. Further to the back were large, misshapen bales, they could be sacks, Kerim memorized their approximate position. As Tony didn't show himself, he crouched beside one of the chests and leant against it. Down here, the wooden object seemed almost familiar.

'Where did you get to?' Tony hissed out of the darkness behind Kerim.

He had not heard Tony come up and turned around quickly. He shone the torch in his face for a moment, saw the forehead gleaming with sweat, the distorted features, and, satisfied, switched it off.

'Stop it,' panted Tony but the light was already gone. 'What did you do up there? Have you gone crazy? Anyone could have seen you!'

Kerim didn't give an answer, well aware of the provocative effect that had on Tony.

'Answer!'

Kerim shrank back, pressed his back against the chest.

'I'm not answering anything. Leave me in peace!'

He was prepared for a violent reaction. To be on the safe side, he gripped the torch and hunched his shoulders.

But Tony didn't move. When Kerim relaxed again, the other said forcefully, but softly, 'Quiet!'

Tony held his breath and listened. There was nothing more to be heard than the dull pounding of the engines. After a couple of seconds, however, as if reaching him from a great distance, the knocking became all too distinct.

'He's looking for us,' said Kerim.

At first, he didn't want to believe it, that a knocking on this ship could have something to do with the two of them. Yet this time, he really did penetrate the noise, made out the irregular intervals between the sounds of knocking and in the end was even certain he could hear them coming closer.

'It's him. We have to separate,' whispered Kerim. 'We each go to a different corner and look for a hiding place.' Tony hesitated but Kerim had already got to his feet and was shining the beam of light around the hold.

Despite the torch, he couldn't orient himself. It was as if the beams of light were sucked up by the darkness. Abruptly, he headed for the spot where he suspected the big bales were. These were untidily piled sacks. When he clambered over them, the contents slid softly away under his feet.

He took cover behind the heap and gasped for air. The thought that he could not know from which side someone would enter the hold suddenly disturbed him. He switched on the torch again and this time he understood why he could hardly make out anything around him. He looked fearfully into the weak beam, the batteries were finished. He switched the torch off.

Dust had risen from the sacks when he had stepped on them and now filled the already oppressive stinking air. Kerim had to cough and sneeze.

When the fit was over, he crawled away from the sacks as fast as he could. Suddenly, he was terribly thirsty. He panted in the darkness, his eyes watered. But he forced himself to calm down and listened for the knocking. After a couple of seconds, he heard it again, still irregular as before but closer. He really is looking for us, he thought and saw the sea before him, just as he had seen it a few hours earlier. Now, however, the dark expanse spread out like a huge puddle over his tiny body. He saw himself from above, a wriggling insect on the surface of an ocean of black ink. I can't swim, the words shot through his head again. He wheezed, straightened up and felt around himself.

Kerim felt the movement of the ship more strongly now. Just as he had reached one wall, on which he felt grooves and pipes, the knocking gave him a start again. This time, he didn't have to listen out for it. It was so close that he instinctively made himself small. Someone was walking past him, and he not only heard him but also felt the vibration of his steps in the metal. He counted three steps, then came the blow, powerfully dealt, yet short, as if its creator was trying to produce a special tone.

Kerim waited until the noises had grown distant before very cautiously stretching out his legs. He had to lie down to catch his breath and felt a draught in his face as his neck relaxed. There must be an opening very close to him. The knocking was hardly audible, the steps had died away. The draught passed over him somewhere above his head. He sat up and, to his dismay, found he was crying, silently. There was no agitation in his body, tears were just running from his eyes. It must be the fear, like a cold fever inside him, and yet he only noticed it when he was completely alone and tried in vain to pull himself together.

I have to get rid of this fear, he thought, but didn't know how. So he crawled around again, feeling the floor and the wall with one hand. Finally, he gave it up and took out the torch. He listened for the knocking that had disappeared. Perhaps the man was playing a trick. Maybe he had turned around and was standing somewhere here behind the wall, very close. Kerim hesitated, chewed the rubber covering of the torch and then risked it after all.

What he saw around him resembled a dungeon rather than a hold. Chains hung threateningly from the walls, set in motion by the pitching of the ship's hull. And he saw an entrance. Next to a row of slit-like windows, a door could be clearly made out. He immediately made his way towards it.

In desperation, he rose to his feet and peered out through one of the slits. He recoiled and, for a moment, thought it a stroke of fate that it was again Aldo whom he saw. The man was standing less than ten yards away from the window on the tween deck, even looking in Kerim's direction. Kerim ducked below the window and counted slowly, very slowly, to ten. During these seconds, he thought feverishly. This man isn't a ghost, he said to himself. He's a human being of flesh and blood. Why am I so afraid of him? He saw Aldo in his mind, just as he had caught sight of him—strong, leaning on a stick, his legs wide apart, the high collar ends of his jacket blown by the wind and flat against his cheeks. Except he couldn't see the face in his mind, it had remained a pale blotch against the darkness of the sky and the sea. He asked himself whether it would have reassured him to see Aldo's features.

When he cautiously stood up again and looked through the window, their eyes met. Aldo was smiling, Kerim even thought he could see him winking.

Immediately after that, the man was at the door. There was a creaking sound. Kerim fled back into the hold. He knew that it was over. His chest was gripped as if by a brace, a feeling he thought he already knew—a mistake, he now realized, as he tried to reach the piled-up sacks. He felt such fear for his life that he could hardly breathe. He couldn't find the stack, threw himself to the floor and crawled on all fours close to something large, soft.

Buzzing, the rows of fluorescent tubes came on one after the other. Aldo followed the tracks of light as they lit up. Taking his time, he inspected the stacks and bales, struck them with the club or merely tapped them. Kerim heard him whistling softly, it sounded like the tune of a children's song.

Aldo searched the hold systematically. Kerim waited and counted his steps. It wouldn't take long now. He had calmed down somewhat. Now that he could see and hear the man, some of his fear had vanished. A new feeling rose in him. It was something like defiance, he could not simply accept the situation he was in. But immediately, despair came to the fore again. I'm poor, I don't have a family any more, who cares if I disappear? he thought. Then, however, he remembered the words of the Teacher, that the Almighty kept watch over every man, that He saw each one, even the least of Believers. 'And as long as He sees you, you are more than a breath of wind.' 'I'm not a rat,' Kerim said to himself and, in a surge of pride and strength, he rose in order to face Aldo.

As he stood and looked the other in the eye, Kerim already regretted what he had done. He had expected surprise, some flicker of emotion. But there was nothing. Aldo looked at him impassively and finally, with deliberate slowness, raised the club and motioned him to come closer.

***

Kerim saw them coming, he was standing at the entrance to the crew's quarters. They had all lost interest in him. Earlier he had been questioned by a technical officer and even by the captain. Sitting at a plastic table, he constantly glanced at the floral-pattern curtain at the window of the cabin and answered only yes and no. There wasn't much to say, he felt, the situation was fairly clear. The captain passed his index finger over his bushy moustache and regarded Kerim with a mixture of annoyance and interest.

After a short time, however, he turned his attention to his crew again, who were organizing the search party that was finally to track down Tony. Kerim now only had one thought on his mind: Would Tony think he had betrayed him? If they had to die now, then that would be his greatest disgrace. Reluctantly, he thought back to Anatol and awareness of his guilt passed through him like a shudder. He felt himself to be small and unworthy because of it, he seemed to deserve nothing, not even rescue from what was about to happen.

When he heard the commotion of voices, he went to the door. Tony was just stumbling against the railing. For a moment, it looked as if he was going to be sick. When the bosun struck out at him, he began to defend himself, at first only a little, then evermore violently.

Kerim saw how they brought him along the gangway. Aldo grabbed Tony and pushed him onto the afterdeck. When he raised the club, Kerim ran over. But Aldo wasn't hitting Tony, only threatening him. Tony remained on the floor, his features were crumpled. He was cursing, and Kerim knew, even if there had been a tiny chance of being taken to the next harbour by this crew, it was gone now. The bosun pushed Kerim into the circle the seamen had formed. Aldo looked down at Tony and cursed back in a language that seemed comically alien to Kerim.

The captain and one of the officers opened the circle and they planted themselves in front of the stowaways. The bosun had to make a brief report, then the captain ordered him to be silent. The wind blew over the deck and left an impression on Kerim's skin, a layer on face and hands which seemed to come away when he screwed up his eyes or moved his fingers. It was still night, the sky was a haze over the dark sea, it swallowed up the board lighting after a few yards.

The captain rubbed his moustache again. He began to speak in broken English.

'You don't understand the problem,' he said in a tired voice. He rubbed his moustache more forcefully.

'No one in Europe wants you. You're not welcome. There are laws. We have to pay a fine if we take you along. A big fine. A lot of money.' He glanced around the circle and nodded to the men, as if he also had to convince them.

Kerim was no longer listening to the words. But he had no difficulty understanding that this situation was staged. The sailors were preparing something and he could foresee what it was. Involuntarily, he made sure the plastic bag with the addresses and the money was still there. He watched the captain in the expectation that the latter would lift the veil. He felt nothing, all his fear was shut up deep inside, ready to break out as soon as this solemn talk came to an end.

'There are laws,' repeated the captain and opened his eyes wide. 'Not ours—European laws. You can't just board a ship and sail to Europe.'

At that moment, Tony began to crawl towards the captain until he could take hold of his lower trouser leg. At first, Kerim thought he was going to attack the captain. But Tony crouched before the man and begged for his life. The bosun wanted to push him away but the captain stretched out his arm to stop him. And he didn't lower his arm as he looked at Tony again. He stood there like a preacher, all faces were turned to him.

'You don't understand,' he said. 'I, too, am a poor man. I, too, have a family, children, many children.' He raised his arm higher, and again all eyes followed him, he took a step back, without being able to shake off the grovelling man. 'No, no—they take our money and we have to starve.'

Kerim looked at it all with a feeling that it was unreal, for which he was almost thankful. He could observe the captain, who had made his decision long ago, as if the whole thing was nothing to do with him, could see Justinus, who kept in the background and whose cracked lips moved unceasingly as if he was saying a long prayer. The rest of the men stared dully ahead. In their dirty jackets and boots, they resembled the desperados in a Western.

The bosun suddenly went off and took one of the seamen with him. Kerim squatted down, in order to pull Tony away from the captain's leg. He looked into the other's face, now twisted into a grimace, rubbed his own face and felt the stubble. It was as if his hand were passing over someone else's skin. Then he became aware of the sound of the winches and saw the derrick begin to move. All the men looked up at the raft of oil drums and planks, held by chains, which swung to and fro above them. They stood almost reverently in front of this spectacle. Kerim realized that they couldn't have constructed the raft in such a short time; it had already been prepared.

'We aren't the first,' he said to Tony, who looked at him astonished.

'No,' said the captain, 'you are not the first. We'll give you water and bread. The mainland isn't far. You'll make it.'

'How far?' asked Kerim, as the men took hold of them.

'Not far,' muttered the captain and shook his head at the same time. As if to distract them, he added, 'We'll stop the engines.' He looked at them expectantly, as if he had given them a present.

Kerim didn't understand but the captain was already pushing him towards the rope ladder. Everything worked as if it had been rehearsed.

The helmsman got his instructions. The raft hung close to the heaving surface of the sea and was lowered once the engines had been shut down. Not until he was on the ladder, Tony a couple of yards below him, did it become clear to Kerim what was happening to him—at every rung, he was hanging further down the vast ship's hull, the water was surging up from below and the wind was making him shiver. He looked up, saw the row of dark heads looking down at him and, above them, the towering structures of the bridge with its projections and railings and dull lamplight in the windows. He paused for a moment at the sight, the indoor lights appeared so homely to him.

The captain gesticulated vigorously. Kerim climbed further down. The swaying hull wanted to throw him off and under him was the void. Up above, two men held the chain by which the raft was suspended and tried to pull it close to the rope ladder. But just like Tony, Kerim had to jump to reach it. He was afraid of the water and didn't dare let go.

'Cone on,' Tony shouted at him, 'they're not going to let you climb up again. Jump!' He held out his arms as if to a child, trying to make the gap between them look smaller.

Once again, Kerim glanced up at the heads that by now were far away under the grey sky. Down here, the rope ladder was bouncing off the hull, he knew he wouldn't be able to hold on much longer. First they explain it to us and then they kill us, he thought, damn them.

He let go, sank down and was astonished at the tremendous noise underwater, so close to the ship. A roaring and crashing as if from the depths of the earth enclosed him and he did not believe he would ever come to the surface again.

5

The raft was so fragile that Kerim thought it was already going to capsize when Tony pulled him on to it. After that, all that he could remember later was his unremitting effort to cling on tightly. He clasped the beam on which he was lying, because he knew that between him and death there was nothing but this piece of wood. He would not even have been able to reach one of the rust-covered drums, they were simply too far away from him.

As if a part of the dark sky was being removed, the ship slid away from them. Tony rowed with his hands and shouted to Kerim that he should do the same. 'I can't,' was all Kerim said and he clasped the beam all the more tightly. He still didn't dare look at the water that now washed over him, cold water in his eyes, nose and mouth. Instead, he looked up. The heads at the rail had disappeared, the ship appeared deserted. Tony rowed even harder than before, panting with the effort.

But the captain kept his word. Only when the raft was far enough away did he start the engines again. When he heard the sound, Tony stopped rowing, sat up and looked back at the still vast ship.

'Row with me,' he called wearily to Kerim. 'The screw will suck us in.'

Yet Kerim didn't relax his embrace, merely shook his head. Nothing could have moved him even to sit upright.

The dawn divided sky and sea as a pale line. Kerim could no longer feel his arms and he was wretchedly cold. Tony, who had crouched in different positions close to one of the barrels, kept moving. He was on constant lookout, pressing the plastic bottle with the water close to his body as he watched. At some point, he nudged Kerim with his foot and indicated he should sit up. He held up the bottle which Kerim was unable to take, as his hands, white as those of a dead man, were still one with the board.

It was hard but his thirst was overpowering. Finally, there was movement inside him. Slowly, painfully, he turned first one hand, then the other. The upper part of his body remained rigid, so that, at first, he managed nothing more than to turn on his back. He lay there, staring into the slowly emerging blue of the sky and waited until he could feel his arms again.

In order to take the bottle, he had to sit up. The terrible, restless surface of the water was close to him. Yet, despite everything, the fear of falling into it had lessened. After he had drunk, he was able to sit up and, like Tony, look into the distance.

'I'll kill them,' he said loudly and was himself surprised at the raw, worn sound of his voice. 'I'll wait for them in a harbour town and kill them one by one.'

Tony only nodded silently. All his attention was on a hardly visible short streak on the horizon that had suddenly appeared, delicate enough to dissolve again at any moment.

'I'll leave Aldo to the end and—drown him.'

'All the same, they gave us the water.'

'He nearly threw you in the water,' Kerim straightened up in outrage but immediately slumped down again. 'Drown,' he repeated, shaking all over, and removed each hand in turn from the beam in order to get some movement into them.

Yet the captain had not promised too much—it was land that they saw. Admittedly, only an island, yet it was a pale grey strip which gradually pushed itself evermore clearly in front of the seam between heaven and water. Tony couldn't take his eyes off it, as if he was afraid that if he let himself be distracted he wouldn't find the island again.

Later, the sun meanwhile beating down on them, they could clearly make out the low, rugged shore of this rock in the middle of the sea. However, the island had wandered imperceptibly to the right. Suddenly, Tony became agitated. He turned to Kerim and began pointing.

'We're drifting past it,' he shouted, fear distorted his face.

'Start rowing! We have to reach the island, or we're finished.'

Kerim pulled himself together and threw himself on his stomach next to Tony. He tried but, lying there like that, he could row only with one hand.

'Do what I'm doing,' shouted Tony and slid into the water beside the raft.

Kerim looked over to the island, saw that it was indeed lying dangerously far to the side and jumped into the sea, briefly went under, thought for those few seconds he would have to die, before his head rose above the surface again. Snorting, he looked around, felt himself sinking again and clung to a barrel. Once he had caught his breath, he began to thrash his legs rhythmically but he didn't get the impression that it was having any effect.

***

An image came to Kerim's mind. It was faint and so remote that he thought he had already seen it at home, on the television which, so it seemed to him now, hung over their heads an eternity ago and produced an unceasing racket in the evenings. He remembered the bearded Robinson Crusoe, saw him standing in front of a beam and carving a notch in the wood. That's how he counted his days on the island.

Here, thought Kerim, that's not necessary. He glanced down at himself and looked at his chest, exposed between the fluttering ends of his tattered shirt. His ribs protruded alarmingly, his bony thorax appeared to have become much larger. His skin was leathery and covered in countless scratches. I don't need a tree, he thought, I've turned into a piece of wood myself. The days could be counted off on him, too, he knew that, and also that there wouldn't be many more.

He had understood that the day the birds stayed away. Only the big gulls could have kept him and Tony alive, if they had managed to catch one.

Kerim placed his hands on his chest. He could hardly feel himself breathing any more; his ribcage was a rigid frame. He looked out at the sea. The sky was grey and overcast. He was surprised he wasn't shivering. His weakness made him sway. He sat down on the stony mussel-strewn ground.

He remembered the first days of their Robinsonade. Glittering sunlight beat down on the island as they ran aground. After they had watched the wreckage of their raft from the rocky shore, seen the pieces gradually scattered in the grey-blue sea around the island, they lay exhausted on solid ground, unable to move their arms and legs. Kerim fell asleep. When he woke up and turned on his side, one of those big birds flew past over him. In the sunlight, there was an unreal glow to the white plumage on its head and stomach, it intensified the light so that Kerim's eyes hurt. For a moment, he found himself looking into the bird's eyes. They were fixed mercilessly on him. Kerim felt his complete isolation. The seagull's shadow brushed over him and immediately after that he was looking at the hard and impenetrable sky.

Kerim stood up and tried to lean against a rock but it hurt, just as the stone everywhere poked against his bones. So he only rested one arm on it. The sea was unsettled that day. The island lay half-sunk in the water like a huge stone. On it, there was nothing but rock and birds, on the beach below lay heaps of rotting seaweed from which crawled swarms of sand fleas.

He looked around and concluded yet again that there was no point in exploring the island any further, there was simply nothing to be discovered. They had already found the spring on the second day, because mossy vegetation distinguished this spot from the other dry rock hollows and sandy valleys. They investigated it and found damp earth which under their digging hands proved to be a water hole. Tea-brown liquid welled up out of it, and they thanked God on the spot for this gift. But disillusionment soon followed. Because the horizon gradually cleared, by the third day they could see the narrow strip of the mainland in the distance. Kerim became painfully aware that it had been a mistake to make for the island. With the raft, they would definitely have been washed ashore there on this long-extended coast. They would have had to do nothing but wait.

'I didn't see it,' responded Tony, at once exhausted and desperate. 'How could I know?'

'It's your fault if we starve to death here.'

Kerim despised himself for having blindly followed Tony's orders. But even more painful was the thought that everything here could easily have been avoided if in Mersin he had boarded the ramshackle, overcrowded boat and not the big ship which appeared so much safer to him. If he had only simply stuck to the instructions of the traffickers and not paid attention to the talk about boatloads of refugees drowned in the sea, he would probably already be somewhere in Europe, sitting in some street cafe and listening to the ringing of church bells.

Tony no longer kept an eye on the strip of land which was becoming evermore visible. He, too, was tormented by the thought Kerim had spoken out loud. Full of anger, he turned to Kerim.

'If you hadn't given me away, I would still be on the ship and you would be drifting somewhere in the sea.'

That was the moment of the break between them. Since then, they hadn't exchanged a word. More than that, they drew an invisible line of demarcation in order to stay out of each other's way, and it had been functioning for days. Only occasionally, from a particular spot on the slope, did Kerim see the other. Tony always crouched or lay in the shelter of the dry bushes, patches of which were to found all over the island. He seemed turned to stone, only the shreds of the rags on his body were touched by wind.

'I'm going to kill him,' said Kerim to himself, 'if I have to go on looking at him any longer.' And he looked at him—thin, the dark skin covered in dust and presumably just as covered in scratches as his own.

'But you don't see scratches on him,' he panted, as he kept on walking.

He was on his way to the spring. Even now, despite his weakening condition, he was aware of the snail-like pace with which he moved. The sun shone down on his helmet of woven twigs and dazzled him.

'You only cower down and almost disappear into the ground.'

Never, so he thought, had he felt the egotism of this man as clearly as here. Tony didn't attack him, in fact, he didn't even cross the boundary. Nowhere, at no point of the route had he ever encountered him. No, Tony's resistance was softer, more vegetative. He crept up wherever he could. For sure, his smile was winning. But the ever-present caution and restlessness of his eyes was also noticeable. That showed his character.

As he walked, he brooded over further observations and peculiarities that could set him against the other. Yet, in his exhaustion, nothing else occurred to him. On the crest of the hill, which was not very steep but cost him a greater effort with every day that passed, he stopped and looked at the mainland. He wasn't quite sure, yet what he could make out infinitely small in the sea in the far distance could only be ships. They were not as big as the *Sea Star* but from up here it was possible to recognize two at once.

He stared at them for a long time. Then he pulled off what was left of his shirt and waved it above his head. Perhaps someone on one of the ships just happened to have a telescope in his hands and was having fun observing details on the island.

After a few minutes, the sun was so hot on his shoulders that he pulled the rag back on again. He stumbled down into the hollow, fell on his knees in front of the water hole and began to dig mechanically. More and more water was revealed in the mushy ground. It didn't bubble up but was separated out from the earth so that a brown puddle appeared. The deeper he dug, the less sand there was in the water and finally one could drink it. Kerim tried to strain it through his teeth and spat after every mouthful. And each time it was an opportunity to think up new ways of cursing Tony. He could afford to lie in his niche in the rocks and only come here at night because he had the water bottle.

Kerim set off on the way back. He no longer felt his steps, hunger dulled his senses. Everything he did was wrapped in an unfamiliar numbness. He looked at the ground. Sometimes he dreamt for an indefinite period of time, was startled by a gust of wind, only to immediately drift off again.

Once, after brooding for hours under his rock, he observed a dead fish that was gradually being washed onto the grey shore. The waves repeatedly detached the cadaver from the stones, carried it a little way into the sea and brought it back again. At some point it lay still, only the tail moved a little. Then something awakened in Kerim, an impulse went through his limbs, just sufficient to get him moving. Keeping his eye on the fish, he stepped forward.

He grabbed the cadaver and finally threw it on land. There he picked it up, looked at it from every side, smelt it and asked himself whether he should bite into it. He briefly had the idea of leaving it to dry in the sun, yet in the end, he gave up the thought and simply threw the fish back in the sea. He was dominated by hunger but as yet it wasn't great enough.

Now, two days later, he was no longer so certain whether he should not have torn out a couple of carefully chosen pieces, let them dry and then hastily swallowed them down. He returned to his place under the rock ledge and let himself drop down, heavy as a sack.

Further down towards the shore, he could see Tony. He lay motionless and unprotected on the ground. Kerim wondered whether he should check how he was. Yet he remained sitting and merely kept his eye on Tony. For minutes at a time, he watched Tony's left arm, without being able to make out the slightest movement. Kerim thought him dead but he simply registered it, without feeling anything in particular. Only the thought that he would now be alone on the island disturbed him. A seagull, the first for days, flew low over the beach. With unreal slowness, as if suspended by a thread, it alighted against the wind a few yards from Tony. Its plumage glowed white among the grey stones and the indefinable colour of the sea. Kerim watched the bird, and now he saw a dead fish lying close to Tony, perhaps it was even the one he had thrown away. At any rate the other had acted more cleverly, by using the cadaver as bait to catch something living. Kerim nodded appreciatively to himself, nodded a long time, like an old man.

The bird, bigger than a hen, cautiously approached the fish, repeatedly putting its head at an angle to keep an eye on the much larger cadaver next to it. Tony didn't move. It must be torment for him to wait on the hot stones in this sun.

So there you lie, thought Kerim, like one of those African street children you talked about. We haven't got far, we have no food and not even glue we could sniff to forget this misery here. We have nothing except brackish water and the time that passes. We just wait, day in, day out.

As he watched Tony, Kerim realized that he couldn't summon up any sympathy any more for the other man. Everything inside him had gone numb. It didn't interest him if the man over there was alive or was about to die. Only his curiosity made him keep on looking, as if like an obsession.

The seagull meanwhile had come dangerously close to Tony, it pecked at the fish, and at that moment the hand of the false cadaver made a grab for its strong, rubber-like legs. The bird was scarcely startled, merely hopped to the side, came back and jumped right over the hand, the big, snow-white wings not spread, only opened a little.

Now Kerim was overcome by an emotion after all—cold contempt for the situation they both found themselves in. He even laughed, amused by the dark hand of the other, repeatedly flailing in the shimmering air and the bird jumping around.

'You'll never catch it,' he muttered to himself and burst out in a throaty laugh again, feeling his teeth completely dry against his lips. 'You always wanted to be smart, like now,' he mumbled. 'But in the end, the bird is going to eat you. Yes, that's just how it'll be—the giant chicken is going to eat you.'

At that, he again remembered the dogs that had attacked him a long time ago. His laughter disappeared into a meaningless grin. He looked around. The sun-bleached bushes rustled in the gusts of wind, the pitiless light seemed to have eaten ridges and edges into the rocks, just as it was gradually dissolving both their skins. Only the great quantity of water, indifferent and equally pitiless, could resist it. Never before had the emptiness of the world oppressed him so greatly, never before had he so clearly seen himself disappear into it. He closed his eyes.

'Almighty God,' he said, 'I have nothing any more, not even a feeling. You feel for me.'

The next day, a boat approached the island. Kerim and Tony had been watching the fishing cutter from which it had been sent for some time. Their enmity was suddenly forgotten, together they crawled almost to the waterline, scratched the sand out of their beards and laughed like drunk men.

But it was a very small rubber dinghy, hardly big enough for the two fishermen. When they jumped onto the beach, Kerim ran towards them and greeted them in English. Entirely taken up with pulling the boat ashore, the men didn't reply at first. Finally, one of them turned around and once again Kerim found himself looking into one of these weather-beaten seaman's faces he had learnt to hate. The man looked around at the island, speaking in a disjointed and partly incomprehensible manner as he did so. As far as Kerim could make out, they only had room for one of them and that was, as he at once realized from the way the man was pointing his finger, for him. Kerim tried to argue, pointed at Tony, and then immediately let his arm fall limply. But the man only repeated again and again: 'Later.'

He stumbled back to Tony and told him. The laughter had long ago disappeared from Tony's face. He scrutinized the fishermen from gleaming, dark eyes, then he looked at Kerim, who stood before him, head bent, and nodded understandingly. He needed a moment, had to clear his throat and then said, 'Just go now. They're not going to wait long.'

'I can't.'

'They'll come back to pick me up, for sure.'

Kerim glanced at the two fishermen, who were already holding the rocking boat in the shallow water again. Their impassive faces suggested nothing good. He could not rely on anything they happened to say.

'What if they don't come back?'

Tony raised his shoulders and wiped his face hard with right hand. 'You must go to them now, listen to what I'm saying.'

Kerim didn't move. 'Why me and not you?'

Tony stretched out his arm. 'We're different. Don't you understand? Look at my skin.'

'No.'

Tony gave a pained sigh. Out of the corner of his eye, he saw the fishermen beginning to push the dinghy towards the open sea. The sunlight surrounded them like a transparent fog.

Tony's face came close to Kerim's. 'Yes,' he said. 'I beg you to go now. Listen, whatever happens, this is important: I know you didn't give me away. None of all this is your fault. You're not to blame.'

PART FOUR

1

A kind of awe overcame Kerim when he found himself facing his almost-legendary Uncle Tarik at the door of his flat for the first time. The gaunt man looked at him silently for several seconds, then came up to him and placed the palm of his hand on Kerim's head before they embraced. It was a meeting full of both relief and melancholy. Kerim could feel the tension of his long journey fall away from him for the moment—arriving at his uncle's home in Berlin was like a homecoming, even if the surroundings were unfamiliar. Uncle Tarik saw in him above all the son of his dead brother, Kerim inevitably seemed like an envoy from that part of his family for which he feared every day. He stepped back, took his nephew by the hand like a child and drew him inside.

Their joy at seeing each other did not last long. Kerim reached Berlin on a Friday. As promised, the driver brought him to the street entry of the tenement where his uncle lived. Naturally, it had been drummed into him to report to a police station as soon as possible and apply for asylum. He did so on the following Monday. From then on, his uncle accompanied him to every appointment with an official. Tarik expressed his disappointment that Kerim had not informed him until he was already in the city, only the thought that he could anyway not have done anything else except wait consoled him. He had the feeling nevertheless that without being to blame, he had neglected his charge, the son of his dead brother.

They spent their first weekend together planning the next steps. Kerim had to be registered, after that he faced a number of examinations. They both knew how slim his chances were of being recognized as entitled to asylum, despite that they painstakingly went over his story. With the help of a lawyer, Tarik had informed himself about what was necessary. So Kerim found out about the curious game that was in store for him. The people who later questioned him pretended to want to know harmless things: Where had he come from and by what route, where were his documents? The answers to these questions were clear—he could not remember the exact route and he had no documents.

The account of his reasons was more complicated. Nasir had already explained that the uncertain situation in Kerim's homeland would not be sufficient in order to be given asylum in Germany. It was important to construct a concrete threat to life and limb. Nasir assured him that he need not have a bad conscience about it, since it was impossible to prove such direct danger for many asylum seekers.

'Even if someone had threatened to kill you, attacked you in the street or held a knife to your throat at night in your home,' is what he had said, 'how could you prove it much later on in Germany? Your enemy is hardly going to provide the information, even if he could be called on the phone. As things stand, one has to think something up, even with people who were tortured.'

It was only in Germany itself that Kerim understood what Nasir had been trying to tell him. It was not so much the truth that counted. Instead, it was more important that he didn't get entangled in inconsistencies, because in the process that was now underway every detail was important.

And so he became familiar with the functionally furnished offices of German authorities, sat, with his uncle and an interpreter, opposite officials who hardly ever looked him in the face. He was examined, his fingerprints taken. During the questioning, what was said was recorded, which made Kerim feel ill at ease.

Although he was well prepared, Kerim changed his approach during the interrogations. He gave detailed information about things that could not be a risk to him, otherwise he was reticent. He did it in a way that was not provocative. He described the Holy Warriors, the circumstances of his abduction as well as his flight in every detail, urgently conjured up the danger of revenge being taken on him, but fell silent at questions about his journey. He made an effort to give the impression of a timid and scared person. Again and again he reminded himself of what Nasir had told him. He really was in danger but the important thing was to make others feel and understand that. That alone was the purpose of his act.

The atmosphere in the buildings intimidated him. There were noises, clacking footsteps on the stone floors of the corridors, banging doors and sometimes voices, too. Yet none of it got through the silence which he felt like a dull pressure in his ears and even on his skin.

Kerim observed his surroundings closely. These people were neither friendly nor unfriendly, the impersonality of their behaviour was something completely new to him. At home, one usually sat opposite someone who, by small gestures, even if they were only feigned, showed that he had a private side. Exaggerated formality and coldness were the exception. Here, however, person and office were not separate, at least not when the people were on duty and were dealing with him, a near-criminal. Because this, too, was clear to Kerim since he had been fingerprinted—by travelling to Germany, he had transgressed a law, one that everyone apart from him knew.

Later, Kerim remembered one of the officials very well, because during the interview Kerim didn't take his eyes off the man's watch. The man studied the documents and spoke from behind a sheet of paper. The watch was evidently made of plastic, with a broad grey strap and a huge digital display, on which a time was never shown. Kerim was able to look at it at his leisure. Abruptly, the man lowered the documents, leant back and looked at Kerim. What part did violence play in his life? he asked.

Kerim responded cautiously. 'I am only a cook,' he said after a while, spreading out his hands at the same time.

The man stared silently at the big scar that Rashid's knife had left, pursed his lips and shook his head slowly.

Finally, he said goodbye to them with surprising friendliness and gave Kerim the feeling that something favourable had been decided in his case. His uncle, too, was optimistic after this appointment. As always, Kerim quizzed him afterwards.

Tarik immediately became matter-of-fact again. It was only about the assignment to a hostel and the fact that the hostel was in Berlin. Tarik appeared relieved and explained to Kerim that he was lucky, he could have been sent anywhere in Germany. Now he was close by and could at least visit his uncle.

Finally, Kerim also learnt that the object on the official's wrist was not an ordinary watch but a pulse watch.

'Some people need something like that,' said Tarik in passing and although his nephew had asked no further questions. 'Perhaps he's ill.'

The course of the interview made Kerim feel confident. He would also have accepted that someone wears a plastic watch without a display, as some kind of jewellery, just as in passing he had seen other people who had bits of metal, rings and spheres attached to their faces. But for many things, there were also reasons that he did not know, he only had to search for them.

However, he had little opportunity to do that in the asylum seekers' hostel. He spent months crowded together with people from countries whose names he didn't even know. The biggest problem was not the bad food they got, nor the unceasing noise and commotion, nor the dirty toilets and the warden who observed them with such suspicion and treated them like convicts. What Kerim suffered from most was that he could never be alone.

When he lay on his bed and tried, through the noise made by the TV, the people in the room and in the corridor outside, to create a kind of space for himself alone, then he thought again and again of the arrival at his uncle's home and the peace and quiet that those two days and three nights from Friday to Monday had granted him. At a stroke, the trials of the seemingly endless car journey were at an end, more quickly than he had expected. Since there was even a small room for him in his uncle's flat, Kerim briefly experienced silence and seclusion, he almost felt lost. He made an effort to see the room as clearly as possible in his mind. Then he slowly opened the door, stepped inside, went over to the window or sat down on the bed. He never switched on the light but imagined himself waiting there for dusk.

At least he could also visit the room in reality, and during his time in the hostel he did so almost every day. Immediately after breakfast, he left the hostel in order to spend as much time as possible with his uncle. Very soon, his fellow occupants envied him this possibility. None of them had anyone to whom they could go. The hostel was the centre of their lives and they did not know the city that they were not allowed to leave.

The only person with whom Kerim had more contact than the minimum necessary was a thin, nervous Albanian who spoke good English and probably suffered from a slight persecution mania. His name was Ervin and he was very proud of it. This name, so he said—and the eyebrows rose in his narrow, small face with the jet-black eyes—was as good as a German name and would increase his chances here. Through his relationship with Kerim and some others, Ervin was evidently trying to create a counterweight to the black Africans who had soon formed a group and of whom he said that they were the real reason for the wretchedness of their conditions, since they literally attracted the hate of the average German. It was from Ervin that Kerim found out why bawling and very unpleasant-looking youths sometimes stood in front of the hostel at night and threw beer bottles over the high fence. To the Germans, the Albanian explained, asylum seekers were the lowest of the low. Kerim understood him like this—none of the Germans could understand why people came to their country, people who were not allowed to work and so were supported by tax money just because once upon a time it had been written into the constitution.

'They have been living without war for sixty years,' said Ervin. 'All they know is tourism, countries they look down on. Few of them can even imagine in their dreams what it's like to have to leave one's homeland. And the politicians do everything they can to make sure we don't have an easy time, because then the electors would punish them. Hence the shitty food and this dump here. . . . Do you have a mobile phone?'

Kerim said he didn't.

Ervin looked around surreptitiously. 'If you ever have one, hide it. Someone once asked me here, in front of the hostel, how I as a poor refugee could afford such a thing.'

The room he was given at Uncle Tarik's faced the backcourt. During his visits, Kerim often stood at the window for a long time and looked down at refuse skips and forgotten, rusty bicycles. The pigeons cooed. He scrutinized the dark sheer firewall with a single tiny window in the middle and wondered what might be hidden behind it.

From the beginning, the cold was part of the quietness around him. A fresh breeze always rose suddenly in the backcourt and blew into the room where Kerim waited for it by the open window, taking a deep breath. His cousin Hussein had occupied the small room but he moved out soon after the death of his mother. He had married meanwhile and lived in Cologne.

It was only after he arrived that Kerim found out that Aunt Sabihe, as he had called her since childhood days, without ever having consciously met her, had died of cancer a few years earlier.

'But she knew you when you were still a child,' said his uncle in a quiet voice as they stood in front of the big portrait photo that hung on the wall in the living room. Kerim remembered that his parents, too, had often told him about seeing her. Yet in the picture he saw only a woman he didn't know. She was middle-aged, a headscarf hardly covered her long dark hair. She had looked at the camera attentively and a little sceptically, as if she doubted whether it worked.

Kerim was not a little surprised to find his uncle was an elderly man. Of course, he could have known from his father's stories how many years separated the two brothers. But he had never thought about it. In his eyes, Uncle Tarik actually was an old man, even if he only outwardly appeared to be one—with his grey moustache, his combed-back snow-white hair and the many little wrinkles that made his eyes look narrow and gave them a crafty expression. Uncle Tarik had got into the habit of walking just as quickly as the Germans. Nor did he seem to expect any particular courtesy on the part of his fellow human beings. Even his son contradicted him unnecessarily when he visited, was silent when he should have answered or at least responded with something inconsequential.

Tarik had accustomed himself to a regular life. On Tuesdays and Fridays, he went to a Turkish market nearby, at least one evening a week he played cards at a members-only cafe.

On several occasions, his uncle, now that he was alone, he would have moved into an even smaller flat if Kerim hadn't come. As he said it, he looked cheerful and appeared relieved. Kerim had the feeling from the beginning that he was welcome even if he always had to go back to the hostel. He was soon popular with the acquaintances who called on his uncle. These were Turks and Arabs who, like their host, had already been living in Germany for a long time. Kerim had to tell the story of his flight countless times. Right at the beginning of his stay, he got to know a Palestinian whose name was Mohammed. He was the owner of a small jewellery shop, a stocky, plump man who liked nothing so much as talk about his children. He was not often a guest but he did come several times, on one evening even with his wife and two daughters. His son, however, about whom Mohammed complained, never came. Mohammed called him a wastrel and good-for-nothing who only caused him worry. He lived here on the same street, had a flat of his own, but he was completely estranged from his parents. They hadn't seen him for months now. Mohammed constantly compared him to his daughters who in his eyes represented the exact opposite. From time to time, his wife softened what he said a little but she never contradicted him. The daughters were somewhat older than Kerim, both of them pretty and petite with big, very dark eyes and, at least as long as they were sitting close together on the settee, rather silly. Kerim supposed that they were twins but he didn't ask. Mohammed enthused about them too much, about their no-doubt successful studies. Except at the beginning, the young women didn't give him as much as a glance whereas Kerim observed them continuously. He was fascinated by the casualness with which they moved, the relaxed way they related to their parents, even their manner while eating. They ate so little, so carefully and so solemnly, it was as if they were afraid of poisoning themselves. Here, as in everything else, they gave an impression of doing something out of the ordinary and basically of being on a visit from another world, that is, their own. Their mother seemed to notice it, too, when she occasionally softly admonished them to interrupt their confidential partly whispered conversations. Since they spoke only in German, Kerim didn't understand what they were saying. Yet even then he felt unnerved at the mere sight of them. He asked himself what they saw when they looked at him, the refugee who had just arrived, and came to the conclusion that he represented something more or less old-fashioned. His flight story, which their father had to translate for them and still followed with lively sympathy, could for them be no more than a fairy tale.

A Turk called Ferid visited far more frequently. He walked with a stoop, leaning on a stick with a glowing blue plastic handle. On the street, Kerim already recognized him from far away by his prayer cap and the appearance, amid all the other people, of a loner, the result of his disability, always gazing at the ground, unwaveringly pushing his way forward. On his visits, Ferid never forgot to light a cigarette before taking his leave and, eyes narrowed, to remind Tarik of the advantages of life together with a woman. After the years of being alone, so he explained it, it was now surely time to take another woman. Ferid didn't permit a response, but merely nodded approvingly at his own words before immediately saying the whole thing once again, this time beginning with Tarik's age. It seemed to be a matter of genuine concern to the man. He was likewise a widower, and it was said of him that only after the death of his wife had he found his way to Faith, very late, but all the more intensely. Kerim had the impression that there was a quiet reproach behind it all. In Ferid's eyes, Tarik had changed and he had changed because he lived in Germany. Living alone appeared to him as something strange, although he himself behaved no differently.

Whenever it got to that point, Tarik pointed to his nephew with a smile, yet Kerim also observed that he quickly glanced at the sideboard in the corner of the room. Behind its ugly doors, there was a mirror and between two little old chains a strand of Sabihe's hair, very long and almost triumphantly dark, as if as a reminder that for her death had come far too soon.

One afternoon, Kerim was standing at the living-room window and looking down at the rainy street. There was a postbox there and he had often watched people as they conscientiously put their letters into the slit for local addresses or the one for all other addresses. This time, a man in a thick anorak stopped his bike in front of it. Several plastic bags were hanging from the handlebars and, at first, Kerim took him to be one of those strange figures who wandered the streets in the area, carrying their schnapps supplies for the evening or even all their worldly possessions with them. To his surprise, the man brought out cloths and bottles of detergent and began unhurriedly and very carefully to clean the postbox. He sprayed, he wiped, took two steps back and then forward again, in order to continue his work. A woman nervously tapped her chin with a large pale brown envelope and nevertheless waited patiently, keeping a proper distance until the man was finished. Kerim started when he noticed his uncle behind him. The latter had been looking over his shoulder and merely gave a quick nod. They saw how, with a cursory gesture, the man granted the waiting woman access to the postbox. Then he wiped it dry with a cloth from a separate bag, packed everything away, stood in front of postbox and began to photograph it. Dutifully, he checked the pictures on the camera display. When he was satisfied, he packed the camera away, cast a final glance at his work and cycled off. Kerim stared at the shining yellow postbox.

'Does someone pay him to do that?'

'I hope so,' said his uncle. 'The Germans love order, but there are not many who are crazy enough to clean one of these postboxes in their free time.'

'He took a photo of it.'

'Yes, because he needs proof that he's really done the work.'

'Does no one come to check it?'

'I don't think so.'

'Then he could show the same photo again and again and actually stay at home.'

His uncle firmly shook his head. 'You saw how much stuff he had with him. He wants to do his job well.'

Kerim guessed that he still had a lot to learn. He began with the German language, had his uncle explain the rudiments and then used old textbooks. One had been left behind from his cousin Hussein's schooldays, Tarik acquired others in a second-hand bookshop around the corner. And again, as during his English lessons, he became excited when the flat letters came together as words which in turn took on meaning before his eyes, as if they suddenly cast shadows into his head. Fascination, too, set in. He saw illustrations of industrial plants, shipyards and famous old buildings in towns, whose names he could not yet pronounce, but his attempts alone already gave him more of an inkling of this new world than his walks through the streets, on which he always only stared at people.

He did that, too, when he stood in his room and watched the windows of the house opposite. In the evening, the noise of traffic, which reached the courtyard as if from a great distance, subsided. Not far from the flat, a steel bridge took the underground trains out of their tunnels into the light and above the street, with houses on either side. Their clattering progress, the squealing of the brakes and the automatic opening and closing of the doors at the station could be heard until late at night.

Kerim did not want to spy on anyone when he switched off the light and looked out. He was simply interested in how these people, who were still strange to him, lived. It was mostly younger people who were still up in the late evening, sitting in front of computer screens or tidying up their empty kitchens. He often observed a couple in a flat at the same level directly opposite. They evidently preferred to spend their evenings together, ate by candlelight and drank wine. She, tall and slim, disappeared near the window at some point. Kerim assumed there was a low couch or mattress there. Her friend or husband likewise bent down at the spot but remained visible in the window. His body moved rhythmically up and down and, as if according to a plan, he carried out further regular movements. At first, Kerim turned away from this scene, full of shame. But gradually, he followed what happened more attentively. As far as could be seen, the man always had his clothes on and was even wearing his glasses. And they always left the light on in the room. Kerim came to the conclusion that it could not be something truly intimate that the couple was doing over there. Only he, Kerim himself, felt an excitement as he watched, which he sought and which he nevertheless did not find really pleasant. Was the man spreading out something like a cloth over the woman? Was she talking to him while he possibly only touched her with his hands? Was that his way of showing her his love?

This view into a small flat led to unanticipated thoughts and aroused in him the longing for a woman, whom he did not yet know, nor how he would find her.

2

Tarik was aware that his charge knew something about cooking but nevertheless didn't allow him near the stove, for months treating him like a guest every time he visited. In his opinion, it was more important for Kerim to settle in. All his acquaintances disapproved of that. They thought he was spoiling him and the young man was consequently in danger of going astray. They knew what they were talking about. Ferid's sons, as soon as they had come of age, had turned their backs on their now-religious father. Living in the same city, they as good as never came to see him.

'It's this country,' he often sighed when he sat at Tarik's. These were moments when he appeared tired and disappointed and yet each time again made an effort to defend his sons. 'They are not ungrateful. They have simply not learnt what a family is, what respect is owed a father. This country has ruined them. They're like all these other boys, without a goal and all alone. They don't even get on with each other and they're brothers—can you understand that?'

Ferid expected a comment about it from Tarik, since his son, too, had gone his own way for a long time. But Tarik merely listened patiently to his friend's laments and didn't say much. For him, it was normal for young people to become independent at some point. He had not been a strict father, had watched and instructed his child but only rarely disciplined him, had made sure that he didn't go astray, which he, too, feared in the foreign land. Children could lose sight of the passage of time and live from day to day without any conception of their future, as happened to many a boy from German families. Or, like Ferid's sons, they could drift into dubious circles, become involved in shady dealings which they never talked about but which governed their days and gained evermore power over them until they were completely alienated even from their relatives.

Ferid had been stricter. He had beaten his sons and locked them in. Once—they were still little more than children—they had fled to Tarik. The two of them came along the street late in the evening and sought refuge with him and his wife. Mute with fear, they had both sat on the settee and waited. They didn't even dare drink the tea that Sabihe had placed in front of them. Finally, Ferid came and fetched them. Silently, he took them, a hand on the shoulder of each boy, and led them to the door of the flat. His heavy footsteps made the cold tea in the glasses tremble. Sabihe tried to calm him down but Ferid only shook his head, annoyed most of all, no doubt, that the boys had dared flee his sphere of control, even if only temporarily. Yet it had all been in vain. Now they were gone.

'You do everything for him, don't you?' asked Ferid about two months after Kerim's arrival.

'What makes you say that?'

'You give him a mobile phone as a present and . . .'

'A new watch,' said Tarik.

'And what's that over there?' Ferid pointed at a shoebox decorated with brightly coloured letters that lay open on the old sideboard. The lid lay beside it and clearly visible were dark brown leather and shiny runners.

'They're skates,' said Tarik innocently.

'What does he need something like that for?'

Tarik smiled to himself. 'He wants to go on the ice with them.'

'I know what you do with them,' retorted Ferid bad-temperedly. 'But why do you have to comply with all his strange wishes? He's not a child any more.'

'I know. But the wishes remain, don't they?' Tarik interrupted himself and tried a different tack.

'Kerim is very ambitious. Do you realize how well he has learnt to speak German within a few months? I'm sure he'll find his way. I'm only giving him a bit of time.'

What Kerim was able to relate vividly and, with time, evermore excitingly, pursued him into his dreams. The dark, deep water swallowing him up, unable to breath, with nothing to hold on to—he never found the right words for that. Sometimes, however, he woke up in the hostel at night with the certain feeling that, in his sleep, he had just drowned. These were strange moments; at once liberated and worn out, he wiped the sweat from his forehead and it seemed to him like the seawater in the most dangerous situations of his flight.

One day, he set out on a long march. It was already winter in the city, he came to a curiously secluded park. He could not yet know that the emptiness there was merely typical of wintertime. These strolls, as he called them, turned evermore frequently into forced marches. Kerim needed them, since at night he could hardly get to sleep in the shared room, unaccustomed as he was to being idle. He brooded as he walked, sometimes he was startled by thickly muffled joggers, then again the cawing of crows flying up alarmed him. Despite the presence of living things, he felt completely abandoned. He was not dressed warmly enough, the wind roared in his ears, the bare trees and bushes around him seemed to be dead, dead under their wreaths of snow which, although feather light, the wind did not appear to touch.

He was all the more surprised suddenly to hear cheerful voices and the laughter of children coming from the direction of a grey, frozen lake. At an inaccessible point, he forced his way through the bushes to the lakeside and, from some distance away, watched the colourfully dressed group of people on skates. They moved fast, in wide circles, spreading their arms as they did so. Children fell on the ice, then stood up again without complaining. On the contrary, it even seemed to give them pleasure. Since he couldn't swim, Kerim would normally never have dared to approach the lake in this way. Yet the sight of the skaters entranced him. So he even risked taking a couple of steps out onto the ice. He was astonished how easily one could walk on the cold surface, how reliably it bore him. The water, too, appeared to be dead; only occasionally, when he looked down very hard, did it stir in the faded depths beneath the ice like an imprisoned animal.

One of the figures in the grey distance detached itself from the colourful crowd and raised an arm as if to signal something to him. Kerim was sure that the reddish figure with a fur hood was waving to him out of high spirits. So he waved back and as he moved forward on the scratched, as if roughly polished icy surface, he for the first time became conscious of his loneliness in this city, in this world. At the same time, he also thought that he would be able to leave his isolation behind at just this moment if he only stepped out with sufficient determination and could reach those people populating the dull haze over there, standing like phantoms before his eyes which had been dried out by the cold. Again the figure waved to him. It moved in his direction and he started walking faster. It must be a woman who was coming towards him, gradually becoming more clearly visible.

Only when a second figure detached itself from the group and likewise headed towards him, gesticulating with both arms, did Kerim halt in alarm. Suddenly, it began to dawn on him that perhaps he misunderstood the situation and instantly he felt himself thrust back into the isolation from which he had just come. A second later, he broke through the ice.

As if he had inadvertently freed the water, it swept up over him and swallowed him. Even more than the cold, he was first of all terrified by the darkness into which he plunged. He fell backwards with arms extended and was certain someone was pulling him further down. Then his fall became slower. Gradually his body righted itself again and slid upwards, to where the dark grey appeared diluted, by a glowing circle that he took to be the unattainably distant sun. Then a contrary thought went through his head: Had he not once believed the sun in Europe was smaller than at home? He opened his eyes wide and numbly floated towards this spot. The higher he came, the more clearly he saw what the circle really was. He made out the hole that he had fallen through by its serrated rim in the midst of the fog of light.

Fearfully, he became aware of the broad, impenetrable expanse of ice above him, a nightmarishly low sky. Then he began to move. He understood that he had to reach the small hole up there when he surfaced and somehow he had to hold on to the ice before he sank down again. So, staring upwards all the time, he began to flail his arms about and he really did manage to get under the hole. Then he saw the light of the winter's day above the ice again.

He stretched out his arms and placed them on the surface of the ice. He was able to get a hold at first, yet he knew that he dare not move, because the rim threatened to break off.

'Hello,' said a woman's voice above him, 'don't move! Keep very still.'

Kerim understood what she was saying and held his breath for a moment. He heard the rustling of material and crawling sounds, shortly after that the woman was in front of him. She had taken off her long jacket and was lying flat on the ice. With a heave, she threw the jacket in his direction, so that one sleeve came to lie close by his hand, while she held the other.

'Don't stand up. Keep lying flat when you come out,' she said. And although this time Kerim didn't properly understand her, he knew instinctively what she meant.

He made a grab for the sleeve but as he did so the ice under him cracked. The slight jolt went through his body and he went rigid again. The woman pulled the jacket to her and repeated the procedure. Now, crawling on his stomach, the man was also beside her, then changed his mind, moved backwards and took hold of her leg. The next time she threw the jacket far enough, the sleeve brushed Kerim's hand. He grabbed it. The material of the outdoor jacket was so strong that it would probably have held two men of his weight. As the two began to pull with combined strength, he thrust himself up, was now lying with his chest on the ice. They pulled him out of the water as quickly as possible.

'Stay the way you are,' said the woman again.

Jerkily, they pulled him away from the hole. Kerim didn't dare stand up before the two of them did. When he was finally on his feet, he was shaking with cold. He looked down and was incapable of taking a single step on the ice. The skaters stared at them from the distance. Kerim could think of nothing except the mass of water under the ice. If the woman had not determinedly thrown her jacket over him and pulled him along, he would have frozen on the spot.

He stared at her as he fearfully walked forward. There was a white cloud of breath in front of her blue discoloured lips. The more the warmth of her jacket, which had saved him, brought him to life again, the more he was ashamed of what had happened.

The woman gestured to the other people that there was nothing to worry about. Kerim was surprised that she evidently didn't belong to them. The man who had helped save him also remained behind. Kerim felt her breast at his arm which she was clasping as if he might at any moment break through the ice again and disappear. She drew him along. He didn't find it unpleasant, yet so unfamiliar, that he simply didn't know what he should do. After a few yards she stopped and turned around.

'I'll take him to my car. He has to dry out,' she called to the man. Then she dragged Kerim along again, as forcefully as if she had just arrested him. She was right, nevertheless—by now, despite her jacket, he was shivering wretchedly again.

She went to the boot and brought out a blanket before sitting him down in the car. She threw it across the seat, Kerim sat down on it and pulled the door shut. The woman got in, paused for a moment, put her hands on the driving wheel and looked through the windscreen, thinking about what to do next.

'My name's Sonja,' she said. 'What's yours?'

Kerim told her, drawing the blanket around him.

'What you did out there was dangerous. You could have died. Didn't you see the barriers?'

Kerim didn't really understand what she meant, and shook his head. Sonja was satisfied with that, thought for a moment once more and turned to him again.

'You know what, I'll just begin driving, so that the car heats up,' she said and started the engine.

Then Kerim had to try to explain to her where he lived. He made every effort, but only when he told her the complicated street name did she understand.

'That's a long way,' she said. 'And you walked it all?'

Kerim said he had. 'I like walking.'

The heater began to make him feel warmer. He gradually relaxed. Sonja was thoughtful again. Finally she glanced at him and a decision flashed in her eyes.

'Show me your hand,' she said.

Hardly hesitating Kerim shoved his still damp hand out of the blanket. Sonja grasped it, pulled it towards the driving wheel, felt and looked at it. Gently she pushed it back and said, 'I'll take you to my place first. I have to make a phone call anyway. Don't have a mobile, you know. We can dry your clothes and have a tea. And afterwards, you can go home.'

Kerim didn't reply. But the prospect of having to undress made him uneasy. At the same time he had the feeling that he was unable to defend himself against this woman.

Less than five minutes later, they were in Sonja's flat. She had him remove his shoes and socks while they were still in the hall, before leading him straight to her bathroom. She went out, left the door ajar and made her phone call. Kerim understood almost every word. She was evidently talking to a man. He stood uncertainly in the bright light of the bathroom and, over bottles of perfume and jars of cream, looked at his face in the mirror. He could hardly get enough of his own pallor, he hadn't got over the shock yet. But at least he wasn't shaking any more.

A big brown cat slunk into the bathroom, meowed encouragingly and let him stroke it. It rolled onto its back, Kerim stared at the animal's pale stomach and drew back his hand, transfixed by a memory of earlier actions. In order to get them out of his mind, he shooed the cat away.

Slowly, with mechanical movements, he began to remove his clothes, having first placed a large white towel within easy reach. He found the whole thing embarrassing, yet he knew he couldn't stand around here wet. Sonja was still talking on the phone, occasionally she gave a short laugh and sometimes there was something almost flattering in her voice. Kerim wondered if he would be able to accustom himself to this voice, to this light, lively voice which seemed to be carried by breath alone.

Before he took off his underpants, he reached for the towel, just in time to hold it protectively in front of himself as the bathroom door was pushed open.

'Yes,' said Sonja into the phone, 'I saved him, and now the survivor has first of all to get dry.'

She didn't take her eyes off Kerim while she was speaking, looked with curiosity, as if she wanted to find out what it was she had pulled out of the water.

Shortly after that she hung up, put the phone aside and came over to him without the least inhibition to dry him off. Her hands went everywhere except between his legs, and yet, or just of because of that, he became aroused. But she acted as if she didn't notice, only kept on drying him much longer than was necessary. Not until then, holding the towel firmly against his shoulder did she suggest that he take a warm shower. A faint smile, half amused, half provocative played around her well-formed lips. But her grey-blue eyes presented themselves to his gaze with complete innocence.

3

From the day of their encounter, he was really only always running after Sonja. He knew it and was himself surprised how little it mattered to him at first. Given his situation, he was guarded and had accepted that he must adapt to it. He quickly got used to the fact that he had to call her six times before reaching her. He carefully prepared himself before each call, said the sentences he would speak to the answerphone before he dialled. He explained her permanent absence with her work, about which he knew next to nothing. He had grasped that in this country a woman could live alone and provide for herself. Except that he didn't know how much she had to work in order to earn a living.

It all amounted to this—that she would summon him to come to her when she had the time and the inclination. That bothered Kerim, yet he accepted it. When he stood in the yard of the hostel, called her on his mobile phone and, at the same time, observed his fellow residents or merely looked back at the corridor, obstructed by dirty suitcases and bags of clothes, then he simply didn't have the courage to make demands of anyone.

He did not tell his uncle anything of the new acquaintance but Tarik noticed anyway because of the many vain phone calls and because his nephew left the room with the phone when he finally did reach some-one. He thought it altogether desirable for the young man to strike roots in his new homeland. In Tarik's eyes, that corresponded to the normal course of things. Also when one day Kerim asked him about the price of a pair of skates and he could only reply that he didn't know, never even in his dreams had he felt a need to buy something like that, Tarik didn't give it any further thought. He granted his charge this wish and told his friends about how they went to a special shop about which he first had to make inquiries.

Mohammed, who for some reason also objected to the skates, at this point recalled the story, the sur-prise, when he had to buy a jockstrap for the birthday of his son, the good-for-nothing, and in the sports shop discovered that this was a kind of close-fitting protec-tion for his most sensitive parts. He described how at the till he quickly dropped the unexpectedly large thing into a bag and fled, feeling that he had bought one those sex toys that were sometimes displayed in certain shop windows. Tarik reminded Mohammed of the harmlessness of a pair of skates, yet for the latter, as for Ferid, the desire for them appeared to be something questionable and capricious.

The nearly fatal adventure on the ice continued to have its effect on Kerim. In the beginning, it was only the shock that overcame him when he thought back to the incident. But this gradually gave way to the wish to be able to glide over the ice like the people he had observed. He imagined what it would be like one day to surprise Sonja with an invitation to go skating and to hurtle across the solidified water, not across that of a skating rink, on which he only wanted to practice, but across a real lake. Once he had got that far, he fantasized, he would have made it, then he would have come to the end of his journey here. This thought made him feel warm and gave him strength when he lay alone on his hostel bed in the evening, eaten up with longing for Sonja's pale hot body.

Just as she guided him in everything, so she also guided his hand. On their first night, he had asked her why she had demanded that he show her his hand. She solemnly explained, that she was convinced that a hand said almost everything about a human being. One could see if it was dirty, delicate, clumsy, if it was good at making a fist. One could tell almost everything from it, except whether the person it belonged to was clever or not. But that had hardly been of any importance when she'd decided to take him home.

So he explored her, his first woman, under instruction. It was as if she wanted to leave nothing to chance. He felt her breasts, her abdomen and her thighs, her hand always on his. At the very beginning, she squeezed his fingers between her legs and held them there. Slowly, she moved up and down and closed her eyes. There was nothing Kerim could do except to kiss her lips, cold from the heavy breathing, and to pull her firmly towards him. Not until she opened her eyes, looked at him and smiled did he have the feeling that he was really there with her. Then she turned to him and Kerim would have been far more able to enjoy all this wonderful, now tender, now fierce touching, of whose effect he had suspected nothing, if his excitement had not constantly made it difficult for him to breathe. When she finally drew him to her, allowed him to harmonize with the rhythm of her body, her breathing and, so he believed, her heartbeat, he was spellbound by her deep, provocative, unfamiliar groaning. He wanted more of it and sucked it in close to her mouth, everything up to that sobbing, almost plaintive note at the end, so intense that it was as if she was finally being overwhelmed by the strength of her own body.

After the first time, he whispered, 'I love you.' And meant it in all seriousness.

She gave a quiet laugh. 'You are . . .' she began and then didn't say it out loud after all. Instead, she kissed the tip of his nose.

Even if he had to return to the hostel again afterwards and Sonja hid herself away for days, the memories of their nights remained, and he fed on them and called them to mind if he missed her very much. Sometimes he paused in fright as he did so and asked himself whether what he did with Sonja and what he felt for her was not forbidden. He had never experienced anything like it before and uncertainty was not long in coming. Without ever thinking of doing without these pleasures, he brooded over them. Finally, he reassured himself with Sonja's dominance—what overwhelmed him here came entirely from her, and everything, her beauty and his longing for it, were part of her power. He went over it in his mind and came to the conclusion that while he had been seduced and made happy he had not been changed.

He still occasionally observed the young couple at the window opposite. But now he saw the mysterious movements of the man, indeed everything that the pair did there in the seclusion of their backcourt flat, with different eyes. He believed that he now shared in what they enjoyed. Sometimes he regretted not to have had the time to experience it all back home with Shirin. Of course, he couldn't tell her any of it. When he heard her small voice on the telephone, distorted by an echo, he no longer connected it with the young woman he knew and with whom, as he now knew, he had been in love with for so long. Sometimes, the receiver at his ear, he shut his eyes and thought he could see her, far away in the distance, as a tiny figure on a hilltop, while the wind alternately carried her voice to him and blew it away again.

Sonja, on the other hand, was closer to him than any stranger had ever been before. He thought he could catch the scent of her sweat if he only thought of her. And sometimes he was afraid of idolizing her too much. Then again he remembered Sabihe's black lock of hair in Uncle Tarik's wardrobe and told himself, This feeling does exist, others can feel it, too.

The more often he saw Sonja, the more convinced he was that she only kept him at a distance because he hadn't got far enough yet, because he still had to prove himself in the strange land, because she knew how many hurdles he still had to clear in order not just to arrive here but also to reach her. This thought filled him with confidence and resolve, it spurred him on to learn German even more intensively, to go out even more often and to get to know this city, this country.

Sometimes, however, she also confused him. Early one evening, she called to tell him she was going to a concert nearby and to ask him whether he would like to come. Of course, Kerim said yes, quickly got ready and went to the agreed place.

It wasn't easy to find Sonja in the middle of the crowd under the bridge of the elevated railway. Lots of young people were standing around, most of them smoking and holding bottles of beer. Finally, Kerim discovered her on the arm of a man older than he was. When she saw him, she did let go of the other in order to introduce Kerim, yet the situation appeared in no way to be awkward for her. Kerim did his best to suppress jealous thoughts. He politely said his name and was as friendly as he could but it was at just such moments that it seemed to him he was separated from Sonja by a glass wall. In all the noise, he saw her laughing with the man, and the invisible sheet of glass pushed Sonja away from him into this frieze of strangers.

Everyone was waiting patiently in the cold evening air. Kerim stood silently beside the other two, counted the hand-sized rivets of the steel bridge, listened to the train that drew away thunderously above them.

At last, the doors were opened and admission began. The room inside was dark, the wallpaper yellowed from cigarette smoke. There were black-varnished tables and chairs and a big bar. The walls were covered to the ceiling with posters. Sometimes they displayed only names and strange symbols, then again the faces of band members, young men, women. On some there were also realistically painted angels, devils, knights with giant axes, pentagrams, machine guns, pirates, skulls, a Satan with long horns and a goat's beard, a fighter plane, a dice shaker on its side, coloured pills in a transparent tumbler and—he liked this best—a big red heart that looked like a balloon and was held in a dog's jaws. It must be about to burst, thought Kerim, who was fascinated by these pictures, when the music burst over them with a roar. It was a quickly dispatched opening number by the band of the evening but that was already enough to make Kerim fear for his hearing. The stage was bathed in dark red light, and he stood immobile, shocked, until Sonja pushed her way beside him and pulled his hands from his ears. She laughed and, in sign language, encouraged him to listen to the music and to dance on the spot at the same time. He saw the pale faces of people emerge and disappear in the red fog, the sleeves of black leather jackets brushed past him and a complete drunk staggered through the crowd and almost knocked him over. But he was most afraid of the cigarettes flitting about in the hands of the dancers. Wrapped in smoke and noise, the singer gave a short address, distorted by the microphone. Kerim did not understand a single one of the words, more panted than spoken. Sonja had just pressed an open bottle of beer into his hand, when the music fell upon him again. The red light made the drifting smoke visible and was reflected by a metal covered door which, for a moment, made him think of one of the butchers to whom he used to go to with his father to buy meat. Quickly he drank a big mouthful from the bottle and hopped around with the others, just to get rid of the thoughts of his earlier life, which here appeared to him like the pointless, oppressive after-effect of a dream.

Instead, he wanted to take in what was new. And he looked around in the flickering light, saw people shaking to the rhythm, gathered together in a kind of collective trance. They too, thought Kerim, know the power of community, they, too, are looking for it, and yet what they are doing is without Faith, without the least obligation. Images like those on the posters were no doubt very important for that and each remained who he was but could forget it here for a short time.

After an hour, during which Sonja constantly made sure to keep him supplied, Kerim was drunk. He clung to her arm and staggered away from the stage. At first, he had felt a liberating lightness, now, however, the inebriation had become heavy, had thickened into a sadness-saturated haze in his head. He thought all the time he was falling, but not until he felt the cool night air outside the door did he actually fall into Sonja's arms. He no longer remembered how he got back to the hostel that night. That unnerved him the next morning when he woke up with an incessant whistling in his ears. Only the smell of Sonja's perfume was still around him and he remembered her thick woollen scarf that he had felt against his cheek. Immediately after that, however, he had the smell of the urine in his nose again, into which he must have fallen under the viaduct of the elevated railway. He felt embarrassed that he had lost control of himself. Even worse was the thought that he had failed—he had not been a good escort for Sonja on their excursion together in this asphalt-grey city. Presumably, the man who had accompanied Sonja had also taken her home. Kerim only hazily remembered his nose ring which had gleamed in the dirty-cold light of the street. Perhaps the two of them had found him comical.

* * *

A couple of days later, he came to his uncle's home and, in the common entry, encountered Herr Patzek, the last German in the house. No one knew very much about him, he lived alone in the flat on the ground floor. He often sat at the open window, looked out into the street, had the habit of keeping an eye on who was coming and going in the house. Kerim had just switched on the light when he saw the elderly man standing in the open doorway of his flat, a cigarette in his hand, his white beard stained yellow around the mouth. He appeared to be a bit drunk, at any rate he didn't hesitate to address Kerim, fixing bleary blue eyes on him.

'And who are you, if I may ask?'

Kerim introduced himself and didn't quite dare simply to walk past him to the half-landing.

'You've not been here long, have you?'

Kerim shook his head.

Luckily, Herr Patzek had more fun talking himself.

'You know, lad, there's one thing you should always remember,' he began, after drawing on his cigarette, 'doesn't matter, if it's where you're from or here, doesn't matter, whether it's under Allah or . . . Jesus. The little man always gets it in the neck. Remember that. It's always the little man that gets it.'

Kerim pressed the light switch once again and nodded.

'Do you understand what I'm trying to tell you?'

Kerim said he did, although it wasn't true.

'It's always the little man who has to carry the can. And that's why, doesn't matter if it's where you're from or in here in this country—you've got to be smart, you understand? Smart, that's what counts. You don't have to be rich, you don't have to be strong—no, the little man has to be smart.'

'Smart,' repeated Kerim.

Pleased, Herr Patzek gave a laugh. 'You've got it—smart.'

He was finished with his lesson and now pointed to the stairs. Kerim took his leave and hastened up. As he passed by, he cast a glance into the flat. It was dark apart from the living room, where a huge standard lamp with a cloth shade bathed the room in a mellow light.

4

Although Ferid encouraged him on various occasions to attend Friday prayers, Kerim stayed away from the mosques. He was unable to admit it to himself but since his asylum procedure had begun, he had become cautious, if not cowardly. He did not want to attract attention in any way—nothing was to influence the confidential course of the procedure in a negative way. So he did not want to join any particular group of people either, no matter who they were. He even found unpleasant his constant enforced stays together with other asylum seekers and he did his best to keep to himself whenever he could. He wanted to stand quite alone, no one should be able to draw conclusions about him by way of strangers.

On arrival in this country, he had detached himself from everything except his Faith. He had renounced violence and tried to strictly separate his memories of it from what he had learnt about the Faith. Secretly, he knew that he would never succeed in doing so, the two things were far too mixed up with each other. And yet he was able to summon up the voice of the Teacher without having to think of his experiences with the Holy Warriors.

So Kerim recalled the words about the Believers in lands unfamiliar to them. At times, so the Teacher had said, they even developed something like fire. Yet it only arose from the fear of losing contact with their home. Hence this fire was closer to homesickness than to the true God and these people had first to be led back. It was different with the younger ones—they were in the process of losing their roots and that was precisely what made them free for the pure Faith. They felt a strong need to stand up against the conformists, against their parents.

Whenever Ferid reproached and reprimanded him, Kerim played the part of the clueless young man who didn't waste any time thinking about religion. Secretly, however, he despised the late-awakened Ferid and his false religious fervour.

Ferid was not the only one he regarded with a degree of distance, even with a certain cruelty. Since the long conversations in the mountains with his Teacher, Kerim especially felt his strength when he watched other people, even more so when he listened to them. How weak and lonely they still seemed. While he gazed impassively at their faces, he saw each and every one as a prisoner, tied up in the dark sack of his own delusions, flailing and twisting, never freeing himself. Kerim knew about the coldness of his gaze, yet, at the same time, he enjoyed the freedom it gave him, freedom from the false protestations and certainties that lurked behind the words of such people. Convinced that he himself would never grow old, that God had granted him only a limited span of life, he always inwardly turned away as soon as Ferid tried to bother him with the insights that age brings.

He thought of the sentences his Teacher had once formulated: 'What makes many—whom you, who knows, will still meet—so unbearable is their slow fading away. In the beginning, they are like a strong, proud and powerful tone, but by the end, no more than a whimper. You have to understand—this slow annihilation is the gauge of their gradual loss of Faith.'

'Do they die, then, as Unbelievers?' Kerim had asked.

A quick yet not fleeting smile on the part of his Teacher was the reply and a nod of acknowledgement.

He still felt his pride at having surprised his Teacher with his intelligence. But the very next moment, everything darkened. Mouth open, he lay on his bed, staring at the grille-encased neon tubes on the ceiling of the dormitory, was again with the Holy Warriors, feeling the hot light on his skin as they made their way over the hills. The sun was high in the sky, and the heat was driving sweat out of every pore. The hill country stretched out around them. From far off they were ghosts, wading through molten copper. Mukhtar, who was little more than a step ahead of them, raised his hand to make the men proceed even more cautiously. Long-dead trees rose up around them, broken, splintered, the rough bark as if ripped by the sharp light. Kerim saw gleaming shards in the ground and, now and then, grey-white bones. There was no wind and the only thing they heard was the low sound of engines in the distance. It was so still that the men didn't dare cough. Rifles at the ready, they crept forward. Then Mukhtar signalled to them and they all stopped. Their leader pointed ahead, the men squinted and saw the flickering silhouettes at last. Kerim remembered exactly how hard it was to make out the three dogs. They were romping around, chasing one another, their tongues hanging, but in the heat they only managed a few yards. They were still young. When they noticed the people, they retreated but reluctantly, ready at any moment to turn back. They weren't feral, a memory, perhaps more, bound them to human beings. It was as if they were waiting all the time for a long unheard word from them, a word that would at last liberate them from the terrors of a freedom to which they no longer belonged. And the word came. Mukhtar called to them with alarming gentleness, his voice vibrated in a kind of song, it hovered over the hills. Kerim had never forgotten the voice, it had touched him as it touched the dogs. They fled, but their circles grew smaller and their heads and ears were turned towards the men. Mukhtar went on calling them until finally they were a few feet away. Then Mukhtar gave the sign and the men fired. All the dogs were hit, they howled and fell before they began to run, their paws dug up the sand, their bodies twisted on the ground, the men hurried up in order to hit them more accurately. Yet the dogs didn't die immediately, they crawled away. Mukhtar gave a sign and they stopped shooting.

Kerim looked away over the landscape and waited until they could gather up the bodies. They threw them over their shoulders and returned to the bigger camp to which they had retreated southwards. Here the scattered groups were brought together. For Kerim, it was a place of fear and oppressiveness. Huge camouflage nets protected the stores, and the supply trucks coming from the Iranian side unceasingly struggled up to them through the mountains.

A ring of mud huts surrounded the central guesthouse. This was where the mobile radio station was housed, though Kerim saw nothing of it except the antenna on the roof. No one had access to this building except the leaders and occasional guests from abroad. It was solidly built and had once been a school. The pupils, however, had gone long ago. Now it was the realm of men like Mukhtar, who taught the many Holy Warriors gathering here that their sacrifice began in the middle of life. Kerim was removed from the protection of his Teacher and he suffered for it, because now Mukhtar pursued him unhindered with his contempt. There were no strategic lessons any more. Only combat training, the regular prayers, the Friday sermon. The latter was given by alternating imams, occasionally also by the Teacher. Yet the sermons remained so vague that the old feelings were no longer aroused in Kerim. He missed them, missed the passion in the words of his Teacher. All that he hoped for was the imminent separation of the groups for the forthcoming operations in different points of the country. To this end, all the martyrs were tested once more—they had to fight, to allow themselves to be beaten, to crawl though the rifle fire of the military instructors. They were left to go hungry and given the Holy Book as food. In the end, the groups were mustered and in such a way that the weaknesses and strengths of the members were more or less balanced.

Kerim never found out if it was bad luck or if someone had interfered, but he was put into Mukhtar's group. Perhaps he only remembered the day with such intensity on which they had hunted the dogs, because it was the same day on which he was addressed both by Mukhtar as well as, after a long time, by the Teacher. One of the mud huts stood a little apart from the others. They called it the Blood House, because here the animals they ate were cut up as well as those they 'prepared'. The house was on a not very steep slope, the blood could be easily washed away through an opening in the floor. Yet this dark room was filled with the smell. Kerim and several other boys, Hamid among them, were sent there with the dog cadavers. They squatted in the half-light that fell through the skylights, cut open the animals' bodies and took out the intestines. They took care not to remove too much, so that later nothing would be noticeable. Unexpectedly his Teacher entered the hut and Kerim raised his head in surprise. The Teacher stood in the bright doorway and swarms of flies gleamed in the light that flooded into the room with him. He inquired as to how Kerim was feeling and looked at the latter's blood-smeared hands as he did so, before finally announcing that they would not stay in this camp much longer. To Kerim, it was as if his Teacher did not want the mysterious bond between them to break, and he felt safe and light after he had gone. Shortly afterwards, Mukhtar came into the hut. He glanced around, came up to Kerim, nudged his forehead with the stick he carried in the camp and pushed his head far enough back so that he could look him in the face.

'I know it and I'm telling you what he's doing by favouring you. He's raising up a coward who will one day be a traitor.'

Kerim saw the man's dark eyes fixed on him, he felt the stick at his forehead and understood that this was a grave threat. Whatever he did, he would never gain Mukhtar's trust. At that moment, so he often thought later, the thought of flight took hold of him. In a strange way, it was as if Mukhtar had turned him into just that traitor he had always taken him to be.

Hamid tried to reassure him, said he shouldn't take it so seriously, but Kerim still felt the tip of Mukhtar's stick for a long time after, exactly at the point on his forehead where otherwise the fervent prayers on the rocky ground left their mark.

And he guessed why Mukhtar hated him so much; Hamid's guilty eyes betrayed it—he had spoken of the schoolteacher in the cave.

When the dog cadavers were ready, they were carried out and laid on the slope to 'mature' until Rashid came with the other bomb experts to fill the hollowed out bodies with explosives and sew them up. It was good if the cadavers stank, because then no one touched them or became suspicious if they were put out on the street.

***

One evening, Kerim and his uncle were startled by a continuous creaking and banging in the stairwell. It came from above them, where a flight of stairs led up to the attic. Tarik had lived long enough in this part of the city and wasn't alarmed, especially as on listening more closely the creaking was accompanied by a monotonous singsong. With presence of mind, Kerim had immediately hurried into the kitchen to fetch a torch while his uncle was still listening at the door of the flat.

'There could be several of them,' he said when he saw what his nephew had in mind.

'I only want to take a look. They're not going to kill me,' retorted Kerim.

'Let's hope so,' said Tarik, looking anxious.

Kerim looked at his uncle and hesitated for a moment. He asked himself what had caused the man to become so fearful in this safe and peaceful country. Tarik seemed to have read his thoughts.

'You never know,' he said and shrugged.

Kerim pushed past him and resolutely opened the door. He switched on the stair light, then the torch, because further up, above the attic door, there were no lights. The last half-landing was always in darkness.

Cautiously setting a foot on each step, Kerim crept upstairs. The beam of light wandering over floor and walls returned him briefly to the hold of the *Sea Star*. The memory was so intense and so detailed that he had to stand still, before it trickled away, allowing him to take in the real space again.

A man was sitting at the top, his head sunk to his chest, his arms clasping his spindly, drawn-up legs. Even when Kerim was standing in front of him and the beam of light of the torch was shining right on his head, he didn't react, his breath came in fits and starts, was a hardly perceptible panting. In-between, he hummed a tune from time to time.

Kerim squatted and poked the man's shoulder. There was no response, so he shone the torch around. A syringe lay on the floor close to the limp hand. The sleeve of his shirt was unbuttoned and there were a couple of small drops of blood on it. The man had wound his belt around his upper arm and loosened it again after the injection. His hand was still on the buckle.

In his lap, a cigarette lighter was wedged in the folds of his trousers, a dirty spoon also lay nearby. Kerim knew immediately what was going on, he had seen enough American films and he was astonished how much the scene resembled the film images.

He took the man's chin and raised his head, shone the torch in his face. In the beam of light, his eyelids began to flicker and the eyes opened just a crack.

'Hello, can you hear me?' asked Kerim.

He didn't expect an answer, yet suddenly, the heavy, unsteady head nodded.

Kerim drew his hand away. He looked around once more. The man had brought old newspapers with him but not spread them out. On the pile lay a cloth bag with his belongings. Out of pure curiosity, Kerim went through the contents. He came upon a couple of plastic bags, a packet of cigarettes and an MP3 player with headphones. He knew things like it from the young people and the joggers in the neighbourhood. Kerim was disappointed, since he had hoped to find something personal. Then his fingers felt something hard at the bottom of the bag. It was a delicate-looking golden ring with a finely set red stone, a piece of jewellery for a woman. Kerim immediately thought of Sonja, his fingers closed around his find and he switched off the torch as if to be alone with the temptation he now faced.

He stood up and shoved the ring into his trouser pocket, looking down at the still only half-conscious junkie.

'Give me back the ring,' whispered the man suddenly.

Kerim needed a moment to master his surprise. His uncle called him softly from below.

'There's someone here,' answered Kerim and, nervous and feeling guilty, took two steps towards the stairs. 'He can't stay here.'

'What do you want to do?' asked his uncle.

'Give me back the ring,' repeated the man on the floor. And when Kerim shone the torch in his face this time, it was as if he was holding a stick in his hand.

'You stole it anyway,' he muttered.

He felt nothing but contempt for the wretched figure who dared to claim rights in this situation. In Kerim's eyes, this drug addict was as responsible as if he was only playing at being poor.

Abruptly, he bent down to the man, grabbed him under the arms and pulled him up until he was standing. With a gentle push, he leant him against the wall, picked up the cloth bag and threw it down the stairs. Then, keeping the man in front of him, he shoved him towards the steps. The latter reached out clumsily for the bannister, Kerim pushed him forward a little bit at a time.

'Go,' he said, 'go and shut up.'

The man laboriously took one step after another. Kerim saw him sway and was ready to hold him, if he should fall.

Tarik moved out of the way when he saw them coming. In the weak light of the stairwell, the junkie looked as white as a corpse. His greasy, dark blond hair seemed to have been cut only recently. Perhaps, thought Kerim, he has a girlfriend who cares for him when he lives his life not under the influence. And perhaps the ring is for her.

Encouraged by Tarik's presence, the man abruptly turned around again. Kerim was just picking up the bag.

In a dull yet loud voice, he said, 'You should give me back the ring. I need it.'

Now anger rose in Kerim. He pushed the man forward so violently that he staggered, only just managing to keep his balance.

'You should disappear,' Kerim growled, 'right now.'

He hung the loops of the bag around the man's neck and gave him another shove.

One floor below, the two Turkish families had been disturbed. The husbands stood in the open doors, their wives behind them. One asked Kerim what was happening. He explained, at which the uninvited guest became agitated.

'You've robbed me,' he panted. 'I saw it.'

Without any coordination, he grabbed at Kerim's trouser pocket, so that the latter recoiled, stumbled and ended up sitting on the stairs. Now the neighbours intervened. The men seized the junkie and dragged him down the stairs by force. When he shouted out in protest, one struck him in the face. A minute later, they had thrown him out of the building.

'He's talking nonsense,' said Kerim apologetically to his uncle.

He was still sitting on the step when the men came back. They thanked him, exchanged a few words in Turkish with each other and disappeared into their flats.

Kerim stood up. 'Curious,' he said to his uncle. 'He was having delusions.'

Tarik said nothing, only looked at him with unusual attentiveness as he went past. But Kerim ignored it.

It's strange, he thought later in the hostel, as he was lying on his bed and examining the ring, I'm free and there are people all around me. But it's not like at home. Here I can do what I want. But he wasn't sure whether this strange anonymity meant greater oppressiveness for him or greater freedom. He had spent the larger part of his previous life in the circle of his family. And he was unable to decide which state he found more agreeable. For sure, he had been alone since his flight. Here, however, everyone lived for himself. It was as if they took care to remain invisible until they had to talk to one another.

* * *

A couple of days later, as he returned from one of his walks, he heard a quiet voice behind him.

'Hey, you, wait a minute.'

Tired from walking and preoccupied with his own thoughts amid the noise of the street, Kerim didn't react. Hurried steps came closer but he went obstinately on, until someone touched him softly on the shoulder. With a start, Kerim halted and turned around. In front of him stood the junkie he had robbed. He was wearing the same shirt as on that other night and the dirty cloth bag was hanging around his neck. Kerim looked at the suntanned narrow face and a feeling of shame shot through him. The man's pale blue eyes were now clear and looking keenly at him.

'I want to have the ring back,' he said with provocative determination.

Something in Kerim froze instantly.

'I don't have it,' he replied. It sounded uncertain but he was already determined not to give in.

'Give it back to me and the matter's settled,' said the man.

Kerim scrutinized the figure in front of him, then his gaze wandered to the street which looked almost idyllic in the late afternoon light. The foliage on the trees was dense. As every day, veiled women sat on wooden benches near the old iron pump and chatted while their children tried in vain to work the pump handle. The doors of the dark house entries, their walls covered in hastily scribbled messages, stood open. It showed a certain degree of courage for this drug addict to speak to him here, perhaps it was even despair. Could the ring really be so valuable? Kerim asked himself before giving the ice-cold answer.

'I don't know you.'

The man became agitated. When Kerim made to go, he grabbed him by the shoulder. They were standing not far from the door of an Internet cafe Kerim had never gone into. Young people from the neighbourhood met there. The windows were covered with opaque foil, as were those of many cafes in which Turkish or Arab men met in the evenings. From outside, the heads of the card-playing customers were always only visible down to the eyes. They seemed masked, like members of a secret society, secluded in these bright neon-lit rooms, sitting under the sepia-coloured portrait of Atatürk, a television or maybe a panorama picture in the middle of which, massive and mysterious, rose the Kaaba.

Coolly, Kerim brushed the hand from his shoulder and took a step back. But the man immediately grabbed hold of him again, more firmly this time, and drew Kerim towards him.

'What do you want?' Kerim shouted.

The next moment, three of the youths from the Internet cafe were beside them. The biggest and strongest was the leader and he immediately took the initiative. Kerim would very much have liked to know why the ring was so important to the man. But it appeared to be too late to find that out.

The leader pushed between them, struck the arm aside. He stood so close to the man that the latter involuntarily stepped back. The other two had meanwhile taken up position behind him. They were wearing white or grey hooded sweatshirts and seemed at once amused and tense. Kerim already knew what would happen now. The leader had challenged the man so determinedly that, in the eyes of his gang, he now had to prove himself.

'What is it? What do you want?' he hissed.

He pushed the man back, who was fumbling nervously with his cloth bag. Out of the corner of his eye, he registered the others standing around him and realized that he was in a trap.

His burning desire for justice gave him strength once more. He stiffened, even jutted his chin and said, 'That guy has stolen something from me. It's got nothing to do with you. I only want the ring back that belongs to me.'

'I fuck your ring, and I fuck you, you whore,' the leader snorted and raised his fist.

Intimidated, the other moved back, though still looking steadily at Kerim over the shoulder of his opponent. The latter was by now regretting the whole business.

'What's so valuable about the ring?' he now asked at last.

'It belongs to my mother,' replied the other.

Kerim couldn't help laughing and shook his head in doubt.

'Clear off, wanker!' interrupted the leader. He was close to hitting the man.

The latter realized it, turned around and fled, getting a kick as he did so. He cried out and looked around in shock but didn't stop running.

'What kind of ring is it?' asked the leader, after he had introduced himself as Amir.

Kerim still had the ring in his pocket like a talisman and handed it to Amir. He took it from the palm of Kerim's hand with two fingers, held it up, inspected it with a professional eye.

'Nice stone, good work,' he then said and handed it back.

Kerim looked at the other two youths in astonishment. Amir's expertise was evidently also unchallenged when it came to jewellery. Then it dawned on him who he was talking to—this must be the errant good-for-nothing, son of Mohammed the jeweller. Kerim asked Amir and the latter merely nodded cursorily. Where the other knew his father from was quite evidently a matter of indifference to him.

5

With his new mobile phone, he could theoretically have called his mother, his brother or Shirin every day at any hour. To his surprise, however, he less and less felt the need to do so. Even the weekly calls from his uncle's telephone began to be an effort for him, the conversations became evermore awkward. Simple things were troublesome to explain, he had to describe what he had experienced in short sentences so that it always remained trivial. It was as if the distance between him and these once-familiar people was becoming more evident with every further week that he spent in foreign lands, as if he shouted over evermore loudly but was able to say ever less.

Since he was often there now anyway, he began to send emails from the Internet cafe which, if at all, were only answered weeks later. With the written words, he was just as far away, they congealed into clichéd phrases which seemed to him drawn in big letters on a board which could be read from a great distance.

He found it a little disagreeable but he was, to some extent, in Amir's debt. Amir was suited to be leader not only because of his physique but also because of his intelligence. His friends talked to him in low voices, almost cautiously. Usually, however, they were only around him, accompanied him and fooled around with one another. Kerim became aware of Amir's loneliness, a certain difficulty with the people who followed him and whom he dominated and who, perhaps for that reason, were no longer enough for him.

Amir's curiosity was insatiable. After he had protected Kerim, he now expected in return that he talk about himself. The first few times, Kerim was still able to entertain them with the story of his flight. He spoke of the war, only fleetingly about his time with the Holy Warriors, about the island, and the young people sat there, mouths half-open, forgetting to draw on their cigarettes. It was already getting dark. The flat computer screens bathed the room in unreal light, on each one, near the bottom of the picture, a little rifle, which otherwise wandered unceasingly through artificial landscapes, but now, for the duration of his story, was immobile.

Amir's dark face was tense. Kerim's story in particular seemed to occupy him, an interest, which had long ago faded, seemed to be reawakened. Kerim felt it clearly but did not know what the interest was. Even if it didn't bother him at first, he remained alert. He liked Amir, not, however, because of his display of strength but because of the sad yet attentive gaze with which he examined his surroundings. This broad-shouldered young man with cropped black hair, who always held himself very straight and always seemed tense, was capable of genuine thoughtfulness.

'The man on the ship,' said Amir, 'where did he go?'

Kerim raised his shoulders. 'I don't know. I don't know anything. I can hardly remember what he looked like.' He said the last sentence more to himself.

'Do you think he is still on this island?' asked Amir and evidently expected an answer from Kerim.

He shrugged again. 'I don't know. I don't think so.'

He had never asked himself the question and yet, at that moment, the thought of Tony had a curious effect on him. He suddenly had him clearly before him, as he had seen him from the rubber dinghy, squatting on the bare hot stones, leaning on one elbow, his posture inappropriately relaxed. Again he saw the dark figure become gradually smaller and he almost felt the nausea again, which the swaying image produced in him. And he remembered how, late in the evening, when the fishing boat had at last entered the little harbour, he had fled, in order to make his way to Germany. He must have annoyed the fishermen by doing so. The thought was an uncomfortable one—perhaps, unintentionally yet again, he had caused harm and prevented Tony's rescue.

* * *

For days, this idea, prompted by Amir, didn't let go of him. He was overcome by a strange mood—he felt lonely and yet full of vigour. He didn't quite know on what he should expend his energy, and so, more often than was good for him, his thoughts revolved around Sonja. For some time now, he had tried in vain to reach her.

At some point, he had had enough of waiting and decided to go to her. The evening was surprisingly cool, a fine rain was falling and strong gusts of wind blew through the streets. For the first time, Kerim was bothered by the many tall houses. He missed the view into the distance, the feeling of standing in an open landscape, and he thought he could feel it in his bones. All he could do was look at the sky which was a curious white colour but broken up by dark patches, like spilt milk.

He walked a few streets further, reached for the ring, his present, in his pocket. The thought, however, of the man from whom he had taken it, depressed him. He stopped at the entrance to the municipal park. This green oasis was enclosed by streets of old and new houses. Their outlines merged into one another in a sky that was becoming increasingly grey. Kerim suddenly felt tired and he would have liked to sit down on one of the benches which were all empty because of the bad weather. But he hadn't gone far enough yet, he was afraid of encountering Amir or even Ferid here. To cross the park, he had to go over a hill. From the top, Kerim had a little bit of a view and he paused to enjoy it.

Suddenly, not only the city but also his life of the last few months was spread out in front of him, blurred and ungraspable, at a distance, at once painful and tranquil. It was an image of futility, he felt, as he emerged from the stream of new impressions and became aware of his loneliness. He knew very well that he had had a great deal of luck and that many of his fears had not come true. All in all, one could say that it had been easier than anticipated. And yet, the constant feeling that he was a guest sickened him.

He looked at the endless rows of windows and wondered whether all the people behind them felt at home. I always feel like that day in Sonja's bathroom, he thought, I'm there for sure but, in a strange way, also far away. God help me, he said to himself, I'm homesick. He almost started at the thought, he had not expected it to be so strong. It made him feel wretched and weak. He had no desires any more to drive him on. He saw the eternal monotony around him—young families, mostly Turkish, German single mothers, aged down-and-outs with weathered faces, looking for useable refuse along the path and in bins; he saw the dog owners and the punks, the scruffy students, always with their beer bottles, and the young girls, staring at the displays on their mobiles as they walked. Everyone had something to keep them busy. Only he was always waiting for a woman to whom he meant nothing and yet whom he couldn't let go, because he was crazy about her.

The heavens seemed to open and heavy rain poured down on him with such force that it seemed to want to drill through the soft surface of the park. Kerim saw little fountains of mud splash up and the rain turn to hail. A few moments later, he was entirely alone. The hailstones struck his cheeks and lips, got under his collar. Now he could have done with his Teacher, only he would have been capable of releasing him from his dejection. The mere thought of him allowed Kerim to breathe a sigh of relief. Which wrong path have I taken? he asked himself. At the same time, he had a quite different thought which lightened his mood: How free I used to be, before I fell into this trap.

He looked along the path which snaked down the slope and led back into the city through a narrow exit in the park wall. He decided to turn back. For the first time, he lacked the strength to walk.

Later that evening, as if having sensed his despondency, Sonja called him. Kerim still found it difficult to keep his feelings under control. Alone in the flat, he had unceasingly recalled his memories and the thoughts of his Teacher, had become intoxicated with them. While only shortly before, the power of the spell of those days had coursed through him, he was now, with Sonja's fine and clear voice in his ear, hesitant and at a loss for tender words. Although he did not reproach her, his silence made her touchy. He couldn't stop her trying to draw a friendly word out of him. To Kerim's surprise, she finally suggested visiting him at his uncle's flat. She wanted to see, she said, where and with whom he was living. Once again, Kerim was speechless. He just about managed to express his agreement. They decided that she should visit the day after the next. When he gave her the exact address, a feeling of unease stole up on him. He impressed on her that she should not tell his uncle anything about the accident on the pond, because that would upset him.

'Wait, wait,' he then said quickly and fell silent.

'What is it, should I not come after all?' she asked uncertainly.

'Oh yes. But wear something that covers your shoulders, OK?' He didn't like having to say it.

'That's all right,' she responded.

'My uncle. You know . . .'

'Don't worry,' she said quickly.

After they had said goodbye, Kerim went to the window. He was glad of the cool rainy weather, which would certainly continue until the evening she came—Sonja would have to wear more clothes. As much as he liked her body, he wanted to hide it from every other man. Now he regretted having used his uncle as a pretext instead of speaking openly. But he brushed the thought aside. His mood had improved. Yet he was annoyed, because she had let him wait once again.

***

On the evening of her visit, the weather was still rainy. There was a musty smell in the house entry where Kerim waited for her. He had been nervous all afternoon, had not managed to keep himself busy in some way. He had spent the last twenty minutes at the street door. He hadn't seen Herr Patzek, wondered whether he might be ill. Now he saw her car, but she had to find a parking space. Further long minutes passed before she at last hurried up through the rain. She was wearing a blue, not-too-short summer dress. Her heels clicked audibly on the pavement. Even if she didn't look provocative in anyone else's eyes, she still looked really good. When she reached him, he immediately put his arm around her and drew her into the hallway. She let out a quiet squeal, tried to brush the wet hair out of her face but, in Kerim's embrace, didn't manage to do so.

He pushed her against the wall. The light went out, he pressed his face against her neck, drew in the damp scent of her skin and felt her pulse under his tongue. As if of their own accord, his hands began to work their way down her body, Sonja didn't want to resist him and, panting, stood there without moving. Yet Kerim couldn't stop, every inch of her rain-fresh skin led his mouth further. When he felt the curves of her hips, he grabbed them and went down on his knees. In the half-light, he saw the almost colourless material of her dress in front of him, he shoved her legs apart and thrust his head under the piece of clothing. He was only able to take a single deep breath before Sonja shoved him away. He let himself fall backwards onto the floor of the hallway and spread out his arms. While she hastily smoothed out her dress, he said, 'You're not good to me, you . . .'

For the first time, he was unable to find something like an affectionate swear word in this foreign language. Finally, Herr Patzek did open the door after all. He had a cold and, coughing, he pointed out to Kerim that it wasn't healthy to lie on the cold floor.

Sonja's visit lasted only two hours. It was noticeable that she was keeping her eye on the time. That evening, Kerim found out more about her than in all the weeks before. That suddenly bothered him but he consoled himself with the fact that they had found other things to do apart from talk to each other.

Uncle Tarik was dissatisfied because he had nothing he could offer the woman. Kerim had deliberately only informed him shortly beforehand in order to prevent things from getting too solemn. They didn't want to lend the matter too great a weight—the plan was to put a short visit behind them, which could be repeated from now on. Yet it had been ill-thought out, Kerim realized, because his uncle was now literally subjected to Sonja's presence—he could offer only tea and pistachios and otherwise sat opposite a woman whom he did not know at all and had nothing with which to occupy himself. He stirred his tea or stiffly placed his hands in his lap and did not rightly know what he should say. He missed those small tasks that even a small snack brought in its train.

Even if it was what Sonja had agreed to, she was nevertheless aware of the unease of the man sitting opposite. So she talked about herself and, in a toned-down version, how she had met Kerim, and about her job plans. She spoke more quickly than usual. She talked about a 'business start-up seminar' she attended. For Kerim, the phrase broke down into three expressions each of which he understood but could not make sense of as a whole. He realized that she learnt something there but he did not understand what it was. Nor did his uncle inquire further. His narrowed eyes and the all-too-steady nodding were evidence of his uncertainty.

Sonja had hardly any opportunity to take in the room around her. The meeting was more forced than she had anticipated. She wondered if it was her fault. The elderly man in front of her was friendly and alert, yet she sensed a certain reserve. Although he spoke very good German, she was all the time not certain whether he understood what she was saying. He didn't ask questions, expressed no opinions, but only listened. She glanced over at Kerim, who seemed very young, sunk so deep in his easy chair and smiling to himself. Perhaps because the situation was threatening to turn into something like a job interview, she realized that although she slept with him she had never taken him quite seriously. He was constantly swinging between an attractive cheerfulness and a cold earnestness, so rigid in each that it was as if he were two different people. He wanted too much from her, she knew that suddenly. As if Kerim had made a confession that changed everything, she was aware at that moment of the gulf between them. I wasn't thoughtless, she silently reassured herself, but it had been temptingly easy.

She then quickly said something about her boss, the head of a small alternative concert agency. She added that she had known him since school and now dealt with all the paperwork in his office, the bookings and the data bank. She swiftly changed to her musicians, who came to Berlin in rattling mini-buses from France, Spain or Britain for their performances, their luggage consisting of nothing more than their instrument cases. On the days of the concerts, she never had much time, she added, as if she wanted to justify herself. As she talked into the silence, her own voice confused her more and more.

'Is that the man with the ring in his nose?' Kerim asked suddenly.

'Yes, exactly, him. His name is Stefan, and he's been wearing the ring as long as I can remember,' she went on chattering. 'He wears other rings too . . .'

'On his hands?' asked Tarik, who was just pouring them some more tea.

Sonja became nervous, looked uncertainly at the alert Kerim. 'Oh, I don't know where. He's . . . he likes men,' she said briefly.

Tarik leant back slowly in his chair. There was something so inquiring in his look that she felt obliged to explain.

'Stefan loves men.'

Tarik no more than nodded and looked into his teacup. Kerim, however, giggled and infected Sonja with it.

***

A little later, he showed her his room. He closed the door, stood right in front of Sonja and admitted his relief about the matter with Stefan. She saw the relaxed expression on his face.

'You mean he's gay.'

'Is that what it's called?'

She said it was.

Instead of embracing her, he told her to sit down on the bed. For a moment, it seemed as if she hesitated, but then he brought out the ring, solemnly took her hand in his and put it on her finger. Sonja was completely surprised, drew back her hand and looked at the ring.

'It's beautiful, really. Are we engaged now?' She drew him to her, kissed him and thanked him.

'What does engaged mean?' he wanted to know, and she explained it to him. 'Yes,' he said then, 'we are engaged.'

She was silent at that and, instead, looked around his room. There wasn't much, the walls were entirely bare, on the empty shelf above the desk there was only a single, richly embellished book. A small, carefully rolled-up carpet leant against the table.

She went to the window and looked over to the neighbouring house. She suddenly had the feeling that she was losing someone by coming closer to him. She thought about the drive here, how the buildings had gradually changed, how generously laid-out estates and houses surrounded by greenery had gradually given way to these densely populated tenement blocks. None of it was new to her and yet she felt there was something almost sinister about this lover and the evening in this flat. She thought about the ring, about the almost childlike way in which Kerim had given it to her, considered that it all seemed rather overdone for someone who was over twenty, and a new thought took hold of her with such intensity that she couldn't get it out of her head again. Suddenly she was mistrustful of Kerim and saw him with different eyes. What, she asked herself, if he was simply calculating, if that was the reason for his curiously split character? At any rate, his residency status would be tremendously improved if he found a German woman to marry him. Everyone knew that, yet if she had asked him about it, he would no doubt have been offended. Her suspicion was aroused.

Kerim came close up behind her and Sonja took a small step forward, simply in order to go on thinking for a moment. Suddenly, she understood what was at the bottom of her vague confusion—she had a bad conscience, because whatever he wanted was much more than she was prepared to give. And with every meeting, it seemed to get worse.

He embraced her, put his hands on her stomach. Over her shoulder, he, like her, looked out of the window. Just at that moment, the man in the flat opposite started his mysterious movements again. His wife kissed him fleetingly on the cheek and then immediately disappeared, as if she had lain down in front of him.

'Do you see,' Kerim whispered close to Sonja's ear, 'they do that almost every evening.'

Sonja saw how the almost fully clothed man over there moved—he was doing something with his arms which remained hidden, however, by the wall below the window.

'What are they doing?' murmured Kerim and his hands stroked her Venus mount. Sonja breathed heavily.

'I think,' she whispered, 'he's massaging her.'

Kerim's hands left off for a moment. 'He's massaging her?' His voice sounded astonished and was a little too loud in her ear. 'You mean, like a sportsman.'

'Yes,' Sonja retorted, 'perhaps she does sport. Possibly she's a dancer. She's got the figure for it.'

'Mmh,' was all that came from Kerim and it sounded like disappointment.

He pushed Sonja's dress up and pushed one hand into her slip. His fingers found their way so skilfully that she reared up and with this movement pressed her backside against his groin. She supported herself on the windowsill, lowered her head and closed her eyes. While her slip which had slid down was almost tearing, she pressed into his hands. Whatever else is not right between us, she thought, it's not this.

6

'You're a philosopher, aren't you?' said Amir, seemingly casual.

'I don't understand.'

Amir leant back and glanced around the Internet cafe. The gang was there, Hanif was staring at the screen three inches in front of him, the mouse under his hand clicked unceasingly. Almost everyone there was wearing headphones.

'I've been watching you,' Amir continued. He looked intently at Kerim. 'You always keep your distance. I mean, you're all right. But there's something about you.'

'I don't understand.'

'You don't say everything.'

Kerim leant back and there was an amused expression on his face. 'You mean, I'm gay,' he said, pleased to be able to use the newly learnt word so soon.

But Amir remained serious. He brushed off the cigarette ash and looked at Kerim again, who was sitting in front of him, one hand on the other, waiting, as if he was in a press conference. That was exactly what Amir was trying to understand. If one simply approached Kerim, then he made an innocuous impression and was like anyone else. If, however, one spoke to him alone and directly, then something froze in him and everything he said seemed rehearsed. Amir scrutinized the other, the face with the gentle features and the restless eyes, the rather slight figure and the surprisingly strong hands. He had told them his fantastic story in every detail and yet it was as if he had never talked about himself. Amir was too realistic and self-confident to be afraid of Kerim. He wasn't one of those big-mouth corner boys and mobile-phone stealers of which there were so many here. He knew cocaine dealers and arms dealers who, when necessary, did not shy away from violence. The man in front of him did not belong to that set of people. This one was straight, but with unfathomable depths. Amir found his company agreeable, perhaps only because he so rarely spoke without being asked. When the others told their jokes, he laughed, too, but the next moment he was wrapped up in himself again. Possibly, Amir said to himself, it was all because he hadn't yet settled down here. But he doubted it.

'I saw your girlfriend yesterday. Not bad,' said Amir. 'Really not bad.'

Kerim looked to the side, embarrassed. 'Yes,' was all he said in reply.

'What's her name?'

Kerim told him.

'Sonja,' repeated Amir thoughtfully. 'How long have you known her?'

'Not long, a couple of months.'

'And, do you get on?'

Kerim felt he was being pumped for information. Nervously, he fidgeted about on his chair and was glad when Hanif came up to the table.

'Hey, Amir, it's boring here. When do we get going?'

Abruptly, Amir turned his head. 'Am I your entertainment manager or something?' he hissed. 'Go on, man, play your game.'

Hanif made a show of reluctance but he obeyed. In an instant, Amir was as calm as before.

'I once had a German girlfriend, too. I mean, I had many. At the beginning, it's good, but then you've got to watch out that they don't take the piss out of you.'

Kerim didn't understand.

'I mean, you have to watch out, they're not like the women back home where you come from. Once they're with you, they want to cheat on you. That's the way it is here. They talk a lot but they're unfaithful.'

Kerim was beginning to find the conversation unpleasant.

'One even reported me to the police.'

'Why?'

'Maintenance.' Amir raised his hand and instantly dismissed the matter. 'Do you actually go to mosque?'

Kerim wasn't prepared for the question and shook his head.

'Why not? Don't you believe in God?' Amir spoke slowly and kept looking at the other's face.

Kerim hesitated, his eyes wandered across the room. Amir knew that he had found the right door.

'So you do believe in God. Then why don't you pray?'

'I pray every day,' said Kerim. It sounded indignant.

'Really?'

Kerim had a bad conscience at this question and, on top of that, knew he couldn't hide the fact. He thought about it, finally clinging to the idea that the new freedom had thrown him a bit off course. Only for that had he sometimes neglected his prayers, because he wasn't at home. Of course he knew it couldn't be any kind of excuse but he didn't want to reflect on that now, not with Amir's attentive gaze on him.

'I don't want to talk about it,' he said curtly.

Amir lit another cigarette. 'Over there, where you come from, you got to know some dangerous people,' he said quietly.

Kerim shrugged. 'But the most dangerous one I know is me.'

Amir winked at him. 'We'll see,' he said. 'Let's go.'

Glad of the interruption, Kerim followed him. They stood behind Hanif in the computer booth. Amir placed his hand on the boy's shoulder and shook him roughly. Hanif took off the headphones but his eyes were glued to the stylized mountain backdrop on the screen, in front of which were houses pockmarked with bullet holes. Hanif's game figure had just taken cover between them.

'Show him the page,' said Amir.

Hanif sighed. With a couple of clicks he left the game and opened a website.

Kerim recoiled involuntarily when he recognized the face. Emir Zarqawi was wearing a belt with explosives and, as always on photographs, appeared at once absorbed in himself and to be looking furtively at the camera. Kerim remembered many similar web pages he had seen. Now, however, so far away from all of that, there was a tumult of contradictory feelings in him. Of course, there was the memory of home, too, but simultaneously also the smell and the taste of the sand in the camp, the distant shouting of orders and, over it all, the smell of burning, of lurking danger. He didn't bother reading the bands of text with propaganda and slogans. Instead, he looked inquiringly at Amir who smiled and nodded at the screen.

There was a film running. The sound came softly out of the headphones Hanif was still holding. The unsteady image of a handheld camera showed an army convoy on a mountain road. The brushwood on the slopes was coloured yellow-brown, impossible to make out whether it was a question of the technology or whether it really was so. Distorted voices could be heard, Kerim understood only odd words. Suddenly, the truck at the front exploded and the camera seemed to be deflected by the force of the explosion. When the person filming had stabilized it again, there was shouting, the cry God be thanked, immediately followed by machine-gun salvos—the rest of the convoy was being fired on.

Kerim turned away.

'What is it?' asked Amir.

‘For you, it’s a game,’ said Kerim. He took a few steps away and deliberately stood under one of the plasma screens on the wall. A soundless football game was taking place on it.

When darkness fell, they were sitting in the car. It belonged to Samir’s father and he should really have brought it back some time ago but Amir still had something to take care of. Naturally, he was the one who drove and had insisted that Kerim accompany them. First, they went to a couple of cafes, all of which looked like gloomy storerooms serving drinks. There were always scantily dressed, bored-looking women behind the bar, and each time Amir went into the back rooms alone, when he came back, he neither had anything with him nor anything to report.

Hanif, Samir and Reda had squeezed onto the backseat. Their mobiles vibrated and rang constantly, each conversation lasted only seconds. Amir drove too fast, they raced down dark streets. Kerim looked out of the window without saying anything. It was a long time since he had gone anywhere by car, so he had immediately been ready to come with them. Now, however, he regretted it, because he had no money on him and now would have to stay with them, whatever they did. He cursed himself for his overconfidence. Amir and his lads had no problem staying in this country, they had everything he still had to fight for and they didn’t think of that for a second. Even worse, however, was that Kerim himself was ready to put everything at risk for a little distraction.

Amir was reticent, behaved as if there was something to hide, which was not a good sign. Soon Kerim lost his sense of orientation amid all the buildings flying by, these were beyond the world he had explored on foot.

After one of his brief phone calls, Samir leant forward and said, 'He's waiting under the bridge.'

Amir simply nodded. Immediately after that, Hanif wanted to listen to music but a wave of the hand from Amir was enough to silence him. Kerim thought with amusement that squashed together like that in the car, the three were like Amir's children.

'They've killed him, haven't they?' asked Amir without warning.

'Who?'

'Zarqawi,' said Amir.

'Yes, he's dead.'

They drove along a canal, the surface of the water calm, almost black.

'You know what I think? The Americans didn't manage it by themselves,' said Amir. 'The Arabs turned him in. And why? Because he took his revenge on Jordan. I would have done the same if I had been in prison there like him and been tortured. But the arm of the Jordanian secret service was longer than he thought. And so, in the end, they gave the Americans his position.'

'Why does it interest you?'

'Lots of things interest me,' replied Amir. 'Or do you think I'm like them in the back, happy playing computer games and hanging around?'

Kerim didn't answer.

'Where are we actually going?' he asked instead but got no reply.

They stopped under a dirty concrete bridge which was as wide as a tunnel. The silhouette of a man appeared at the other end. Amir switched off the light and made no move to get out of the car, only lowered the side window. Mild air came in, the chirruping of birds and the wind in the treetops could be heard. It was as silent in this tunnel as if they had left the city. Kerim wondered what was at the other side. The man's footsteps came closer.

'Who is he?' asked Kerim.

Amir waved the question aside. 'Some arsehole from around here.' He said quietly.

Then the man's face appeared at the window. Kerim was astonished that he was a German. Like the others, he wore a sweatshirt with a hood which cast a shadow over his face.

'Are you sure they don't work for one of our people? Are you completely sure?' asked Amir.

The other seemed intimidated. 'Yes,' he said. 'They're three blacks, sorta Rasta types. I've never seen them here before. How do I know who they're doing it for. Perhaps they're even asylum seekers doing it on their own account.'

Amir undid his seatbelt and opened the door, pushing the man aside as he did so. Over his shoulder, he said to the three on the backseat, 'Are you ready?'

They all said yes.

When he was standing beside the car, he turned to the German again. 'You know there aren't any asylum seekers, only ones that have just arrived or dealers.'

Smiling as if at a joke, he went to the boot and rummaged around. Everyone got out, only Kerim was uncertain. Finally, Amir opened the door on his side.

'Of course that wasn't about you. What's up?' he asked almost exhilarated. 'There are only three of them. We're going to scare them a bit. Come on, hard man from the war zone, get out and give us a hand.' He shoved a telescopic baton into his pocket.

Kerim did what he was told.

They strolled unhurriedly to the end of the tunnel, the German followed a couple of yards behind. In front of them lay a slightly sloping meadow, definitively framed by the shadows of a semicircle of trees. Somewhere between the trees, there was a path, patches of lamplight marked its course.

'Where have they got to?' whispered Amir.

The German pointed in a direction and at that moment the mobile in his sweatshirt began to ring.

'Turn the fucking thing off!' Amir shouted at him.

The man reached hastily into his pocket and fumbled so violently it was as if he had to kill a small animal. At last, the phone fell silent.

'The rest of you turn your things off too,' said Amir and gave a sign to get moving. Walking, he spoke to the German again. 'There are only three of them, you're sure?'

The other said yes. 'They meet here every evening. Sometimes there are a couple of alkies with them. But they're not part of it. Only the blacks.'

'Good,' said Amir, 'now shut up.'

Just before they had reached the trees, they separated, so that at a signal from Amir they would break through the bushes to the path at different points.

The three were sitting in a row on the backrest of a bench, their feet on the seat. Two of them were wearing brightly coloured knitted caps, their faces hardly discernible in the darkness. Next to the bench, there really were two ragged older men who stepped back in alarm when the group came onto the path in a semicircle around them. Everything happened very fast. Hanif and Samir pulled the man on the left off the bench from behind. He tumbled onto the ground like a sack and they held him down. Reda and Amir dragged the man beside him onto the path, which left one for Kerim.

He was certain that Amir wanted to test him and he was just as certain that he would pass the test. His opponent was confused, didn't rightly know whether he should fight or flee. Whatever was going on inside him as he was standing there, his hands in front of his body at waist height, it cost him the time he would have needed to defend himself effectively. Kerim's fist struck him on the side of the chin, so hard that he went down. Kerim sat on his chest and made sure he got the other man's arms under his knees. He placed one hand on the man's face and pressed his head into the grassy soil. Briefly, Kerim saw the dark profile between his fingers and couldn't help thinking of Tony.

'Be quiet!' he whispered reluctantly.

Amir appeared beside him. 'Have you got him?' he asked.

Kerim didn't answer, pressed the man's head down more forcefully. Amir glanced over at the two bearded alcoholics who were standing close together five yards away. They were looking on, at once attentive and dispassionate, as if, no matter what might happen, there was in any case no other place on earth for them except this park.

With a metallic sound, which seemed out of place in the silence, Amir flicked the baton. 'You said scare,' said Kerim.

Amir stepped up to him, nodded exaggeratedly, 'It's what I said and what I'm doing.'

He went around to the man's legs and hit his knee with the solid metal tip at the end of the baton. The man flinched under Kerim, tried to turn his head. Like an animal trainer, Amir walked over to each of the men and did the same.

'Is that what you want?' he then asked loudly.

One of the men managed a strangled no, Kerim's man tried to shake his head under Kerim's hand.

'Then don't come here again,' said Amir. 'You won't want to go to the parks in the east. Try it in the north—but not here.'

He gave instructions to take their drugs and money off the men and to let them go. Everyone stood up almost with a degree of solemnity. The three blacks retreated into the darkness, one picked up his knitted cap and brushed off the dirt. The group stood around the bench and watched them disappear. Kerim wiped the blood and saliva from his hand and caught a glimpse of his victim's hate-filled gaze.

'And you just go on and have a nice drink,' Amir called over to the two old men.

They were standing arm in arm. 'Right you are, mister,' they replied and raised their bottles.

'What have we got?' asked Samir.

Amir held up one of the little packets close to his face. 'The usual plus any amount of E,' he said.

Kerim never found out how much money they had got away with that evening apart from the hash and the pills, there had been nothing on his man. Yet the German was paid, just as he was. Kerim had got his first wage in this country.

When they were sitting in the car again, they were all euphoric. Reda had already rolled a joint which was passed around during the drive. Kerim had just taken a deep drag and coughed and spluttered when Hanif said, 'These guys are victims.'

'Yes,' said Amir grimly, 'and we're the winners.'

He switched on the music. It was an Arabic love song at thunderous volume. The houses flew past Kerim, and for the minutes the drive lasted, they were standing in the void, with no connection to him, cold and indifferent as the ocean he had once seen.

***

From now on, Amir sought Kerim's company. Whenever he saw Kerim on the street, he came over or at least whistled at him. Once he even rang the doorbell and Tarik opened to him. Others also noticed Amir's changed attitude. Kerim showed Amir where he walked and, as if in return, Amir took Kerim to his flat. Kerim had already heard that he lived there alone since separating from his girlfriend. No one, not even Amir's mother, had visited him there.

Kerim entered the flat with a mixture of curiosity and uncertainty. He didn't know why Amir was insisting so determinedly that they spend time together but he followed as if out of habit. The two rooms didn't quite give an impression of neglect but there was something unlived-in about them. Amir evidently always spent his time here in the same way, few things appeared to have been used recently. Among those that had been was the hubble-bubble beside the settee in the living room. Tobacco and aluminium foil were lying on the table in front of it. There were no photos or anything on the walls, the few pieces of furniture were largely bare. Amir switched on a lamp in the corner of the room, threw himself down on the settee and told Kerim to take a seat. He immediately reached for the hubble-bubble and prepared it. When he had lit it, he smoked silently for a while before beginning with the questions.

Kerim was surprised that they were sitting in a room with drawn curtains in the middle of the afternoon. The atmosphere reminded him of Herr Patzek's flat. Amir didn't offer him anything but only puffed away at his pipe. As he did so, he looked at the wall and his eyes narrowed.

'What are we doing?' asked Kerim after a while.

Amir didn't let himself be hurried. He checked the pipe once again, handed it to Kerim, who declined it.

'I want to know a couple of things from you,' Amir said at last.

He asked about the Holy Warriors, but in very general terms, and Kerim didn't quite know what he should say. Unlike other conversations, this time there was nothing of an interrogation about it. Instead Amir merely wanted to feel a closeness to those past events because they fascinated him. Kerim told him about the night in which they had had to dig up the Sufi grave and get rid of the bones of the old sheikh. He tried to describe what he and the others had felt, that they were crossing an invisible boundary. No one would have followed them there, no one would even have understood what they were doing. Together they had stepped into a shadow realm.

Amir didn't understand at first.

Kerim explained that everything he had learnt amounted to this—to see life as prelude to real existence in Paradise, to see through the error of clinging to the life in this world with all its misery and suffering. For that reason, concluded Kerim, one certainly didn't have to build mausoleums for dead saints, not least preachers of some false doctrine or other, and then go on pilgrimages to them. Kerim summed up everything he had learnt back then. And once he had begun, it poured out of him. He was surprised at how present all those ideas and events still were for him. He saw himself again in the circle of his fellow fighters, heard Hamid's whispering and the calm voice of his Teacher. Without being aware of it, he lost himself in his memories, paid hardly any attention to Amir.

'But you don't believe in it any more, do you?' asked Amir at the end, after a few seconds of silence. 'You've run away from all of that.'

He found it difficult but, finally, Kerim agreed.

'It was still the beginning of the revolt back then, it was still developing,' he emphasized, feeling a need to make his involvement appear less significant. Not least because he was already asking himself about the effect of what he had said on Amir, who was sitting on the settee with an impenetrable expression and had, at any rate, evidently heard enough for this evening. He turned his attention to the water pipe again. Kerim reassured himself. What could it all mean to the young man, here in a distant country? It was no more than distraction for him.

PART FIVE

1

Kerim spent more than eight months in the asylum seekers' hostel. He got to know African, Indian, even Chinese cooking—as they had nothing else to do, the inmates devoted much effort and time to preparing dishes they were used to. Usually they ate late in the evening and sometimes these meals turned into real banquets. It was as if here the cooks celebrated their sole triumph in having, for a few hours, the familiar aromas around them again.

One morning in autumn, Kerim got the notification that he had been granted asylum in the Federal Republic of Germany. It was communicated to him matter-of-factly and without any great ceremony, yet Kerim thought he sensed something like relief, even on the part of the stern woman, one of the officials whom by now he had known for so long. His uncle began to thank her, as if it all been her doing. Kerim, however, sank deep in thought, looked past the little, yellow-striped cat which hung like a growth from the woman's computer monitor, saw the trees outside the window and felt a deep calm. He was already looking back at the hostel, the unceasing murmur of voices and patter of footsteps, the holdalls tied up with cord and stuffed under beds—it was behind him. And before his inner eye appeared the room at Uncle Tarik's, about which he had so often thought. Now he could at last move into it properly, could sleep there and learn there.

The experience of this curiously neutral act of hospitality made him feel grateful. He was intoxicated by the idea that the right of residence had now finally made him another person, someone different from the inmates of the hostel. I'm going to make a completely new start, he said to himself many times, I'm going to do everything differently and nothing is going to connect me to the past except the people I really love. He saw himself crossing the street, inconspicuous among many others, going into shops, walking around parks—he already had a presentiment of the new freedom he had won.

His uncle was pale with pleasure. He placed his hand on the back of Kerim's head and pushed him through the asylum seekers' hostel, as if he was afraid his nephew could after all, at the last minute, get lost in one of the corridors of the ugly building. He was so intent on leading him onto the right path that he even announced to Kerim that he must now, at some point, have a serious word with him. Kerim said nothing to that, feeling as he did how greatly his uncle's concern was borne along by the feeling of joy.

Kerim did not find it hard to take leave of his roommates and the others, even if they congratulated him and were happy for him. Kerim found embarrassing the pessimistic undertone of so many of them. It was as if he had used up all the good luck for which they had hoped. He packed his things. When he was already standing outside, he put everything down again and looked for Ervin. The latter had just noisily shut his locker and was coming from the washroom. At first, the news seemed to be a shock to him. Kerim almost immediately understood, however, that in losing him the Albanian was losing something that had become familiar and found that hard to bear.

'When will we see each other again?' he asked and a mocking expression crossed his lips.

'Perhaps I'll come and visit you,' said Kerim.

Whether he believed it or not, Ervin nodded firmly and embraced him.

As they were standing there, Kerim's gaze wandered again over the unlovingly furnished rooms. Yet it wasn't the time he had spent here that was on his mind. Instead, it was a single conversation with Ervin, it had taken place only a couple of weeks earlier. The Albanian had been drinking and felt the need to talk to Kerim in a fatherly way, at the same time, expressing an exaggerated admiration. His chin sank to his chest, yet he went on speaking, hurriedly, as if he feared his thoughts would escape him.

'If anyone,' so he said, 'has a chance, then you do. You are so, so—pure, you have no past to spoil you, and everyone can see that. They have to take account of your honesty, they simply have to!' He reached for Kerim's arm but missed it, raised his searching hand and continued, 'You haven't even tried to use your girlfriend—what was her name?—Sonja, yes, you haven't even tried to use her.'

Kerim asked how he could have done that and learnt that marriage to a German would have automatically secured a right to stay. At first, he hadn't thought any more about it but, with time, a suspicion had arisen in him: What if this had been the reason for her reserve in all these months? Had she simply distrusted him, without saying a word about it? With this idea on his mind, which didn't let go of him, he felt himself deceived by her.

His uncle called him and Kerim felt dejected as he hurried along the dark corridor to the exit. Once again, he had to leave someone behind whose chances were poor, yet this time he found it easier. Here he had not associated himself with anyone, not with Ervin either, had formed no friendships, unlike many of the others, and now he was glad of it.

***

One afternoon, Kerim was sitting with his uncle, drinking tea and talking, and what, at first, seemed spontaneous in the conversation increasingly appeared to Kerim to have been raised deliberately.

'I've heard that you've found some friends here in the neighbourhood,' said his uncle, after a short pause had appeared.

Kerim was instantly alarmed but he only nodded.

'Do you think these layabouts are the right company to keep? You've had a lot of luck and should appreciate it. What they get up to is no business of yours. What do you think?' His uncle's voice had grown sterner.

'I simply got to know them because they live around here,' said Kerim.

'I know. I even know where they come from, every one of them. But that's no answer to my question.'

Kerim waited for a moment and then said, 'No. They probably aren't the best company.'

'Probably not,' repeated his uncle. 'You know it and I know it. Listen,' he said and leant towards Kerim, 'I'm glad that you know this German woman. She's nice. But Amir and his people are not the right friends for you. You must see that.' He made a dismissive gesture with his hand.

'They're local boys,' Kerim tried to appease his uncle.

'No, no,' said his uncle firmly. His gaze was insistent. 'You don't know the way things are here.' Shaking his head, he leant back in the easy chair. Then he began to speak again. 'I left it up to you for a long time. But I think that was a mistake. In this country, you have to try to get ahead. One has to be clever . . .'

'Smart,' said Kerim.

Tarik frowned.

'If you like, yes, smart. And you are.' He tried to smile encouragingly and then continued, 'Do you remember the man who was cleaning the postbox? We laughed about it. But remember this, you can stand in the street in a suburb at three o'clock in the morning and wait for the bus—and it'll come. Perhaps it will be a couple of minutes late but it'll come. That's the way it is here. When you're young, that doesn't mean much. But the older you get, the more important it will be to you. At home, if you stand on the street at three in the morning, you can't be sure that you'll live to tell the tale.'

Kerim sipped his tea. 'Especially now,' he said.

His uncle looked at him from the side, as if he had to think about what had been said. Finally, he showed his agreement with a gesture. 'It's bad now. But even in my day, I once had to jump into the bushes from the road one night and lie flat on the ground because a couple of people thought it was fun to shoot at me from a passing car. They could easily have hit me.'

He looked straight at Kerim again and indicated that he should wait for a moment. He got up and went to his bedroom, Kerim heard him rummaging around. When he came back, he was holding a stack of letters in his hand, there must have been about twenty.

'Did you know that your mother wrote to me?' asked Tarik.

Kerim shook his head, let himself fall back and immediately felt homesickness and pain. He shut his eyes for a moment and swallowed several times.

Tarik saw his nephew slump down in the easy chair and knew exactly what the encounter with the past triggered in him.

'I know it's difficult for you,' he muttered. 'I waited with these. But she wrote me a couple of things about you.'

Kerim had opened his eyes again and nodded without saying anything.

What followed now was something like a journey into the past. His mother talked about him in Uncle Tarik's voice. He could only listen and be astonished that he had never really been aware of her fear for him. The boy whom she praised for his hard work and about whom she also complained—that was him, he realized.

Uncle Tarik read, '*Kerim has disappeared, and we are all very worried. I don't know what has occurred. These are uncertain times. I don't want to think about what could have happened to him. He didn't come back from the trip and has now been gone a week. I pray that he will return.*'

His uncle looked up. 'What did you do?' he asked.

Kerim was still holding the empty tea glass and didn't know how to reply. His uncle leafed further. All the letters he laid on the table were short, the paper was written on in large, unsure handwriting. He held up one of the letters close to his reading glasses, briefly looked for a sentence and then continued reading:

'*Today Kerim came back to us and I thank God for it. He has grown thin and doesn't speak to us. He has changed greatly, his eyes glow. But he is alive. I think he was in great danger, he looks much older. I won't ask him any questions. I shall remain silent. I shall slaughter a sheep, happy that God has given him back to us.'*

Tarik took off his glasses and looked at Kerim. He let a couple of seconds pass.

'I won't press you to tell me about it. I, too, content myself with being glad that you are here. You have experienced a lot for your age. But whatever it is you brought from over there, whatever you still carried with you on the ship, you now have to forget it and begin something new.'

'I haven't brought anything with me,' responded Kerim in a weak voice.

He stared at his uncle. In front of his eyes, he saw clearly and distinctly the road to Diyala, just where it ended at a marketplace. The stones crackled in the heat. It was forenoon, and people crowded under the projecting tin roofs that gave shade to the square. At the front, by the roadway, a fruit seller had set up his cart. He was an old man, letting prayer beads run between his fingers, and paid no attention to Hamid. The latter walked towards him in a leisurely way, was still about twenty yards from him. Like this, it would be child's play.

'Have you got him?' Rashid squinted and poked Kerim's shoulder.

Kerim shrugged him off and hissed, 'Yes, but if you push me the picture will shake.'

'More than that is going to shake in a minute.'

They were lying flat at the edge of a hollow, at a sufficient distance. They could crawl back whenever they wanted but, as he had to film, Kerim had made himself as comfortable as possible. The figure drawing further away was clearly in the middle of the viewfinder. With great care, he tried to follow him using the zoom. That wasn't so easy, because Hamid wasn't walking in a straight line but making his way towards the fruit seller on a winding path. He was possibly avoiding obstacles they couldn't see from here. It was more likely, however, thought Kerim, that, so close to his death, he was going weak at the knees.

'He's taking his time,' whispered Rashid and blew the sand in front of his lips as he did so.

On the other side of Kerim crouched Mukhtar. He was holding the radio control with which he would ignite the bomb. It was the first time they were trying out this method.

Kerim concentrated entirely on the viewfinder. Even if only a light breeze rose, sand was blown in front of Hamid's figure. The boy looked almost normal, only a little fat around the hips. The loose, dark robe he was wearing concealed everything. Hamid reminded Kerim of himself not so long ago, a fat boy on his way to market.

'What is it?' asked Mukhtar.

'Everything's all right. He's on the road now,' answered Kerim.

They didn't use any binoculars in order to avoid unnecessary reflections.

Mukhtar crawled forward and stretched his head out of the hollow. When he's past the fruit seller, five seconds, that's what they had said to Hamid. That meant he would quicken his pace in order to get among the people at the market as quickly as he could. Hamid had seemed dazed during his final hours with them, but he had listened and agreed with everything. He did not want to take the two pills every martyr got before his last journey. Offended, he pushed the hand offering them aside. Mukhtar had to repeatedly explain to him that they were necessary, not because someone doubted his Faith but because with some the weak, earthly body failed them at the last moment. Only the Teacher, when he was called over, could convince the boy.

He had volunteered days before, had begged to be the next to go. Kerim had long before noticed the change in him. A deep sadness had taken hold of the boy, he cut himself off and fled into prayer. Sometimes, when he was struck or kicked in passing, he kept still as a donkey. Kerim thought he was storing up the pain inside himself.

Once, when they were cleaning the blood house, Hamid had said he only now understood how much the life here below was only a preparation for Paradise. He had had several discussions with the Teacher. Perhaps, Kerim later often thought, the boy also had a bad conscience because of his betrayal of him and Kerim regretted not having talked more about it with Hamid.

Quite unexpectedly, he finally became carefree. He had never been sad, he said to Kerim, who asked him about it, but, full of joyful anticipation, had taken his leave of this world.

He would do his job well, Kerim was sure of that.

Hamid had reached the fruit seller.

'He's stopped,' said Kerim.

'Why?' growled Mukhtar.

'I don't know,' answered Kerim. 'He's talking to the fruit seller.'

He operated the zoom. The old man was sitting on a stool, still moving the beads in his hand. Hamid chatted with him. That's unbelievable, thought Kerim, but said nothing. He gripped the camcorder more firmly. He would follow Hamid until he disappeared behind the fruit barrow, but then zoom out as fast as possible in order to have the whole explosion in the picture. That was quite hard to do. If he acted skilfully, he could just about hold the camera still.

'Now,' said Kerim loud and clear, and Mukhtar began to count.

Kerim's heart beat against the wall of earth on which he was lying. His left hand clutched the small casing of the camcorder. He zoomed away, had the whole approach to the market, the houses and even the hills, hazy in the heat, behind the town in the picture. Then Mukhtar flipped the switch.

For the length of a brief, terrifying intake of breath, nothing happened. Then the bomb exploded.

Although the detonation only shook the ground a little and Kerim was able to firmly hold the camera, he had to zoom more than he had expected. He forced himself to stare into the viewfinder and not to pay attention to a single square inch of the world around him. Only the little preview window saved him from thinking about what he was seeing. The old man and his fruit barrow were hurled right onto the road. A low, dark cloud of dust and rubble spread across the marketplace. In the middle rose the fireball of the explosion. Kerim could clearly see body parts whirling around. And above it all hovered something which he was certain was a head. Hamid's childlike head. For a moment it was up there above the houses, just as if the explosion itself was his new fiery body. For a second, little Hamid had become a giant, swollen into a monster in the middle of the market square which, however, no one could see apart from the three of them out here. After the explosion had died away, seconds still passed, until, like a whimpering, the distant screaming began. Mukhtar gave Kerim a vigorous shove as a sign that he should now stop filming. This part of the action was of no use to them, so Kerim switched the camera off. Mukhtar had already got up and, bent low, hobbled across the hollow. Kerim and Rashid followed. They hastened away through thistle bushes and across loose rocks. As always, Mukhtar hurried ahead of them. Sweat was pouring down their bodies as they reached the white pickup whose engine the driver had already started.

'I didn't bring anything with me,' said Kerim and set down the empty teacup, his hands trembling.

Tarik thoughtfully stroked his white moustache.

'I won't ask you about it,' he repeated. 'I know from your father that you don't talk much. Keep it to yourself, lock it up somewhere inside you, close the door. . . . Look, the people who came here are a strange lot. It doesn't matter whether they're Turks, Arabs or Kurds—as the years go by, they lose their relationship to their homeland. They can travel there and spend their holidays there, visit their families. But even for those at home, they are no longer the people they were. It's the same with all of them, Ferid and his sons, me. Sabihe felt it, too. Not everyone finds his way. They dig themselves in, live only here.' He pointed to the window. 'Because you are so young and because you learn so quickly, I'm telling you—free yourself of what lies behind you. Believe me, later on, you will have plenty of time for your memories. But now you must learn, learn. Now you are at last allowed to get a job. Or you finish your studies. Your girlfriend can help you there. Talk to her.'

Kerim saw that his uncle was worried and he also felt how he was trying to hand over responsibility to him. In Uncle Tarik's eyes, his German girlfriend must have been a real stroke of luck, Kerim told himself, they need not have been so worried before Sonja's visit.

The next day, as if in a mysterious way she had become aware of Uncle Tarik's concern, Sonja arranged to meet Kerim in the city centre. Although she had very little time, he went there on the stifling Underground. It was a warm day and humid despite the sun. Sonja was already waiting for him. He was meanwhile convinced that she had not been honest with him. But he decided not to talk to her about it, because he didn't want to hear her attempts to justify herself.

She was sitting on the edge of a fountain basin, one hand in the water. With the other, she pressed her laptop bag to her body. Given the temperature and unlike many other women Kerim had seen on the underground she was very modestly dressed. The white, high-necked top combined with her tied-back hair gave her a serious appearance, only the washed-out jeans and the trainers provided a slight contrast. Kerim had to look twice before he recognized her. With it all, she was wearing a pair of very dark sunglasses. She seemed to be nervous because of a couple of small children playing on the other side of the fountain.

'I've been afraid the whole time, they could get it into their heads to soak me,' she said after they had kissed in greeting.

He took a step back and said, 'You look different.'

'I was at my course, you remember, I told you about it.'

Kerim gently but firmly took the notebook bag from her. Sonja wanted to add something but Kerim seemed distracted as he shouldered it.

They found a cafe with a nice terrace. Sonja briefly looked suspiciously towards the entrance and concluded that inside it looked like a corner pub. She shifted her chair so that she could look at the passers-by on the street. She took off her sunglasses, put them on the table, tugged her hair into place and began to ask Kerim questions. This time not about his earlier life or his journey but about what he had been doing recently. Kerim told her honestly about his new friends from the Internet cafe. After a little hesitation, he described to her in every detail his experiences in the park.

Sonja's face darkened visibly but that didn't stop Kerim continuing with his account. When he was finished, Sonja put on her sunglasses again and said, 'So you go around with this gang and beat up drug dealers?'

Kerim nodded.

She shook her head. 'I find you more and more strange. How is that compatible with your religion?'

Kerim said nothing.

After a couple of seconds she broke the silence. 'I really think we have to find something for you to do. I'm going to take care of it.'

'Yes,' said Kerim and beamed at her.

She removed her glasses again, leant across the table and gave him a kiss.

When the waitress came to their table, both looked up simultaneously. She was a big blonde and took up position right beside Kerim. She put down her pad and leant over, her hands on the tabletop. She was wearing a strapless, pale yellow top which, stretched almost to breaking point left, her stomach exposed and barely covered her large breasts. With it she wore a white miniskirt split at the sides. She didn't so much as glance at Sonja but smiled at Kerim. The smile moved because she was chewing gum. She leant there casually, one leg a little behind the other, playfully lifting her heel from the shoe.

'What can I do for you?' she asked and went on chewing.

Made speechless by her presence, Kerim was still staring up at her. His gaze wandered uneasily over the upper part of her body to her narrow face with its thin plucked eyebrows. He breathed in the sweet body-smell of the woman, saw the pale down on her lower arms, the dark discoloured inner sole of her shoe and glanced again and again at the cleft between her breasts which bulged towards him. From one second to the next, she had come so close to him that he could no longer move.

'You can bring us two *cafe au lait*s and that's it,' said Sonja, irritated.

The woman didn't take her eyes off Kerim and pushed herself off the table. 'My pleasure,' she said, turned around with a swing to her hips and tripped back into the cafe.

Kerim swallowed and didn't know what to say. Sonja, however, was annoyed. She put on her sunglasses and folded her arms.

'Did you have to stare at her tits like that,' she said quietly but sharply.

'No,' lied Kerim.

'Why do you do it then?'

'I don't know. Don't other men do it, too?'

'Not like that,' said Sonja tersely. She evidently wanted to close the subject. 'They try not to, at least,' she added.

After a bit, she smiled and placed her hand in his. She was wearing the ring he had given her and it really suited her. Kerim pushed it up and down a little, positioned the stone in the middle of her finger and leant his head to the side. Despite his bitter suspicion that she had only adopted him like a toy, it made him happy to see her wearing the ring.

When he heard the waitress coming back to their table, he didn't look at her. She put the big coffee cups down in front of them, but bent down so far towards Kerim that he became rigid once again.

'Now go on, tell him your cup size and then leave us in peace!' Sonja snapped at the woman.

She drew herself up to her full height, held the tray in front of her stomach like a shield. 'Cup size,' she repeated almost thoughtfully.

'For heaven's sake,' said Sonja, once she had disappeared, 'what was that about?'

She remained disgruntled, even after they had put the money on the table and left unnoticed.

Sonja had only explained to him why she had to see Stefan at the office right away when they were already at her car. Just before they said goodbye, Kerim asked her what the big white building on the other side of the street was. People were constantly going in and out of the glass revolving doors and the walls around the entrance were plastered with peeling posters.

'That's the Technical University,' said Sonja.

'I thought so.'

'Do you want to go over, take a look at it?'

'Why not? It's something new.'

She drew his face gently to her and stroked his cheek. 'But to go to university, you need a school-leaving certificate.'

'I know,' said Kerim morosely.

'You can catch up on it,' she said encouragingly. 'You can do it.'

'Will you help me?'

'If I can.'

2

Kerim told two versions of his university visit. When he was sitting with his uncle and Ferid, he described the wide, dim corridors along which he had wandered. He was astonished at how empty the big building appeared, despite all the people walking around inside. Outside some seminar rooms, there were plastic tubs on the floor in which the students had put out their cigarette ends. Kerim had admired the rows of huge windows. He had stood in front of a large notice board, in front of announcements, telephone numbers of students looking for flats or work, news of forthcoming concerts, of reading groups, cultural events, readings and also of things he didn't understand. These notices were carefully designed, with logos in every possible colour. They were flyers, as he knew from Sonja, who had such things made and had sometimes asked him for his opinion.

He saw students flooding out of their lecture theatre, each seemed eager to get away as quickly as possible. The big old building with the courtyard in the middle had no side wings. Instead, annexes, which might once upon a time have been modern, grew out of it. Now they were like the foyers of run-down theatres, somewhere there was even a huge cloakroom which no one used any more and on the plastic-panelled walls, there were forgotten signs like

'Maintenance H.D.' and 'Inventory Number 17448'. It was already late enough for the Turkish cleaners. They passed heavy vacuum cleaners over the endless strips of floor covering. They were sweating and, after every yard, they wiped their hands on their smocks. They ignored Kerim just as they ignored everyone around them, talking unceasingly among themselves, they stayed in their own world.

Kerim left the new building, looked for a long time and finally found the courtyard again. He stood in the narrow space, looking at the wall, and was just making up his mind to go when one poster caught his eye. On it, in Arabic lettering, were the words 'God Is Great.'

Up to this point, he related what he had seen and did so mostly to please his uncle. He was supposed to see that his nephew had not forgotten his admonishing words. Secretly, however, Kerim hoped to dispel the impression he must have made on his uncle during the earlier conversation. He cursed himself for having lost control and for briefly having shown weakness. Only his peculiar situation far from home could excuse it.

That evening, Tarik's son had also come to stay for a couple of days. To celebrate his arrival, Kerim had cooked rice, white beans and lamb, a standard dish which was not much effort for him to prepare. Hussein was a slight man of medium height, who not only looked like his father but also behaved like him in many respects. He radiated the same patient calm and, just like Uncle Tarik, screwed up his eyes when something was on his mind. Kerim liked that in his cousin just as he did in his uncle. It leant weight to whatever one said, it never felt inconsequential. And the short interval of time between the screwing up of the eyes and the reply was a moment of contemplation. Kerim had not known this kind of conversation before. In his family, there had not been much talking, and when his parents told stories of earlier days the children looked this way and that and listened in silence. From his father, he had got really only instructions or explanations. It had been just the same at school or with the Holy Warriors.

Tarik was visibly happy at the presence of his son. Again and again, he cast glances at him that were full of pride, to which, however, the latter did not respond. Hussein sat there, his legs crossed, turned his Marlboro packet in his hand and looked at Kerim. He once more related the story of his flight, only making sure that he didn't just reel off the details.

When Kerim was finished, Hussein pulled a face as if to say, Quite a story! But what he said gruffly was: 'You can cook. What else can you do?'

'He can speak German,' crowed Ferid, interjecting. 'Truly, in this short time, he's speaking like a German.'

'You've got a talent for languages,' said Hussein approvingly.

Kerim shyly waved his hand in denial. His uncle knew the truth; in fact, he still communicated with Sonja in a mixture of English and German. If he was stuck, which, as far as he was concerned, happened all too often, he changed languages.

'And he has a German girlfriend,' his uncle didn't forget to add.

'Well, aren't you in a hurry,' said Hussein. 'Who else have you got to know, since you've been here?'

As Kerim hummed and hawed, his uncle brought up Amir and the boys from the Internet cafe.

'Our Amir, from around the corner?' asked Hussein, surprised. 'I've known him since he was a kid.' Hussein related how shortly before he had gone to Cologne, Amir had began kickboxing. And that he had actually expected Amir to make it to world champion in the discipline. 'He does everything one hundred per cent, absolutely. Didn't he have a son with a German woman? What's he doing now anyway?'

Kerim said he was hanging around and left it at that. Hussein shook his head.

'In a foreign country, one has to be mediocre,' he said. 'You just learn whatever's necessary and no one envies you for what you achieve. Stay away from Amir. He's got problems. By the way, the family originally comes from somewhere around Beirut. There's a rumour that his father is supposed to have become rich during the civil war through the hold-up of a security van. But I don't know if it's true. Have you ever seen his sisters?'

Kerim nodded.

'But no doubt he prefers to keep them away from you boys. They must be beautiful girls by now.'

‘Do you really think that they’re rich?’ asked Ferid.

‘His father always drove a brand-new Mercedes. I don’t think he earns that much with his jewellery shop.’

They were now drinking tea and Tarik had put a big box of cakes of every different kind on the table, when Hussein reinforced his warning. ‘Stay out of Amir’s way. He’s just as ambitious as you but doesn’t know what to do with his strength. One day, he’ll probably,’ Hussein paused and grinned as he scratched his chin, ‘begin working for a private security firm, because the police won’t have him or he’ll kill himself driving his father’s car.’

‘Or he’ll set up a business like you,’ said Tarik.

Hussein turned red instantly, spread out his arms and said, ‘Dad, I deal in cars—there’s nothing illegal about it.’

His father merely muttered.

***

When he saw Amir again the next day, the first thing Kerim asked him was why he had given up kickboxing. Amir’s expression was dismissive. He didn’t ask where Kerim had heard about it. He showed Kerim his hand and pointed to his knuckles.

‘I got callouses from the training. It looked as if I had thick warts everywhere. My fingers were crooked. My girlfriend didn’t like it.’

'The German one?'

Amir smiled and shook his head. 'No, another one.'

It was early afternoon, the lads were still at school. Only Kerim and Amir had, as always, time on their hands. They were walking to a kebab shop two streets away. Amir wanted to invite Kerim for a meal. When he asked Kerim what he had been up to recently, the latter hesitated for a moment. He put all his strength into staying in control, into doing what he had been doing for so long—showing himself to others only up to a certain point but hiding the other part without arousing any suspicion. Yet, surprisingly, he didn't manage it this time. There was nothing special about the day and the person who had asked, it was only Amir, and yet it burst out of Kerim. He talked about his visit to the university but began the story with the misshapen stone angel in the courtyard and the poster for the prayer group. He said how he looked at the clock and, for a moment, felt lost somewhere between the afternoon prayer and the one at dusk, how he went down the broad stairs to the basement and looked for the place where they met and how finally, in a bare, neon-lit room, he came upon a handful of Believers, Arabs from every possible country, also Turks, Pakistanis, Afghans and Indians, one of whom said to him that the time didn't matter, he could come whenever he wanted.

They were already sitting in the snack bar before Kerim stopped talking. Once again, something warned him against his words to this man whom he really did not trust. The place was empty apart from them. Down the street at the next entry was a gloomy bar whose customers were mainly Germans and from which loud rock music boomed. At the door, Kerim and Amir had seen the hippies who were getting on in years, squatting there, drinking beer and sucking at their roll-ups. Most of them looked as if they had seen far better days. With gestures and shouts, they were communicating with a group of down-and-outs who met in front of the supermarket on the other side of the street every day. There was a kind of unspoken agreement among them as among the survivors of a vanished epoch.

The owner of the snack bar was arguing loudly with his wife. He was standing behind the counter, she was sitting on one of the chairs for customers. Their alternating shouts rose and fell, there were gaps between the exchange of words but one of them always picked up the thread again. Nevertheless, Amir succeeded in placing their order. The man disappeared into the back room and roared out his responses to his wife's remarks which, to judge by the shrill tone of voice, could only be reproaches. When the food arrived, Kerim was sunk in thought again and described to Amir the rest of his experience. How, at a stroke, he had the feeling he was among friends, a feeling he had not had for a long time. Kerim struggled to find words when he wanted to tell Amir something of the intimacy which only belief can give a community. The bare room with the shiny floor became part of that still timelessness of which Kerim had experienced a little in his own prayers, but whose full, comforting power had only been present in shared prayer. He had praised God's name in so many places, by rushing mountain streams and on boulder-strewn lunar landscapes, on the hot plain just as in the bowels of a ship and in his quiet, dark room. And all these places became one with each new prayer. That was what he wanted to tell Amir when he said, 'The moment I entered that room downstairs, I found again what I had been missing for a long time.'

The quarrel of the married couple entered the next round. The woman, who was wearing a long, pale grey coat and a headscarf, didn't budge from the spot but her voice seemed to dance around her. She uttered short, piercing sentences, and after each one she fell silent again. Two seconds passed before the husband screamed out, as if his wife's words were causing him physical pain. He paced up and down behind the counter, threw his tea cloth into the corner and yet could not make up his mind to come out from behind it.

'Do you understand what they're saying?'

Amir shook his head. He had stopped eating and was looking steadily at Kerim. Kerim sensed that something mysterious was going on inside him. His face had become a mask, not even his eyelids were moving. Kerim related how he had been invited to the university refectory by an Algerian, how they had sat in that ugly hall and watched students as they pushed aside the leftovers of their predecessors on dirty tables and wiped the seats before sitting down in order to eat and afterwards likewise leave behind their own leftovers. The man explained to him that this place had for many years been the meeting point of every conceivable political group—anarchists, Maoists, Trotskyists, communists, PKK people and all the shady types who were always to be found around these groups without anyone knowing what they lived on. The Algerian had already been in Germany for a very long time and he laughed about what he was saying. Kerim went on to tell how in the early dusk they had returned to the prayer room which had filled meanwhile and where the prayer mats now lay on the smooth floor as on the surface of a frozen lake. Now the Believers were even closer to one another, now they shared everything that was important.

Again the woman raised her voice. This time the husband did come out from behind the counter and stormed towards her. Kerim was afraid he was going to hit her but the man came to an abrupt halt a yard in front of her chair before starting to scream again. The wife still didn't budge, only stared straight up at him and waited for his torrent of words to end. Again there was a brief pause, then the whole thing was repeated. Several times the man wanted to go back behind the counter but never got very far. Each time his wife began to speak and he turned on his heel to stand in front of her.

'The essential point,' said Kerim, 'is unity.' And in order to explain that to Amir, he quoted the Teacher.

'A shard can never be anything else but the memory of the glass from which it was broken. The West is unceasingly striking us. It wants to smash us to shards and after that into shards of shards, into ever-smaller fragments. It wants all of us, every one of us, to forget the glass. The glass is unity and one doesn't have to search for it, doesn't have to philosophize about it. One can experience it, feel it and be a part of it—in prayer.' That was what he had felt again. 'My father never understood that. He was a man without true Belief.'

'Like mine.'

'After that, I talked to the Algerian for a long time.' Kerim thought about how in a moment of unmediated closeness, he had told the Algerian much more about himself than would have been necessary. 'At the end, he told me, there was a mosque which I should go to. A particular one, not the PKK mosque near here, not one for normal believers, the conformists. He described the way to it exactly. And that we could see each other there again.'

The quarrel behind them went on, but Amir suddenly jumped up, his chair scraped across the floor with a penetrating sound. He turned to the man and said loudly and in German, 'We're eating. How long is this going to go on?'

The man gestured disparagingly, barked something at his wife and this time managed to get back behind his counter. The woman, at any rate still defying her husband, merely glanced impassively over at them. Suddenly, it was surprisingly still in the snack bar, only the beat of the music from next door could still be heard. Amir sat down but didn't touch his food. He stared at Kerim and scratched his forehead.

'Unity—what does unity mean?'

Kerim didn't know what to say. But Amir didn't wait for him to finish his reflection.

'I'll drive you to that mosque. Whenever you like, let's go there together.'

It had grown dark. On their way back, they met Reda and Samir. The two of them had placed bottles on top of a wall and were trying in turn to hit them with a 'scissors kick', as they called it. As in a karate film, they jumped in the air and, before the kick, twisted to the side. When they saw Amir, they challenged him to join in. Reda suggested teaching it to them. But Amir said nothing, waved them aside and simply left them standing.

He said goodbye to Kerim at entrance to the latter's house.

'Let's go right away, tomorrow,' he said.

In a gesture unusual for him, he had placed his hand on Kerim's shoulder and kept it there. Kerim had the feeling that after all his confessions, he could now demand something of Amir.

'I've heard you have a son?'

Amir said yes. 'Who told you that?'

Kerim jerked his head up towards the flat.

'From Hussein. Do you remember Hussein?'

'Sure, Hussein. What's he doing?'

'He's dealing in cars.'

'Car dealer,' repeated Amir absent-mindedly. His gaze was already on something else, distant. One might have thought that the string of lights on the awning of the Kurdish baker two hundred yards away had drawn his attention.

3

Kerim had not called his family for some time, nor had he sent them any emails. Because of his own worries, he could no longer bear their fears about the evermore numerous assassinations and suicide attacks, the evermore threatening terror in the country.

He sat on the bed in his room for a long time. He had stood up Amir and for the next few days hid away from him.

He was holding the Holy Book in his lap. How was it possible, he had been asking himself for an hour, still to interpret the words in such a simple way? They're holy words, he thought. On the other hand, the Prophet had been a Chosen One, a man who was in touch with the Almighty. Perhaps I, a simple man, cannot understand his words properly. He looked at the book. He felt the cover, with its embossed letters, on the palms of his hands.

As the Teacher had said, was not really everything that one had to know there on paper in front of him? Questions did not help, they took him no nearer to the printed words. Kerim lowered his head over the book and he saw the texture of the paper in the black print and the smell of the paper rose to his nose. Yet if a small part of the Higher Knowledge which inspired the Prophet were not also in us, how then could we understand his words at all, how would we have any idea at all of the Faith? And is it not consistent, that someone like the Teacher, who tried to bring his life and his thinking in line with the precepts of the Prophet, is also closer to that Higher Knowledge than an ordinary Believer was, to say nothing of the Unbelievers?

Kerim thought about the words of the Teacher, about how the knowledge would grow in him of itself, how the seed would of necessity sprout.

He looked up from the Holy Book and slowly closed it as if it were a jewel box. Not even his father had ever spoken to him like the Teacher. His father had not known much about the Faith and not thought about it either. Entirely devoted to the things of this world, he always only worried about the next day, the next week. Yet nothing of all that had remained—he had disappeared, just as everything and everyone in Kerim's life disappeared. When he thought of his father today, he seemed like a man who one does not recognize but whose shadow one perceives when he passes.

What remained of Kerim's brooding was the profound longing for a purity of belief which would be a purity of life. In the evenings, when he lay on the bed in his room, as he often did, the window open to the echoing sounds rising from the courtyard, the rattling of the dustbins, someone tinkering with a bicycle, the distant sound of a train and occasionally even the long tooting of a barge, then it did him good to think about his life so far, about his family, the time of his childhood. He thought about the English teacher, the school and all the prospects that then he still thought he had and how, after the death of his father, he had been thrown off course and had simply not found his way back. He searched for a meaning in what he had seen and done. It also distracted him from tormenting thoughts about Sonja but, more important, it brought him back to his concerns about himself, to the salvation of his soul and to his inner peace. It also gave him back the holy resolve with which he had listened to the words of the Teacher. He realized once more that while the words had always inspired him, the deeds had frightened him. Am I so weak that I cannot act in accordance with what I believe, in accordance with what I feel? He reproached himself and reconstructed every occasion in his life on which he thought he had failed. It all began with Anatol, then followed the death of his father, his flight from the Holy Warriors and the theft. He also felt responsible for Tony who perhaps had never been picked up from the island. His false life here weighed on him. He had even stolen the ring he had given Sonja, and the sight of the junkie whom he sometimes observed among the down-and-outs in front of the supermarket repeatedly reminded him of it. This ring meanwhile seemed to him like the symbol of a false love for Sonja, which he had wormed his way into, and also of her suspicion of him. The longing to be free of everything that was unspoken and free of his guilt awakened in him once more.

Sometimes on those evenings his mobile phone rang and he could see that it was Sonja. Agitated, breathing heavily, he didn't answer, snapped the device shut and threw it down on the bed beside him. Even my love of her, he thought, is not pure, it is full of lechery. Without ever having to marry her, without even knowing her any better, he believed he could have lusted after Sonja for ever. It was so much a celebration of the unfamiliar, of which he wanted to take possession, his need to do so was so powerful—he was not certain whether he might not have been able to kill this woman out of desire. The thought made him shudder. Yet there were those moments of frenzy in which he had wanted to throttle her in order to keep her for ever.

He thought of her and tried to understand what she expected of him. Suddenly, it became clear to him, that their life together would be a chain of ever-new arrangements to meet, that her love, their future together would be based only on that. Everyone here was free, there was no fixed order on which one could rely, that's why one constantly had to be asking questions about everything, had to go hunting things down and try to offer oneself, that's why there were losers in this game, those who had too little to offer, the ugly, the stupid or simply the clumsy. When one was at last with someone, then one even had to fight for time together and, on top of that, even be afraid that the time was too boring. Was not this never-ending struggle at the very heart of that bleak freedom, about which his Teacher had sometimes spoken, that freedom which leads to loneliness and also has just that purpose, to detach people from one another, to separate them from the unity, so that they spent their lives straying through empty space? Kerim remembered his words exactly: 'And think of the women. Everyone in the West tells you they should have the same rights, that they should be free. But no one is really free. What they want to achieve is that men and woman stand in opposition to each other instead of being there for each other. They try to persuade us that it's freedom, when each person only follows his own interests, only does what benefits him. And again it is objects whose slaves they become because they want to have more and more of them.'

'Why do they try to persuade us of that?'

'That's how they destroy order, the family, and make people, men and women, lonely. They marry, and when they divorce they fight each other like strangers for their property and their children. It's always about money, believe me, they're obsessed by it. It makes them cold and hard and yet it's the only thing they really believe in. They can't behave any other way, it's how they've been taught. Even if their films and books maintain the opposite, it's money and the things one can buy with it, that's their pitiful faith. They say they love freedom but their freedom is loneliness. They say they love life but this life is greed. They say progress but this progress only prepares the terrain which tomorrow they will exploit and destroy, untiring, empty and insatiable.'

Kerim thought further. Sonja and his uncle and, in an unpleasant way, perhaps also Amir, were the only people by whom he felt looked at, whose paths led not through him but to him.

Kerim came to a decision and asked Tarik for a carton big enough for all his things. The latter readily looked one out without asking any questions. He found a cardboard box, took out the packets of rice and tea and brought it to Kerim who carried it to his room without saying anything. He put everything he could find into it, his mobile phone, his watch, even the skates. In the box, they looked like two shiny crossed blades. It wasn't much that he had in front of him. He looked in his pockets for money and put that in too. Then he stood up, fetched the Holy Book, held it in his hand and decided to keep it. He kissed the cover and put it back where he had got it. It wouldn't have meant anything to her anyway. He closed the flaps of the box and stuck them down with tape. After that he sat down on the bed and stared at the carton. Yes, he encouraged himself, I want to be a different person, and this here is to be the past, I don't want to wait any longer.

He thought of the prayer group and the Algerian, who had behaved as if they had been friends for years. Again Kerim felt how powerfully he had heard the call of the Faith. The gentle, warm feeling of a trust wanted to rise up in him, spread around the room, and out through the windows and doors into the city. But it didn't happen. I allowed Hamid to go, he thought, I watched as he was blown to pieces and so many others with him. I am cursed to lose people. All who were close to me disappear behind me, that is my fate.

He stood up, closed the window, took the cardboard box under his arm and left the flat without saying goodbye to Tarik.

* * *

'Have you tried calling his uncle?' asked Stefan.

'Yes, no one answers,' replied Sonja.

'You know,' he said seriously, 'at some point, you should think about how often you've already said no.' Stefan was standing right up against her desk and leaning with one arm against the shelves along the wall, packed with software packages and files. The office window was open, and behind the heavy metal grate protecting the ground-floor rooms the birds were chirruping.

'I find him strange,' repeated Sonja.

'He's dark, he's slim, he's both naive and serious—everything we want, or isn't he?'

She glanced angrily at him.

'Why do you find him strange? Because he prays?'

'You don't understand, he's quite different. Everything about him is different.'

'So what? Basically everyone is different. The familiar is an illusion.'

She shook her head reluctantly and Stefan didn't let go. 'It's still a very, very long way off and it's an unpleasant thought, but one day, even your beauty, I don't mean to say it'll fade but—it could change. I don't know how many of the boys here have chatted you up. And you've always been a good girl and stayed with your cat. And then one day, just like that, you take up with someone you find strange.'

'It was something superficial—you won't understand—it was easy, it didn't take much. But now I'm afraid of him. I don't know who he is, I don't know what he does. You can't talk to him the way the two of us talk. And then he leaves this big cardboard box in front of my door, full of stuff. At first, I felt let down—does he believe in things so much? Does he perhaps want to please me with it?'

'And then?'

'Then I thought, it's a sign. The things must mean something to him. At any rate, he wrote his name on it.'

Stefan took his arm off the shelves and scratched his throat. He went around the desk to the window and gripped the bars of the grating with both hands. 'It's a sign.'

'OK,' she said, 'and what does it mean?'

Stefan began to rattle the bars. 'Maybe something like: Rescue me? It must touch your heart somehow, or not?'

'Goodness me,' she muttered. 'I'm stopping this now, Stefan. Is that OK?'

He went on looking out through the grating. 'Yes, leave the computer on, I'll do some more on it.'

'You could hardly interpret the sign more theatrically, could you?' she asked.

He thrust himself away from the bars and turned to her. 'Well, what do I know?' he said. 'No idea how someone like that ticks.'

'You know,' said Sonja, as she rose from her chair, 'I like being with him. But when I am with him, I always feel a bit sorry for him at the same time. What I'm doing isn't good.'

'You're not taking him seriously. To listen to you talking, it's as if he were a child. If you want to change something about that, you should respond to the box.' Stefan threw himself into the office chair and spun right around once. 'Well,' he said then, 'you're probably quite out of practice, when it comes to men.'

Stefan rose quickly, went quietly to the door of the room and flung it open. Startled, her colleague Till jumped back and his hand went up to the side of his big black glasses. He had evidently been eavesdropping.

He was already on his way back to his desk when he stopped, briefly shook his purposefully unkempt hair and, ignoring his boss, said to her, 'You better watch out, Sonja, maybe he's a fundamentalist. He'll make you have eight children and you'll have to wear a headscarf. I'm serious. Something like that happened to a woman I know.'

'Nice one, Till. You know that your opinion is almost as important to us as your work,' said Stefan, waited till the other had sat down behind his computer screen and carefully shut the door.

***

Kerim heard the doorbell. Shortly after that, as so often before, his uncle knocked cautiously at his room door. The light from the hall burst into the room. Dazzled, Kerim screwed up his eyes. Sonja was standing there, holding the cardboard box. When Tarik had closed the door behind her, she put the carton beside the bed, took off her shoes and squatted in front of Kerim. Gently, she took his face in both hands and raised his head.

'What's wrong? I've been worried about you. What are you doing here?'

Kerim didn't reply. He looked at her and saw her, although she was so close to him, as if from a great distance. Even if he had wanted to, he would not have been capable of telling her.

'Are you lovesick because of me?' she said and stroked the cleft of his chin with her thumb. She was so close that he could not have moved without touching her.

It was the first time Kerim had heard the word and he understood it immediately. It was a lovesickness that he felt but in quite a different way from what she meant. He had been abandoned. It was as his Teacher had once described.

'You will lose confidence when God leaves you. Confidence is His strength in you. Then you will be very lonely, a leaf in the wind, detached from the tree, a shard in the sand.'

Kerim remembered how proud he had been that his Teacher at times made such an effort with him, just to explain things. There was a sparkle in his eyes on those occasions, the ever-new words he found for his thoughts made him happy.

He didn't respond to her hand which, as so often before, gently felt its way up his thigh. This time she couldn't seduce him, she did not succeed in casting her spell over him, which on other occasions had placed him at her mercy. She stood up and looked down at him and he sensed her uncertainty. She glanced around the room, as if she was looking for something familiar, something to hold on to. But he let her go without a word of encouragement. Later, he would try to look for and find the right words of comfort. He heard her footsteps outside in the flat and sank, heavy as a stone, back into his memories. He was lying once again on a hill. From there, the burnt ruins of the village could be clearly seen. The rise of the hill provided them with just enough cover so that they could not be seen from the highway. It was empty and cut through the hills in a straight line before dissolving in the blue-grey haze of the horizon. Mukhtar told them to pass the binoculars from man to man, each should have a good idea of the place where they would face the foreign devils for the first time. The operation was for training purposes—they were not filming.

Kerim focused the lenses and swallowed, his mouth was dry. He was unable to hold the binoculars steady. His hands were shaking and they were shaking with fear. His gaze passed over the charred beams of the houses, the scattered plastic tanks, blackened walls, a pale, unharmed stepladder and the grey-brown corpses lying around, staring at the sky open-mouthed, their eyes dark splotches. Some seemed to be grinning, all appeared small. Beside their heads, it was as if tar had run into the sand from the black gaping cuts in their throats. Finally, he saw his own car, the old Toyota, at an angle to the road, two tyres in the sand, yellow with dust and seemingly forgotten by everyone.

Kerim swallowed again, raised the binoculars, saw the ridge of hills beyond the road and the narrow procession of trees on the crest, as if the true inhabitants were leaving the village there. He heard Mukhtar wheezing beside him and himself breathed even more softly. He had seen what this man was capable of. A couple of days earlier, they had entered the village to kill the inhabitants. No one knew why but now, after the invasion, they were at war and, the Teacher repeated it again and again—anyone who cooperated with the occupiers, or even merely tolerated them, was an enemy.

Their opponents were unprepared. With a couple of salvos, they had driven them together on the narrow approach to the highway. Mukhtar ordered them all, men, women and children, to kneel and killed them one after another with his knife. If there is something like blood lust, then, so Kerim had known since that day, he had seen it in Mukhtar's eyes, insatiable.

Afterwards, Mukhtar had shown each of them the bloody knife. He stopped in front of Kerim, looked into his eyes and saw his horror. He waited for a moment, shaking his head, and then wiped the blade on Kerim's cheek. Kerim was certain that he had been marked. He would be the next in the series of self-sacrificing martyrs, because with every operation Mukhtar trusted him less.

Now Kerim was looking down on the destroyed village and waiting with the others for the American patrol which was responsible for this area. He was about to pass on the binoculars as the sound of engines became audible. Mukhtar immediately gripped his hand and pressed it down in the sand. Two Humvees, broad, armoured general-purpose vehicles, came racing along. They were coming from the nearest town and had let some time pass before making their visit. When they came level with the destroyed village, they braked and rolled forward at walking pace. Like the others, Kerim gripped his rifle more firmly, in order, as they had learnt, to open fire after the explosion. The soldiers in the Humvees hesitated. Rashid was ready, his glasses in one hand, in the other the mobile phone which he was using for the remote-controlled detonation this time. They were still too far from the booby-trapped car, however. Then they did something no one had anticipated—they accelerated and raced past Kerim's car. Nevertheless, Rashid made the attempt. The detonation half-flung the rear vehicle off the track but they all knew immediately that the attack had failed. Both Humvees came to a halt, it was a few seconds before the armoured doors on the far side opened. Mukhtar still waited. He pointed at the vehicles, as if to say, That's what happens when the explosion misses them. In fact, not a single American was to be seen.

Kerim almost regretted it. He would at last have liked to see the Crusaders in the flesh, these men from a distant country with sky-high buildings, the country that ruled the world. These people who believed only in the worst in everything, who were convinced that with their money and their weapons they could subjugate every other culture, who marched into foreign lands without bothering about the inhabitants, who profaned everything they touched and even took pleasure in it. The Teacher had shown them in films, had talked about their contempt for other nations but, above all, for the Faithful. They were the embodiment of unbelief, spreading in its messengers like a disease. All that he saw, however, were these general-purpose vehicles with curved gratings in front of the radiators and the small bulletproof glass slits in the doors.

The Anwari brothers wanted to know whether they should open fire, Mukhtar signalled them not to. Keeping low, the group stole along the top of the rise. Where the hill came to an end, a couple of broken-down walls gave them cover. They crouched in a row, leant back against the remains and waited for the order to run. Mukhtar made his way up the hill and glanced down at the Humvees. He returned and told them the Americans had a free field of fire in the thirty yards until they could get behind the next rise. He instructed the brothers to draw the Americans' fire on the hill and then to quickly follow the others at a suitable moment. Mukhtar assumed that the Americans wouldn't pursue them out of fear of booby traps, all they had to manage were those thirty yards. The brothers took up position and, at a signal, opened fire. The others began running immediately. At first, nothing happened, Kerim only heard the shots from the hill. Then the answering fire began but it didn't seem to be aimed at those who were fleeing. Kerim stayed behind Rashid—even if he had wanted to, he would not have been capable of overtaking him. They had almost reached the rise when Kerim became aware of the bullets striking around him and, in a surge of panic, realized how accurately the Americans were firing at this distance and with what rapidity. As he ran, thoughts chased through his head—we're poorly armed; and—I don't want to die. He was ashamed but he couldn't stop thinking it. Mukhtar struck him on the back with the flat of his hand because he was falling behind. Never more than now did Kerim feel that he had lost his way. He drew his head down between his shoulders, screwed up his eyes and expected at every moment that he was going to be hit.

Yet nothing happened. They went into position behind the next hill and Mukhtar ordered them to keep on firing at the Humvees until the brothers had reached them. The pair almost made it. In the last few yards, a bullet struck the older brother in the face. Kerim clearly saw something small flying through the air. The man uttered a suppressed cry, remained on his feet, didn't collapse, but began to stagger, holding both hands to his cheeks. His younger brother was beside him immediately and pulled him along.

Behind the rise, Mukhtar wanted to pull the hands away as the man looked at him with huge, fear-filled eyes. However, he didn't manage to. His trembling, blood-smeared fingers on his cheeks, the man spat blood into the sand. His brother asked him if he could open his mouth, but he just shook his head. He couldn't speak, wheezed, and Mukhtar calmed him with astonishing care. To all appearances, the bullet had gone through his cheeks. Mukhtar grabbed the man's wrist and pulled him to his feet and, for a moment, the absurd hole could be seen as on the punctured photo of a face.

***

When Kerim left his room again, he tried to behave as normally as possible with his uncle and Hussein. They made it easy for him, had probably agreed not to bother him. Even over the meal, they only chatted about all kinds of trivia.

The next afternoon, Tarik had gone to the market and afterwards wanted to go to his member's cafe. Kerim and his cousin were sitting over a game of backgammon. The windows were wide open and Hussein was enjoying the freedom to smoke whenever he wanted. The doorbell rang and Kerim got up, certain that he would have to get rid of a sales rep. Usually they were from Internet companies. This time, however, it was two Arabs, in suits and ties. They had just been deciphering the names at the door and now straightened up.

Kerim was immediately ashamed to be standing in front of these gentlemen—they were in their best clothes while he was still in his pyjamas. Both men were carrying slim leather cases and the older of the two immediately began to address Kerim. He skilfully used their common language as a bridge. He was very polite and finally explained that they were Jehovah's Witnesses. Kerim had no idea at all what that meant, so he asked. Gratefully, the man took up the question and used it as an opportunity for an explanation. Then followed a short pause during which Kerim didn't exactly know what he should do. He felt it was now probably appropriate to invite the two of them inside. He himself was curious, he hesitated principally because of Hussein. The man said it wouldn't take long but if it wasn't suitable just now, they could come again. In the end, Kerim let them in.

In the hall, the men took off their shoes. They also introduced themselves to Hussein who, slouched on the settee, had been watching the TV with the sound down and now, startled, stood up. They sat down at the low living-room table, placed their cases in front and opened them. They did it simultaneously, as if it had been rehearsed. Each took a couple of brochures out of their case, snapped it shut again and placed the papers on top. The man who had spoken to Kerim was evidently the boss. The younger one, who had an almost sickly pale complexion, constantly glanced at the other who was talking and insistently gesticulating. Kerim was certain that the younger man wanted to learn what the other had already mastered. Except that Kerim wondered what that might be.

He went into the kitchen to make tea. From there, he heard the older man begin to chat. He talked a little about his childhood in Damascus, asked about Hussein's origin, then went on to outline the odyssey of his life, which had taken him by way of the US to Canada, Great Britain and, finally, Germany. Then he got down to the point. As Kerim brought in the tray, placed the tea and the remaining cakes, distributed on two plates, in front of the pair, the man was asking whether they had ever thought seriously about the end of the world. Kerim and Hussein looked at each other and shook their heads. The man had just taken a bite out of a piece of cake and was still chewing as he continued. He spoke of a war that came at the end of the world, about which men had known since ancient times and which in the holy texts was called Armageddon. He paused and looked searchingly at Hussein. The latter said he had never heard of it. Armageddon, explained the man, was no war like those they all knew more than enough about. No nations, generals, states would fight each other, no terrorists and armies. Instead, all the kings, generals, heads of government, all the rulers of the world would join together to fight against the 'hosts of heaven' which were commanded by Jesus Christ. Silence fell. The pale man relaxed a little and drank some tea. He made an effort not to slurp. The older man leafed through his brochures and then quoted: '*Jeremiah declared in his prophecy, that those slain by Jehovah will lie scattered from one end of the earth to the other end of the earth.*' Again there was a short silence. The man said that, even if no one knew when precisely, this War of the Last Days was close. Biblical prophecies, which had been fulfilled, definitely proved that since 1914, humanity had been living in the Last Days of its epoch. They, the Jehovah's Witnesses, knew that the great destruction was imminent and they could point the way for them to survive this catastrophe. Because for a God-fearing person, this war was exactly what he had already been anticipating for a long time—the decisive battle by which God would enforce his claim to rule the earth.

Hussein nodded. The man allowed a few seconds to pass, then, open-mouthed, he bit off another piece of cake and followed it with a mouthful of tea. He really seemed to like it and that pleased Kerim. The man took off his glasses and polished the lenses with a handkerchief. Outside the window, the bottle bank was noisily emptied. The exhaust fumes of the truck could be smelt even inside the flat. Since the man realized that Kerim and Hussein didn't know what to make of what he was telling them, he offered to leave information material with them, gave them an address and indicated to his student that the show was over. He rose, said he would be very happy if they were interested in finding out more and got ready to go.

At that moment, Hussein switched on the TV sound. The news came white on red in big letters from CNN. The 'Number Two of the Al-Qaeda Network' had been wounded and taken prisoner in the border area between Afghanistan and Pakistan. After the news-reader had announced that, the programme switched to a correspondent who half-faced the camera, half-faced the mountain landscape in the background.

The two visitors listened only briefly, then took their leave. Kerim accompanied them to the door. They said goodbye with a few polite phrases and immediately turned their attention to checking the nameplates of tenants for Arab-sounding ones.

When Kerim came back into the room, Hussein had changed to a German channel. As it turned out, military circles had already confirmed the detention of this important leader of the organization. Unconfirmed, on the other hand, was a rumour that German secret service agents had a hand in the capture. There was no evidence of their active involvement, yet it was reported by various, usually well-informed sources.

Hussein stared mesmerized at the TV, drawing nervously on his cigarette, but appeared in no mood to talk about it.

Only later did Kerim grasp the importance of the event. In his time here, he had seen many TV news broadcasts, he had followed the violent protests during the Muhammad-cartoons controversy, as it was called and, with a mixture of disbelief, astonishment and a kind of pain of loss, watched the all-powerful Dictator of Baghdad take his last walk. This time, however, the far-distant events reached directly into his own life.

When his uncle returned home in the evening and was just as tight-lipped as Hussein, Kerim imagined he could sense the quiet threat that was in the air. Tarik merely shook his head when he asked him about it.

'For us here, none of that is any good,' he said. He was about to turn away but then added, 'When I was young, these religious people were regarded as backward and wrong-headed. Not even Ferid would have joined them. And today, the whole world is preoccupied with them. What does it mean?'

When his uncle saw the brochures lying on the table, he asked who had brought them and Kerim told him. Tarik leafed carelessly through them before finally concluding, 'The stuff is printed in America.'

He took the pile into the kitchen and threw it away.

The feeling of tension didn't disappear and became even stronger the next day when Kerim, late enough, after he had hidden himself away for so long, went out to look for Amir. But it was Reda whom he ran into, smoking outside the Internet cafe. He had always had the feeling with Reda of not being really accepted.

This time, too, he remained completely indifferent when Kerim spoke to him. He didn't even turn his head but looked away from him down the street.

'Have you seen Amir?' asked Kerim. 'Is he inside?'

Reda shook his head. His hair was different from before. It was completely shaved off at the sides.

'Where is he?'

Reda raised his shoulders.

Kerim glanced into the cafe through the open door. The others were sitting in front of the screens, but only Hanif raised his hand in greeting.

'How long is it since you've seen him?'

'A while.'

Kerim thought. 'Is he at his flat?'

'No. No mobile phone, nothing. No one knows anything.' Reda spat on the pavement. 'Perhaps he's dead. We don't know,' he said finally, stepped on his cigarette end and went inside without saying goodbye to Kerim.

4

A week passed during which Kerim didn't stop wishing that he could stuff back into his mouth the words he had said to Amir. The sentences had burst out of him more than he had spoken them and he very much hoped that the strident argument of the couple in the snack bar had made them ordinary and smaller. Amir's reaction, however, made him fear the worst. He had absorbed these words like long-parched earth soaking up a torrent of water. It worried Kerim to hear that Amir had disappeared, and his disquiet was constantly intensified during those days by the warnings of terrorist attacks in Germany, one following on the heels of the next. If one watched the TV news, one could get the impression that well-hidden but always active government agencies were trying to outdo one another in the art of unsettling the population just enough to make sure that it would still keep quiet. Airports increased their security checks, public buildings were cordoned off almost to the point of inaccessibility, there were warnings about attending large-scale sports events and concerts. But the life of people in the quarter went on as before—for them, nothing seemed to have happened.

Kerim didn't find a solution for his own problem either, he simply became a bit calmer. Sometimes he watched Uncle Tarik going about his daily tasks, preparing food in the kitchen, reading the newspaper and commenting on world events, taking his leave and going to his cafe. Secretly, he admired him for his equanimity in all the business of living. Was not Uncle Tarik, too, Kerim asked himself, a refugee? Had not he, too, early on, burnt all his bridges behind him in order to begin a new life here in Europe? Even if he kept in touch with the homeland, he really had very little to do with the people there. Having settled down long ago, it didn't seem to bother him that, in all likelihood, he would end his life here. He had never talked of going back, not even for just one visit. This thought didn't leave Kerim in peace, so once he asked his uncle about it.

Uncle Tarik reflected.

'Yes, perhaps one day, when the situation improves. But I'm old.'

Kerim asked him if he never felt homesick, and his uncle answered, 'Earlier very much so, but then not for a long time, and now it's slowly coming back. You'll see, if you stay here, it'll be exactly the same for you.'

Kerim was not very satisfied with the reply. The thought—whether in time one could not perhaps, after all, learn to forget the things that lay behind one—preoccupied him. Then again he had to think of his father who had died without true Faith. Something much the same would happen to Uncle Tarik, even if in a different way.

Finally, he decided to go and look for Amir. While everyone still told him that he had disappeared, they seemed quite indifferent about it. It was probably Amir's strength and reserve that freed them from any concern.

Kerim found out where the jeweller's shop of Amir's father was and went there. It was small place, squeezed between a betting office and a second-hand clothes shop. There was one small bargain shop after another and the pavement was crowded with people, one had to watch where one walked. All kinds of gold jewellery as well as watches were on show in the security-protected display window, the heavy door was fortified with a grille. Once he was standing in the shop, Kerim felt as if he was at home again. The people hurrying past outside, the very slight smell of carnations in the air and the silence between all the small things displayed for sale in subdued light, which actually looked as if they had all been forgotten, filled Kerim with melancholy and pleasure.

Behind the glass counter, there was a passageway, its entrance screened by a plastic string curtain. Kerim clearly felt someone watching him from there. Two hands pushed through the strings, parted them and Mohammed stepped out. It really was hard to believe that, in the distant past, this man could have carried out an armed robbery. He placed his hands on the glass table and greeted Kerim. The latter briefly described what was on his mind, not forgetting to mention that he was worried about Amir. The man's smooth features darkened. He pushed out his lower lip and there was something about his expression that seemed he'd been offended. He told Kerim that he had guessed he was not here to buy wedding jewellery. He knew nothing about Amir's whereabouts. Looking mistrustful, Mohammed asked once again where and how exactly they had met. Kerim said something about a chance meeting on the street where he lived. He hadn't finished yet when Mohammed was already shaking his head and he began to talk about his son, just as if he had, for a long time, been waiting for someone to whom he could confide it all. Distractedly, he fumbled for his cigarettes, held out the packet to Kerim. After the latter had declined, he put the packet aside and quite simply forgot to smoke himself.

Mohammed related that Amir, his firstborn, had always got privileged treatment, emphasized that he had had all the material conditions to grow up decently. And in the beginning, everything appeared to be going well, he was very ambitious. But then something had happened to him, something mysterious. It was not that his ambition had left him but all the things that ambition was directed at were suddenly no longer enough. Perhaps, speculated his father, it had at some point become too easy for him to get recognition. Whatever he did, it didn't challenge him enough. He found life boring. The man raised both hands defensively. He had never asked of Amir that he become a doctor or a wealthy businessman, nothing of the kind. But he should surely have had to do something. He looked past Kerim, as if he was trying to remember, then he began again. It was no use being strong, he said. Here in this country, one had to be patient and smart, learn a lot. He talked about the kitchen of an Arab restaurant in which Amir had been a temporary worker. One of his colleagues challenged him, said the lentil soup would taste better if there was a little blood in it. At that Amir cut open his hand with a butcher's knife and held it over the soup pot.

'His blood in the food,' said the man. 'And that in these days. The intrepid hero, he didn't stick it out at anything. His sisters have turned out so well, the opposite of him.' He shook his head. 'If he has an idea, any idea, and he believes in it, even briefly, then he does it.' He met Kerim's eyes and raised his forefinger. 'Once I said to him, so that he understands: Life is like this Internet, you must want something definite in order to be successful. If not, you can have a bit of fun with it, but really you're just wasting time. Be careful with him, he does everything without reflecting. It was the same with his son. He had known this woman for a month. He'll have nothing. In the end, he'll have nothing.'

Kerim had long ago grasped that he had come here in vain. He cautiously began taking his leave, saying that he wanted to keep on looking. He had to promise Mohammed that he would come back and report. When he finally left the shop, he was firmly resolved to go to the mosque the Algerian had told him about. If he didn't find Amir there, he thought, then he wouldn't find him anywhere.

He stood on the street and his gaze wandered over a ninety-nine-cent store, a shop for paints and artist's materials, a sex shop, kebab shops, greengrocers. In the distance, he spotted a clock and realized that he could still get there in time for evening prayers. He walked, taking exactly the route that the Algerian, at his request, had described.

* * *

After one and a half hours, he reached the trading estate. It consisted of extensive groups of buildings protected by fences and video cameras. The roads were deserted. There was a background rumble and the smell of tobacco in the air. Right in the middle of the factory buildings, there were detached houses with flat roofs and large windows. Kerim saw the light behind the thick curtains and imagined how, in the mornings, the people there stepped out onto their plant-covered balconies and had a view of stacks of wooden palettes, of railway tracks which ran along the roads from factory to factory, of excavators and trucks. Not far away, an illuminated Marlboro man, as tall as a house, towered up, a lasso in one hand, the cigarette in the other. On the horizon, a block-like silo was sharply outlined against the reddish-violet sky. A tiny window shone at the very top.

He walked through the tunnel of light of street-lamps and looked for the side street the Algerian had told him about. The rhythmic sound of a moving train was audible in the distance. He was more and more confused by the abandoned landscape. He stopped, looked around, saw a gatehouse about as big as a kiosk. It was brightly lit up but empty, a paper cup on the plastic table and a tobacco pipe. Next to the little building was a parking lot, above it the glass front of the main building bathed in neon light. In the factory hall, hoses hung in folds from the ceiling like strange beasts, their huge jaws sunk into machinery casings. He saw a jumble of struts, pipes. Behind that, gratings and yellowish lockers. Not a soul far and wide.

Along the factory fence, he followed a sandy footpath between bushes and trees. There was a lonely traffic light, it showed red. The leaves on the trees, the grass, in fact, everything, was covered in the unreal gleam of the streetlights. Kerim noticed the security camera on the wall of the building which, as if moved by an invisible hand, turned in his direction. In front of a low section of the building, he looked into the rooms for the workforce. Linoleum floors, yellow light, a red drinks machine. Here, too, everything was deserted. He saw clothes hooks on a frame which ran above benches in the middle of the room. Posters on the walls, a rabbit, a basket overflowing with kittens. He remained standing for a moment, became aware of a quiet clicking and discovered another remote-controlled camera.

He passed roofed gates, loading ramps, dark windows, carefully marked-off strips of lawn, neatly planted with young trees and flowers, and signs that warned against stealing the plants. He saw many more of the deserted gatehouses and of those lonely, lit-up windows. And it all reminded him of the deck of the *Sea Star*, as he had, only briefly, seen it on the night he crept on board. Then, too, he had heard the unceasing noise of machinery and everything he saw around him had been guarded and yet unprotected.

He recognized the mosque from the distance because of the many parked cars in front of it and the people going in. It was a flat-roofed building like all the buildings here, it looked like the casing of a machine. Kerim's need for something familiar in this landscape intensified the closer he came to the building. Because he didn't feel like the newcomer in a strange community, he paid no attention to the groups of people, to the alert and curious glances cast in his direction. All his attention was focused on the unadorned building at the far end of the parking lot, the open heavy double door. The murmur of voices from the prayer room drew him irresistibly on. A couple of men stood casually at the entrance, only an older one looked closely at him. Their eyes briefly met and the thought went through Kerim's mind—what would it be like to meet someone else here he knew, someone apart from Amir? His movements became slower, suddenly uncertain, he placed his shoes with the many piled against the wall and took his time doing it.

The prayer room, a former factory hall, was well filled. Here he was now among all the people from this part of the city that he didn't know. Kerim saw nothing of what the Algerian, in his conspiratorial fashion, had suggested. Around him there were only ordinary men such as one could see everywhere in the streets here, family men, men like his uncle, looking for conversation with others of their generation, and very young men who, wherever they were standing, spread the atmosphere of a youth club. Kerim's eyes scanned every corner of the room, searching for someone who looked special or behaved in an unusual way. Yet, even by the two sets of shelves with pamphlets and books, and even in front of the shabby desk, an old, yellowish, tarnished computer screen on it, he saw only inconspicuous visitors. No one here knows you, he told himself, reassured and resolved, after prayers, to ask a couple of these men about Amir.

At the other end of the hall, a fire door, on which a faded sticker showed a crossed-out flame, opened. The imam appeared. Kerim craned his neck to catch a glimpse of the neighbouring room but without success. The imam was a slight man. He was wearing light, rimless glasses that made him look like a teacher. His shirt under the black woollen waistcoat was as snow white as his turban cloth. His beard was not exaggeratedly long, dark brown with a few red strands through it. He gave a friendly nod to those around him and, without any further instruction, the faithful formed up in several rows in front of him. The imam raised his hands and began the recitation. The prayer took its course and Kerim once again entered the community of Believers, which here, in this place, seemed more abstract, more remote from everyday concerns than ever before in his life.

In the next few minutes, he was briefly filled with the old fervour and, as so often before, his injured self-confidence was renewed and his heart swelled. This time, however, he didn't quite manage to lose himself in the prayer. His eyes wandered over the backs of the men in front of him. Only during the prostrations did he close his eyes. When he had straightened up, he once again began looking closely at those standing around him. As if he had a foreboding that his earlier reassurance had been premature, he was still searching for anyone he knew. And indeed his glance settled on a younger, very slim man two rows in front of him. His posture alone, a presentiment of his profile, seen at an angle from behind, and a small part of his spectacles frame were enough to startle Kerim. His next impulse was to leave the prayer room instantly but he could not do that without attracting attention.

After the prayer, he went on observing the man but kept his distance. He was always facing away. He seemed to be well known among the Believers, went up to a number people and had short conversations with them. Several times Kerim changed his position in the room in order to get a better view but without success. Despite his talkativeness, the man gave the impression of being in a hurry. Kerim observed him glancing over at the fire door more than once before turning back to the person he was talking to and raising his hand apologetically. Finally, after a few words of goodbye, he left the room. He kept his eyes on the floor and really did seem to be in a hurry. Kerim waited until the other had drawn level and walked parallel with him at a distance of a few yards. Now he saw his full profile, the narrowed slits of eyes behind the spectacles. He recognized Rashid. Yet could hardly believe it, torn between irrepressible joy at seeing him again and paralysing fear. The man left the room in the direction of the parking lot, Kerim remained standing and considered what he should do.

He stuffed his shirt back in his trousers, straightened his waistband and looked for people he could ask about Amir. There was nothing else he could do except address someone at random. So he went over to the imam who was standing in the middle of a group of young men. When the prayer leader saw Kerim, he interrupted the conversation with a gesture. He looked at Kerim with an open expression and the latter put his question. The imam reflected for a moment and then called over a big, fat man with an imposing moustache, who came over immediately. He folded his fists in front of his stomach and lines furrowed his forehead as if the question, which the imam now repeated, was difficult to understand. He puffed out his cheeks and shook his head. Kerim looked at the men around him, no one seemed interested in replying. As a result, he could only take his leave and accept that he would leave worried but without having accomplished anything.

Outside in the parking lot, men were still standing in groups and smoking. The evening air was pleasantly cool and the smell of tobacco blew over in gusts from the cigarette factory.

Kerim was already on his way back. The creaking of a door abruptly interrupted his thoughts, he looked in the direction from which the sound came. About twenty yards away, several men were leaving the building by a side-entrance. Rashid was also among them, and Kerim was immediately certain that the big man walking at the front, who was already holding the keys to a new utility vehicle in his hand, was Amir. Kerim couldn't bring himself to call out to him, he was too agitated by the fact that fate had brought these very two together. Just as he was about to do so nevertheless, his gaze went back to the smaller man who had remained a few steps behind. This time he looked over at Kerim. As their eyes met, Kerim was finally certain and only now was he shaken by an icy shudder. The shock made him gasp for air, he recoiled, as if he wanted to hide behind the curtain of cigarette smoke. He quickly turned away and took a few steps in the opposite direction. He stopped, looked at the ground, tried to pull himself together and again looked towards where the man had been standing. But he was already gone. The utility vehicle was started, the engine roared and, tyres squealing, it raced past, no one could be recognized behind the dark windows. The vehicle braked sharply once, at the gate, before disappearing.

Kerim's heart was racing, helplessly he looked around and didn't know what to do. He saw me, he thought again and again. He felt so tense that he couldn't leave the parking lot. Nothing could help him apart from time and the sight of these unknown men, for whom nothing had happened and who, little by little, took their leave of one another and went to their cars.

Suddenly, there were warning shouts and exclamations of surprise from the direction of the street. Everyone looked towards the fence around the place, by which a column of police vans was drawing to a halt. In no time at all, the police stormed the mosque grounds, two at the rear shut the gate. The policemen pushed those still standing around aside and headed straight through the open door of the prayer room. Cries of protest rose, hasty steps could be heard. Two of the policemen who had remained outside discovered the side entrance. The shouts from the prayer room became louder, one voice literally cracked with rage. Kerim went back inside.

The policemen were standing in the factory hall and looking around. He had the impression they were surprised at what they found. What on earth can they have expected? he thought, as he saw these men, who in their helmets and protective suits seemed to have come from another world and unfortunately landed at just this place. The fat man, whom the imam had waved over when Kerim asked his question, shouted the loudest. Probably he was a hall attendant, he looked at the floor and harangued the policemen in Arabic without stopping. They eyed his every movement suspiciously and didn't understand that he was, above all, upset about their boots, with which they were soiling the great carpet. The general uproar could only briefly distract Kerim from his shock, it returned again like the intense memory of a nightmare. He moved away from the group which was vacillating between curiosity and anger, took a few steps to the side and simply lay down on the freshly mown grass beside the entrance.

As he couldn't leave the site anyway, he closed his eyes and tried to breathe as calmly as possible, but his fear, and on top of that the police raid, inevitably led his thoughts back into the past. In the early days, they only found shelter in the villages close to the frontier. Here, where the foothills of the Kurdistan mountains gave way to a dry steppe landscape, the country was flat, crossed only by a few highways. Patrols in this region were especially dangerous for the occupiers. The land provided no cover, so all they could do was race past the settlements. They hardly ever strayed into one of these little towns. Here the resistance groups had their supporters, many of their own free will, some out of fear.

They maintained a kind of provisional headquarters in the house of one large family. The head of the household was a wealthy, curiously nervous and yet reliable supporter. People like him feared the new order, they feared for their property, their family, their future. The group was given a room with several computers at the back of the house. When the Holy Warriors gathered there, they spent the time in the middle of the man's family, his parents, his wife as well as his eight children. While the members of the group prepared the films, which others would later put on the Web, they were surrounded by the shouting of children; sometimes one could even hear them on the finished clips. It was clear to Mukhtar that the propaganda was just as important as the operations themselves. Consequently, he left Rashid and Kerim in peace when they worked at the computers. Kerim remembered how much he enjoyed the air-conditioned rooms of the house despite the noise. Rashid taught him everything he needed to know. During the editing and when they added sound using militant songs which they recorded and then mixed in at appropriate points, he had the feeling that he was himself again. Of course, he could not talk about how he was shocked by the things their group was doing, least of all to Rashid who, good-natured and friendly as ever, worked beside him. But he was able to reflect. About the fact that during a power cut, when half out of curiosity, half by chance, he had been in the family's big bedroom on the floor above, he had come upon the casket with the money. He had at once thought that the drawer in the old sideboard was unusually heavy and, when he saw the iron box, he already guessed what was inside. He didn't look for the key but simply found it because it was lying next to the box in the same drawer. The windows in the big room were open, yet the draught was only sufficient to stir the light brown curtains drawn across them. Kerim had never seen so much money and yet it wasn't that alone which made the scene unforgettable for him. It was the feeling of domestic security, the peaceful everyday atmosphere that suddenly enclosed him and made him aware of how far away he had been from anything like it in the preceding months. A room, the mild light of a late afternoon, the smell of dried carnations in the air and, from outside, the steps of people hurrying past, busy with quite different things—all that made him suddenly both tired and melancholy. Then, as today, he would not have been able to say whether the decision to flee had to do with what he had been forced to see or whether he was quite simply exhausted.

When the power came on again, he sat at the computer with Rashid and worked on the pictures of the killing of the villagers. Since the purpose of the clip was to spread fear and terror among enemies and all those who were willing through treachery to become so, they could only edit out long shots. So again and again, he saw Mukhtar going along the row of kneeling, bound villagers—each time, Mukhtar gripped one after another under the chin from behind, pulled up the head and cut the victim's throat. They lowered the volume of the sounds of horror, the gurgling choking of the dying, the bubbling and whistling of their breath suffocating in blood, saw Mukhtar grabbing and holding the head of the last in the row, a young man. Carefully, following the throat as it protruded further, he separated head from trunk and held it up. Kerim again saw Mukhtar's fist and the half shut eyes of the dying face, and again he felt the hot wind, filling the silence and making it difficult for him to breathe.

Only his fear of Mukhtar still made him behave as if nothing had happened. Kerim suspected that the leader was waiting for the sign from him that he would be the next to sacrifice himself. But even if he said nothing, he was lost.

His moment came much earlier than he had expected. The family had gone out, only their ten-year-old boy had been left behind to look after the house. The children of the neighbourhood, who had been keeping watch for them all day in the unlikely event of a patrol approaching, really did raise the alarm early in the evening. Rashid instantly leapt up and ran out of the room to hear what had happened. Mukhtar was waiting for him outside and said he should disappear through the back door. All the other men had already gone. Mukhtar didn't wait for Kerim, perhaps he simply forgot him. He heard the footsteps fading away, calmly got up from his swivel chair, left the room and went upstairs. There he met the boy who was playing with a wooden pistol. Kerim pushed the toy out of his hand and loudly ordered him to go down and see if the Americans were coming. The boy obeyed, Kerim hurried into the bedroom and discovered that the drawer was locked. His heart cramped with disappointment. Then he broke open the lock with his combat knife and lifted out the casket. He was prepared to take the whole thing away with him, but it was open. He grabbed the bundle of banknotes and, still holding it, went downstairs.

Outside, foreign-sounding shouts and the heavy tread of feet could be heard. They know exactly where to look, thought Kerim, an indication of how many traitors there were in the town. The boy came back, just as Kerim had returned to the computer room to fetch Rashid's cloth bag which was still hanging over his chair. The son of the house watched as he stuffed the money into the bag but didn't seem to understand what he was seeing. The boy said the foreigners were at the courtyard gate and, at that moment, Kerim already heard them beating and kicking against the metal. Perhaps now, he thought, I will finally see them—the desecrators of the holy places, the masters of the world, who have stepped down from their glass towers and space stations and have come here in planes and ships to fight me, Kerim, the cook.

The iron gate gave way at the very moment he jumped into the open through the back door. He could clearly make out the prints Mukhtar's boots had left in the sand, they were unnaturally broad, as if he had stepped in each one twice. He followed the garden walls until he came to a crowded alley. He knew that the American raid could give him the vital start he needed in order to survive. The members of the group would scatter and no doubt sit tight for quite a while before they gathered again.

He still saw the footprints, went in the opposite direction and walked, not too fast, not too slow, his heart racing, knowing that now, with the money in the bag he was carrying, there was no way back for him.

He opened his eyes, repeatedly he said to himself, It can't be, it's completely impossible. The whole of the last week, the doubts of Sonja's love, all of it makes your nerves flutter. He thought back on the wearisome proceedings he had gone through. How could Rashid contrive to walk around freely here? And the longer he talked to himself, the more he believed it. The footsteps and the shouting around him were still unsettling, but the one whom he had thought he had recognized, who was so closely bound up with his past life, faded away into a phantom.

5

Not until weeks later did Amir return to his flat, and he came late in the evening, so that no one saw him. It was very likely that this would be his last visit, because from now on he would have to be prepared. That was on his mind as he hurried up the dark stairs, looked around once again on the steps as if he wanted to take leave of even the most unremarkable things. He unlocked the door to the flat and switched on the light in the hall. He didn't need any more illumination than that. He went into the room and saw the three most important objects there: the mattress on the floor, the wide-screen TV and his water pipe.

He stepped over to the window, pushed the old curtains aside and looked down into the evening street. Scratching his already luxuriantly sprouting beard, he remembered how often he had looked out here, in how many different moods, from despondency to indifference. To him, the room meant restriction, loneliness and also an untenable kind of freedom. For a very short time, they had been a family, here, in an flat that was far too small. As he thought about it now, he gave a bitter, silent laugh. He had never felt any of it. He had known for a long time that he had never believed in this idyll, that he had always been waiting for it to fail. He had tried so hard in the time after that to see the reason for his wretchedness in the separation. Everyone around him, his friends, his family had zealously encouraged him to believe it. How ignorant he had been and, with him, everyone he knew. But he had found a Teacher. The true cause lay much deeper. It was his Teacher who had opened his eyes to the abyss at the edge of which he had been standing all his life. And not he alone. The isolation he had always felt, the inadequacy he experienced, it was nothing but the inner desert of unbelief and how long he had strayed through it! He thought of Kerim and how he, Amir, had, from the beginning, had a presentiment that the meeting with him would be a fateful one. Even when he had only observed him day after day through the window of the Internet cafe or from up here. Now he saw Kerim as an unfortunate envoy of heaven, dispatched on an impossible journey, only in order at last to awaken him, Amir. Really, he should have been grateful to Kerim for everything that he had unknowingly brought him. He had not seen the barren landscapes which Kerim had told him about but he knew the desert inside himself all the better.

Amir went over to the low bookcase and gathered together books, catalogues, all the printed paper. He carried the pile into the bathroom and threw it into the bathtub. He switched on the light. In fact, he had intended to burn the paper. But now he was afraid there would be too much smoke and that it would alarm the people in the house. He went back into the room and looked around for things that might be useful. He pocketed the small packet of drugs he had taken from the black man in the park, he looked for and found his passport and the money he had set aside for something, for what he could no longer remember.

While he was rummaging around in the dark room, he came upon a corner of wallpaper sticking out from the wall. He had pressed it down dozens of times and tried to jam it behind the skirting board. Now he pulled at it until the corner became a length of wallpaper coming away right up to the ceiling. He tore the whole piece off and threw it down. A dark irregular crack now seemed to open in the wall. Amir stared at it as if at a discovery.

What would his father say? he asked himself. His father would no doubt soon hear about him. He saw his father in his mind's eye, during one of the few fundamental discussions they had had, gesturing dismissively, turning his face away. Amir heard his voice: You young men, you want to do things, but you want to do things without thinking, without believing. No one can control you, not over there and soon not even here. He was right, thought Amir, as a Believer to act without thinking, that was what he had learnt in the short time from the man with the gentle but nervous face who had become their emir. He thought about how he had gripped him under the chin, how his dark eyes in their narrow slits flashed behind the lenses of his spectacles as he said, 'Can you do it without any fuss? Can you do that?'

And how he wanted to nod fervently and was unable to do so because of the hand at his chin.

'He knows me,' the emir had said softly and urgently and, instantly, there was no longer any doubt that his, Amir's deed, too, was indispensable to their operation.

Once again he went over to the window. Briefly, he thought about his mother and his sisters, who were his father's pride and joy, in their world beyond anything that concerned him. But he pushed the thought aside. The night-time silence of the street always surprised him anew. So many Believers, he thought, who have made their peace. And then so many Unbelievers, whose unattainable desires only cloaked their fear of the void, which they all bore within themselves. Just rest, he thought, just take a good rest until you're awakened.

He went into the bathroom and now did, after all, take the topmost piece of paper out of the tub, crushed it and set it alight. It was his own writing burning there, a page left over from his driving test years ago. In the flame, the handwritten words writhed for a moment before collapsing and disappearing in the fiery edge. He dropped the rest of the piece of paper into the tub and watched as the fire went out. Then he left the bathroom and paused at the door of the flat. There was someone on the stairs. Amir waited.

Occasionally, he was still unexpectedly overcome by a quiet fear. But he could always get over it, much more easily than he had ever imagined. He remembered how he had entered the prayer hall for the first time. Cautious in a way that he usually never was, he observed the others so as not to make a mistake. After prayers, he remained there, sat leaning against a wall and waited. When the majority of people had left and only individual groups of Believers remained, a man of his own age spoke to him, courteously and almost shyly at first, then gradually more resolutely. He finally embroiled Amir in a conversation about questions of belief. Naturally, Amir was unable to say very much about that. Yet it didn't seem to bother the other. On the contrary, the quieter Amir was, the more verbose the former's address became. Amir scrutinized him, the round face, gleaming as if from a fever, the soft beard. He inspected him from his white prayer cap down to his dark socks. He remembered very well how, at the beginning, he had still been possessed by the familiar feeling of physical superiority. Everything about the other appeared to be the attempt to compensate for the weakness of the body. Amir was so preoccupied by this thought that for a while he didn't hear what was being said to him. At some point, the imam came up and Amir rose to his feet out of courtesy. He stood in front of this friendly man who looked like a schoolteacher, introduced himself, exchanged the usual phrases and still had his feeling of strength which was simultaneously a kind of condescension towards these people whose principal activity was evidently talking. Whether they sensed his distance or not, they stopped talking at him at the right moment and, instead, simply welcomed him, here in these rooms and to their group. That's how it began.

Already on the first evening Amir had liked this place, where one could pass the time without having the usual faces around and where there was indeed an atmosphere of scholarliness that he had known neither at school nor in his family. He understood that here the word ruled with unlimited power and he needed time to open himself up to it. He only succeeded when the feeling of strength began to wane. Yes, he thought, when I became weak, I began to listen. No one set out to make him weaker and, at first, no one demanded of him that he submit. And yet he did so, because everything that depressed him, and also everything he hated, was linked to this strength. It was like taking off a suit of armour, piece by piece. He learnt not only how to pray but also how to make the prayer a part of life. From then on, he really learnt.

The more he submitted, the weaker he allowed himself to be, the more quickly the pressure that had always accompanied him lifted. The little things of life, of which he had become increasingly unaware, took on significance: The month, the day, the hour, the meal, the ablutions and with whom he spent his time—it all became part of the larger story and assumed all the more weight, as the story was not very long and only unfolded towards the End, towards the sacrifice that he, too, would at some point have to make.

Rules he had hardly known—and if he had, he had always flouted them—began to give his life order.

He craved to obey them evermore strictly, to change himself. And soon he got to know other people, Believers tested in battle, who received help from many quarters. His brothers had collected the parts of the armour which he had removed in order to receive instruction in the Faith, and carefully stored them. Finally, they brought these to him and reassembled them. So he became strong again but his core was transformed. The distance he kept from the others had not entirely left him. In particular, the Germans who had found their way to the Faith and whose missionary zeal at times knew no bounds filled him with mistrust. Yet in the new community, all that was no longer important.

Sometimes he even asked himself whether it was really God he was following, as many of the others said of themselves. But he didn't brood on it. If indeed the rules were perhaps even more important to him, Amir, than God, then they nevertheless pleased Him. That was enough. He was not born to be a teacher, and so he felt closer to those fighters who came from the Holy War in Iraq and found shelter in the homes of chosen members. He was allowed to pray with them at the mosque, sometimes now even to sit with them. Only gradually did he understand what a far-reaching significance their presence had. They were very cautious in initiating him. Then, however, events followed fast and furious and Amir was certain that he would have to pass a test unexpectedly soon, in order to show how far he was willing to go.

The lamp was humming quietly above him and he glanced up. He knew very well that as yet he was no more than an underling. The people who had arrived in recent weeks let him feel that. And yet no long-winded instruction was necessary. Kerim had been right—it thought itself, it was outside book wisdom, all books but the one only existed to obstruct the clear view, to confuse thoughts, to make one forget the unity.

Once it was quiet, he switched off the light and left the flat.

***

While he was on his way to the agreed meeting place, it began to rain. Where he left the car, there was nothing but the wet cobblestone street and the stench of the nearby canal. He waited. In the distance, there was a tall office block with the illuminated sign of an insurance company. For some reason, he expected someone to call to him from the dark bushes. But nothing happened. Fine, cool rain fell on him.

At some point, a car turned into the street and raced towards him with a clattering sound. The driver braked sharply and the car skidded past. Amir went over. The man inside raised his hand and pointed to the passenger seat.

They drove down the street by the canal in silence. He looked at the wet-gleaming trees, knew that he had nothing to fear and nevertheless felt the cold entering him. Apart from driving, the only thing the man beside him did was occasionally wipe over his nose with his shirtsleeve.

They drove for about twenty minutes. The canal bank had become broader and there was enough room for a scrapyard. Iron arms rose up out of the piles of wreckage. Opposite, on the other side of the street, there was a three-storey house, which—one could tell from the windows—was empty and, in part, badly damaged by fire. Amir had not imagined it all to be so shabby.

They got out and the driver led him to the house. The nearer they got to it, the more rotten it smelt. Amir was surprised at this completely isolated building. There was something temporary about it, although it was quite solid and several storeys high. The entrance was nothing more than a hole in the wall, the torn-out frame lay in the hallway behind it. Inside, there was a light somewhere and, stepping over indefinable objects, Amir headed towards it.

The light was somewhere by the stairs. The Moroccan came towards them. The driver now had a big torch in his hand, he shone it into the stairwell, where Amir made out someone kneeling. His head was lowered, his arms bound behind his back.

The Moroccan, another newcomer in this city, looked at him with unblinking eyes and abruptly gave a firm nod—something that had long ago been decided was now going to be carried out. He took out his knife and, with a degree of solemnity, gave it to Amir, handle first. To him, everything appeared clear and necessary. Why, if not out of hate for the informer, who had so nearly betrayed them, should Amir have insisted on being present? Yet Amir didn't hate this man. He raised his hand defensively and went towards the stairwell. The driver followed with the beam of his torch. The huge shadows of Amir and the Moroccan rose up the walls.

Amir looked at the big, fat man, who had been a kind of factotum at the mosque and whom he had never seen close up. The man pressed his chin to his chest, his face could not be made out.

Around them was the smell of shit and mould, the rain produced a crackling sound up above, where the grey sky could be seen through the ruined roof. The man was kneeling below a row of metal letterboxes. Amir squatted in front of him and looked into the face of a frightened boy. He must have tried to shave off his moustache and had cut himself in several places. He started when the driver shone the torch in his face. Briefly, there was something defiant in his expression but it immediately gave way again to that tension which the burden of the dwindling time produced.

'Just what did they promise you?' Amir whispered. The man didn't react. 'Money? Residency? A job, maybe?' A laugh burst out of Amir that was more like convulsive giggling. 'They have nothing here in their world that they could give you. It took me a while to grasp that.'

The driver was becoming restless, he came up to them and had evidently given the Moroccan a sign, because the latter began to fumble in his jacket. The breathing of the kneeling man became heavier, he turned his head to the wall. A whistling sound came from his lungs. The driver drew Amir back as the Moroccan pressed a pistol to the man's head. The barrel pointed like an iron finger at the fat man who screwed up his eyes. The shot echoed through the room, the tin of the letterboxes rattled quietly. The driver shone the torch at the head of the heavy man, who had fallen forward and whose face was now lying on the right cheek. The barrel was still pointing at him. But it was over.

It was not until they were outside the house that what he had seen became clear to Amir. The thought of it contracted his stomach. From one moment to the next, he was forced to vomit. The two others stopped, turned around and waited. When Amir was finished, tears were running down his face from the release of the tension, as if a sorrow that had not been felt demanded a sign nonetheless.

They drove him back into town as far as the street where his car was parked. Without another word, he got out.

'Be trustworthy,' said the driver softly. He held up two fingers, pulled one slowly back and kept his index finger raised in admonition.

Then he drove off. Amir watched the car disappear. Cold rain fell on him and the bad taste in his mouth refused to disappear. He spent the rest of the night in the car.

ε

Tired out but tense, his mind completely clear, Amir waited for his moment. As he could not let himself be seen in the street, he posted himself on the route that Kerim took on his walks. Here, along the Spree, the riverbank vegetation was so thick that there was no getting through the undergrowth. Rusty fences cut through an overgrown park, demarcated plots of land around once-beautifully-situated buildings, which today were ruins, with bushes growing out of the broken windows. Kerim's walks led him away from the water along one of these fences. The remains of an amusement park decayed behind it. The brightly painted seats of a carousel lay overturned in the grass. There was even an old Ferris wheel on the site. Most impressive, however, were the remains of a burnt-out roller coaster. The charred cars hung in this scaffolding like terrifying black fruit. This abandoned park presented an image of terror which was only mitigated by the woodland twittering of the birds.

The air was humid on this autumn evening. Amir had pulled the hood of his sweatshirt over his head, it hid so much of his face that he felt safe. He followed the path as far as the half-wrecked ticket offices, disfigured by graffiti, in front of which visitors must once have queued. Amir secretly enjoyed these signs of downfall and mute destruction. It gave him a feeling of liberation. It was all part of the legacy of a state which came to an end long ago, about which Amir knew little more than that it had been a Godless, anachronistic thing, warlike, with walls, barbed wire and watch towers which he could still vaguely remember from his childhood. Amir went into one of the little buildings to shelter from the drizzle that had begun again. He leant against a wooden beam which divided the room and got ready to keep an eye on the path until darkness fell.

***

Tarik stood in the street in front of the house and waved at Hussein's car as it drove off. He had just said goodbye to his son. He still felt their embrace and knew that he'd have to wait a long time for the next.

He turned away to go upstairs again, casting a glance at the Internet cafe as he did so. Three boys were standing outside and smoking. They were all wearing big, unshapely white trainers. They paid no attention to him.

It's strange, he said to himself, I wouldn't dare just speak to them. And yet they're just Arab boys. How remote they have become from older people like us!

As he slowly went up the stairs, he thought again about his nephew Kerim. He wondered why Kerim behaved so strangely, why he insisted evermore obstinately on his walks and today had even avoided taking proper leave of his cousin because of it. Tarik had the feeling that his nephew was slipping away from him. He wished Sabihe were still there. She would surely have got closer to Kerim than he was able to do. In a roundabout way, and very belatedly, he was now having a very similar experience to the one his friend Ferid had always told him about. Ferid had once said that he had always believed that the strength to find their own way would, through God's will, grow in his children of its own accord. He had never thought much of the way the Germans brought up their children. A few basic principles, he had been convinced of that, would be sufficient, and the rest would take care of itself, because the foundations were there and man had no influence over them. Yet, in short, Ferid concluded that he had been mistaken. Very little developed of its own accord and one could almost get the impression that, actually, a child was a sensitive plant that one had to tend and care for if it was to have any chance at all of growing. And naturally, Ferid had only shaken his head at it all, had scratched his unkempt moustache and then, in the end, lamented the many alien influences.

Tarik opened the door to the flat. He went straight to the kitchen, took some of the salad he had prepared in the afternoon and shuffled into the living room with his bowl. His back straight, he sat on the settee and began to eat. The noise of his own chewing seemed so unpleasantly loud that he wanted to switch on the TV. He already had the remote in his hand when he became aware of a sound like the ringtone of a mobile phone but far away, as if it were coming from one of the neighbouring flats. He put the remote back on the table, placed the bowl beside it and listened. The longer he listened, the more certain he was that it was coming from some corner of his home. He got up and the first place he looked was Kerim's room. He opened the door and the sound was indeed already much louder. He switched on the light and looked round the bare room. Finally, he looked behind the door and on the floor, at the foot of the bed, saw the cardboard box he had given Kerim. He lifted it onto the bed, it had been stuck down and then opened again. He pulled it open, carefully removed the skates, reached for the mobile phone, flipped it open and answered.

Sonja was at the other end, evidently quite confused because no one had responded yet. She asked after Kerim and Tarik told her he had gone for a walk. As he said it, he noticed the watch at the bottom of the box and he was overcome by a strange feeling of unease. It was so strong that he had difficulty following Sonja, who kept on inquiring after his nephew. In the last few weeks, he had become ever stranger—that was all he said and ended the conversation.

***

Sonja switched off the phone and put it away. She was sitting with Till and the singer of an unknown American band at a metal table in the courtyard of a hotel. Despite the already-quite-low evening temperature, the man was wearing nothing but a shiny black leather waistcoat on his torso. There was a degree of ambiguity, if not suggestiveness, to everything he said to Sonja. He listened eagerly, and with a knowing gaze, to everything she said. Sonja looked at the small tattoo on his upper arm. Immediately, the singer placed his big hand over it, as if he wanted to touch her. But Sonja remained cool. It's just me and my cat again, she thought. Stefan was right, I'm probably too demanding. The giant beside her raised his beer glass and was briefly distracted by Till, since he had to raise his thumb as commentary on the former's T-shirt text. 'Todo para todos' was the message written there in big, black letters. Till pinched the material in two places, pulled it away from his chest and spread out the letters. He smiled as the singer tried to translate the words first into English, then into French.

Dissatisfied, Sonja glanced at her glass of mineral water. She had been unable to bring herself to visit Kerim again at his uncle's home, to stand facing him in that room of a belated adolescent. She did not want to reveal to herself once again, what Stefan had accused her of, that is, from what a distance she regarded this person, how little in truth they had in common. And she was too smart to think that what she had felt there was a patient, forbearing love that had somehow slipped too far towards motherliness.

It was time, the singer had drunk his 'German beer'. They stood up and walked to the car. Adroitly, with what appeared to be a practised movement, the man took Sonja's arm. His hand touched the side of her breast but only as if by chance. She tried to find a balance again between distance and attention.

* * *

Lost in thought, his eyes on the ground in front of him, Kerim came along the path, looking just as Amir imagined a philosopher to look. He was walking quickly, there was already an evening calm to the day, and even the birdsong seemed muted. Amir let him pass the little building. His liking for this man, who, at first, had seemed so mysterious, indeed, whom he had even admired, was briefly rekindled. As he crept up behind him, the attraction gave way to disappointment and contempt, yet was still pervaded by it, as was his determination—it was the secret source of the hurt that drove him forward. Amir quickly glanced around, then grabbed hold of Kerim and pulled him into the bushes. It wasn't hard to get on top of Kerim. With one hand, he squeezed his throat, with the other drew his knife.

'What do you want?' Kerim said, his voice choked, and tried to push the heavy body away.

'You could have been a hero,' panted Amir, with anger and accusation in his voice. 'But I know now what you are—a thief and a traitor.'

He stuck the knife in, Kerim gave a loud groan but Amir's thrust was sure. He drew the knife out, holding Kerim firmly on the ground until he lay there, quiet.

'And I know what you are,' whispered Kerim.

Amir let go of the other's throat and rolled to the side. Kerim's hand went to the huge wound at the level of his liver. He was unable to distinguish the long slit edges of clothing from flesh and doubled up. Amir wiped the blade on the grass, shoved the knife in his belt and pulled out the little packet of drugs. Carefully he pressed it together and pushed it deep into Kerim's trouser pocket.

Kerim lay there without moving. His cheek on the damp woodland floor, he stared in front of him.

'Just go away, all of you!' he gasped.

Amir glanced around. The path was deserted, a heavy stench rose from the water. With one bound, he was on his feet. Relieved, Kerim heard his steps receding.

Worse than the pain was all the blood that welled through his fingers. He turned on his back and looked at the grey evening sky between the branches. He thought of everyone he had known and, for some reason, had lost. He thought of his Teacher, just before the air raid.

'It is a thought that thinks itself,' the Teacher had said. 'It has a secret power. Like something living, it is, at first, unable to look after itself. Minute, it hovers in the air, it is an invisible seed and you breathe it in, unaware. Yet this germ is the belief in a miracle. Not the memory of it—it is unimaginably more. Because its roots are not in the past, like everything earthly, the spirit, too. No, it is divine, its roots are in the future. It is a bright wound in the dark, a barely visible light, a prefiguration of what will be, and you bear it within you as we all do. Perhaps once, sometime, the wind blew it onto your breath, or perhaps you brought it with you—who knows? You bear it with you and it grows. Very slowly, new thoughts spring from it. But these are not thoughts like the ones you usually have. No. They don't lead back, they lead forward. As if the night were to cast off its stars, as if the rivers were to turn back and flee the ocean, as if the mountains were to grow down into the earth—as if the tallest buildings would fall.

'Oh yes, I have seen it in distant New York. I worked in a school for the blind there for a long time. It was a beautiful day. The children and I, we were in the street when it happened, they looked into the sunlight and I wiped the snot from their noses. Then I had to explain to them what was happening. And as I talked and talked, I myself understood what I was seeing. My suspicion, my presentiment, my most hidden hurt, my quietest question, not even whispered in despair—all of it had grown big in me, had long ago filled me, had grown, before finally leaving me and taking shape there, there before my eyes. The very old, small thought had become a deed, the hardly audible word, muttered, as if with a dying breath, for every one of us, it had finally reached the ear.'

'What is the word?' asked Kerim fervently

'You know it,' said the Teacher. 'Come, let us take a few steps. The flowers are blooming so magnificently here in the snow, as if next spring would never to come. See how they struggle, see the wretched hut there and how the sun lights it up, as if it wants to carry off every one of its crooked stones. Along here, stay with me just a little while. I have seen the giant Twin Towers collapse, yet only this isolated hut touches my heart.

'Did you know that the last colour someone losing his sight sees is green? And what else is happening to all of us, except that we are slowly losing our sight, across the years?'

Kerim closed his eyes.